HEART OF RAGE

HELENA NEWBURY

FOSTER & BLACK

Heart OF RAGE

HELENA NEWBURY
NEW YORK TIMES BESTSELLING AUTHOR

Foster & Black

Cover by Mayhem Cover Creations
Main cover model image licensed from (and copyright remains with) Wander Aguiar
Photography

Third Edition

ISBN (Paperback): 978-1-914526-30-5
If there are types of content you'd rather avoid, you can check the content advisory for
this book on my website:
https://helenanewbury.com/heart-of-rage-cw

ALSO BY HELENA NEWBURY

All my books can be enjoyed as standalone titles, but I've grouped them by theme here so you can find things easily.

Aristov Bratva

Frozen Heart

Heart of Rage

Other Russian Mafia

Lying and Kissing

Kissing My Killer

Kissing the Enemy

The Double

The O'Harra Brothers

Punching and Kissing

Bad For Me

Saving Liberty

Outlaw's Promise

Brothers

Stormfinch Security

No Angel

Off Limits

Guarded

Capture Me

1

ALISON

It didn't start with love. It started with hate.

I leaned hard into the corner, my knee an inch from the asphalt. The big motorcycle teetered on its wheels, a tenth of a degree from tipping and crushing me. At the very last second, I twisted the throttle and the bike roared like a bad-tempered bull and rocketed forward, trying to pull itself from between my legs. We swept around a delivery truck, so close I nearly cracked my head on its side mirror, and then we were speeding away up the street, slaloming between the slow-moving cars just for the hell of it.

It's lucky that I don't spend much on clothes or make-up or going out, because my bike drinks oil and demands a constant supply of eye-wateringly expensive spare parts. But it's worth it. I have this...*rage* inside me, a toxic pressure that builds and builds. It powers me, non-stop: keep working, keep moving, keep pushing, and the only thing I've ever found that quiets it is *this*.

I leaned into the next corner, sliding around an SUV like an ice skater. I straightened up, glanced ahead to plan my next move, and—

An icy hand grabbed my heart and crushed it so hard it couldn't beat.

Further down the street, an army of firefighters was spraying water into a bright orange glow. Clouds of steam and smoke cloaked the building, but I knew what was there.

I cranked the throttle and accelerated, praying. *Please no. Please let it be the one next door. Please!* But as I neared the police barricades, my stomach dropped. The flames were shooting out from between beautiful, white stone pillars. *No!*

I slowed and pulled up beside a police cruiser. As soon as the cooling rush of the slipstream fell away, the June heat wrapped around me. Even at nearly eleven at night, it was stifling. I quickly unzipped my leather jacket, then stashed my helmet on my bike and ran towards the police *Do Not Cross* line. An officer raised his hand to stop me, then waved me through when I flashed him my FBI badge.

I found Mrs. McCullen by a fire truck, tear trails cutting lines through the soot on her face. A poster for this season's play, *Much Ado About Nothing,* was on fire on one of the pillars, and the charred pieces were wafting down around her.

She turned to me and opened her mouth, but she couldn't find any words. I threw my arms around her and hugged her close. Over the top of her snow-white hair, I watched the fire gut one of the most beautiful buildings in Chicago. The place was over a hundred years old, and everything, from the mosaic on the lobby floor to the amazing, vaulted ceilings, was original. But that wasn't why my stomach was in a tight knot, seeing it on fire.

Mrs. McCullen runs the Chicago Community Theater, a non-profit that puts on plays with the help of volunteers, most of them from disadvantaged backgrounds. It's a place where anyone can practice a talent or learn a skill, a supportive place where you can escape your problems a few nights a week. I've seen a former addict get and stay clean as she worked away sewing costumes. I've seen a broken, silent guy who lost his kid in a car crash finally come out of himself as he learned to dance for a part in *West Side Story.* All of that was being turned to ash. But that wasn't what hurt the most, either.

Before it became the Community Theater, the building had been the Chicago School of Dance, run by my mom, and I'd been practically raised there. The memories rushed in: sitting on the cool stone floor of my mom's office, coloring in a coloring book while she finished work; my dad lifting me up to hang tinsel in the main hall; standing at the barre doing my stretches when I was old enough to start ballet myself.

Then, when I was twelve, my whole life changed in a heartbeat. My parents were ripped from me and this building became the only shred of my past I had left. That's why I'd always supported the Community Theater. I wanted the place to stay open, stay alive...and now it was gone forever. It felt like someone had reached down inside me and torn out part of my soul. Tears pricked at my eyes, and my breathing went tight.

A firefighter emerged from the building, coughing, and stumbled over to the fire chief. "No one inside," he told the chief. "But you better get the arson team in here, I could smell the chemicals. Definitely deliberate."

I was still hugging Mrs. McCullen, and I felt my body tense against hers. The rage inside me woke and expanded, heating to a fierce scarlet.

The theater wasn't *gone*. It had been *taken from us*.

And I knew who had done it.

I lifted my head from Mrs. McCullen's shoulder and looked along the street. There was a row of empty, derelict buildings, and then the entire rest of the block was taken up by a single massive structure, a flattened slab of polished granite with no windows. The casino. The man who owned it had been wanting to expand for years. He'd bought up all the other buildings in this street, but the Community Theater had held out. So he'd torched the place to force them to sell.

The anger flared brighter, hotter...and suddenly, I was letting go of Mrs. McCullen and stalking through the police and firefighters and onto the sidewalk. Sniffing back my tears, I marched down to the entrance of the casino at the end of the block.

I threw open the glass doors and waited while my eyes adjusted to the gloom. The owner kept it dark inside, and hot as the pits of hell. Heat meant people drank more, and the waitresses could wear less, and it was easier to separate drunk, ogling men from their money.

The security guys at the door frowned suspiciously at my leather jacket and leather pants, but let me pass. I headed straight through the jungle of blaring, rattling slot machines, then crossed the rowdy main floor, past roulette wheels and craps tables. I scanned left and right as I walked, searching the mass of people, but I couldn't see him anywhere...

And then suddenly, ahead of me, the crowd fell silent and started to split in two, people scuttling white-faced to clear a path. Someone was approaching, and there was only one person who'd scare everyone like that.

He appeared, marching straight towards me, scowling at everything and everyone. Blackjack dealers snapped to attention. Waitresses swallowed and held their trays a little straighter. Everyone knew about this man's temper and the violence he could unleash. His gaze took in every detail, ensuring that his money-making machine was wringing every last dollar out of every single customer, and that no one was being stupid enough to try to cheat him.

I'd heard what he did to cheaters.

His suit was so dark it was almost black: it soaked up the light, and it was only when he moved that you could make out the sheen of the expensive fabric. His shirt was the deep red of spilled blood, and his collar was open, revealing the tattoos that wound their way like a lover up his chest and around his neck. By rights, he should have been ugly: the exterior should have matched his poisonous heart. But his Russian heritage had blessed him with a strong, square jaw glossy with stubble, and gorgeously sharp cheekbones. His eyes were like pale gray ice, beautiful but so cold it almost hurt to look at them. And the way his full lower lip jutted as he scowled was pure sex.

Terrifying, dangerous, and sinfully tempting. If the devil walked the earth, he'd look exactly like—

"Gennadiy Aristov." My voice was raw with anger, even as I fought to keep it level. I *hate* the *Bratva,* the Russian Mafia. They're so much worse than the normal criminals. They've weaponized crime, turned it into a tool to amass power. And the Aristovs are the worst of all: they have judges and politicians in their pockets: even, supposedly, the mayor. As well as the casino, Gennadiy ran all of the family's illegal operations: the guns and the drugs, the protection rackets... And over the last year or two, his brutality had spiraled out of control.

Gennadiy's gaze raked over me, studying me like a bug. "Yes?" he asked, his voice disdainful and scalpel-sharp. The two Bratva guys who walked alongside him moved their hands to the guns under their jackets, but they didn't draw them. I'm 5'4" and small-built: even in biker leathers, I'm not exactly intimidating.

We stopped, only a few feet apart. I could feel the rage straining to break free. "You burned down the theater," I blurted.

Gennadiy lifted one perfect, dark brow. "I have no idea what you're talking about." That *accent!* It caressed each word like a paintbrush dipped in liquid silver. But it didn't hide the undercurrent of smug satisfaction. It *had* been him. And he wanted me to know it.

The rage slipped loose, expanding, consuming me. I didn't have a plan. I didn't think about how many people he'd killed, or how much trouble I could get in. I just knew he'd ripped away the only part of my childhood I had left, and destroyed something precious and beautiful, and he didn't care, *no one cared,* and no one was going to do a fucking thing about it, and—

I punched him in the face as hard as I could.

2

GENNADIY

Two minutes earlier

LET ME TELL YOU SOMETHING ABOUT POWER. THE MORE YOU HAVE, THE more people there are trying to snatch it from you. You want to hang on to power? You better be ready to fight every day of your life. And to fight, you have to have something that drives you.

Business was good. The Aristov empire stretched right across Chicago, and we had cars, mansions, money...everything we'd dreamed of when we were three starving kids in Russia. But our size made us a target. Our enemies were constantly hunting for weaknesses, there were hundreds of illegal operations to oversee, *and* I had to run the casino, a full-time job in itself. It was too much for one person, but my brothers had their own responsibilities, and I didn't trust anyone outside the family enough to let them help. I was already working eighteen-hour days, and as we expanded, it was reaching the point where something had to give.

But I had a secret weapon. The thing that pulled me out of bed before dawn, that kept me going until the early hours.

Anger.

It's been with me too long to be an emotion. It's a force of nature, a storm made of darkness that rises and falls but never dies away completely. It started in a borstal in Vladivostok, and it's been building ever since. The anger let me become what I needed to be: a prince of darkness, the most ruthless of all my brothers. It lets me do the things I have to do: threaten, blackmail, kill. The one thing it won't let me do...is rest.

So I never stop. I'm constantly moving: speeding around the city, dealing with enemies, solving problems. And when I'm here at the casino, I don't sit in my office having meetings, I prowl the floor, checking for issues, and my men run up to me and mutter questions in my ear.

"Two of our guys got picked up hijacking a truck in the eighth precinct last night," one of them told me. "Cops were supposed to keep away from that block. Commander Meggitt says he's sorry."

I know the name of every cop on our payroll. "Meggitt...he's the one into woodworking, isn't he?"

"Yes sir. Builds dollhouses in his downtime."

I walked on, past the roulette wheel. "Woodworking's such a *dangerous* hobby. Those table saws...you could lose a finger before you knew what was happening. Pay Commander Meggitt a visit, remind him to be more careful."

"Got it." The man ran off.

I marched over to the craps tables. Another of my men hurried over to me. "We caught the guy who was dealing in our club. But he won't tell us who his supplier is."

"Throw him into the foundation of Radimir's new building and start pouring concrete."

"And once he's talked?"

"Keep pouring."

I held up my hand to pause the craps game, picked up the dice, and turned them in my palm, checking the weight: just last week, we'd had a guy swap in loaded dice. But these were fine. I rolled them, waved for the game to continue, and moved on.

My brother Valentin appeared from the shadows. "You asked me to find Iosif Kalugin. He's holed up in a motel, south side." Valentin paused. "You want me to..." He reached under his long coat and brushed the hilt of one of his knives.

"No." I thought about what Kalugin had been doing and the disgust rolled through me like thunder. "I'll do it personally, tonight. Get a boat and some heavy chains."

Valentin nodded and peeled off into the crowd. I marched on, the crowd parting in front of me—

And that's when I saw her for the very first time.

A woman, a small one, but marching towards me with utter determination. "Gennadiy Aristov," she growled.

She'd heard of me, but she wasn't scared. That irritated me...but it made me curious, too. "Yes?"

"You burned down the theater."

I had to think for a second. That old wreck, down the block? Yes, I *had* sent someone to deal with it, one of the three places that would burn this week alone. Why did she care? The theater was a dump, and the space would make an excellent high-stakes poker area. "I have no idea what you're talking about," I told her.

She glared up at me, and I glared down at her. She looked even smaller because she wasn't wearing high heels, like the women I'm used to seeing. She was wearing leather biker boots, scuffed and worn from riding, and black leather pants that hugged her legs like a second skin. Her eyes were deep blue, and they caught the light, flashing and glittering. They made me think of sapphires dug from deep in the earth, beautiful but incredibly hard.

I could feel the anger gathering and darkening in my chest, and I wasn't sure why. Yes, she was an insolent little thing, marching into my casino and accusing me of things, but it was more than that. I know my rage like a sailor knows the ocean. This anger was too fast, too bright. She made me irrationally angry, and I'm *always* rational. *What's going on?*

I had the weirdest feeling, like her being here, *me* being here, were unshakable certainties, like I was a planet and she was a comet slamming into me, our paths determined millions of years before.

I inspected her, coldly analytical. I looked at the small breasts that pushed out her black vest top. The wisps of black hair that had escaped the tight little bun at the back of her head fell to caress her neck. She was glowering up at me, furious, and it was making her lips pout in a way that was—

That was—

I looked up, meeting her eyes.

Her fist slammed into my face.

I went staggering backwards. At first, there was just numbness and shock. Two of my men who'd been near me stood frozen as well. None of us could believe someone would dare to hit me.

Then the pain arrived. The whole side of my face started to throb. *That actually hurt.* She was small, but she had power. *I'm going to have a bruise.* Worse, people were looking. Casino staff, Bratva, customers...they'd all just seen Gennadiy Aristov get punched in his own casino by this...this tiny little thing. I let the anger expand in my chest, filling me, and stepped forward,

My men finally woke up and overcompensated for being caught off guard. One of them drew his gun, and the other ran forward to hit her.

She just...*flowed* sideways, gripped the wrist of the first guy and twisted, and he screamed and dropped his gun. The second guy tried to punch her, and she spun and brought her knee up, and he crumpled to the ground, cradling his balls.

Now *everyone* was looking. The rage darkened, becoming thick, black clouds that crackled with energy. *How fucking dare you?*

I jumped forward and grabbed the woman. She twisted, and for a second her breast brushed my forearm, soft and warm through her vest top, and I froze. Then she grabbed my arm and pulled it in a way it wasn't supposed to go. *Ow!* I released her, grabbed her again, and she broke free again. I tried again, and again, but she was so fast, it felt like she had about six arms.

I finally wrapped her up in a bear hug from behind, trapping her arms against her. *There.*

She stamped down on my shin. I managed not to cry out, but my face went scarlet with pain and anger. I lifted her fully off the floor so that her legs were kicking helplessly in the air. *There!*

She threw back her head and yelled at the top of her lungs. *"Get off me, you—"*

I clamped my hand over her mouth and—*finally*—she was under control.

I stood there panting and furious, and took stock. Her long hair had been shaken half out of its bun, and it was so deeply, coolly black it was almost blue-black, and so fine that it looked like black smoke where it waterfalled down over my arms. Her head was only a few inches from mine, and I could smell the soft cherry scent of her shampoo. Her back was pressed so tightly against my chest that I could feel every breath she took. Her leather pants were superhero-tight, and the firm half-globes of her ass stroked against my cock every time she wriggled. She was still trying to talk, and the feel of her lips and hot little exhales against my palm made me feel...*odd.*

The anger felt different. Like there was something in those dark clouds, little flecks of gold helplessly caught in the howling winds. The angrier I got, the more they billowed around, gleaming bright...

I suddenly remembered all the people watching. I growled, turned away from them, and carried her across the casino and into my private office.

I marched across the room and around my desk, my anger building with each step. I dumped her into my big leather chair and then slammed my office door. Instantly, the noise of the casino disappeared. I saw her body go stiff with shock as it sank in: she was alone with me, and the office was as good as soundproof. No one would hear her scream, in here.

I stormed over to the chair and loomed over her, gripping the top corners and caging her in with my arms. She was panting, scared. But then she lifted her chin and glared up at me, defiant.

She was irritatingly pretty. Those deep blue eyes were so hard, so strong...just for a second, I wondered what it would take to make them weaken. "Who are you?!" I demanded.

She panted a few more times while she considered, her chest rising and falling. "Brooks," she said at last. "FBI."

My hands tightened on the top of the chair, and I felt my jaw clench. I *hate* the FBI. They're so much worse than regular cops. The FBI is a shambling, slow-witted giant, its legs tied together with red tape, and its sole purpose is to crush the lean, efficient business my brothers and I have built. The FBI might be American, not Russian, but it's still part of the same corrupt government machine that tore the Aristov family apart.

I leaned in. "Let me educate you, *Agent Brooks.* I am not a man you raise your voice to." The chair creaked as I tilted it back. "I am not a man you disrespect." I leaned even closer, close enough that I could smell the soft, vanilla-sweet scent of her skin. I lowered my voice to a whisper, my lips so close they almost stroked her ear. "That FBI badge will not save you, little one. If I drop you in Lake Michigan, it will just be extra weight, dragging you down."

She caught her breath. Then, "I'm not scared of you."

The fury swelled, a hurricane inside me. *Everyone* is scared of me. I glared down at her. She glared up at me, stubbornly brave—

That flutter of gold, again, tiny pieces glittering bright in the darkness. My eyes went to her lips, soft and pouting with righteous indignation, and the anger whipped the gold flecks faster and faster...

I wavered for a second. Then instinct took over.

I wrapped my hands around her throat, my tattooed fingers brutish against that smooth, tan skin. "Are you scared *now?*" I asked.

I felt her throat bulge under my hands as she panic-swallowed and her blue eyes widened in fear.

The door flew open. Valentin stood in the doorway, his long coat flapping around him. His eyes went from me to her and back to me.

I let go of her throat and stepped back. "Get out of my casino," I told her. "And don't come back."

She stood, white-faced and shaky, and felt her way around the desk to the door, her eyes never leaving me for a second. In the doorway, she stopped. "The theater was almost out of money," she told me. "Another six months and they would have had to sell. You didn't have to burn it."

"It's my city," I told her. "I'll burn what I fucking like, and there's nothing you can do about it."

She stared at me...then stood tall, lifted her chin, and glared at me. I silently cursed: *Chyort! No one* stood up to me like that.

Then she turned and walked away.

Valentin looked at me and raised a questioning eyebrow. He was already turning to follow her, his hand on one of his knives.

I considered. She certainly infuriated me enough to consider it. True, killing an FBI agent would bring a world of pain down on us, but only if they found out it was us. Valentin could follow her home and make it look like a mugging gone wrong: he was good at that. We could wipe the security cameras that showed her coming here, and no witnesses would be stupid enough to go to the cops. One quick slash of a knife and Agent Brooks would be taken care of.

But... I inhaled, catching the last, lingering trace of her scent. "Let her go," I told Valentin. "She's not worth the trouble."

I had no idea, then. Not of how valuable she'd become to me or how much trouble she'd bring.

3

ALISON

I PUSHED THROUGH THE GLASS DOORS AND OUT ONTO THE SAFETY OF the street, then stood looking back at the casino, making sure no one was following me. Even the muggy night air couldn't chase away the chill between my shoulder blades. His threat was still echoing in my mind, each syllable made silvery by his Russian accent.

I'd lied. I *was* scared of him. Especially when I'd felt those powerful fingers wrap around my neck. What had I been thinking, walking in there alone and yelling at him? My heart crashed against my ribs. He really *could* have killed me and dumped my body in Lake Michigan.

But for some reason, he hadn't. He probably didn't view me as enough of a threat. God, he was so arrogant: he'd actually called Chicago his city. Until tonight, Gennadiy Aristov had only been vaguely on my radar. Now I hated him, despite the fear. Maybe *because* of the fear. I resent anything that makes me feel weak.

And there was something else. When he'd loomed over me, trapping me in the chair with those thickly-muscled arms, his shirt drawn tight across his pecs... When he'd glowered down at me with those brutally hard, gray eyes...

He had no business looking so good. Or *sounding* so good: that accent, each syllable painted gleaming silver as his deep growl carried them right to the core of me...

I shook my head and stalked back down the street to where I'd parked my bike. The fire was still raging at the Community Theater, the glow of the flames painting long orange tongues of light all the way along the polished walls of Gennadiy's casino. My steps got smaller and smaller as I drew close, the loss of the place throbbing through my chest.

It's my city. I'll burn what I fucking like and there's nothing you can do about it.

I stood there staring into the flames. They were blurring behind tears, and I didn't dare blink, or they'd spill over, and people would see.

Inside the burning building, something creaked and then crashed to the floor with a tinkle of glass. The pain spread through me, reverberating...

And then it hit some tiny, stubborn part of me, and that part hardened into granite.

I sniffed and felt my jaw tighten. If I'd been back in New York, my old FBI partner Sam Calahan would have said *Uh-oh. You've got that look.*

Gennadiy Aristov was wrong. Yes, this was his city. Yes, he could burn anything he liked.

But there *was* something I could do about it.

I climbed onto my bike, put on my helmet, and roared away into the night.

The next morning, my boss, FBI Assistant Director Halifax, walked into his office, turned to close the door...and jumped back, spilling his coffee, when he saw me standing in the corner. "*Jesus Christ, Brooks!*"

"I want to go after Gennadiy Aristov," I told him.

"What? No. Why are you in my office?" He started trying to wring coffee out of his dripping shirt cuff.

"Their network is huge." I unfurled a roll of paper across his desk. It showed a complex tree diagram. "Just since last night, I've identified at least a hundred businesses that are likely owned by or part-owned by—"

"Have you *slept?*"

"—the Aristovs, together with—"

Halifax sighed. "The Aristovs are too big. I already have you working on the Irish and the Italians."

"Since when did organized crime get *too big* for us to investigate?" I snapped.

Halifax gave me a warning look. "You know what I mean."

"You mean it's politically inconvenient because they have senators in their pocket."

"I mean, we have limited resources and we have to pick our battles." Halifax took a deep breath, and his tone softened a little. "You're a good agent, Alison. But you're not going to get anywhere with the Aristovs. No one ever has. They're too smart, too careful."

"I want to try."

Halifax glanced through the glass wall of his office to the desks outside. "Where's Hutchins? Goddamn it, is she late again?"

Agent Caroline Hutchins is the one close friend I've made since moving to Chicago from New York. She's a single mom, and recently she'd had a run of being late for work because she kept getting stuck in traffic dropping her kids off at daycare. Unfortunately, Halifax is a real stickler for timekeeping, and he doesn't care that she makes it up at the end of the day. "I saw her downstairs, sir," I lied. "She was going down to Records."

Halifax pinned me with a look. "Don't bullshit me, Brooks."

I swallowed but stood my ground. Caroline's youngest kid, Jack, was born with a heart defect. He's doing better now, but about a year ago, it was touch-and-go, and she went through it all on her own. The poor woman deserved a break. "I'm not bullshitting you, sir. She's in Records. Now, Gennadiy Aristov..."

Halifax dropped into his chair, ran his hands through his hair, and groaned. "You're not going to let this go, are you?"

"No."

"Even if you *were* going to go after the Aristovs, why would you want Gennadiy? Isn't his brother, Radimir, the *Pakhan?*"

I could tell I was wearing him down. "Yes, Radimir's the big boss, but he keeps his hands clean, running their property business and being the public face of the family. It's Gennadiy who runs all the illegal operations. And over the last year or two, as the Aristovs have expanded, he's gotten more and more ruthless. Arson. Murder. Remember that gang that robbed the jewelry store last September? Well, they did it on Aristov turf and didn't give the Aristovs a cut. Gennadiy stole the haul and executed all four of them." I leaned in. "He gunned down six Mexican smugglers. He caught a guy stealing and *cut off his hands!*"

"I still don't think—"

"I've prepared a briefing," I told him. "Shouldn't take more than two or three hours." I pulled my laptop out of my bag and fired it up.

Halifax put his hands up in defeat. "*Alright.*" He sighed. "What would you need?"

"Six good people and six months."

"You can have three, and three months."

Fuck. That was going to be near-impossible. "Thank you, sir."

"And two of them have to be Hadderwell and Fitch."

My heart sank. Hadderwell and Fitch are both less than a year from retirement, and they're phoning it in at this point, doing just enough to make sure they still get their full pension. They weren't going to love taking orders from a woman, either. But I forced myself to smile. "Fine. And can the third one be Caroline?"

Halifax waved me out of his office. "Fine. Take her."

Yes! Caroline was outstanding at the sort of deep research we'd need to take Gennadiy down. "Thank you, sir. You won't regret this." I hurried out of his office before he changed his mind.

$\sim$

The first job was to understand who we were dealing with. I found photos of the Aristovs and pinned them to the wall. Gennadiy, the murderous crime boss we were focused on. Radimir, his older brother, with his three-piece suits and permanent icy scowl. Valentin, the younger brother, who was thought to be the family's hitman. And then there was Mikhail, the brothers' uncle, an older man who did most of the liaising with the rich and powerful and never went anywhere without his pack of Malamute dogs.

"Gennadiy Aristov?" Caroline twirled a lock of golden hair around her finger and blinked up at me nervously from behind her glasses. "I heard some guy once...*displeased* him and he beat him so hard, they couldn't identify the body."

Hadderwell sighed. Tall and balding, he was leaning against the wall, one eye on the stock trading app on his phone. "Brooks, you have no chance of taking this guy down."

His buddy Fitch—short, squat, and with a thick, ginger mustache—put his feet up on a desk and grunted in agreement. "The guy's *serious.*"

I crossed my arms and lifted my chin. "So am I."

Early the next morning, I pulled up outside Gennadiy's house, ready to start surveillance. I leaned forward, arms on the steering wheel, and just stared.

The place was massive, a beautiful three-story mansion at least a hundred years old, built from gray stone. What must a place like that cost, especially here, within easy driving distance of the city? Tens of millions, easily. And all of it from guns, drugs, and gambling. I felt the anger bloom in my chest, tensing my shoulders and then rolling down my spine. He'd got where he was by trampling the little people, by not caring who he hurt. Well, *enough.* My fingers squeezed the steering wheel. *I'm taking you down.*

One thing I had to grudgingly admit: the mansion was far more tasteful than the showy, tacky palaces most criminals spent their money on. He was a ruthless bastard...but he had class.

Then I got my second shock of the day. Gennadiy emerged from the mansion in a thunderstorm-gray suit and marched over to his BMW. *He's leaving already?!* It wasn't even seven a.m. yet! I'd gotten there what I thought was crazy early to make sure I caught him, but I hadn't imagined him leaving for at least another hour or so. Apparently, he was an early riser, like me.

Gennadiy ran a hand lovingly over his car's roof, then climbed in and drove off. I quickly started up my unmarked car and followed.

Usually, when we're tailing a suspect, we'll stay three cars behind them and keep passing them off between different agents so they don't notice they're being followed. But right now, I was staying close: I *wanted* Gennadiy to see me. I wanted him to know he was under surveillance.

He was sharp. Within just a few minutes, he was checking his mirrors. Then he made a couple of unnecessary turns, just to see if I'd follow, and I did.

At the next red light, our cars stopped close enough that I could see him glaring at me in his rear-view mirror, his gray eyes absolutely furious. I smiled sweetly, feeling a little thrill of victory. I wanted him pissed off and shaken, I wanted him *pressured*. Pressured criminals make mistakes, and mistakes are how I catch them.

At first, I thought it wasn't working. He drove with mechanical precision to the gleaming skyscraper that housed Aristov Incorporated, the massive property company run by his brother. I waited for him outside, then followed him to the casino. Then to the docks. Aside from the scowls he gave me each time he climbed out of his car, it was like he was pretending I wasn't there.

But no criminal can be calm with a cop breathing down their neck. As the day went on, I saw his shoulders start to hunch with tension and his driving becoming jerky. I was getting to him.

And then, just as the sun was setting, it happened.

He turned suddenly down an alley, and I missed the turn and had to reverse. For a second, I thought I'd lost him. Then I saw his car, down at the end. I accelerated...and then had to pull up fast when I realized his car was stopped. Too late, I saw that there was no one inside.

I saw movement in my peripheral vision, twisted around...and saw Gennadiy standing next to my car. He stared at me through the glass, his gray eyes breathtakingly cold. I swallowed. He was much, *much* taller than me, even when I was standing. Sitting down, it was like having a giant towering over me.

He put his hands on my car's roof, like he was planning to rip it off. His fingers began a slow, deliberate drumbeat on the metal. His expression said, *What are we going to do with you?*

An iron band tightened around my chest. We were all alone in the alley. No one would see. Suddenly, following him on my own didn't seem like such a great idea.

Gennadiy's eyes flicked down to the window controls, then back up to mine. I debated, my heart hammering. If he wanted to, he could punch straight through the window anyway, and wrap those tattooed fingers around my throat again.

I thumbed the switch. The window hummed down, intrusively loud in the silence. A breeze swept down the alley, toying with his hair, and I caught a hint of his cologne. It was smooth and subtle, but it had a deep, rich finish of sandalwood and vanilla that was the most primally sexual thing I'd ever smelled. It was like being wrapped in strips of silk and then hauled in and smooshed against hard male muscle. My face heated, and a thread of energy corkscrewed down to my groin. *Damn,* he smelled good.

His eyes raked over me. They seemed to linger on my chest, even though there isn't exactly much to see there, then carried on down over my gray suit pants. That magnificent, full lower lip curled. "So this is what you look like when you're not all dressed in leather." Maybe it was just his accent, but *leather* sounded teasing. He leaned in a little closer. "Why are you following me?"

"Why do you think?" I felt the anger rising: everything he was, everything he'd done, everything *people like him* had done. "Consider yourself put on notice, Mr. Aristov. The FBI is watching you very, *very* closely."

He shook his head slowly, his eyes locked on mine. "Don't try to take me on, Agent Brooks. You have no idea what I'm capable of."

My stomach flipped, fear pushing aside the anger, and I fought to keep my voice level. "That sounds like a threat."

"Threats are for people who are afraid to take action."

He glowered down at me, willing me to back off, and I was scared enough that I almost did. He'd tensed in anger, and as his shoulders pulled back, his tailored shirt had pulled tight across the broad curves of his pecs. The physical presence of him was intimidating as hell, and coupled with that legendary rage... He could end me without a second thought.

But that stubborn part of me right down at the center of my soul wouldn't give in. I owed it to my parents. "Better tell that private chef of yours to start cooking you some prison food," I managed. "Ease the transition."

He blinked exactly once. Then his jaw set and—

I felt something. Like after years of drifting through space, I'd suddenly collided with my perfect opposite, and we'd just locked together with a firm, magnetic seal, a human yin-yang symbol.

He's my nemesis. That's what it was. And as we stared at each other, I saw something change in his eyes. *He feels it, too.*

Then, without a word, he turned and stalked off towards his car, muscled shoulders swaying from side to side, his suit jacket tight across his broad back. My heart was hammering. *It's the adrenaline.*

He started his car, and I threw mine into gear. He glanced in his rear-view mirror and for a second, our eyes locked again. Then he sped away...and I followed.

4

GENNADIY

One week later

I WAS STRIPPED TO THE WAIST, MY BODY GLISTENING WITH SWEAT. THE punchbag twisted and swung, its chain creaking, as I hit it full strength, again and again. But I wasn't looking at it. I was looking past it, through the window, and down to the street outside. I was looking at her.

It had been a week since the FBI started their surveillance. I'd seen three other agents following me: two men, one fat and one thin, and a woman with long blonde hair. But most of the time it was her. I'd done some digging and managed to get her first name: *Alison*. So simple and plain next to the *Svetlanas* and *Ekaterinas* I was used to. And yet my mind kept going back to it, like a smoothly perfect stone I couldn't stop stroking.

I hated her. I hated her for being a cop. I hated her for being so slickly efficient that I couldn't shake her, and so doggedly determined that she wouldn't give up. I hated her for not being scared of me and for having the arrogance to think she could take me on.

Most of all, I hated her for being on my mind every minute of every day. I scowled. *Of course* I thought about her constantly; she was always *there,* following me in her car or on that big, cherry-red motorcycle of hers. I was having to move all my meetings indoors, away from her prying eyes. And I couldn't just go and inspect a growhouse, or a pill factory, or check on a cache of guns, because I'd lead her straight to them. I had to rely on my men to do the legwork and report back, and for a control freak like me, that was agony. So far, I'd managed to keep the investigation a secret from the rest of my family: this was my problem, and I'd solve it. But I had no idea how.

I cursed. *Blyat'!* I had better things to do than evade an FBI agent! There were deals to be done, new territory to take, enemies to eliminate...the anger inside me powered me, but it needed to be fed, too, and every day it demanded more and more blood.

I thumped the bag, and it rocked and spun. Alison Brooks was a royal pain in the ass, and the *worst part* was...I couldn't stop looking at her.

I scowled down at her car in the darkened street outside. I had the lights off and the blinds open in my home gym so I could watch her without her seeing me. The streetlight outside was busted, so I had to strain my eyes to see. I could just make out the pale curve of her neck and the dark mass of her hair, pinned up into its tight little bun. Her face was hidden in shadow, so I couldn't see her mouth. I slammed my fist into the bag again. That teasing, insolent mouth, gloriously wide, her lips blush pink and just slightly pouting. I whacked the bag with a left hook. *Maybe I should get that streetlight fixed.* It was bad for security to have so many shadows.

Her white blouse was just a slash of white against the dark lines of her jacket, but I'd spent enough hours glaring at her over the past week that my mind could fill in the details. Those upthrust little breasts, just two gentle hillocks in the white cotton. I couldn't stop imagining how she'd look naked, how her breasts would feel under my tongue as I lathed around and around her nipples until she was straining and begging.

Then there was that lean, athletic body. The door of her car blocked my view below her waist, but I knew how those long, elegant legs looked in her pant suit...and best of all, how that tight ass looked as she walked. I remembered how it had felt as she struggled against me at the casino. Was *that* why I was getting obsessed with her, because she was a woman who could actually hold her own against me in a fight?

I felt my forehead crease. Whenever I was around her, I could feel the anger building in my chest, that dark storm begging me to let loose and destroy her. But there were gold flecks caught in the hurricane, and the faster the anger whirled, the more I wanted to destroy her in another way. Grab her and slam her up against something and mash my lips down on hers. Rip her blouse and bra away and feel those pert little breasts stroke my bare chest, her nipples hard. I'd pull her legs around me, fingers sinking into her ass, and plunge deep into her, that pouting mouth wide and gasping, moaning my name—

I punched the bag so hard the eyebolt it hung from creaked, and a crack appeared in the plaster. *Chyort!* I stood there scowling down at her car, panting like a bull. *What's wrong with me?*

Just kill her. That was the sensible move. Wrap my hands around her throat again, and this time not stop until her eyes lose their light. Or even easier, call Valentin and have him slip a knife between her ribs. It wasn't as if she was hard to find; she was eight feet away from me every second of every day. I grabbed my phone and weighed it in my hand, still staring down at her...

And I thought what I'd thought every night that week.

Tomorrow. I'll kill her tomorrow.

5

ALISON

One week later

I PULLED UP OUTSIDE THE CASINO, OPENED THE DOOR...AND LET OUT A kind of *oof* as all the cool, air-conditioned air escaped and city air as thick and hot as soup rushed in. The city was sweltering in a brutal Chicago summer, every bit of concrete scorching, every metal door handle hot enough to burn. Even now, in the late afternoon, it was barely any cooler. I hurried over to Caroline's car and leaned in as she lowered her window. "Anything?"

She shook her head mournfully and showed me her notes. She'd been following Gennadiy all day, but he'd stuck to his usual haunts. I cursed under my breath. I'd been running this operation for two weeks now, and we had nothing actionable. "Thanks," I told Caroline. "Good work. Go on, get out of here."

She smiled gratefully and drove off to pick her kids up from daycare. I ran back to my car, shut myself inside, and cranked the air conditioning up to max... but like all of the vehicles from the FBI pool, it was built for utility, not luxury, and the blowers barely worked. I flapped my blouse against my skin and scowled at the casino's smoked glass doors. I'd taken the first shift, from six a.m.

until noon, and after working in the office for a few hours, I was back on until midnight tonight. Or, more likely, I'd wind up staying on until the morning, afraid that we'd miss something if I dared to catch a few hours' sleep.

The problem was, surveillance takes a lot of manpower, and our little team didn't have it. Normally, we'd have two or three people on each shift, but that was impossible with only four of us. Worse, Hadderwell and Fitch refused to work overtime, and Caroline's kids meant she couldn't work late either. So most of the time it was just me, sitting outside Gennadiy's mansion in an FBI car or following him through traffic on my bike. I watched him even when I was meant to be off duty. I was *determined* to bring him down...and it wasn't like I had anything better to do with my evenings.

The casino's doors swung open, and Gennadiy emerged, scowly and gorgeous, moving fast towards his car. He might be an evil, uncaring son of a bitch, but I had to admit he worked his ass off. He was always up and out of his mansion by seven, and he barely stopped all day, racing around town to visit the family's various illegal enterprises. He never made it home until the early hours. The man was a *machine.*

Gennadiy spotted me. His dark brows lowered, and he gave me one of his million-watt glares, his gray eyes like lasers. I glared right back, loathing him...and trying not to think about how his new suit really showed off the V-shape of his upper body, or how soft his coal-black hair looked today. Then he climbed into his car, and I started my engine, ready to follow.

Watching him had become my entire life: Caroline joked that I spent more time with him than with a husband. When you're around someone that much, you start to notice things. Like the fact that he favored his left leg when he walked. And that when he climbed into his BMW, he stroked the roof affectionately with that big, tattooed hand. And that sometimes, when he glared, and that tidal wave of hate slammed into me...it felt like there was something else, a current going in the opposite direction, trying to tug me closer even as the main wave pushed me away...

I scowled. *Don't be stupid.* Why would he want *me?*

When I wasn't watching him, I was working with Caroline to map his network of illegal operations and front companies. A few days ago, we'd finally gathered enough to convince a judge to authorize a phone tap. The first time I listened to one of Gennadiy's calls, I was full of hope.

But the calls I'd intercepted so far were worthless: the casino manager telling him about a new consignment of poker chips, the dry cleaners telling him his suit was ready. Gennadiy was too smart: he probably had burner phones we didn't know about, and he only used his regular phone for unimportant stuff.

Gennadiy drove off, and I tailed him to a bar called Worship, which the brothers had taken from a bunch of Armenians earlier that year. I followed him in and sat in the corner sipping a ridiculously expensive alcohol-free beer, but it was useless: the Aristovs disappeared into a VIP area upstairs, and I wasn't getting in there without a warrant. *Goddammit!*

When he finally left the bar, it was nearly midnight, and I was exhausted. I followed him back to the mansion and set up in my usual location outside. *Weird...wasn't that streetlight broken before?*

I reclined my seat as far as it would go. I didn't dare sleep, but I could at least get comfortable...or as comfortable as it's possible to be, in a car with only tepid bottled water and a stale takeout sandwich.

Suddenly, the laptop on the seat next to me bleeped. Gennadiy was making a call! I grabbed my earbuds, hope rising. It was the middle of the night; no way *this* was the dry cleaners.

A voice. Russian-accented, female, and... excited. "Are you almost here?"

A long-suffering sigh from Gennadiy. "I have to cancel, Avelina. I'm sorry."

"*Gennadiy!* Nooo!" She drew out the 'o' into a moan, and I grimaced. I could picture her, lower lip pouting. In my mind, she had long blonde hair and catwalk-model looks. I hated her already. It was something about his name in her mouth.

"You know how it is," he said tiredly. "A problem with work."

"There's *always* a problem with work."

I winced. I'd had this exact conversation with boyfriends in the past, when I had to work late at the FBI. They just didn't understand that—

"It's important," Gennadiy told Avelina. I nodded in agreement.

Avelina's voice became sulky and sing-song, like a spoiled princess. "Sometimes, I think you just don't care about me."

There was a scraping sound, and I realized Gennadiy was running his hand over his stubble. "Avelina, you went into this with your eyes open. I told you, no getting involved. Just sex."

I blinked. Was that really how he ran his life? It sounded so...stark. And lonely.

There was a rustle of covers and a *wump*, as if Avelina was lying in bed and had melodramatically flopped onto her back. "Fine. Tomorrow night, then. But...Gennadiy?"

"Yes?"

"Tell me what you'll do to me."

I could almost hear the smile spread across Gennadiy's face. "That depends. Have you been a good girl, Avelina? Or a bad one?"

The faint creak of the bed as Avelina shifted her weight. "A very, very bad one," she whispered.

"Then I'm going to have to bend you over your kitchen table again," Gennadiy told her. "Pull your dress up over your hips. Rip away your panties."

I felt my face heating. *I should stop listening.* Clearly, this wasn't about work. But my hand wouldn't move to the *Disconnect* button.

"Then I'll push your legs wide apart." Gennadiy's Russian accent made each word a silvery weight that sank through my mind and plunged straight to my groin. "Shove my face between your thighs."

I glared at the laptop. *I hate him,* I thought determinedly. *I'm going to destroy the bastard.*

But...

There was something different about the rage he sparked in me. I'm used to my anger, it's a poisonous black ooze that wells up from deep inside me, filling me, crushing my lungs until I can't breathe, squeezing my brain until I can't think, until I have to find some way to release it. But with Gennadiy, it was like the dark liquid heated as the pressure built. The more I saw of him, the more I heard his accent, the hotter the anger got, boiling towards a flashpoint where it would just explode.

"I'll pin you to the table," said Gennadiy. "And press my tongue right up inside you. I'll tongue-fuck you to the very edge. But I won't let you come. Not until you're a thrashing, moaning mess. Not until you beg me to let you."

Avelina's breathing had gone trembly. So had mine.

"And then I'll push two fingers into you and feel you squeeze them as you come," said Gennadiy.

I could see his thickly perfect, tattooed fingers in my mind. I shifted my ass on the seat. I was practically lying down, it was dark— well, dark*ish*—and no one was around. One hand wandered down to my thigh. Then I snatched it back. *No! Jesus, what's wrong with me?*

"What will you do then?" said Avelina, asking the question I couldn't.

"Pick you up," said Gennadiy. "Carry you through to the bedroom."

I'd experienced his arms wrapped around me, the press of his pecs against my back. I could imagine exactly what it would feel like to be carried like that.

"I'll throw you on the bed," Gennadiy told us. "Pull your dress down and suck a breast into my mouth."

My hand started to wander downwards again. Then a movement in my peripheral vision caught my eye. The drapes were open in one of the mansion's upstairs windows, and a hulking, suited figure had walked into view, a phone pressed to his ear. I froze, staring. I could see his mouth move as his words filled my ear. "I'll rake my teeth along your nipple, feeling it harden against my lips. And my hand will be on your throat, pinning you to the bed." The figure turned, and my heart jumped into my throat. He was staring out at the street, staring at *me!*

"I'll spread your legs wide," said Gennadiy in that silvery Russian accent. "And let my cock just kiss the lips of your pussy. That way, I can feel you getting wetter and wetter as I lick your breasts. I'll watch you grind your hips and arch your back. Trying to get me inside you. Needing me."

I hated him. But waves of heat were rippling down my body, making me crush my thighs together. My nipples were achingly hard, and I could feel I was getting wet.

Gennadiy paused, still staring right into my eyes. *He has no idea I'm listening. Right?*

"Do you need me right now?" asked Gennadiy.

Silence.

"Answer me!" growled Gennadiy.

I felt my lips form *yes.* Then Avelina whispered it, and I jerked in shock: I'd almost forgotten she was there.

"And then I'll bury my cock in you," said Gennadiy in my ear. "Deep, deep in you."

He's speaking to her, I repeated again and again in my mind. *He's speaking to her.*

"And I'll fuck you. Hard. Fast. Feeling you flutter and slicken around me until you're clawing at my back, until you're grabbing my ass to pull me into you. And then I'll ram myself into you to the root and kiss you while I shoot deep inside you. I will banish every man who's ever fucked you. You. Will. Be. Mine."

I lay there panting in the darkness, panties soaked. I detested this man. But apparently, my body hadn't gotten the message.

He was speaking to her. Right?

Gennadiy ended the call and pulled the drapes closed. But it was a long time before I stopped staring up at the window.

A few weeks later, at the end of the operation's first month, assistant director Halifax breezed into our office. "How's it going?" he asked.

"Great!" I beamed and waved at the wall of photos pinned to the wall, at the tree diagram of front companies and illegal enterprises we'd drawn. "We're closing in."

"Outstanding, Brooks." Halifax headed for the door. "Glad to hear it."

The instant the door closed, I let out a groan and slumped forward, resting my head on my keyboard. The truth was, we weren't any closer to bringing Gennadiy down. Some of it was a lack of resources. Caroline worked her ass off and was really great at tracking down information and making connections. But Hadderwell had to be asked three times to do anything, and Fitch was surly, obstructive, and spent most of his time staring at my ass.

The main problem, though, was that Gennadiy was just too smart. We had plenty of information, but no smoking gun that would let us arrest him. Most criminals are actually pretty stupid. A few are clever and organized. But Gennadiy was *exceptional.* He worked his ass off, and he never let his guard down.

Caroline patted my shoulder. "We'll get him."

"I have no idea how," I mumbled into my keyboard. "He's just so...*focused.*"

"Reminds me of someone," said Caroline. *What's that supposed to mean?* "Look, you mind if I head out?"

I checked the time. It was after six, and unlike me, she had a family and a life. "Shit! Sorry, Caroline. Go, get out of here."

She squeezed my shoulder, grabbed her purse, and headed out, leaving me as the last person in the office. I got up and paced, too stressed to sit still. *What the hell am I going to do?* Maybe Halifax had been right. Maybe Gennadiy *was* impossible to take down. If I failed, if three months went by and I still hadn't got him, I could kiss my career goodbye. But, worse, Gennadiy would get away. He'd keep getting more violent, keep building his empire, keep crushing the little people under his feet.

I caught a glimpse of my reflection in a computer monitor and stopped. *The little people.* Like my parents.

I looked quickly away, eyes roving across the tree diagram of Gennadiy's businesses. As I stood there wracking my brain for a way to bring Gennadiy down, I felt myself slowly rise up on my toes...and then sink back down. It's an old habit left over from dancing, and it helps me think, but it looks dumb, so I only let myself do it when there's no one around. I rose up...sank down. Gennadiy's empire was vast and it connected to others too: Konstantin Gulyev, Luka Malakov...sometimes, the Russian Mafia felt like an infinite, sprawling beast...

I frowned. *Russian* Mafia. I'd never thought about that part. Before they came to the US, the Bratva had operated in Russia. How had the *Russian* cops fought them?

I ran back to my computer and started typing, first looking on the internet, then connecting to the State Department and sifting through their files. I went down a rabbit hole, and when I emerged three hours later, I had my answer. The Russian government had tried everything for years. Nothing worked. And then one man changed everything. His name was Viktor Grushin.

I found a photo of him, a tall man in his late fifties with silver hair and a short, pointed beard: good looking, in an older man kind of way. He wasn't a cop, he was former GRU, Russian Military Intelligence. A frickin' *spy*. Almost all of his file was classified, but he'd had a busy career, from the Middle East to Africa. And when the government brought him in to break the Bratva, he'd done it. He was like the Russian Elliot Ness, the one guy who'd been able to beat the gangs. I scanned quickly through his file, leaning forward in my chair. Was he still around? Could I get in contact with him, ask for advice?

Damnit. He'd died a few years ago. But he beat the Bratva. It was *possible.*

As I closed the file, the exhaustion suddenly hit me. It was after eleven, and my day had started at six that morning. I stumbled downstairs and changed into my motorcycle gear, and a few moments later, I was scything through the streets on my bike.

Normally, I love riding. When you're driving a car, you move in staccato, ninety-degree movements: pull out, overtake, pull in. On a bike, you chain together a series of long, sweeping arcs, blasting past the traffic like it's standing still. There's no feeling like it in the world, and it's the only thing that lets me vent the toxic anger that builds up inside me.

Except...in the last few weeks, even riding hadn't been working. Being around Gennadiy fed my anger, and the more he made me mad, the more I obsessed about him. He was like the loose tooth my tongue couldn't stop jiggling. Even now, as I wove between cars on the Clark Street bridge, he was on my mind. I could see the wind ruffling his black hair, feel the kiss of his Russian accent against my ear. There were plenty of Bratva bosses. Why did this one rile me so much? Because he was arrogant? Because he'd destroyed part of my childhood and my mom's legacy? Or something else?

I thought about the way his blood-red shirt pulled tight across the curves of his pecs. About the infuriatingly addictive scent of him. About those thick, tattooed fingers and how he'd described thrusting them into me. I could almost feel them, parting my damp lips and sliding up inside—

A truck horn sounded, so close it vibrated through my entire body. I was in the wrong lane with a semi-truck thundering towards me, the driver bug-eyed with fear, waving for me to get out of the way. But my mind was still trying to catch up, and there wasn't enough time. The truck's headlights painted me white as we raced towards each other at a hundred-and-twenty miles an hour.

Fortunately, my body knew what to do even if my brain was frozen. My hands tugged the handlebars, and I instinctively leaned right. The bike drifted in behind a car, and the truck roared past an inch from my left elbow. I slowed and sat there panting, furious at myself. I *never* lost focus like that. *What's the matter with me?*

At home, I clomped up the stairs to my second-floor apartment, then peeled off my leathers and sighed. I was starving, and I knew the refrigerator was empty. There were still packing boxes in the corner of the room from when I'd moved back to Chicago, two years ago. The problem was, I was never home.

I stumbled through to the bathroom, stripped off, and got into the shower. Long hot showers are my one indulgence. If anyone asked, I'd claim it was something to do with relaxing my muscles. But the truth is, I'd found that if you run the water hot enough and stand there for long enough with the water really hammering you...it's almost like getting a hug.

When I got out, I wrapped myself in a towel and let myself fall full length on the bed. I was so exhausted, I instantly felt myself sinking down into black warmth.

But my mind was still spinning too fast. It wouldn't let me come to rest in that peaceful darkness. It powered me on, down and down.

Down into my own personal hell.

6

ALISON

"WE'RE GOING TO BE LATE," I MUTTERED FROM THE BACK SEAT.

"We're *not* going to be late, honey." My mom turned around and laid a gentle hand on my knee. "We left plenty of time."

My dad, who was driving, peered through the falling snow at the nose-to-tail traffic that stretched all the way to the next intersection. He didn't say anything, but I saw his jaw tighten: he wasn't so sure. My stomach knotted.

"It'll be fine, honey," my mom told me. "Want to run through your routine again? I can play the music."

I shook my head. I'd practiced the dance—as best I could, in our small apartment—since I woke up that morning, and I'd been running it on loop in my head since we left. I was as ready for the exam as I'd ever be. I just hoped I was ready enough.

"You got this," my mom said softly, and patted my knee. "You're gonna do great. And we're proud of you no matter what."

My mom was a ballet teacher, but back in the day, she'd been a pretty legendary dancer. She'd gone to the famous Fenbrook Academy in New York, toured with a big ballet company, had her picture on posters outside theaters... But she'd never pressured me to follow in her footsteps. When I was six, and she took me to my first ever class, she made it clear: "Try it. If you like it, do it. But don't do it for me."

As it turned out, I loved it. I had freakishly good balance, and transitioning from a *plié* to an *arabesque* felt natural; it felt *right*. And the attention to detail, thinking about every angle of my body, down to the pointing of my toes, appealed to my obsessive brain. Plus, deep down, I *did* want to be like Mom. I didn't have her calmness or her people skills, but I did have a little of her grace, and even if I'd never be as good as her, I wanted to dance. So I enrolled at her school, and I practiced every day alongside the other students. Mom made sure that I didn't get any special treatment for being her daughter. Six years on, I was a gawky twelve-year-old on her way to her first big external exam, and I was a bundle of nerves. "We're not even moving," I mumbled.

"You know what?" said my dad. "You're right. This traffic sucks. Fortunately, *I have a plan.*"

My mom and I rolled our eyes and smiled. *I have a plan* was one of my dad's catchphrases. A big, bearded guy, he had a softly rounded belly and an enormous heart. He was a middle school English teacher, and a lot of people couldn't figure out how someone like him had landed someone like my mom. She liked to tell the story of how she'd visited his school to talk to the kids and been utterly smitten by his gentle kindness.

My dad turned the wheel, and we broke out of the line of traffic and entered an alley. "We'll follow this to the next street over and miss the traffic, it'll save us ten, fifteen minutes. We'll be *early*. I deserve a cinnamon bun when we get there."

"How about a *kiss* when we get there?" my mom said. "Your doctor said to moderate the cinnamon buns."

We turned left and right, following the alley. "I saved the day," my dad mumbled, mock-grumpy. "I feel a cinnamon bun is more than warranted."

"A kiss from your wife isn't enough?" my mom asked, clapping a hand to her chest.

We turned out of the alley and onto a street...which was blessedly clear of traffic. *"There,"* said my dad, "Baby, a kiss from you is priceless. I'm just saying that there are times when a man—"

A flash of movement on my left. A dirt bike with two people on it, the visors on their helmets down to hide their faces. As they passed my dad's window, the glass disintegrated into tiny pebbles. At first, I thought they'd accidentally caught it with their wing mirror, but then they hurled something through the hole.

Time seemed to stop.

All three of us stared at the glass bottle as it tumbled. I could see it in exquisite detail: the colorless liquid that sloshed inside; the stained, red rubber band that secured the burning strip of rag. We knew what the thing was; we'd all seen them in movies. But none of us could process the thing being in our car. Then, as it went neck-down, glugging liquid, the tang of gasoline hit my nostrils. And the raw horror of it became real.

The bottle hit the dashboard, just in front of my mom, and shattered. Gasoline sprayed the windshield, the roof, my parents' clothes...followed a split-second later by flames. The outside world disappeared behind an orange sea of fire.

My mom screamed as flames raced up her sweater and down her legs. My dad's face, hair, and beard caught fire, and the car swerved violently. There was a sickening crunch, and suddenly we were lifting and spinning. As the car corkscrewed through the air, burning gasoline fell like rain. Some of it reached the backseat, and I screamed and ducked, covering my face with my hands.

The car landed hard on its roof, and I blacked out for a second. I woke to agonizing pain in my left leg.

I was hanging upside down, held by my seatbelt and—

I was in a leotard, and even though the car's heater had been on, my mom had wrapped a blanket around my legs to make sure I stayed warm. The blanket had come loose from my right leg, but it was still around my left...and the blanket was on fire.

I screamed and kicked, trying to slither out of it. Which is when I discovered the blanket was made of some man-made fiber, and it had melted and stuck to my skin.

In the front seats, my mom was screaming hysterically, non-stop. My dad wasn't making any sound at all. Every surface was covered with roaring flames, and the car was filling up with choking white smoke.

I hit my seatbelt release and collapsed onto the ceiling, which was now the floor. My leg was a solid mass of white-hot pain. I could barely see through the tears, and every choking sob filled my lungs with smoke. I somehow managed to find the door handle and pulled it, spilling out onto the snowy sidewalk. Blessedly cold air bathed my body, but the blanket was still on fire. I remembered something about rolling on the ground, but it hurt too much to move. I scooped snow over my leg instead, and the flames finally went out.

Now I had to save my parents. I gritted my teeth against the pain, rolled onto my front, and started crawling back towards the car—

The wind cleared the smoke for a second. I saw my parents...and started screaming.

I fought my way up out of the nightmare and woke still screaming, my lungs raw. I scrambled across the bed and hugged myself into a fetal ball in the corner.

The police found me lying on the sidewalk. They rushed me to the hospital and then to a specialist burn unit. My leg's bone and muscle were intact: when I healed, I'd be able to walk with no problems. But...

I ran my hands over my left leg in the darkness. From toes to mid-thigh, the skin was a mass of swirling, shiny scars.

The cops figured out what had happened pretty quickly. Two mafia families, the Torrisis and the Emilianis, were at war. The Torrisis had targeted an Emiliani lieutenant called Stefano, and he drove the same model and color car as my dad. The guys on bikes had been chasing him and briefly lost him. Then we happened to turn onto the same street, right in front of them.

If I hadn't been going to a dance exam.

If I hadn't been nervous, and made my dad take a shortcut.

Everyone knew that the Torrisis were responsible, but the cops couldn't prove anything. No one went to jail.

With my parents gone and no other relatives who could take me in, I wound up in a group home in a shitty area of the city. All the other kids were already involved in petty crime, or drifting towards it. As the lone kid from a nice neighborhood, I was an instant target. I found that out the first morning, when I dug my spoon into my oatmeal and found a dead cockroach.

I gave up on ballet. There was no money for lessons, plus who wants a ballerina who makes the audience cry out in horror—or pity —when they see her leg? For a few weeks, I had this forlorn hope that someone would adopt me, like in the movies, and I'd get a whole new family who loved me. I soon learned that people want to adopt adorable babies, not traumatized, scarred twelve-year-olds.

The de facto leader of the other kids was a boy called Wyatt. He alternated between beating me up to impress the others and pressuring me to get into shoplifting because, as a girl, I could hang out in the cosmetics aisle and fill my bag with valuable, easy-to-sell make-up. But I kept thinking of my mom and dad. Somehow, it felt even more important now to make them proud. So I said no, even when it meant Wyatt leaving me with black eyes or, once, a broken finger.

There's something about living without affection—without anyone hugging you, without anyone asking how your day was or comforting you when you're hurt—that hardens you, and not in a good way. I put up walls to keep everyone out and became silent and withdrawn at school.

Then, when I was fourteen, Wyatt started making noises about a different way I could work for him. There were men he could introduce me to, he said.

I ran out into the night, in the middle of a downpour. I wound up sobbing my heart out on the curb a few blocks from the group home. I just wanted my mom's scent and my dad's hugs. *How is this my life?*

I hit rock bottom. I hit it so hard that something inside me cracked, and what leaked out was a dark fury.

It was *wrong.* A gang snatched my family away from me and left me stranded in this place, and no one did anything about it. And now I was going to be forced into that same criminal world, and some guy would—would *buy* me...

The anger welled up inside me, and I let it fill me, power me. Being mad was better than being scared.

I slowly got to my feet, soaked to the bone but standing tall. And I walked further down the block, to a place I'd passed many times, a small building with a faded sign that said *Master Sun's Tang Soo Do.* Classes were finished for the night, but I found Master Sun sweeping the mats. He was in his late fifties, but aside from his gunmetal-gray hair, you wouldn't have known it. He had that lean toughness that comes from fighting your entire life. "I need you to teach me," I told him.

"I'm sorry," he said gently. "All my classes are full. Come back in September."

I stepped closer. "I *need you,*" I said, my voice cracking, "to teach me."

He looked at me more closely: at the fading bruises around my eyes and the fresh ones on my arms, and his mouth tightened. Then he nodded.

"I can't pay," I warned him.

He nodded again. "That's okay."

My chest seemed to open and lift: it was the first time anyone had shown kindness to me in years. "W—When can we start?"

He laid his broom against the wall. "Now."

Master Sun trained me, and I discovered that martial arts, with its precision and speed and endless practice, wasn't so different from dancing. My freakish balance helped, too. I trained every day, getting stronger and faster. After a year, I was good enough to break Wyatt's arm when he cornered me in a hallway, and he left me alone after that. But I didn't stop learning. That anger I'd unleashed needed to be let out, or it would consume me. So I sparred with Master Sun every night, all through my teens.

The guy who ran the group home had an old scooter, and as soon as I was old enough, I started delivering pizza so I could pay Master Sun. But he refused to take my money. "Save it," he told me. "Use it to get out of this neighborhood."

As the end of high school approached, people started to ask me what I wanted to do. I already knew: I wanted to stop the gangs. So I joined the Chicago Police Department.

At the Police Academy, I discovered I was lousy at the parts of policing that required gentle, tactful diplomacy and other people skills I'd missed out on learning. But I excelled at unarmed combat, and my obsessive brain meant I'd follow up every last lead until I finally made progress. I eventually made detective and threw myself into my work, even picking up a few commendations.

But what nobody saw was that I was achingly lonely. Those walls I'd built around myself in the group home left me unable to trust, unable to make friends, and I didn't know how to dismantle them. I became known for always being the last one still working. Partly, it was my obsessive brain: I couldn't quit until I'd caught my target. But partly, I was burying myself in my work because I didn't want to come home to an empty apartment.

Then my success caught the attention of Carrie Blake, head of the FBI New York office, and she encouraged me to join. For the first time, I felt like I'd found a home. An agent named Sam Calahan took me under his wing, and for years, I worked with him, Kate, and Hailey. They accepted my weirdness and became my friends.

But one by one, they all found love and moved on. First, Kate met Mason and moved to Alaska. Then, even perpetual bachelor Calahan fell in love with the mathematician and hacker, Yolanda. I could feel my new found family disintegrating, and I was terrified of being the last one left. So when a position opened up at the Chicago office, I transferred. And now here I was: burying myself in my work because it was all I knew how to do. I'd found a friend in Caroline, but her kids meant she didn't exactly have time to go for after-work cocktails.

And it wasn't like I was going to meet a guy. Even before the fire, I wasn't much to look at. I don't have the curves men love: hell, I've barely got *anything* up top. If a man *is* interested in me, he gets scared off as soon as he finds out I'm an FBI agent, let alone when he learns that I can kick his ass in a fight. And if by some miracle we do get to a second date, I have to gently tell him about my leg. Do you know what it's like to dig up the courage to reveal something like that to someone you really like...and then have him stop calling you? After it happened three times in a row, I just stopped dating.

Plus, there was my obsessive nature. Sure, if I did have friends and romance, I'd cut back on work a little. But I'm always going to be pushing myself and working late, and no halfway normal guy is going to be okay with that. Sometimes, I think the only man I could be with is someone who understands. Another workaholic, someone as obsessive as I am. And where the hell am I going to find someone like *that?*

7

GENNADIY

July

I PUSHED THE PEDAL TO THE FLOOR. THE TURBOCHARGER WHINED AS IT sucked in air, and then unleashed it in a melodious roar that shook the windows of the downtown stores around me. The car surged forward, and a smile played across my lips. My brother Radimir likes his big Mercedes, but I've always loved my BMW. When we were teenagers in Moscow, living on scraps, I used to see the oligarchs driving past in their shining BMWs and dream of owning one. Now I have one, and on a summer day like today, blasting down North Michigan Avenue while it's still empty of traffic, there's no better feeling in the world.

Except—I checked my rear-view mirror and my knuckles whitened on the steering wheel—I couldn't relax and enjoy it because Alison was there, following me in an unmarked car. Silky black hair secured in an efficient little bun at the back of her head, blouse tight over her small, high breasts. She was wearing the blue blouse today, the one that matched her eyes.

I shook my head in irritation. She was better at this than any cop I'd ever known. She stuck to me like glue, even when I was up before dawn or rolling home in the early hours. She couldn't be doing all this for a paltry government salary. What was driving her?

I sighed and turned into an underground parking garage. A few moments later, I was strolling through Conroy Mall. It's just your standard shopping mall: clothes and home furnishings, piped music, and coffee shops...and weirdly, it's one of my favorite places to go. I've never been able to figure out why.

I'd managed to lose Alison briefly as I left the parking garage, and for a brief, glorious moment, I thought I'd slipped away for good. Then I saw her reflection in a cookware shop's window, and my shoulders slumped in disappointment. She must have gone to the security office and tracked me down on the cameras. I glared at her in the glass as I pretended to adjust my collar, my eyes running down those long, graceful legs. Why does she never wear skirts?

I marched over to a coffee stand and bought a cup, killing time until my meeting with Radimir. Then I glanced over my shoulder and—

Alison wasn't looking at me. She was staring off to the side. I blinked, my ego bruised. What was more important than me? Her whole job was watching me!

I followed Alison's gaze. There was a gang of teenagers outside the make-up store, one slightly older boy of about fifteen, and a bunch of younger kids. The boy was leaning over, snarling at one of the girls and pointing towards the store. The girl looked like she was about to burst into tears.

I recognized the setup because it was the same in Moscow and in every other city in the world. An older kid using the younger ones as *krysy,* as rats. He forces them to shoplift and takes the profits, and if one of them gets caught, then he can just walk away.

I turned back to Alison. She was still watching the kids. I frowned, bemused. What does she care? Shoplifting wasn't exactly an FBI-level crime.

I took a slow, careful step away. This was my chance, while she was distracted. I could get away and actually have five minutes of blessed privacy with my brother.

But then I stopped. I had to know what she was doing.

Alison marched over to the kid in charge and grabbed his shoulder. He took a swing at her, and she swayed and hooked his leg, and he went face-first into the floor. She pinioned him there with a knee on his back. What the hell is she doing? Shaking them down, maybe? I could imagine that with a drug dealer, but this kid probably wouldn't have much money. Did the FBI pay that badly?

Then she showed him her badge and started speaking into his ear, quiet and very, very serious.

I felt my jaw drop. Is she...GIVING HIM A TALK?! Like some cop in a wholesome Christmas family movie? The kid was nodding frantically. And now she was talking to the girl, probably telling her something like he won't bother you again, and the girl was nodding gratefully and scurrying away...

I stared at her in amazement. All the cops I knew in Moscow were on the take. Even in the US, I'd always presumed most of them were corrupt, or at least just out for themselves. But apparently, I was being hunted by—the words tasted strange—an honest cop.

Alison got to her feet and saw me watching. She looked surprised that I was still standing there.

I gazed at her, shell-shocked. I still hated her: she was still one of them, one of the enemy, and she was still trying to tear down my whole world. But I'd always presumed that deep down, we were the same, just on opposite sides of a war. I'd never considered she might be...good. I braced, waiting for the attraction to flicker and die, now that I knew her character.

Except that isn't what happened at all. The attraction fucking exploded like I'd just dumped a gallon of gasoline onto the fire. Every muscle tensed. My cock rose. I actually took an involuntary step towards her. I wanted her more than ever.

Her whole buttoned-down appearance made it even hotter. My vision telescoped in to the exact point, just in front of her bun, where I'd have to sink my fingers into her hair to rake the hair clips out of it and let her hair fall free. I could see tiny slivers of tan skin between the buttons of her blouse, together with scraps of her white bra, and I could imagine exactly how her stomach would feel, warm against my fingers, as I slid my hands up and ripped that blouse open so I could cup her breasts...

Her goodness was a magnet. All I could think about was plunging deep, burying myself in her, filling her with bad. I'd fuck the good right out of her.

I felt my face heat. *Chyort!* Apparently, I had a thing for good girls.

Alison frowned at me, and I realized I wasn't doing my usual scowl. I didn't know what I was doing. I gave her a glare and turned away, stalking over to the food court and taking a seat.

She took a table in the corner, and I couldn't help but look again. For a second, I was back in my office, caging her in my chair with my arms. Let me educate you, Agent Brooks. Except now, it had a whole new dimension. I imagined her over my knee, naked, moaning and squirming, breasts rubbing against my legs, long hair tossing as my hand rose and fell on her ass, teaching her a lesson—

My view was suddenly blocked by a broad, muscled chest and an expensive waistcoat being tugged straight. I looked up into Radimir's cold blue eyes. "We have our own nightclub. Fourteen bars. Membership at three different private clubs. Why do you always insist on meeting here?"

I coughed, embarrassed, and forced all thoughts of Alison away. Then I smiled at him. "Because it annoys you, brother. How's Bronwyn?" He'd gotten married earlier that year.

Radimir grinned. He never used to smile. "Good," he said with feeling. "Very good. I never thought being married would be so..." He shook his head, unable to find the words. "I'm going to surprise her. While she's away this weekend, I'm going to build her bookshelves."

"Bookshelves?"

"Bookshelves." He spread his arms wide. "Big white ones. Floor to ceiling. The whole wall."

I frowned. "I thought women wanted shoes."

Radimir shook his head smugly. "Bookshelves."

I shook my head in wonder. I couldn't imagine ever being so

besotted with a woman. "It's good to see you happy, brother. Next thing, you'll be making me an uncle."

Radimir held my gaze, suddenly serious. My eyes bulged, and I nearly spat out my coffee. Was he actually thinking about it? Him, a father?

"Let's talk business," said Radimir, quickly changing the subject. We both leaned in. "The Irish..." he began.

I sighed, then glanced at Alison over Radimir's shoulder. She was too far away to hear us over the noise of the food court, and we were speaking in Russian. "I still think this is a mistake. I don't trust them."

Radimir put his elbows on the table and cupped one big, tattooed fist with his other hand. "They're the only ones who can do what we need. Finn is reliable."

A few months ago, we defeated the Nazarov brothers and took over their territory and all their operations. That left us with a problem: the Nazarovs handled most of Chicago's drug trade. We didn't have the resources to take it over, but we didn't want to leave a power vacuum, either. The only option was to partner with another gang. Radimir had chosen The Irish Mafia, led by Finn O'Donnell

I scowled. "I don't like them."

Radimir nodded. "I know. But you'll do the deal? For me?"

I sighed. "Of course, brother." I don't always agree with him, but he's still my Pakhan. We discussed the details, talking in code just to be sure: bricks of heroin were sandstone, cocaine was marble. I pulled out my pen and made notes in the little notebook I carry in my jacket. I don't trust computers or smartphones. I take paper notes, and at the end of each day, I burn the pages. I glared at Alison. Try hacking that.

Radimir blinked at me. "Everything okay?"

I snapped my gaze back to him and nodded. I still hadn't told him about Alison. He had enough to deal with, heading the family. Plus, if he found out I had an FBI agent on my tail, he might want to kill her.

I frowned. Why did that thought make something twist uneasily, deep in my gut? I wanted to fuck her, but I didn't care what happened to her...right?

Killing her would draw too much attention, I decided. Yes. That was it.

Radimir leaned forward. "I'm worried about you."

I shook my head and sipped my coffee. "I'm fine."

Radimir sighed. "We've expanded so much over the last year, and you've taken on more and more. All you do is work. And..." He leaned closer. "The way you're operating, Gennadiy." He dropped his voice to a whisper. "The fires. The killing."

"I do what's necessary," I told him stiffly.

He shook his head. "You're becoming..."

"I'm becoming what I need to be, to protect us. And I told you, I'm fine." I knocked back my coffee, even though it was still so hot it burned my mouth. Then I embraced him and got out of there.

Before I met Finn, I had to shake off Alison. I led her on a winding path through back alleys, but she stayed with me. I drove around a huge underground parking garage, but she was still there. When we stopped at a red light, I sat watching her in my rear-view mirror, my gaze searing into her as the anger roiled and churned inside me. How dare you! How dare you try to destroy everything I've built? She was so small, so insignificant, and yet so irritating, like a little bird peck-peck-pecking at a bear. With her gray FBI suit and that tight, tight blouse, and those lips so insolently pouting as she glared back at me. I just wanted to...wanted to...

She cocked a perfect eyebrow at me as if to say, Well?

A horn honked behind me. Fuck! The light was green. I stamped on the gas, my face heating.

I roared across the intersection with her right behind me. Then right, down a side street. Left, into an alley. She was still there. I was panting with adrenaline, pissed off and cursing and—

Alive. More alive than I'd felt in years. I'd never had a worthy opponent before.

Ahead of me, a garbage truck was reversing across the alley. I floored it and shot through the closing gap...

There was an ugly screech of metal on metal as the prongs at the back of the garbage truck clawed at my car. Then I was through, and she was left behind, stuck behind the garbage truck. Finally! For the first time in weeks, I was free of her.

Then I checked my side mirror. A long, ugly scratch ran almost the full length of my beloved car. I thumped the steering wheel and cursed. *Yebat'! Pizdets blyat'!*

Finn wanted to meet at the dog track, where his gang had gotten its start years before as illegal bookmakers. It was hot, loud, and the ground was littered with discarded betting slips soaked in spilled beer. In my Armani suit and Italian leather shoes I didn't exactly fit in.

"There he is!" yelled Finn, slapping me on the back. His white shirt was rolled up to the elbows, showing off thickly muscled forearms covered in twisting tattoos. He gave me a wide grin, green eyes flashing, and pushed a bottle of whiskey into my hand. "Let's walk while we talk. This one's running in the next race." He rubbed the fuzzy head of a greyhound and set off, the dog trotting alongside him.

I sighed and followed. I've never liked the O'Donnells. They're our polar opposites, casual where we're professional, emotional where we're reserved. We're skyscrapers, expensive vodka, and a silenced shot in the night. They're rowdy bars, whiskey and headbutts.

The crowd parted ahead of us. This was Irish turf, and everyone knew the O'Donnells: the men bobbed their heads respectfully and avoided eye contact; the women blushed and smiled at Finn. He swaggered, a king among his people.

"We're ready to do the deal," I said in a low voice. "You can keep seventy-five percent of what you make."

"Feck, always straight to business with you, isn't it, Gennadiy?" He had just a hint of an Irish accent, like a spinning coin twinkling as it catches the light. A pretty young redhead heard it and turned, wide-eyed and breathy, and Finn grinned at her. I rolled my eyes. I've never understood his effect on women.

Finn took a pull on his whiskey and looked at my bottle. "You're not drinking."

"It's eleven in the morning."

"You Russians would have a lot more fun if you pulled the sticks out of your asses. I want eighty-five percent, Gennadiy, and that's me going so low my balls are brushing the ground. And they're big balls, I'll grant you, but that's still fucking low."

I was about to argue when one of Finn's brothers rushed over and grabbed his arm. "Eyes on us. Ten feet back, gray suit."

I groaned and crumpled. I didn't even have to turn around to know it was her.

Finn looked over my shoulder. "You brought a tail?" he demanded, furious. "A *fed*?"

"I thought I'd lost her. She's...annoyingly persistent."

"Fuck this. C'mon, boy." He started to lead his greyhound away.

"Finn, wait!"

He turned and jabbed a finger into my chest. "Deal's off. Come back when the feds aren't crawling all over you." And he walked away.

Chyort! I hurled the bottle of whiskey at a wall. Radimir was going to be pissed, and it was all her fault. I finally turned, and there she was, casually leaning against a wall. She glanced towards Finn and made her eyes go big with mock concern. *Oh, did your meeting not go well?*

I marched over to her as hot, dark rage spread through my chest. "Why are you doing this?!" I snarled in her face.

She gave a quick little intake of fear as I loomed over her, but then glared up at me, blue eyes gleaming. Even through my anger, I was grudgingly impressed. "It's my job," she told me.

"Bullshit. No one's this devoted." I searched her face. "This isn't just about a theater, is it?"

For a second, her eyes flickered. There was something else driving her. I leaned closer, scowling down at her...

And then I blinked in shock. Turned and marched away, shaken. Just for a second there, I'd glimpsed something. What was driving her wasn't some noble, idealistic cause. It was hate. *Anger.*

Just for a second, it had been like looking in the mirror.

I climbed into my car and slammed the door. Then I ran a hand through my hair and scowled, calming my breathing. It didn't matter if we were somehow alike. All that mattered was, she'd gone beyond annoying. She'd become an actual problem.

You want to play, Alison? I threw my car into gear. *Fine. We'll play.*

8

ALISON

August

GODDAMN HIM.

It was three in the morning, and I was on a Coast Guard patrol boat, hanging onto the rail as a summer storm made the deck heave under my feet and then drop away sickeningly. Three coast guardsmen with boat hooks were hauling a dark mass over the rail. It fell to the deck and rolled to a stop under the beam of my flashlight. A body, wrapped in chains. "You think your guy did this?" asked one of the guardsmen.

I nodded. "You were right to call me." Technically, Caroline had been on call, but I hadn't been about to drag her away from her kids in the middle of the night, so I'd taken it. As the boat headed towards shore, I sighed. We'd check for clues, but Gennadiy wouldn't have left any. He never did.

I was into my third and final month of surveilling him, and I still didn't have anything concrete. In that time, there'd been three murders, one bank robbery, four more cases of arson, and countless gun deals I knew involved him, but I didn't have any hard evidence.

He was too smart, too careful. He never used his own gun, the one he was licensed to carry. The only time we'd ever found bullets from it was when he'd fired it in self-defense at Radimir's wedding. I was desperate. If I didn't get a win soon, my boss would close down the operation. I was working sixteen hours a day, seven days a week, and my only breaks were to visit Master Sun, who wasn't doing well. He was seventy, now, and in the hospital, fighting cancer. It was heartbreaking: we'd sparred at least twice a week for over ten years. He was the closest thing to family I had.

When I got back into my car at the docks, I turned off the interior light, made sure no one was watching, and then screamed long and loud, hammering my fists on the steering wheel. Then I sat there panting in the darkness, utterly drained. In all my years in law enforcement I've never encountered someone I couldn't bring down. I was starting to doubt myself. Am I just not good enough?

I'd never felt this way about a target. At home, I had a life-sized martial arts training dummy, and it was Gennadiy's arrogant face I saw when I punched and kicked it. But afterwards, when I fell into bed and tried to sleep...Gennadiy's face came to me then, too. Those high cheekbones and that full, sinful lower lip. I knew his face better than any lover's. I knew every tattoo on every one of his fingers. I'd started daydreaming about what he looked like under his suit, guessing the shape of his pecs and abs from when the wind plastered his shirt across them.

I knew I shouldn't be attracted to him. But there was something about the way his lips tightened when he scowled; the way he walked, like he was crushing his enemies underfoot. I kept remembering the feel of him against me when he had me imprisoned in his arms. There was something about all that seething, angry power that was magnetic. I could still feel the heat of his cock as it swelled against my leather-clad ass...

I frowned at myself in the rear-view mirror. *Focus!* Viktor Grushin, the Russian cop who'd become sort of my hero, would never have been weak like this. I'd read everything I could find on his successes:

he'd busted over twenty Bratva gangs in Moscow, although the articles were always frustratingly vague on how he'd done it. What I did know was, he hadn't done it by moping...or fantasizing about his target.

I took a deep breath, then threw my car into gear. It was almost four am, too late to sleep. Might as well make an early start.

Later that day, I finally got the break I needed.

Her name was Monica Aiken, and she worked for a small freight company. The cops had picked her up for speeding and found enough coke in her car to put her away. She'd told them she had information that she'd trade to make the charges go away. And then she dropped the bombshell: it's about Gennadiy Aristov.

He'd visited their freight company and arranged to ship some crates from New York to Chicago. They were being delivered to one of Gennadiy's front businesses, a bathroom supply company. They were arriving in the dead of night, and Gennadiy was meeting the truck personally. I'd known Gennadiy was bringing guns into the city for months; I just hadn't known how. *This is it! This is how I catch him!*

That night, running on two hours of sleep and bad coffee, I hunkered behind a wall along with the rest of my team and assistant director Halifax. We were all armed and in body armor, and we had five of the FBI's Tactical Response guys with us in full combat gear with assault rifles. This could turn into a firefight, and we weren't taking any chances.

Just past midnight, Gennadiy's BMW showed up. He'd had it lovingly resprayed and polished to remove the scratch. I smirked. *Waste of time, Gennadiy. You won't need a car where you're going.*

He climbed out, together with his brother Valentin and two heavies, and they gathered in front of the building's loading dock. A moment later, the truck turned into the parking lot. We all checked our weapons.

The truck reversed up to the loading dock. Gennadiy and Valentin lowered the tailgate and—

I sprinted out from behind the wall, heart hammering, gun pointed right at Gennadiy's chest. "FBI! Hands where I can see them!" Behind me, the tactical team spread out, covering me.

Gennadiy stepped back and calmly raised his hands in the air.

We moved forward, slow and careful. Only when I was sure that all of Gennadiy's gang were under control did I holster my pistol and climb up into the truck.

Six big wooden crates. I grinned at Caroline, and she grinned back at me. We got him. She passed me a crowbar, and I levered the top off a crate...

A sea of cheerful, bright yellow plastic. I blinked. Ducks. Hundreds of rubber ducks.

It's cover, in case anyone opens the crate.

I plunged my hands inside, waiting to feel the cold metal of an assault rifle. But there was nothing, even when my fingers brushed the bottom of the crate.

Well, obviously, they wouldn't put them in the crates at the front! I levered open the second crate. More ducks. The third crate. Same thing. The fourth and fifth. Now there was only one crate left, and a sickening realization was sinking in. *Oh no. Oh, God, please no...*

I pried open the last crate.

Hundreds of little yellow faces stared up at me.

I stared in raw horror. Then my heart suddenly lifted. The crates have false bottoms! I heaved the crates over onto their sides. Thousands of rubber ducks spilled into the bed of the truck and waterfalled down to the ground, forming a spreading yellow sea.

No false bottoms. No secret compartments. Nothing.

I waded through the ducks, jumped down from the truck, and marched over to Gennadiy. "What the fuck is this?!" I demanded, shoving one of the ducks into his chest.

He took the duck and examined it. "You play with it in the bathtub," he explained innocently.

"Why would you need thousands of them?!"

He pointed to the sign on the building behind him. "It's a bathroom supply company. We're planning a promotion: a free duck with every purchase."

"Why would you arrange delivery for midnight?"

Gennadiy shrugged. "Is there some law against working late?" And just for a second, the corners of his mouth twitched. The bastard was trying not to laugh.

Monica Aiken. She'd been a plant. He'd paid her to get arrested, told her exactly what to say to the cops. He'd baited the hook, and I'd swallowed it. We'd spent all our time and resources here, while the real shipment of guns was happening somewhere else.

Halifax walked over. "You and your men are free to go, Mr. Aristov." Then he looked at me and shook his head, furious.

The next day, Halifax called me into his office for a long lecture on not leaping into action without all the facts. The bust had cost the FBI tens of thousands of dollars plus countless hours of paperwork, all for nothing. "We agreed three months," he warned me. "You've got four weeks left."

When I got back to my desk, there was a new picture on the wall. Someone had snapped a photo of me standing in the back of the truck, looking utterly crestfallen, knee deep in rubber ducks. Hadderwell and Fitch were chuckling like schoolkids. Only Caroline looked sympathetic.

Then a package arrived, addressed to me. I opened the box...

A rubber duck. There was a note, in looping, confident script.

For when you are naked in the bath — G.

I stared at the thing, my chest rising and falling as the rage filled me and threatened to overflow. He'd screwed me, seriously denting my career, either to try to get rid of me or just for fun. I squeezed the duck so hard the plastic squished...

But I didn't hurl it across the room. That was what he wanted. I took a deep breath and placed the duck beside my computer, a reminder to never underestimate him again.

You want war, Gennadiy? You got it.

9

GENNADIY

"She's watching us again," Yakov told me mildly. "Your little bird."

I grunted and poured zavarka into my cup, then added hot water to the concentrated tea and finally a thick slice of lemon. It was noon on a gloriously warm day, a few days after the rubber duck incident, and I was in a plastic lawn chair, stripped to the waist, letting the sun soak into my bones for maybe the last time before the summer ended.

Yakov Beletski was one of the first people I met when my brothers and I came to Chicago a decade ago. He's in his fifties now and looks more like a college professor than a gangster, with his slim build, graying hair, and gold-rimmed glasses, but he's run the Chicago docks for almost twenty years, quietly—sometimes viciously— defending his turf against everyone who's come along. If you want to bring anything through the docks, you talk to Yakov.

He'd become my best friend, and sitting up here on the concrete roof of the dock's control center with him had become a tradition. My life has become smoothly privileged: luxury cars, expensive suits, and shaking hands with politicians. It doesn't hurt to remind yourself where you came from and enjoy a simple pleasure at the same time. I sighed and closed my eyes.

"I can take care of her, if you like," Yakov told me.

I opened one eye. We were both wearing big, aviator sunglasses, and as Yakov leaned forward to take the teapot, I could see Alison reflected in his lenses. She was lying full-length on top of one of the enormous cranes that moved containers around, watching us through binoculars.

It was strange: whenever I realized she was still there, I felt my anger flare and rise. But lately, the anger settled to a kind of warm peace, as if she belonged there. And when I did occasionally manage to slip away from her, the thrill of victory had a coldness beneath it, almost like a pang of anxiety.

She must have ridden her motorcycle to the docks because I could just make out the glint of the sunlight on her leather pants. I wondered how warm the leather would be to the touch right now, like a black cat that's been basking in the sun. I imagined putting my hand on her ankle, running it all the way up her leg, and squeezing her ass, warm and soft, and then pushing my hand in between her thighs and cupping her pussy as she moaned.

"That won't be necessary," I mumbled to Yakov.

"It's no problem. I can have one of my men waiting for her when she comes down." Yakov grinned, jovial as always. "He takes her head, one quick twist..."—he mimed it—"*krrrk!* Then he carries her back up and drops her off the top—"

"No."

"—everyone will think she slipped on the ladder!"

"No!" I said it a little more sharply than I'd meant to, and Yakov cocked his head curiously. I searched for an explanation. "They'll just send another agent," I said. "It's easier to keep tabs on this one. I know her face."

"Mmm," said Yakov. He dipped his head and looked at me over his sunglasses. "It's a very pretty face."

I scowled. "I hadn't noticed."

～

That afternoon, I went with Valentin to pick up the weekly money drop from the Irish. A few weeks before, I'd finally managed to shake off Alison long enough to do the deal with Finn, but it had taken an entire day, with Mikhail driving my BMW as a decoy, to pull it off. Finn had thought it was hilarious that a woman was giving me so many problems. *I can distract her, if you like*, he'd offered. *Charm the panties off her and keep her busy all night long.* I don't know why that bothered me so much. I'd had to stop myself from punching him right in his grinning face.

The drop was at a storm drain on the edge of town, somewhere we were sure there were no cameras. By the time we got there, the sun was low in the sky, throwing out long shadows of the two of us as we walked over to the drain. I kept watch while Valentin climbed up into the huge, concrete tube. A moment later, he was back...but without the two sports bags of cash I'd been expecting. "It's gone," he said, his face pale.

"What do you mean, it's gone?"

"Someone's taken it."

Not possible. No one knew about these money drops; we'd been ultra-careful. "Finn must not have made the drop," I muttered. Which was strange because, even though I hated to admit it, Radimir had been right: Finn was usually reliable.

Valentin shook his head. "He left it there for us. Someone took it."

"How do you know that?"

Valentin held something out. "Because they left a note!"

I stared at the envelope in his hand. *What the ACTUAL FUCK? Who would dare to do this? The Italians? One of the cartels?*

I ripped open the envelope and pulled out the card inside. A single one-dollar bill was taped to it.

In case you find yourself short on cash.
-A.

I turned away from Valentin, crushing the note in my fist. The anger swelled in my chest, spinning faster and faster until it was a scorching hurricane. That scheming, sneaky little—

It wasn't the money. A couple of hundred thousand dollars: we'd make that back in a week. It was the embarrassment. I'd have to tell Radimir.

I'd made her look bad. So she'd made me look bad.

It was even worse because I knew that she hadn't just kept the money, like any normal, corrupt cop would. Then I could have at least blackmailed her and gotten her on my payroll. No, I knew Alison: she'd handed every single bill in as evidence, building the case against me. How do you fight that kind of...*honesty?!*

I opened my fist and stared at her signature, at that teasing little 'A', and the anger built and built...and as it peaked, I felt it sear something permanently into my soul: a grudging respect.

I wanted to obliterate her for doing this. But I couldn't deny how slickly she'd pulled it off. I wasn't even sure how she'd done it.

Alison Brooks wasn't any normal cop. She was my equal.

What was it the Americans said? I'd met my match.

10

ALISON

"You sure you're up for this?" asked Calahan for the fourth time. He twisted around in the driver's seat and looked at me, worried. "There's still time to change your mind."

I rolled my eyes. "How many undercover operations did we do together, back in the day? It's fine." I'd only arrived in New York an hour ago. My old FBI partner, Sam Calahan had picked me up from the airport and brought me straight here, to a backstreet in Little Odessa. Calahan needed someone to go into a strip club undercover, and all of his female agents were too well known to the local Russian mafia, so he'd called me and asked for my help. "Who is it you're after?" I asked.

Calahan showed me a photo of a man with a mostly-bald head and a thick, messy beard. "Amvrosy Inkin," he told me. "He's Bratva, been running the club for years. Not a very nice guy, violent, but strictly small time, not really of interest to us. But he has a brother, Daniil, who we *are* interested in, because we think he's selling explosives to a domestic terror group. He's gone off the grid, but we know Amvrosy is pretty close to his brother, so we're hoping he'll lead us to him."

I nodded. "So what do you want me to do? Go into the club and plant a bug?"

"No," said Yolanda, his girlfriend, from behind me. "We've got something much better." She leaned forward from the back seat and passed something over my shoulder.

"A phone charger?" I asked, turning it over in my hands.

"It looks like a phone charger," Yolanda said proudly. "But it doesn't just charge your phone. It sucks all the data off it and sends it through a transmitter hidden in the plug. Everyone's always looking for a phone charger. If you leave it in the office, sooner or later, Amvrosy is going to plug his phone into it. We'll get all his contacts and messages."

I turned and stared at her, amazed. "That's pretty freakin' cool," I said with feeling. Yolanda flushed and smiled, and I smiled back. I still remembered when I'd encouraged her to go for it with Sam, together with a *you'd better not break his heart* speech. I was so glad they'd gotten together.

"It should be pretty easy to get inside," Calahan told me. "The club is closed during the day, so there'll just be a couple of people there: cleaning staff, mostly. Amvrosy only hangs out there at night, when he can stare at the strippers. Say you want to dance there, then sneak downstairs to the office and leave the phone charger there." His jaw set, and his voice became a protective growl. "And don't worry, I triple-checked: they do scheduled auditions on Saturdays, when Amvrosy is there. You're not going to have to actually strip or anything."

I smiled affectionately. He'd always been like a big brother to me, and even now, he was still protecting me. Inside, my chest ached a little: this whole thing reminded me of the weird little family I'd had, back at FBI New York. I didn't have that in Chicago, and I wasn't sure I'd ever find it again.

I looked down at myself. I hadn't been sure what a wannabe stripper would wear, but I'd eventually settled on black leggings, a ribbed white sleeveless top that was cut high to show my navel, and the highest heels I owned. "See you in five," I told them, and climbed out of the car.

Calahan had parked a few streets away from the club so he wouldn't be spotted. It was a beautiful August day with a bright blue sky reflected in the puddles of last night's rain. I was smiling as I click-clacked down the street in my ridiculous heels, on a high from confiscating Gennadiy's drug money a few days before. I couldn't link the cash definitively to him, so it still wasn't enough for an arrest warrant, and I was still running out of time on the case. But every time I thought about how furious he must have been when he found his money gone, I couldn't stop grinning. Why did baiting him feel so good?

The Black Cat had stood on the same street corner for over twenty years, and its age was showing: the glossy black paint was peeling, the window sills were rotted and crumbling, and the vertical neon sign of a cat swishing its tail was askew. When I knocked on the door, a heavyset man in a white tee opened it an inch and looked at me suspiciously. That was weird: he looked more like a bodyguard than a cleaner. "I want to dance here," I told him.

He frowned and had a brief conversation in Russian with someone across the room. Then he reluctantly cracked the door open and let me in. He parted the velvet drapes behind him, and I saw the bar that occupied the first floor. "Leave number with him," he told me, pointing to the bartender. His voice was tight with stress.

I nodded obediently and strolled across the bar, my mind working overtime. Something was up. Why was there a bodyguard on the door? And why was the bartender there, in the middle of the day? Next to the bar were a set of stairs leading down to the basement, where I needed to be. The drapes had fallen back into place behind me, so the bodyguard at the door wouldn't see me if I tried to sneak down there. But the bartender would.

The bartender was Russian, too, but he spoke English better than the bodyguard. He handed me a notepad and a pen. "Write your number on there. Auditions are on Saturdays. We'll call you and tell you what time to come in."

I scrawled a fake number. "Can I sneak a look at the club?" I gave him my best pleading eyes. "I'm really nervous. It'd be nice to see where I'll be dancing, before the audition."

The bartender glanced at the stairs and shook his head. He sounded stressed, too. "Not today." He snatched the notepad and waved me towards the door. "We'll call you."

Fuck. Something was definitely off. He couldn't get me out of there fast enough. I knew I should abort and go back to the car. But then Calahan wouldn't get the information he needed. And his case sounded serious...

I made a split-second decision. Glanced at the bar and the bottle of expensive vodka waiting on a tray...

"Okay, thanks! Bye!" I turned to go, swinging my purse up my arm and over my shoulder. I felt it hit something, but I forced myself not to look...

The bottle shattered on the floor. I squealed and spun around. "Oh my God! Was that me?!"

The bartender was cursing in Russian as he stared down at the mess of broken glass and vodka on the floor behind the bar. "Just go!" he snapped.

I took a few steps towards the door...then, as soon as he knelt down behind the bar to start cleaning up, I veered off and crept down the stairs.

I could hear muffled voices, but it was hard to tell where they were coming from. Heart hammering, I passed the main room with its T-shaped stage and stripper poles, then a series of curtained booths...

There. A door at the end marked *Private.* I snuck over and put my ear to it, but I couldn't hear anything. I cracked open the door, barely daring to breathe—

A messy desk and an overflowing filing cabinet. Definitely the office. I grabbed the phone charger from my purse and plugged it into an outlet, temptingly close to the desk. I was just about to leave when I saw a name scrawled on a Post-it note, half-hidden beneath a stack of papers. Daniil. Amvrosy's brother. Wait, was it possible that...had Amvrosy just *scribbled down his brother's phone number?!* Could I just—

I moved the stack of papers so I could see the whole thing. *Yes!* There was a phone number. I grabbed my phone and snapped a picture. Sometimes, in this job, you just catch a break.

And sometimes, you don't. "Who the fuck are you?" asked a voice from behind me. "What the fuck are you doing in my office?"

I spun around. A tall man in a suit had just come out of a side room, and I recognized the balding head and messy beard instantly. Amvrosy Inkin. And he was pulling a big, chromed handgun from under his jacket.

Fuck. My heart jumped into my throat. Why was he here in the middle of the day? What the hell was going on? I searched for an explanation. Should I admit I was FBI? Normally, that would keep me alive, even if it meant blowing the operation. Even the Bratva think twice before executing FBI agents. But Amvrosy was violent and half drunk: I could smell the vodka from here. And if he realized I was after his beloved brother, he might just kill me to protect him. "I want to be a dancer," I tried, staring at the gun. "I came down here looking for the bathroom!"

"Bullshit!" roared Amvrosy. "I saw you taking a photo!" And he raised his gun to fire.

"Wait!" The voice came from the side room, low and calm and loaded with authority. Amvrosy and I froze.

Gennadiy stepped out into the hallway, scowling and magnificent. "She's with me."

11

ALISON

WHAT THE FUCK? I JUST STOOD THERE, STARING LIKE AN IDIOT, AS MY brain struggled to process *him, here.*

"She's with you?" The barrel of Amvrosy's gun wavered. "She wasn't with you when you arrived."

And suddenly I realized why Amvrosy was here during the day, why he had a bodyguard watching the door upstairs, and why the bartender had been twitchy. The Aristovs must own this place: they must have hung onto it when they left New York. Amvrosy ran it for them, and today the big boss had shown up, probably at short notice. No wonder everyone was on edge.

Gennadiy's eyes ran over me. "I met her this morning. She works in the coffee shop down the street. I told her she was pretty and that she should audition here."

I tried to keep my face neutral. Inside, my mind was whirling. Is he...*saving me?!*

Amvrosy frowned doubtfully...then, to my relief, he lowered his gun. "She's pretty enough," he said, as if I wasn't standing right there, "But she doesn't have much in the way of tits."

Gennadiy stormed forward, forcing Amvrosy back against the

wall and making him gulp in fear. "Some men like small breasts!" Gennadiy snapped.

An unexpected bomb of warmth went off in my chest. Then Gennadiy looked at me, and I drew in my breath: the anger in his eyes, coupled with the sheer imposing size of him, was terrifying. Suddenly, stealing his money didn't seem so smart.

Amvrosy extricated himself from between Gennadiy and the wall and turned to me. "You shouldn't have gone in there," he told me, pointing at the office. "Why were you taking a picture?"

I looked at my toes. "I was looking for the bathroom. I went in there by mistake, and then I saw the club's phone number on a bill, and I realized I didn't have it, so I thought I'd just take a quick photo." I tried to sound scared, which didn't take much acting: Amvrosy still had the gun. "I'm sorry, I didn't know I was doing anything wrong."

Amvrosy stared at me for a moment, then grunted and finally holstered his gun. "Fine," he told me. "You want to audition, you can audition." He grabbed my wrist and pulled me towards him, his voice roughening with lust. "You can give me a lap dance."

What?! Oh crap. He pulled me towards one of the VIP booths, and I stumbled after him, off balance in my ridiculous heels.

A big, tattooed hand smacked into the wall right in front of Amvrosy's face. Amvrosy froze, looked at the arm that blocked his way, then followed it up to Gennadiy's face.

"I own the place," Gennadiy reminded him. "I found her. She can dance for me."

12

ALISON

"Put on some music," Gennadiy ordered, and dragged me down the hallway and into the nearest VIP booth. As he turned away to tug the drapes closed, a thumping R&B track filled the club. My eyes flicked around the booth, but he was standing in front of the only exit. Then he turned back to me, and I gave an involuntary yelp of fear: even in my heels, he was so much taller than me, and his whole body was tensed in anger—

He grabbed my upper arms and pulled me to him. His grip was like warm iron and the raw, brute strength with which he tossed me around...it should have scared me but, just like at the casino, there was something about it that made me heady.

He put his mouth so close to my ear that with each hard, Russian-accented syllable, his lower lip stroked against me. "You're out of your mind," he snapped. "Amvrosy would have killed you."

I blinked. This close to him, the sandalwood scent of his cologne was working its magic on me, and it was difficult to think straight. I looked up into his furious eyes...and saw the sharp edge of concern around the anger. He was mad because I'd put myself in danger.

"What if I hadn't been here?" he demanded.

Each word was a hot current of air against my ear, and they

tumbled my brain until I couldn't think at all. *He...cares about me?* Ridiculous. A man like him didn't care about anyone.

Except...the day before, we'd learned a little more about the guy we pulled out of Lake Michigan, wrapped in chains. Iosif Kalugin, a small-time gangster, someone who'd barely register on Gennadiy's radar. Apparently, he'd been trying to set himself up as a pimp, and he'd been beating up local escorts. Was it possible that Gennadiy had been protecting them?

"I would have figured something out," I muttered. And then, even though it felt wrong, even though he was the enemy, "Thank you."

"We'll stay here until the song ends," Gennadiy told me. "Long enough for a lap dance." A smirk pulled at his lips. "I'll tell Amvrosy you were...talented."

I scowled up at him, my glare lava-hot. If I glared hard enough, maybe I could block out the ribbon of heat that had shot straight down to my groin at the idea of me grinding away on him.

Gennadiy looked down at me, then around at the run-down, seedy club. He shook his head. "Why do you do this?" he whispered, sounding genuinely confused.

He wouldn't understand. He had no idea what it was like to have your parents ripped away from you. All he cared about was amassing more power and wealth, building his empire. I lifted my chin. "Why do you?"

Before he could answer, the drape behind him was wrenched open. "You haven't even started yet?" Amvrosy asked, dismayed. He stared at me. "Why do you still have your clothes on?"

Gennadiy glared over his shoulder. But Amvrosy was drunk or horny enough that he didn't back down. "I have to run this place," he reasoned. "I have to deal with it if she brings my profits down. If you're having all the fun, I should at least get to watch."

That was difficult for Gennadiy to argue with, without raising suspicion. He sighed. "Fine." He moved around me and sat down on the leather couch. I stared at him. *Wait. He's not seriously suggesting...*

"What are you waiting for?" Gennadiy asked. "Dance."

13

ALISON

I STOOD THERE FOR A MOMENT, STARING. *But I— I can't—*

Gennadiy gave me the tiniest of nods. I had to, if I wanted to walk out of there. And then I saw those cold gray eyes gleam and heat. He might not have wanted it; he'd even tried to save me from it, but now that it was happening, he was going to enjoy it.

That ribbon of heat twisted down to my groin again. I was uncomfortably aware of how glad I was that it was Gennadiy sitting there, and not Amvrosy, even though it shouldn't have made a difference. *He's just another gangster, just like all the rest...right?*

The idea of doing this for my arch enemy, becoming his lipsticked, fawning sex toy, draping myself submissively all over him...the anger welled up inside me righteous and indignant, but then folded in on itself, becoming a confusing, dark energy that lashed down between my thighs.

I began to move to the music, shuffling on the spot and awkwardly bucking my hips. I had no idea what I was doing. How I was supposed to just...dance when I didn't know the track or the moves or—

"She's terrible," said Amvrosy from behind me. "Loosen up! Make it sexy! Can't you even dance?"

And something happened: I got mad.

Maybe it was stored-up resentment from when I had to give up ballet. Maybe it was pain at what I'd become: a stiff, suited FBI agent who'd forgotten how to be sexy. I wanted—needed—to prove him wrong. *They want me to dance? Fine.*

I closed my eyes, stopped trying to perform, and just let the music take me. Each long, keening wail by the singer made me arch my back and sway like a snake. Each slow drumbeat made me twitch my hips, changing direction with my ass until I was tracing sultry figure-eights. I let the music be my lover, running my hands up my thighs and over my hips, crisscrossing over my breasts and then up my neck to my hair. I plucked away my hair band and let my hair spill free.

"Now that's fucking sexy," muttered Amvrosy.

I half opened my eyes for a second. Gennadiy was watching, and his expression was a mixture of shock, lust, and awe. I closed my eyes, a strange warmth soaking through me. It shouldn't have mattered that he was impressed. But it did.

I turned slowly on the spot, letting Gennadiy watch my ass as I writhed and thrashed. I got so lost in the feeling of dancing that it was a shock when Amvrosy's voice cut through my haze. "Time to start peeling."

I opened my eyes and glanced down at myself. At my ruined leg. *Boy, are they ever going to be disappointed.* But I might as well get it over with. I fumbled with the waistband of my leggings, trying to figure out how best to strip them off mid-dance. I was already bracing myself for the disgust, the laughter. *What happened to you? You fall into a deep fat fryer?*

"Leave the leggings," said Amvrosy. "Too awkward. Next time, wear a dress."

I let out my breath, sagging in relief. But that still left my top half. I turned back to Gennadiy. I couldn't explain it: even though I hated him, I wanted it to be him who saw me, not Amvrosy.

Gennadiy's eyes had turned absolutely molten, and they climbed slowly up my legs as I swayed to the beat. They lingered on my bare midriff, then moved higher, over my breasts, up to my face. I'd never seen him so...hungry. It was like I could see into his mind, see myself spread and naked and moaning as he ran through all the ways he wanted to fuck me.

How dare he?! I let the anger build, using the outrage to mask the treacherous heat that was thrumming down to my groin. I locked eyes with him as I gripped the bottom of my crop top. *I hate you, Gennadiy Aristov.*

I inched the fabric higher, my eyes never leaving him. I felt it move up over the cups of my bra, but Gennadiy's eyes didn't move from mine. I pulled the crop top into a narrow band of fabric, then lifted my arms and pulled it up over my head and dropped it to the floor. His eyes still hadn't moved. I could feel my breathing getting faster, and the heat was building, becoming a living thing that stole all control. At the same time, there was a sick fear, as I thought about him seeing the breasts I'd always been insecure about. I stirred the anger, thinking about how much I hated him to power me through it. *Fuck you, Gennadiy.* I reached behind me and unclipped my bra, then shrugged it off my shoulders. Our eyes were locked. *Fuck you, Gennadiy. Fuck you. Fuck you—*

I dropped my bra to the floor...and his eyes finally flicked down to my chest. The anxiety hit me, stealing my breath—

But then I saw the brooding, angry mask he always wore drop away and, for a second, he was open and unguarded. He sucked in his breath...and smiled like it was Christmas morning.

He doesn't look disappointed. I blinked in shock. *He looks...*

His eyes narrowed in lust. His fingers sank deep into the cushioned leather on the couch's backrest, and he exhaled, loud enough for me to hear it over the music. His eyes darted left and right, as if he couldn't work out which breast he liked most. Then he finally managed to tear his gaze away and look me in the eye again, and the need I saw there made my knees go rubbery. I'd never been wanted so hard: not ever.

I hate him, I reminded myself. *Hate him.*

Everything else: the club, the mission, even Amvrosy, seemed to drop away. There was just Gennadiy, staring up at me from the couch, and me dancing topless in front of him. And as I moved to the music and watched him watching me, everything seemed to flip around. I'd been thinking of this whole thing as humiliatingly submissive, a slave girl dancing for a king. But...

His eyes were running over my body, now: he'd lost the fight to keep them on my face. *I'd* done that to him. I swayed left, and his head followed, his attention locked on me. I lifted my arms, momentarily hiding my breasts, and heard him grunt in frustration.

I had the power, here.

I took a step towards him, then another. God, the size of him, the sheer muscled power of him... I bit my lip as I gazed down at the X-shape of his body: broad torso, lean waist, and thighs thick with muscle. I looked at those big, tattooed hands that gripped the back of the couch. At any second, they could just grab me and pull me to him. It felt like teasing a bear.

I told myself I had to do it. But that wasn't the reason I took that final, dangerous step, the one that brought me close enough to touch. I could feel that...*gravity* again. I hated him, hated everything he was. But there was something about him that drew me helplessly in.

His eyes raked up and down my body, bathing me in warmth. Our eyes locked again, and he leaned forward ever so slightly. He looked just as helpless as I did.

I turned my back to him, sank down, and straddled one of his legs. My leggings were so tight, and the material so soft, that I could feel the firmness of his muscled quad and the heat of him soaking through the thin fabric of his suit. I slid forward, riding his leg as I moved to the beat, then glided back until my ass kissed his abs. He caught his breath.

The blood was pounding in my ears. I braced my palms on the couch, either side of his legs, and shifted my ass inward, knowing what I'd find. I lifted myself and then lowered myself, right into his lap. At the first hot touch of his cock, I jerked, feeling it throb and harden between my ass cheeks. A wave of heat rushed up my body, flaring in my cheeks. My mortal enemy was getting hard from touching me. I should have been mad, I *was* mad, but—

But every touch of him, every rasp of his breath in my ear, made my groin ache and pulse with needy heat. Heat that was rapidly turning to wetness.

I pushed my ass back, stroking along his cock, and felt it surge upward through his pants, stiffening even more. *God, he's big.* I pressed my naked back to his chest, the hard curves of his pecs warm through his shirt. I arched my spine and thrust my breasts up towards the ceiling. My head kissed his shoulder, my soft hair stroking the rough stubble on his cheek. It was meant to be a lap dance, impersonal and emotionless. But leaning back over him, half naked and vulnerable, it felt so intimate, so trusting. I closed my eyes and my whole world became the slow rise and fall of his body as he breathed, and the heat of his gaze as it roved over my breasts, my face, my lips....

The music shifted, and I moved with it, stroking my ass back and forth along his cock. After a moment, I heard the creak of leather and half opened his eyes.

His hands were lifting from the back of the couch.

I watched them coming towards me, knowing that he was about to cup my breasts. I knew I had to stop him, but I couldn't seem to make my voice work. His palms were only inches from my breasts when I finally managed to croak, "No touching."

He froze...and then reluctantly put his hands back on the top of the couch. I let out a shaky breath. My brain was running a continuous loop of exactly how it would have felt if those big hands had landed on my breasts: I could feel my nipples scraping his palms. If that had happened...

I wasn't sure which I was more scared of: him losing control, or me.

I pushed off from the couch and turned around to face him, straddling his legs. My leggings might as well not have been there: I could feel every inch of his achingly hard cock. The arrow-shaped head was throbbing right up against the lips of my pussy.

I leaned forward and braced my hands either side of his head, still bucking and writhing to the music. We stared into each other's eyes, and the raw heat in his gaze made my breathing go tight. The temptation to run my palms over those stubbled cheeks and lean in for his kiss...

His lips parted. I saw his eyes flick to my lips. *Oh God...*

I snapped myself out of it and quickly climbed onto the couch, kneeling up so that my mouth was out of range. But that brought my breasts dangerously close to his face. I went light-headed and just swayed there to the beat for a moment, imagining his lips on me.

Amvrosy. I suddenly realized that I hadn't heard anything from him for a while. *Maybe he's gone. Maybe I can stop.* "Is he still watching?" I whispered to Gennadiy.

"Understandably, his eyes are still glued to you," growled Gennadiy. "Keep going."

I swallowed and glared at him; at some point, I'd forgotten to keep glaring. I lowered myself atop him, his cock grinding between my thighs, and arched my back, thrusting my breasts forward. Then I leaned in. Both of us looked down at my breasts, watching them come closer and closer to his chest.

They brushed the firm muscle of his pec, shockingly warm even through his shirt. I could feel my nipple starting to pucker and harden. We stared into each other's eyes, watching each other react to each new sensation, connected on a level I wasn't sure I'd ever reached with anyone. *I hate him*, I repeated in my head. *I hate him.*

My ass was circling in time with the music, my pussy grinding against the head of his cock in a way that made me mushy. My upper body started circling, too, helpless, and my breasts stroked his chest, my nipples like pebbles, now. His breathing went shaky. "*Yebat'*," he cursed. "You sexy, crazy little witch..." His cock hardened even more and twitched, pressing right between my folds, and I went heady. I felt like I was being carried on the tip of a huge, warm wave, and there was nothing I could do but hang on.

I reared up higher on my knees, bringing my breasts towards his face. I stared down at his gorgeous, sensual lower lip and went trembly, thinking about how it would feel when my nipple dragged across it. He'd lick me. And then... My breathing quickened. We were about to cross a line. Once his mouth was on my breast, his hands would be on my ass. And then...and then...

I rocked forward and moaned in pleasure as my nipple stroked across his cheek, heading for his mouth. At the last second, I glanced over my shoulder to see what Amvrosy was doing.

Amvrosy wasn't there.

It was like waking from a dream. I jumped off Gennadiy's lap and grabbed my bra from the floor. "How long has he been gone?" I hissed.

Gennadiy looked me right in the eye. "A while." His voice was rough with lust.

"You lied to me!" I whispered.

He smirked. "Did you forget what I am?" He sat back, still breathing hard, and watched as I dressed. I glared at him as I pulled on my bra and crop top and then stormed out of the booth.

Amvrosy was at his desk in his office, doing paperwork. "You were in there a long time," he said, and grinned. "I don't want any of that when you're working here. Not unless they pay extra."

I scowled at him, then marched off up the stairs. I let the anger rise inside me, hoping it would wash away what happened in the booth. What *had* happened in there?

I did what I had to do. That's all that happened. I had no choice. I had to grind in that evil, arrogant bastard's lap and stroke my breasts all over his—

His chest. Smooth slabs of muscle, gloriously warm and firm through his tailored shirt. Glimpses of caramel skin and the dark swirls of tattoos through the gaps between his shirt buttons...

I tore my mind away from the memory, my face heating. I was uncomfortably aware of how slickly wet I was. Well, that was natural, when I'd been grinding along his cock, and he was so hard and so...big.

Jesus, I hated that man. Why did someone so evil have to be so hot?

And why had he saved me? He could have just let Amvrosy shoot me, and I would have been out of his hair for good. But he'd covered for me. And he'd seemed almost protectively angry that I'd put myself at risk.

My steps slowed. Was it possible that he...

No. I shook my head and carried on walking. A monster like him? He wasn't capable of feeling anything, for anyone, least of all his enemy. Maybe he'd just wanted to make sure it was him, and no one else, who killed me.

He hates me.

And I hate him. Right?

When I climbed into Calahan's car, he let out a sigh of relief. "Finally! I was just about to come in there. What happened?"

"Nothing," I said weakly. I showed him my phone. "Here. I got Amvrosy's brother's phone number."

As Calahan stared at the photo in disbelief, Yolanda leaned forward between the seats. "What really happened in there?" she asked gently.

"I told you, nothing."

Yolanda chewed on her lip for a second, glancing down. "Then...why is your top on inside out?"

14

GENNADIY

"A LAMBORGHINI HURACÁN IN MANTIS GREEN," SAID VALENTIN. "Should fetch around $400,000." When I didn't respond, he looked at me over the top of his clipboard. "Gennadiy?"

"Hmm?"

He sighed. "Brother, concentrate!" He walked to the next car, a sleek red wedge. "A 1987 Ferrari Testarossa. Worth about $200,000. We could sell it, but I think we should send it to that senator in LA as a bribe. He's always wanted one." He waited. Sighed. "Gennadiy!"

"I was listening."

"No, you weren't. Where's the Ferrari going?"

"...Dubai?" I guessed.

"No! What's the matter with you? You've been distracted all day." He frowned. "Is it a woman?"

I looked away. "No!"

Valentin crossed his arms and frowned. "It's ever since you came back from New York." His face fell. "Tell me you haven't started something with Konstantin's girlfriend!"

"No! Of course not!"

Valentin's eyes went wide. "The Black Cat! You were going to stop in there! Did you get a lap dance from one of Amvrosy's girls?" My poker face must have slipped because he covered his mouth with his hand, half shocked and half delighted. "You did, didn't you?"

"So what if I did?" I snapped and looked away. "Perk of the job. No big deal."

Except that it had been a week and I hadn't been able to *stop* thinking about it. The soft push of her small breasts against my chest, the way her warmth soaked through my shirt. The silken kiss of her hair, finally released from that tight bun. The way we'd locked eyes as she'd climbed all over me: her body was gorgeous, but the most hypnotic thing had been her eyes, and the battle going on in them.

I caught my breath as I remembered the feel of her soft folds stroking my cock through just a few thin layers of fabric. That feeling was now on a permanent loop in my head, and it had turned me into a pawing, snorting beast bored of anything but sex. Before, I'd wanted her. Now, I *needed* her. I needed her on the hood of one of these cars, naked and spread, my cock ramming into her—

"Gennadiy!"

I looked up. Valentin had moved onto a blue Porsche and was looking at me despairingly.

I sighed. What was it about this woman? I've been around plenty of beauties, but I've never felt like this. The shirt I'd worn for the lap dance still smelled of her, of her cherry shampoo and the soft, vanilla scent of her skin and... I hadn't been able to bring myself to throw it in the laundry, yet.

I was...*addicted.*

Now, whenever I spotted her watching me, I was torn between hating her...and slamming her up against the nearest wall and burying myself in her. Luckily, I'd managed to give her the slip for a few hours. I took a deep breath and forced myself to focus.

We were at what I call *the garage.* It's my second-favorite out of all the businesses we own, after the stables, and it consists of two halves.

The first half of the business is an upmarket restaurant in the center of downtown. It turns a healthy profit, plus the waiting staff overhear insider information from drunk businessmen and pass it on to Radimir, who makes millions from it. But the real moneymaker?

That's the combination of rich customers who drive supercars...and valet parking. While the customers are eating, the valets pass their car keys to a couple of hackers I recruited from the Illinois Institute of Technology, who steal the codes and pass them back. Then, weeks or months later, a team of car thieves steals the car from their driveway in the middle of the night. And we bring it here.

I was standing in the underground parking lot of a half-built apartment building. Radimir used it as a tax write-off: it had been under construction for over five years but never actually completed. That meant no one ever came down to its basement parking level. If they had, they'd have gotten quite a shock.

I turned a slow circle. Eighteen cars gleamed under the cool white lights, and every one of them was the sort of supercar people dream about. Lamborghinis, Ferraris, a Pagani Zonda...there was even a Bugatti Veyron. Some of the cars we sold for cash, but most were used as bribes: some people are rich enough that they're immune to money, but no one can resist their childhood dream car. The garage had become like my own personal museum. Cars came and went over the months, but the overall collection felt like mine.

I smiled and ran my hand over the flank of a beautiful silver Aston Martin. "What's our plan for this one?" I asked.

Valentin sighed, relieved that I had my head back in the game. "That's being shipped to India, to one of Selina Kirk-Hughes's sales —" he broke off. "Is that...?"

I looked up at the ceiling. I could hear it, too: a police siren, coming closer. "Probably just passing by."

We waited for the Doppler shift as the siren went by us. But it just kept getting louder, and now I could hear others, a rising chorus. "It can't be us," I said. "No one knows we're down here." From the outside, the building looked like a dark, disused construction site.

But then the sirens reached full volume...and stopped, right above us.

"*Chyort*," breathed Valentin. We both started looking for an exit. Except...this was a basement. All the exits led upwards, towards the cops. We looked at each other in horror. Radimir owned the building through a complex series of holding companies: no one could tie it to us. But if we were caught down here with four million dollars' worth of stolen cars...

Voices, upstairs. Coming rapidly *down* the stairs.

Valentin, ever resourceful, ran to a drain cover and levered it up. Both of us recoiled as the stench of the sewer hit us. Valentin climbed in and started descending the ladder. "Come on!" he hissed. "You want to go to jail?"

I hesitated, looking around. I couldn't lose all this. Not my *cars!* My brain refused to accept that the raid was happening. *No one knows about this place. They can't have found it, it's not possible!*

Then I heard a familiar female voice, rising above the others. "You two, down there. The rest of you on the south side!"

Alison! And suddenly, it *was* possible.

I scrambled into the sewer and slid the drain cover closed above my head. Before I could even climb down the ladder, boots clattered above me as cops swarmed the garage. I hung there, squeezing the rungs in silent fury. *Goddamn you, Brooks!* The drain cover had a couple of tiny square holes in it and when I shifted my head, I glimpsed her: hands on her hips, scowling at the cars. "They must be here somewhere!" she yelled. "Search everywhere!"

Very, very quietly, I climbed down the ladder into hip-deep, stinking water and crept away.

Valentin and I had to wade for half a mile before we could climb back up. We emerged down the street from the garage, filthy and coughing from the smell. I wiped my hands on my suit and looked at the ring of red and blue lights encircling the garage.

Gone. Four million dollars' worth of cars. Four *million!* It wasn't just the money; it was the power they could have bought us. They could have been used to smooth things over with district attorneys or bribe judges. And in some stupid, childish way, they'd been *mine.*

The anger expanded in my chest, and I paced, unable to stand still. *Alison.* She must have figured out, somehow, that I was behind the car thefts and found the common link between the owners: they'd all visited the same restaurant. She'd probably put a tracker on one of the cars, let me steal it, and then follow it to the garage. *Yebat'*! How dare she? How *fucking* dare she?! I drew in a shuddering breath, every muscle tight with rage. I'd never hated anyone so much, but, even now, the memory of her soft skin, the feel of her pussy caressing my cock through those tight, tight leggings...

"*Blyat'*!" I yelled. "*Blya, blya...Blyat'*!" I picked up the drain cover and hurled it at the nearest parked car, caving in its hood and shattering the windshield. The alarm started to blare.

Valentin put his hand on my arm. "Gennadiy?"

I spun around. "Leave me alone!" I roared.

He stumbled back...and the look on his face made me freeze. He was shocked, wounded...even a little afraid. And that felt like someone had punched me in the stomach. The anger blew away like mist and, for the first time in months, I saw clearly.

This woman had worked some magic on me. Ever since she walked into my life, I'd been making mistakes, losing money, jeopardizing deals, all because...what? Because she was beautiful? Because I wanted to fuck her? And now things had gotten so bad, I was taking it out on *Valentin*, on my baby brother?!

I grabbed him and pulled him into a tight, tight hug. "I'm sorry, brother," I told him, my voice rough with emotion. "I'm sorry." I closed my eyes. How could I get mad at him? The one I'd sworn I'd always protect...because I'd failed to protect him when he needed it most.

I released him, took a deep breath, and started walking towards my car. The emotion had hardened into rock inside me, blocking out any doubts. "Come on. Let's go."

"What are you going to do?" asked Valentin.

"What I should have done back in the casino."

I was going to kill Alison Brooks.

15

GENNADIY

Except I couldn't find her.

After I'd dropped off Valentin and changed my clothes—my suit was so badly soaked with filth, I had to throw it away—I drove back to the garage. The area was still swarming with cops, but Alison was nowhere to be seen.

By now, dawn was breaking, the sun weak and barely visible behind thick gray clouds. I drove around town for a while, waiting for Alison to show up and start following me: she was never out of my hair for long. But she didn't show. Radimir called again. He was calling every ten minutes, wanting to know how one of our most important businesses had been taken down. But I wasn't picking up. I didn't want to speak to him until I could tell him she was dead.

I made sure to drive past some traffic cameras, so she could pick me up that way if she was searching. When that didn't work, I drove right past the FBI headquarters. *I'm here! Come and get me!*

Nothing. I thumped the steering wheel in frustration. How was I going to kill her if I couldn't find her? *Where the hell is she?*

Was it possible that...she had the day off? But she was like me; she *never* took time off. And why would she choose to go on vacation *today,* the morning after a major bust?

The gray clouds had spread across the entire sky, now, and a heavy, cold rain started to fall. I spent the entire morning searching. *Is this what it's like to be her, looking for me?*

And then, out of nowhere, I saw her. If she'd always used unmarked cars, like a normal FBI agent, I'd have had no chance. But thanks to all those nights when she'd followed me on her bike, I spotted its cherry-red bodywork instantly. She was turning into...a churchyard?

I parked on the street and sat there uncertainly, fingering the unregistered gun I'd brought. Was she here for a service? A wedding? I climbed out for a closer look and saw her disappearing into the church, still in her biker gear. *Chyort!* I couldn't follow her in there, or she'd see me immediately.

I got back into my car to wait, checking the time every few minutes. *How does she do this all day?*

After an hour, the doors of the church opened, and people started coming out. I sat up in my seat, my fingers curling around the gun. Now all I had to do was follow her somewhere quiet and—

Wait. Everyone was in black.

Alison emerged. Except...she didn't look like Alison. She must have changed in the toilets because she was in a simple black dress that fell almost to her ankles. And she didn't prowl like she normally did; she walked with small steps, head down.

I got out of my car and moved to the edge of the church's graveyard, watching through a set of iron railings. The gun was still in my hand under my jacket, but the resolve, cold and hard as granite in my chest...it ached. Alison and the other mourners followed the coffin to the grave site. She passed within ten feet of me, with no idea I was there.

I skulked to the other end of the graveyard, found a gate, and slipped inside. Then I crept towards the funeral, using a copse of trees for cover. The rain was hissing down, and Alison was getting soaked, but she didn't seem to notice. She was staring at the coffin as it was lowered into the ground. The rain was sluicing down her cheeks, so I couldn't be sure, but...*is she crying?!*

I felt a hairline crack open up in that hard resolve. I squeezed the gun's grip. *Don't be stupid.*

The service ended, and the other mourners walked away, leaving only Alison standing by the grave. She still hadn't seen me.

I looked around. It was perfect. We were all alone, there were no cameras, and the rain would keep everyone inside and help mask the sound of the shot. Hell, the grave hadn't been filled in yet: I could roll Alison's body into it, shovel the dirt on top, and no one might ever find her.

I pulled the gun out from under my jacket...and then hesitated, staring at her hunched, soaked body and red-rimmed eyes. Something deep inside, something that I hadn't let function in years, was aching.

I replayed the moment I'd yelled at Valentin, squeezing the memory to make the guilt well up. *She's fucked up everything. Everything was fine until she showed up.* I took a deep breath, lifted my gun, and aimed at Alison's chest...

My finger rubbed against the trigger. It didn't seem to want to move.

She took my car. She humiliated me. She almost lost me the deal with the Irish. I took another slow breath and took aim again...

Alison gave a sudden, wracking sob and crumpled, and now I could see the tears spilling down her cheeks even through the rain.

I gritted my teeth and squeezed the trigger harder and harder... and then released it. *Yebat'! Blya, blya...Blyat'!* I shoved the gun back under my jacket and stood there panting, running my hands through my hair, feeling the resolve shatter into pebbles. *What am I—What do I—*

Alison's eyes were squeezed shut in agony. She wrapped both arms around herself, and it was the saddest thing I'd ever witnessed, like she had no one in the world to hug her, and—

Suddenly, without consciously willing it, I was marching towards her. As soon as I left the cover of the trees, the rain plastered my hair to my head and soaked my shirt.

Alison opened her eyes and jumped back, startled. "H—*Here?* You come to a freakin' *funeral?*" She shook her head, crying and sniffing. "Why, to *mock?* Jesus, Gennadiy, that's pretty low even for you."

I opened and closed my mouth a few times. "I didn't come here to mock," I said at last. I nodded towards the coffin. "Who were they?"

She looked down at the coffin, and all the fight drained out of her again. "My *seonsaeng.* My teacher." Her voice went small. "My friend."

I stared at her. She looked so...broken. I rubbed at my face. "What happened?"

Her lips pressed together tightly. "Cancer."

Blyat'. A cold earthquake of memories rumbled through me. Without meaning to, I said, "My mother died of cancer."

Alison looked up at me in shock. And God, she was so *small* and defenseless and—

Something took hold of me. "After this," I said tightly, "we go back to normal."

"After *what?*"

I put my arms around her and pulled her to my chest. She yelped and jerked, but I wrapped her tight in my arms and held her small, soaked body against me as thunder boomed overhead and the rain drenched us both, and after a moment she relaxed. And then I felt her body jerk again, this time with a sob, and then another and another. Even though I could feel her breasts soft against my chest, it wasn't sexual. It was about comforting her, soaking up her pain and...

I knew it was just one way. She was hurting, and she needed someone, and I could help her, just for a moment. But...

But deep inside me, there was a cold place, like some windswept, barren island that's never touched by anyone because the ferocious storms all around it keep everyone at bay. Just for a second, that place felt...connected. I remembered crying myself when I heard my mother was days from death and I wasn't allowed to visit her. I squeezed Alison tighter and, for a second, it *wasn't* just one way.

Then I released her, turned, and stalked off into the rain without looking back.

16

ALISON

"WATCHA READING?" ASKED CAROLINE, WALKING IN FROM THE BREAK room with two mugs of coffee.

I snapped the paper file shut. "Nothing!"

Caroline passed me my coffee, and I thanked her, my cheeks heating. *Why am I embarrassed?* I'd been reading about Gennadiy, which was exactly what I was *meant* to be working on. Except...

Except I'd been reading about his early life. It was a few days after Master Sun's funeral, and I'd managed to get hold of a file from Russia's social services. Gennadiy's mom *had* died of cancer. And Radimir, Gennadiy, and Valentin had spent their teens locked up in a borstal in Vladivostok: I hadn't been able to find out what for, but the place sounded pretty grim. *Is that what set him on this path?*

Was I starting to feel sympathy for him?

My phone rang, and I grabbed it, glad of the distraction. It was Nate, a Chicago PD homicide detective I'd worked with a few times. "You're on Gennadiy Aristov, right?" he said by way of greeting.

I sat up straighter in my chair. Seizing the bags of cash had put me back in my boss's good books, and impounding millions of dollars' worth of stolen cars had made the FBI look *great*. But I hadn't been able to tie either of them definitively to Gennadiy, and I was still nowhere near being able to arrest him. I only had a few weeks left. If Nate had a tip, I wanted it. "Yeah," I said eagerly.

"Well, I'm looking at a picture of him right now. Found it on a guy we just arrested who works for the Barroso cartel. Also in his pocket was a ticket to the Low Low Blues and Jazz club: that mean anything to you?"

My eagerness evaporated. "Gennadiy goes there," I said. I knew his routine by heart, now. "Nine O'clock. Every Thursday." My heart started slamming in my chest. It was Thursday *today.*

"Figured you should know," said Nate sagely. "You take care, Brooks."

I ran to Halifax's office. He was on the phone, but I wasn't waiting. "The Barroso cartel's going to take out Gennadiy tonight."

Halifax sighed. "I'll call you back," he told the phone. Then, to me, "What?!"

I told him about the man Nate had picked up. "The only reason a member of the cartel is carrying around a picture of someone is if they're going to assassinate them." I'd tailed Gennadiy into the jazz club a few times, and it was the perfect place for an ambush: twisting hallways and lots of shadowy places for an ambush.

"Well, Chicago PD caught the guy, so it's over, right?"

I leaned over his desk. "No! The cartel will know their guy was arrested. They'll send someone else."

Halifax just looked at me.

"Sir, we have to stop this. They're going to kill him."

Halifax picked up a pen and started playing with it. "We don't know anything for sure."

I felt my jaw drop. "You don't *want* to stop it."

"What would you have me do? Put agents' lives at risk to protect a Bratva boss? This is the guy we're trying to bring down, Brooks!"

"Bring him down, not—"—my voice cracked—"*kill* him!"

"We're not killing anyone," he said testily. "But honestly, if these assholes want to wipe each other out...I'm not shedding any tears." He frowned at me. "Have you forgotten about the bodies we keep pulling out of Lake Michigan? He's a killer. Maybe karma's finally catching up to him."

It was like someone had slapped me awake. Gennadiy *was* a killer. I'd known that, at the start. At some point, had I forgotten?

"Don't interfere," Halifax told me. He narrowed his eyes, watching me. "Brooks? That's an order."

I nodded quickly. "Of course, sir." I walked back to my desk on legs that felt numb and waxy. *Does Halifax suspect? Suspect* what? *I haven't done anything wrong. I want to bring Gennadiy down. I just—*

I thought of Gennadiy's arms around me, by the grave. *I just...*

I tried to work, but I kept glancing at the clock in the corner of my computer screen. 6pm. 7pm. The office cleared and, as usual, I was the last one there. 8pm. Gennadiy always went to the jazz club just in time for the start of the main set at 9pm.

I looked at my phone. *I can't.* I'd be in serious, serious trouble.

The clock reached 8:30pm. *This isn't right.* Weren't the FBI meant to protect people...even Bratva? Maybe Halifax had been doing this so long, he almost didn't see Gennadiy and his family as people anymore. Hadn't I felt the same way just a few months ago?

8:45pm.

"Fuck," I told the empty, dark office. "Fuck, fuck, fuck." And suddenly I was up and running. Out of the office. Pounding down the stairs. Out into the street. *Payphone, I need a payphone.* Except there weren't any payphones anymore. *Fuck.*

I ran to the first person I saw, a guy in his twenties, and flashed my badge at him. "FBI! I need your phone!"

He handed it over, gaping. I'd tapped Gennadiy's phone so many times by now that I knew his number by heart. As I punched it in, the clock on the phone read 8:55pm. *He'll be driving. What if he doesn't answer? What if he's early and he's already inside the club, and it's too late? What if he's lying dead?*

"Yes?" said Gennadiy suspiciously.

"Don't go to the jazz club!" I blurted. "The Barroso cartel has sent someone to kill you!"

He was silent for a few seconds. When he spoke again, he sounded shocked...and just a little vulnerable. "Thank you."

I didn't know what to say, so I ended the call. Then I handed the phone back to the guy I'd snatched it from. He was looking at me in adoring wonder. "That's the coolest thing that's ever happened to me!" he told me, and wandered off.

I slumped against a lamppost. I could finally breathe again, and it made me face up to just how scared I'd been. I hadn't just been doing the right thing.

I... cared about him. And I hated him even more for that.

First thing the next morning, Halifax called me into his office. "I talked to Chicago PD," he said, his eyes boring into me. "No reports of any trouble at that jazz club last night."

I stood in front of his desk, chin up. I had my hands clasped together behind my back so I wouldn't nervously twist them. "I guess you were right, sir. The cartel didn't send another assassin after all."

"I checked the security cameras at the club. Gennadiy's car pulls up a few minutes before nine." His voice was shaking. I'd never seen him so angry. "But he leaves without going in."

Fuck. I tried to make my voice sound innocent. "Sir, I—"

"Save it, Brooks!" He yelled, loud enough to make the window shake. "I know what you did, I just can't prove it!"

I was very glad I hadn't used my own phone.

"I can't fire you, but I can throw you off the case. I'll take over the team for the final few weeks." He lifted a thick file from his desk and almost threw it at me. "Go back to looking into the Cantellis." He shoved a second, equally thick file at me. "And the O'Donnells."

My stomach dropped. "Sir—"

"Don't push me, Brooks! Be glad you still have a job!"

I turned and slunk out of his office, my eyes prickling. How had everything gotten so messed up?

17

GENNADIY

I HEARD HER BEFORE I SAW HER. THE SNARL OF HER BIKE'S ENGINE, rising and falling as she dodged through traffic, had become her theme song in my mind. At first, my shoulders had tensed in anger every time I heard it coming up behind me. Now, it made something in my chest wake and *lift*.

She came into view, leaning into the corners as she wove through the early morning traffic. She was so graceful when she rode: more than once, I'd nearly driven into another car because I was too busy watching her flex and bend and grip the bike between her thighs in my rear-view mirror.

I was watching her from the top of a small rise in Lincoln Park. In a few hours, the grass would be full of kids and picnicking families, but at seven in the morning, we had the place all to ourselves. It was a bright, clear day, and we had an uninterrupted view out over the sparkling blue of Lake Michigan.

She braked to a stop beside my BMW, pulled off her helmet, and marched into the park. She stopped about six feet from me, watchful and cautious. *Is she scared of me? Or scared of what might happen?*

I took a second to just look at her, staring into those flashing blue eyes. But then the breeze started playing with loose strands of her fine black hair, and it turned into *more* than a second...

I tore my eyes away. Something was happening to me. It had started back in the strip club, when I'd seen her in danger and felt this *need* to protect her. Then I'd seen her in the graveyard, broken and vulnerable, with no one in the world to turn to, and I'd suddenly understood how lonely she was. Maybe because it felt so familiar.

And then she'd risked her job to save my life.

Maybe it *hadn't* started in the strip club. Maybe it had started back when she was following me all over town, and I'd realized how smart and tenacious she was. When I realized I finally had a worthy opponent.

Or maybe it started right back in the casino, when I'd snarled at her, and she'd lifted her chin and defied me. All I knew was, there was a part of me that had been dark, silent, and cold for years, and she made it spin to warm, colorful life.

I had no idea what the fuck I was going to do about it. After the graveyard, I'd had to apologize to Radimir and persuade him that killing Alison would bring too much heat down on us. He wasn't happy about leaving her alive. He'd completely lose it if he knew we were meeting like this.

"You got my message, then?" I asked, my voice carefully gruff.

Alison snorted—somehow, when she did it, it was *milyy*, cute—and looked away. Could she feel it too?

"An anonymous tip to the FBI hotline," she said. "Giant yellow duck sighted at these coordinates."

I smirked. I'd been proud of that. But then my smile faded. "I haven't seen you in a week."

She went over to the railing and leaned on it. "I'm off the case. Someone else will be tailing you, now."

I looked around. We were alone. "Clearly, they're not as good as you."

"Clearly."

She turned and looked out across the lake. I joined her at the railing and did the same: this close to her, I didn't dare look at her, or

I might do something stupid. "I may be able to get you back on the case."

I felt her look at me. "What?! How? No: why. *Why* first?"

"Because it's my fault you're off it."

"But you hate me. This is exactly what you wanted, you're rid of me."

You hate me. It was right there, dangling in the air. I could say something...

Instead, I sucked in my breath and turned to her. "I want to beat you," I told her. "I'm *going* to beat you. But not like this."

She stared at me, challenging me to say more. I stared back at her, stony-faced.

She dropped her eyes. "Okay," she said. Wait, was that pain in her voice? *Should* I have said something? "How?"

"There's a container arriving on a ship in two days' time," I told her. "Refrigerators. Except, inside the casing of one of the refrigerators is a small package of radioactive cesium. You can tell your boss and catch some terrorists. You'll be a hero."

"How do you—"

"I have a friend at the docks."

She nodded. "Yakov Beletski."

I forgot, sometimes, just how well she knew my life. "Yes. He knows everything that passes through. Terrorism...that isn't good for us, for you, for anyone. So when he hears of something like this, he passes word to the authorities. That's why they leave him alone."

"So why doesn't he just tell the authorities himself this time, too?"

Chyort, she was like a dog with a bone. I looked away and ran a hand over my stubble. "I...requested that he let you tell the FBI instead."

I could feel her staring at me. "What did you have to do in return?"

The price had been admitting to my best friend *why* I wanted to help her. I'd stood there scowling and red-faced while Yakov laughed so hard he could barely breathe. "That's not important," I told her stiffly. "Here." I held out a slip of paper with all the details on it.

She stared at it for a moment, then took it. Her fingertips brushed my palm, and the sensation jolted through my body, right down to my toes. "Thank you," she mumbled.

I dug in my pocket. "And take this." I held out a brand-new burner phone. "It's got a number programmed into it. One of *my* burners. Just in case you need to reach me."

She took it and frowned at it. "What happens if you throw away that phone before I call you?"

I smiled tightly and pulled another phone out of my pocket. "I won't. I'm keeping this one just for you."

She looked up at me doubtfully. Then she stared at the piece of paper for a moment. "All this does is make us even," she said at last.

I nodded silently.

She stepped closer, close enough that I could smell her perfume, and looked up at me, worried. "You realize that if this works, if they put me back on the case...I'm coming right after you. I'm going to take you down."

I cocked my head to the side and lifted one brow. "You mean you're going to try." I stared at her lower lip, soft and pouting, oh-so stubbornly. And for a second, I thought I saw *her* eyes flick down...

Then she was turning and running back to her bike, and a second later she roared off into the distance. My chest ached with this kind of...*loss*. "*Yebat'!*" I muttered under my breath. "What have you done to me, woman?"

18

ALISON

One week later

"Okay," said Caroline, grabbing her purse. "I'm outta here. Now remember, you're meeting Edgar at eight. Don't be late. And wear something...you know...nice." She looked at my gray trouser suit. "Maybe a skirt?" she said hopefully.

Not her fault. She didn't know about my leg. "I'll think about it," I lied. Edgar would get jeans and like them. "Go!"

She finally left, and I sighed in relief. It had been a week since Gennadiy had given me the tip about the cesium. I'd taken it to Halifax, claiming it came from a confidential informant, and it had paid off. The counter-terrorist unit had arrested three guys, and it had been a big win for the bureau and for our office. Halifax was delighted and had put me back in charge of the case.

All was good...other than I now only had three days to catch Gennadiy...and Caroline had decided to set me up on a blind date with a single dad she knew from her kids' school. I'd told Caroline, firmly, *no.* But then she'd given me big, pleading eyes: she just wanted me to be happy, and she'd gone to so much trouble to set it up...I'd caved and said I'd go. I scowled at the Post-it note she'd stuck to my computer monitor: *Edgar, 8pm.*

Then my eyes tracked down to the rubber duck Gennadiy had sent me.

I'd been going over and over why he gave me the tip-off. *Because he wanted me back on the case: better the devil you know. Because I saved his life and he has some weird Bratva sense of honor.*

Because he cared about me?

I glared at the duck. Everything had been a lot easier when I'd just hated him.

I thought of the bodies we'd found. I thought of my parents. All the innocent lives lost to the fighting between families like the Aristovs. *He's still the enemy.*

But he was seeming more and more human...and more and more like me. He'd had a shitty start in life, too. And it had turned him into an obsessive workaholic, too. If my life had been just a little different, if Master Sun had turned me away that night instead of helping me, could I have wound up on a very similar path?

It was getting harder and harder to hate him. And without the hate, there was nothing to hold back the attraction that had been there from the start. Now, every time I saw him, it was like my whole body woke and came to breathless attention, as if the time in between was just a waste. And then it would start: my eyes darting everywhere, racing over his suit, his shirt, sneaking looks at the triangle of tattooed, tan flesh at his shirt collar. I'd catch his scent and have to dig my fingernails into my palms because I was imagining sliding my hands around his waist, feeling the hard, warm ridges of his abs through the soft cotton of his shirt.

Then he'd speak, and I'd have to force myself to focus on what he was saying because each low growl resonated right to my core, each word a little bomb that exploded there and sent liquid silver racing straight down to my groin. And it was more than just lust. Whenever I was close to him, my right cheek—always my *right* cheek—would prickle with the memory of how his pec had felt when he'd hugged me against his chest at the graveyard. I'd been bawling my eyes out, but the warmth of him, the solid *wall* of him, protecting me, had been the best thing I'd ever felt.

I put my head in my hands. "What are you doing, Brooks?" I muttered. Was I really so lonely and fucked up that I was starting to feel things for a gangster?

Yes. Yes, I just might be.

I screwed my eyes closed and gave a silent scream of frustration, then sat up straight in my chair. *Focus!* I'd printed out a photo of Viktor Grushin, my Russian counterpart, and stuck it beside my monitor, for moments like these. *He* wouldn't let himself get...*distracted* like this. He would have had Gennadiy locked in a cell by now. *God, I wish you were alive.*

Maybe it was because I wanted to shut out the thought of my blind date, but I brought up Viktor's file and idly flicked through it, wondering how he'd died. *Heart attack.* He'd only been in his early sixties but he'd been a smoker, so that made sense...

Then I saw something that made me lean forward in my chair.

I'd been looking at the scan of the autopsy report, which was in Russian. My computer was helpfully translating the text into English, overlaying it on the Cyrillic. But there was one line right at the bottom that stood out because it wasn't translated. It was just a filename, a string of numbers and letters. And part of it was the date and time the autopsy report had been created.

The date was two weeks *before* Viktor's death.

I sat there staring at it. *Maybe the date was wrong on the pathologist's computer?*

Or maybe this was someone else's autopsy report, and they'd copied it and changed the details to Viktor's, but not noticed the date code at the bottom.

What if Viktor had faked his death? I turned the idea over in my mind. This was a guy who'd put some of the most notorious criminals in Russia behind bars. A national hero...but someone every gang wanted dead. The man couldn't just retire and go fishing; he'd be dead in a week...unless everyone thought he was already dead.

I started typing in searches, digging deeper and deeper. The FBI is hooked into a lot of databases around the world, and I knew exactly what I was looking for: a man of Viktor's age, with Viktor's face, but with a different name. And eventually, I got a match.

I sat back in my chair. "Holy shit," I said aloud.

Viktor Grushin was living under a new name, pretending to be a Polish national. And he was regularly flying between Russia and New York, LA...and most recently, Chicago. *He's alive.* And he was right here in my city. I tried to download a copy of his file, but hit a server error, so I settled for snapping a photo of my screen with my phone. Could I contact him? Maybe ask for his help? He was retired and probably wouldn't take kindly to someone blowing his cover, but maybe if I pleaded...

My eyes fell on the post it note on my monitor: *Edgar, 8pm.* The clock on my computer said 7:51pm.

Shit! I was going to be late! And I couldn't just not show up and leave the poor guy sitting there. I looked down at my suit. There was no time to go home and change. *Well, at least I skip the agonizing about what to wear.*

When I showed up at the restaurant in my biker leathers, the staff thought I was a delivery driver and tried to give me a takeout bag. I found the bathroom and scrambled out of my leathers and into my suit, then looked despairingly at myself in the mirror. I put on some lipstick, then unbuttoned a button on my blouse. *That'll have to do.*

I hurried back into the restaurant, and a waiter showed me to the table. Whoever this guy Edgar was, I had to grudgingly admit he had good taste. The place was classy but not too formal, dark and cozy enough that it felt private but not so quiet that there'd be awkward silences. There was a great view across Lake Michigan with the lights of the city reflected in the dark water, and the food looked and smelled amazing. I couldn't remember the last time I'd eaten something that wasn't takeout or instant noodles.

We rounded a corner, and I saw him, waiting at the table. *Oh, he's cute!* Edgar had pale golden hair and beautiful, expressive blue eyes. I mentally shifted gears. I'd been dreading this; now I was wondering if I still remembered how to flirt.

Edgar jumped up when he saw me and gave me a big, honest smile. He pulled my chair out for me, which was old-fashioned but sort of sweet. We ordered and started talking. He'd been divorced about two years, had two kids he obviously adored, and his weaknesses were Godzilla movies and red licorice.

He was nice. And attractive. I decided to get this over with before I got my hopes up too much. "I want to tell you right up front," I said, "I work for the FBI."

Edgar grinned, which gave him dimples. "Cool."

I blinked. "Really? That puts most people off."

He tilted his head to one side. "Mine's worse."

"I doubt it."

He cleared his throat theatrically. "Investigator for the IRS."

My jaw dropped. "Oh. Okay, yeah. That's way worse."

"Does it put *you* off?"

I locked eyes with him and smiled. "No. No, it doesn't."

He smiled back at me, and then both of us reached for the bread, and we bumped fingers and laughed, and *maybe this could work* and—

I froze. *You have got to be fucking kidding me.*

Marching out of the shadows was Gennadiy.

I started to get up, but he was already at the table, looming over us. And he was *pissed*. "Who is *this?*" he demanded, glancing at Edgar.

I just stared up at him, dumbstruck.

"I'm Edgar," said Edgar, uncertainly. Gennadiy didn't even look at him. Edgar looked at me. "Is this your...ex?"

"No!" Gennadiy and I both said as one. I was annoyed at him showing up like this, but Gennadiy was *seething. What's his problem?*

I managed to shake off my shock. "What are you doing here?!"

"My family owns this restaurant." He looked between the two of us. "What are *you* doing here?"

I looked at my hand, still touching Edgar's. Gennadiy and I had spent three months in close proximity, but this was the first time he'd ever seen me with a man. *Oh God, is he...jealous?!*

I jumped up from the table. "Don't move," I told Edgar. I put my hands on Gennadiy's chest and guided him back across the room, which felt like being a mouse pushing a bull. He was looking annoyingly amazing in a midnight-blue shirt, and I could feel his heart pounding under my palms. He kept glancing back at Edgar, a murderous look on his face, and that stoked my own anger. Partly, it was that Gennadiy had no right to be jealous. Partly, it was that there was a weak little part of me, deep down, that was melting at the fact that he *was* jealous. I hated myself for that.

I pushed Gennadiy up against the wall, and he scowled down at me. "You're really on a date with that *zanuda?*" he snapped.

"Yes! Gennadiy, what is this? You can't just—"

He was turning scarlet. I'd never seen him so angry, not even when I first met him at the casino. "After dinner, what happens? You're going to go to his place and—" He broke off, panting, too angry to say it.

But I was pissed, too. "Yes!" I hissed. "Yes, I'm on a date with him, yes, I like him, and yes, Gennadiy, if everything goes well, then I might just go to his place, drop to my knees and worship his dick!"

His eyes flared, the gray ice turning so bitterly cold it was frightening. Then he turned and walked away. I stood there panting, my palms still warm from the heat of his chest. *Jesus.*

I walked back to the table and, before Edgar could speak, I grabbed my glass of Chardonnay and glugged half of it. Then I gave a huge sigh. *Better.*

"Was that guy...someone from work?" asked Edgar gently.

I nodded, my heart rate still slowing. "In a manner of speaking."

"Are you okay?" He sounded genuinely concerned. And even a little protective, which was all the sweeter because he was half Gennadiy's size.

I nodded firmly. "Yes. I'm sorry about that. But don't worry, it's all over. I dealt with it. Now...where were we?"

He smiled, and I smiled back. But I felt a flutter of unease in my stomach.

I dealt with it. Right?

19

GENNADIY

I'D ONLY BEEN PASSING BY THE RESTAURANT. IT'S ONE OF OUR legitimate businesses and turns a good profit: it's the secret gambling den upstairs that I was there to visit. But then I'd seen Alison and that...that *pridurok*.

I'd never thought about her fucking anyone else. Now I couldn't get it out of my mind. Her tossing that long, silky hair back over her shoulder and leaning in to take his cock between her lips—

All the feelings that had been building for months boiled up inside. She was...she was...

She was *mine*.

I barged through the double doors into the kitchen. Inside, it was the usual pandemonium. Giancarlo, the chef, was ranting at his underlings, half in Italian and half in English, and eighty percent of it cursing. They were scuttling to wash, chop and broil, wincing every time he bellowed.

Then one of them noticed me. "Chef?" she said quietly, pointing in my direction.

Now it was Giancarlo's turn to go pale. He waddled over to me, wiping his hands on his apron. "Mr. Aristov! What—"

"The couple at the table in the corner. The dark-haired woman and the idiot with the blond hair. Where is their food?"

Giancarlo assumed they must be honored guests. "Coming *right now,* sir!" He waved at the plates. "They both ordered the same thing, the linguine." It looked and smelled amazing. "On its way!" Giancarlo waved frantically to a waiter, who grabbed both plates.

I put a hand on the waiter's chest. "*Wait.*"

I reached into my jacket and took out the little bottle I always carry. I twisted off the cap and dripped exactly three drops onto the plate on the right. Guns and bombs are for amateurs. In Russia, dispatching one's enemies is an art form.

I gripped the waiter's chin between finger and thumb. "This one is for the man," I told him, pointing to the food I'd doctored. "*This one.* Get this wrong, and you won't see morning. Do you understand?"

He nodded as best he could, sheet-white with fear. I released him, and he hurried off with the food.

20

ALISON

THE FOOD ARRIVED, AND WE STARTED EATING. THE LINGUINE WAS delicious, with a velvety red sauce rich with tomato and lobster. And Edgar was great. Good looking, gentle and polite...

But there was something missing. There was no charge, no spark. My pulse was stuck firmly in idle. *What's the matter with me? He's a perfectly nice guy.*

"Do you want dessert?" I asked as we finished our pasta.

Edgar shook his head. He'd started to look a little pale.

I was suddenly stubbornly determined to make this work. "Or we could maybe go to a bar, or—"

Edgar shook his head again. I looked closer at him: he was sweating.

"Are you—" I began.

Edgar slid off his chair, and before he'd even hit the floor, he was throwing up. I jumped back out of the way, then ran around and knelt down to help. He was groaning and apologizing, and I rubbed his back and told him it was okay. *What the fuck is going on?*

Then I saw a familiar pair of legs across the restaurant. Gennadiy was standing watching us.

There was a slow, horrible moment of realization. For a second, I fought it. *He wouldn't.* Then: *it's Gennadiy, of course he would.*

I stormed across the room, ignoring all the people staring at me. I grabbed his big hand with my smaller one and towed him into a quiet corner. "You *poisoned* him?!" I hissed.

Gennadiy glowered down at me. "It's nothing, he'll be fine in a few hours."

I stared up at him in disbelief. "Why would you do this?"

Gennadiy adjusted his cufflinks. "He's not right for you," he said dismissively.

The anger rose inside me like black, boiling oil. "You don't get to decide that! *I* decide who's right for—"

He leaned down to me. "I didn't like the idea of you sucking his cock."

My face flared hot. "You—You don't have any say in whose—" I swallowed and glared and tried to ignore how my pulse had skyrocketed, how being this close to him made me feel almost drunk. "What are you going to do, murder any man who looks at me?"

He leaned even closer and pointed to the water outside the window. "It's a big lake. Try me."

I searched his face, but he was stone-cold serious. It should have scared me: it *did* scare me. But there was another feeling, like strong arms locking protectively around me. I realized I'd been waiting for this feeling my entire life, and that scared me even more.

This is crazy. He's a gangster. No different from the men who'd murdered my parents. So why did it feel like I was...*tumbling*? And his cold gray eyes were flaring, switching between anger and something else entirely. *He feels it, too.*

Both of us leaned in...

Then I shook my head and managed to clear it, and reality crashed back in like a freezing wave. *What the hell am I doing? He's my target, I'm meant to be putting him in jail!*

I ran back to Edgar, called him a ride, and waited with him until it arrived. When I checked over my shoulder, Gennadiy was gone.

Once Edgar was safe, I headed home alone. I took a shower to try to unwind, but it was no good: my mind kept running over everything. *What would have happened if I'd kissed him?*

I crawled into bed, but I could only manage a fitful, broken sleep. Maybe that's why I came awake so easily when I heard the noise. I knew instantly what it was: the soft tinkle of the wind chimes in the living room, blowing in the breeze.

Someone had just opened the door from my balcony.

Every muscle in my body tensed. But I took a shuddering breath and forced myself to move slowly: I didn't want the intruder to know I was awake. I reached into the nightstand and grabbed my gun, then clicked off the safety. Feeling better, I slid out of bed and crept across the room in just panties and a nightshirt.

At the bedroom door, I held my breath and listened. Nothing.

I waited, willing my hammering heart to slow. Still nothing. I began to relax. *Maybe it was a random draft or—*

A creak from the hallway. *Fuck.* I got my gun up and hauled open the door. I was braced to see somebody there, but it still made my stomach lurch when I saw the silhouette of a man standing ten feet from me. *"FBI! Hands where I can see them!"* I yelled. I aimed right at his chest. The figure threw its hands in the air.

And then realization hit. We'd nearly kissed at the restaurant. Now he'd come here to finish what we'd started.

Relief sluiced through me...and in its wake, I could feel traitorous, silvery excitement unfurling in my chest. I quickly lowered the gun and tried to sound mad. "Jesus Christ, Gennadiy! I almost shot you!"

Both of us stepped forward. The light coming through the window fell across him.

It wasn't Gennadiy.

21

ALISON

THE GUY WAS ALL IN BLACK, WEARING A SKI MASK. I TRIED TO GET MY gun back up, but we were too close, and he was too quick. He grabbed the gun in one meaty hand and slammed it against the wall. My knuckles banged into the hard plaster, and the gun went flying out of my hand.

Fuck. I took two running steps backwards, trying to open up some space and give myself some thinking time. Everything was happening too fast, and it didn't help that my mind was awash with a hot wave of humiliation. *You let him get close because you were weak-kneed at the thought that Gennadiy was here to fuck you. You fucking idiot, Alison.*

And then it got worse: the guy reached behind him and pulled a gun out of his belt. Now he was armed, and I wasn't. My stomach dropped, and I pushed the shame aside. I could beat myself up later. I had to focus, or I was going to die here.

I jumped forward before he could aim and kicked him hard in the shin, then followed up with a vicious punch to his kidney. He grunted, but he didn't stop. The barrel of the gun moved towards my face, and I grabbed it and pushed it up–

The gun went off, and plaster fell from the ceiling. Then again, and this time the barrel was so close to me that I smelled my hair singe. He wrenched left and right, trying to break my grip on the gun so he could aim right at me...

I suddenly stepped back, pulling him off balance. As he stumbled forward, I snapped out a front kick that hit him right in the face.

He fell to the floor, and I dodged past him, then sprinted to my front door and grabbed the handle. The gun boomed again, and the bullet missed me by inches, digging into the wall. I threw open the door and sprinted down the hallway and out of the building, barefoot–

And then the universe must have decided to give me a break because a Chicago PD cruiser was driving down the street, no more than fifty feet away. "*Hey!*" I yelled, waving my arms. "*Hey!*"

A half hour later, I was standing outside my building, now dressed and nursing a takeout coffee. Caroline had arrived first, screeching to a stop in her blue minivan with toys littering the backseat. She'd hugged me for about a minute straight, refusing to let go. Then Halifax, Hadderwell, and Fitch had shown up. My apartment was now a crime scene, being crawled over by lab techs. There was no sign of the intruder. The cops I'd flagged down had raced inside with guns drawn, but the guy had already fled.

Halifax was pacing around, furious that someone would dare to attack one of his agents in her own home. "I'm getting a warrant for the son-of-a-bitch's arrest," he told me. And he pulled out his phone and started talking.

I frowned. "Who?" We hadn't identified the intruder.

Halifax frowned at me. "Gennadiy Aristov, who do you think?"

I felt my eyes go wide. "It wasn't Gennadiy!"

"How do you know?" asked Fitch.

"Yeah, you said he had a ski mask on," said Hadderwell. Both of them sounded gentle and...*nice*, for once. In law enforcement, when one of you gets hurt or attacked, all the bickering and infighting stops because *it's one of us.*

"I saw your description; it fits Gennadiy perfectly," said Halifax. "White guy, same height, same build...you didn't hear him speak..."

I felt like the ground had tilted and everything was sliding helplessly sideways. "But...it wasn't him," I mumbled. "He wouldn't do this."

The others looked at each other, confused. Halifax put his phone call on hold for a second. "Alison, he hates you. Your entire job is trying to bring him down. He's Bratva, he's a killer...what am I missing, here?"

"But...I know it wasn't him!"

Caroline frowned. "How?"

I opened my mouth, but nothing came out. *Because I know Gennadiy's walk as well as I know my own, and this guy walked differently. Because he wasn't wearing Gennadiy's cologne. Because...*

Because we...

There was no way I could explain. Not without telling them about him hugging me in the graveyard and the secret meeting where he'd given me the tip about the cesium and me warning him about the attempt on his life. Not without explaining that, somehow, my mortal enemy had become...something else.

"I just know," I said lamely.

Halifax put his hand on my shoulder. "You're shaken up," he said softly. "It's okay." He squeezed my shoulder, then turned away and went back to his phone call.

I looked around at all the concerned faces, then turned and looked at my apartment building, awash in red and blue lights. Reality set in and it felt like someone had just dropped an ice cube through my soul. *Are they...right?* Everyone was so sure. Was I just blind to it because I didn't want it to be true?

Gennadiy was a killer, I knew that. And while a lot of high-up Bratva guys don't do their killing personally, Gennadiy *did* get his hands dirty: he'd said as much to me, more than once. This *could* have been him.

I bit my lip. Just because we were attracted to each other didn't mean he couldn't just snap and decide I was causing him too much trouble. Hell, maybe he decided to end me *because* he felt something for me.

I started running back through the attack in my mind. The guy *had* been Gennadiy's height and build. The ski mask had covered everything except his mouth, and it had been dark. Was I *that* sure he'd walked differently, *that* sure he'd smelled differently? Every fact I grabbed at turned to smoke.

What if it *was* him?

I walked a little way from my apartment block, where it was quieter, and thought. I thought about the feel of his arms around me in the graveyard. The look in his eyes when I'd said, *but you hate me.* All the way back to his cold, protective fury at the strip club. The memories were like a river's current, washing away all the uncertainty and leaving only immovable rock.

Gennadiy was a killer. And that seething, vicious temper of his was scary. But hurt me?

No. He wouldn't hurt me.

I took a deep breath and looked around me. Dawn was just breaking, the sky turning from deep blue to pink and gold.

Halifax was after the wrong guy. I had to stop him.

But the police still had questions for me, and by the time I was finally allowed to leave and go to work, it was after ten. I met Halifax, Hadderwell, and Fitch on their way out of the FBI building.

"I got the warrant," Halifax told me, brandishing it. "We're leaving to pick up Gennadiy now."

I gave him a weak smile and watched him go, my toes nervously dancing inside my biker boots. The irony wasn't lost on me. A few months ago, I'd been desperate to bring Gennadiy down. I still wanted to bring him down. Just not for something he didn't do.

Relax, I told myself as I changed out of my biker leathers and into my suit. Halifax could arrest Gennadiy, but they'd have to let him go. There was no evidence it was him in my apartment because it *wasn't* him.

I frowned at myself in the bathroom mirror. So why was a sick fear spreading through me? Why did it feel like I was missing something?

I stood there gripping the sink, staring down at its clean whiteness without seeing it. My cop brain started grinding. I felt myself rise up on my toes and slowly sink down. *No evidence. No evidence...*

I froze, still up on my toes, as everything suddenly reversed in my head. *That means there's no evidence that could prove it* wasn't *him, either.* The intruder had been super-careful not to leave any. He'd approached my building from a side where there weren't any security cameras, so there were no pictures of him. He'd worn a ski mask so I didn't see his face. He'd worn gloves, so there were no prints. He was covered head to toe, so no DNA was left behind. In fact, the only evidence he'd left was...

The bullets that were dug out of my apartment's walls and ceiling.

And it all snapped into place. "Oh, fuck," I whispered.

I ran out of the bathroom and raced downstairs, to the evidence room. I searched through the racks of boxes, looking for one we'd received from Chicago PD, back when I first started the case. Bullets recovered from Radimir Aristov's wedding, bullets that came from Gennadiy's gun, when he'd fired in self-defense. They'd been dug out of a wall, too. Seven of them.

Except—I held up the evidence bag—now, there were only four. Three were missing. The same number that the attacker had fired at my apartment.

I felt a cold sweat break out across my back. I'd been scared plenty of times in my life, but I'd never felt so utterly disturbed.

Someone was trying to frame Gennadiy. Someone at the FBI.

I dug out the burner phone Gennadiy had given me and dialed. The line rang two times. Three times. *Fuck.* It was twenty minutes since Halifax left. He could be arresting Gennadiy any minute. *Pick up! Pick up!*

"Alison?" It was the first time I'd heard him say my name, and despite everything, the sound of it in his Russian accent sent a silvery tremble straight down to my groin.

"Get rid of your gun!" I told him. "They're coming to arrest you!"

I could hear the frown in his voice. "My gun is clean."

"Not anymore, it's not. Someone switched out the evidence. They'll run ballistics on your gun, and it'll tie you to a crime scene. Get rid of it!" I was wincing, listening to myself. I didn't want to think about how many laws I was breaking, telling a suspect about an active investigation. If anyone found out, I wasn't just out of the FBI, I was going to jail.

"Why are you doing this?" asked Gennadiy.

"Because someone tried to kill me last night," I said breathlessly, "and the one thing I'm sure of is, it wasn't you."

Silence for a moment. Then he started to say something, but he was interrupted by the rising wail of police sirens.

"Gennadiy?" I asked, panicked.

"I have to go."

A door banging open. Raised voices. "Gennadiy?!"

But he was gone.

22

GENNADIY

/

THEY LED ME OUT OF THE CASINO IN HANDCUFFS. *ME.*

They took me to the FBI office and shut me in an interrogation room. There were three of them: two agents called Hadderwell and Fitch, and Alison's boss, Assistant Director Halifax. They demanded to know where I was between three and four a.m. the night before. I told them the truth, that I was driving around, doing business. I couldn't prove it, but they couldn't disprove it. And thanks to Alison, they had nothing that placed me at her apartment. I'd passed my gun to Valentin seconds before the FBI burst into my office, and by now it had been sawed up, melted down, and probably buried for good measure.

"This is bullshit!" yelled Halifax. He'd been grilling me for an hour, and he was red in the face, his tie askew where he'd pulled at it to loosen it. "We know it was you!"

I scowled at him. I was having to recite the alphabet backwards to keep from lunging across the table at him. Someone in the FBI was trying to frame me. The familiar hatred of cops bloomed in my chest, clouds of anger spreading and darkening. But now there was a new element I'd never felt before, a rawness within the anger that flashed hot as lightning.

Whoever was behind this, they'd tried to kill Alison. My eyes burned into Halifax. *Was it you?* I looked at Hadderwell and Fitch. *Or you? Or you?*

The door crashed open. Silhouetted in the doorway was six-foot-four of muscle wrapped in Armani, topped with the sort of tousled surfer curls that make women sigh. Conrad Bryce stared at Halifax and the two agents in mock-horror. "Are you *questioning my client without counsel present?!*"

"Just a friendly conversation," grumbled Halifax.

Conrad marched across the room and set his leather briefcase down on the table, a wall between the FBI and me. "Which is now over," he told Halifax firmly.

Less than ten minutes later, I was walking out of the interrogation room a free man. This is why it's worth having the best defense attorney in Chicago on permanent retainer. And it doesn't hurt that we have a hold over Conrad that's more powerful than money.

I wasn't ready to leave, though. The cold ball of fear in my stomach wouldn't let me. I'd spoken to her on the phone, so I knew she was okay. But I wasn't going until I'd *seen* she was okay.

Halifax and the two agents walked me down a hallway, into the lobby...and my heart lifted. Alison was walking in through the main doors with a takeout coffee. She must have had a friend—my money was on the blonde with glasses–tip her off when the interrogation ended so she could be in the lobby just as I passed through.

Alison gave me a cold glare as we approached, and I did the same, keeping up the pretense. Then, as we passed and I looked back over my shoulder, there was a brief second when the others couldn't see.

Her expression changed in a heartbeat. Fear. Panic. And something that reached right down inside me and hit me where I lived: concern. She'd just survived an attempt on her life, and she was worried about *me.*

Park, I mouthed, and she nodded.

～

An hour later, Alison roared up on her bike and pulled in next to my car, then hurried across the grass to me. We were in the same spot where I'd given her the cesium tip, but today a cold wind was blowing across the lake, cutting straight through my suit, and winding cold fingers around my bones.

Alison pulled off her helmet. "We'd better make this fast. My boss thinks I'm at the sandwich store. What the fuck is going on?"

I stepped closer and, immediately, I could feel myself reacting to her. The base instincts, first, my cock hardening in my pants at the sight of her legs in that tight leather. Then the more complicated feelings: the ache in my chest when I saw the lock of hair that had escaped her tight bun and fallen across her cheek, the temptation to hook it with one big, clumsy finger and brush it back behind her ear... God, the pull towards her was off the charts, now.

She saw me staring and frowned. "What?" She crossed her arms, tough as ever. But I could hear the tiny tremble in her voice that gave away how scared she was. And that brought out the most dangerous feeling of all, the one that made me want to pull her to my chest and shield her from the entire fucking world. When I thought of someone breaking into her apartment, pointing a gun at her... *I am going to find this man. I am going to find him and personally remove him from this world–*

I blew out my breath through my nostrils. A few months ago, I'd hated this woman. Now, the idea of someone hurting her made me crazy.

I looked away and forced my voice to be level. "One of my rivals must be trying to get rid of me. They know you're investigating me, so if you're murdered, I'm the prime suspect. They send an assassin to your apartment, then have someone in the FBI fake the evidence so it points to my gun. If you hadn't told me to get rid of it, I'd be in jail for the next decade."

"So who are your rivals?" Alison asked.

I rubbed at my stubble. "That's a long list." I looked sideways at her. "A better question: who is their inside person at the FBI?"

She sighed and looked out over the lake, thinking. After a few seconds, she did something I'd never seen her do before: she lifted herself up on her tiptoes, stayed there for a moment, and then slowly sank back down. It was hypnotic and not just because of her leather-clad legs flexing gracefully. It was like I was seeing some private part of her, something that she only did when she was alone. Which meant, in some weird way, that she trusted me.

At last, she turned to me. "I don't know. But I'm going to find out."

I stepped closer, and now I could smell that cherry and vanilla scent of her. *Chyort,* I wanted to just grab her waist and bring my lips down on that pouting, stubbornly determined mouth...

She's a fucking FBI agent. The enemy. I repeated it and repeated it in my head, but even then, I had to bunch my fists to stop me reaching for her. And there was this...*ache* in my chest. I didn't want her to go. Didn't want her anywhere but securely in my arms, where I could protect her. I took a deep breath. "Be very careful," I managed.

She nodded, pulled on her helmet, and ran to her bike. The wind had turned bitter, sending my suit jacket billowing out behind me and making my forehead throb with the cold. But I stood there watching until she was a speck in the distance.

23

ALISON

That afternoon, I sat at my desk pretending to work while my stomach tied itself in knots. I wasn't just scared, I felt utterly lost. I'd spent my entire career in law enforcement, and there'd always been an unspoken bond, a kind of family. Sure, cops argue, but we always have each other's backs. But now...

Someone at FBI Chicago had conspired to kill me. And most likely, it was someone on my team: they would have had easiest access to the evidence.

I felt like a tree someone had torn out of the earth, roots jangling like exposed nerves. I couldn't trust anyone, and I just wanted—

I wanted to feel Gennadiy's arms around me again. It made no sense. The man was a killer...but that moment in the graveyard was the first time I'd felt truly safe in years.

I closed my eyes for a second and forced the feeling down inside. *Focus, Alison. Who's the traitor?*

I opened my eyes and sneaked a look across the room at Fitch. He was a sexist prick who didn't like taking orders from me, but *murder?* I thought back to just after it happened, when I was standing outside my apartment building. He'd been nice, concerned. Did that rule him out, or was he just a good liar?

Or what about Hadderwell? I turned the other way and watched him through the open door of the break room as he poured coffee, swiping through stock graphs on his phone. He was always boasting about playing the market and picking winners. What if he'd been picking losers instead? Maybe he was in debt and had taken a bribe...

The air started to feel hot, the room shrinking, threatening to crush me. The traitor was *right here* in the building, probably in the same room, and every instinct wanted me to run, but I had to stay passively in my seat and wait for—

A hand thumped down on my shoulder. I yelped and spun around in my chair.

"Sorry." Halifax scrunched up his brow in concern. "Didn't mean to scare you. You okay?"

I sat there panting for a second. No, I most definitely *wasn't* okay. But I couldn't tell him why, even though I'd known him for years, even though I counted him as a friend, because...

Because it might be him. I hated the thought, but I couldn't discount it. He'd been so quick to blame Gennadiy. "I'm fine," I croaked. "Just...you know. It was a long night."

Halifax nodded somberly. "You shouldn't even be at work. Go home, get some rest. We'll keep trying to find something to tie Gennadiy to your apartment. We'll get the bastard."

I nodded weakly and stood up. It was almost quitting time anyway, and I couldn't stay in the office another second. Caroline gave me a worried look as I passed by her desk. *Should I tell her?* I could really use a sounding board. She could keep her eyes open, maybe help figure out who the traitor was...

But telling her would put her in danger, too, and she had kids. No, I had to figure this out on my own.

I rode home, stopping on the way to get Cantonese takeout, then clumped up the stairs to my apartment. It was weird, being home so early. *What do normal people do all evening?* Maybe I could find a movie to watch.

I put the takeout bag down on the coffee table and started unpacking cartons...then stopped.

The rug was out of place. One end was all rucked up, like someone had tripped on it. That wasn't weird in itself: about a million people had been through here the previous night, dusting for prints. Except...I'd straightened the rug before I left. I was sure of it.

I pulled out my gun and moved slowly into the hallway, breathing quietly. I checked the bedroom: nothing. But the door to the bathroom was closed, and I *never* leave it fully closed. My heart started pounding. I edged towards the door, wishing my leathers didn't creak so much.

I listened. Nothing. Were they waiting for me, on the other side?

I took three quick breaths, then turned the doorknob and threw the door wide—

The bathroom was empty.

I let out a long sigh, put my gun away, and leaned back against the wall, breathing hard. There was nobody here, but I was sure there had been. I could feel it. *Why break into my apartment a second time and just..leave?* Nothing seemed to be missing.

I huffed and sat down on the toilet to think. As I sat, something metallic caught the light and glinted under the sink. I got down on my hands and knees and found a small, silver screw lying on the tiles. *Where did that come from?*

I looked around. My bathtub is boxed in with a cheap, white plastic panel to hide the plumbing. And one of the screws was missing.

I started to get a bad feeling.

I ran and got a screwdriver, then unscrewed the remaining screw and lifted away the plastic panel. "Oh shit," I said aloud.

I was staring at three plastic-wrapped bricks of what I guessed was cocaine.

And at that second, someone banged on my front door. Halifax's voice, stressed and urgent. "Brooks? Open up!"

24

ALISON

I SHOVED THE PLASTIC PANEL BACK INTO PLACE AND SCREWED IN BOTH screws. Then I opened the front door. Brooks was there with a bunch of agents, none from our team. This wasn't a social call. "What's up?"

Halifax showed me a search warrant. "Some...*items* are missing from evidence."

I pretended to read the warrant while I thought. I'd gone light-headed with panic, the room spinning around me. I was being set up. They'd tried to kill me last night but failed, so now they'd found another way to take me out of the game.

We'd had it all wrong. Someone wasn't trying to take out Gennadiy; they were trying to take out *me*.

Halifax's face softened, and he looked genuinely concerned. "Alison, talk to me!"

Fuck. What do I do? If he wasn't behind this, I should tell him everything. But if he was, I'd just be showing my hand.

One of the agents was slashing open my couch cushions. I could hear another one rooting through my bedroom. No one had gone into the bathroom yet, but as soon as they did...

I had to make a decision fast. If they took me in, I'd be questioned and charged. Once I was locked in a cell, it'd be next to impossible to get anyone to listen to me, let alone convince them I was innocent. And I didn't like my chances in jail, once the other inmates found out I used to be FBI. But the alternative wasn't any better. If I ran, I'd be a fugitive.

An agent walked into the bathroom. *Fuck.*

Halifax turned away for a second. I started to back towards the sliding glass door that led to the balcony.

I heard the sound of a screw hitting the tiled floor. I pressed up against the glass door, feeling for the handle...

The sound of plastic wobbling as the panel came off. A low whistle from the agent in the bathroom. "Found it!"

Halifax whirled around, frowning accusingly...and saw me standing at the door. I turned the key, wrenched the handle down, and shoved the door open. Then I was out onto the balcony.

"Alison, stop!" yelled Halifax. Then, "Get her, she's running!" into his radio. I could hear him sprinting towards me.

I climbed over the balcony's railing, dangled for a second and then dropped down to the parking lot. It was only one floor, but when I hit the concrete, the jolt still rattled my teeth. There was no time to shake it off: cops were already running towards me. I swung my leg over my bike, hit the starter, and shot forward, weaving between them and twisting away when one of them got his hand on my shoulder. Then I was out of the parking lot and roaring down the street.

Almost immediately, sirens wailed behind me and red and blue lights lit up the night. I turned left, right, trying to throw them off, but after a few seconds, the glow behind me returned, relentless. *Is this what it's like for Gennadiy when I'm tailing him?*

The panic had taken hold, clawing at my insides. I knew that by now, Halifax would have called it in. Cop cars would be scrambling to head me off. Roadblocks would appear. They'd get a helicopter up and pin me with a searchlight. I darted down side street after side street, but I couldn't shake them, and the closer the lights behind me got, the more my breathing tightened.

I turned into the next street. *Think!* I could feel I was close to hyperventilating, my breath fogging my visor. I had to be calm, I had to be calm *right now* because if I kept panicking, I was toast. *How do I lose them?* I thought about procedures, search patterns, everything I knew about how a search like this was conducted.

I had to lose my beloved bike.

I turned into the next alley, then into another, narrower one, too narrow for the cop cars to follow me. They screeched to a stop, and I knew they'd be radioing ahead, getting the alley blocked at the far end to trap me.

Except...I wasn't going to the other end. I ditched my bike behind a dumpster, pulled off my helmet, and ran, slipping between two buildings and sprinting until I hit the street. I was in luck: it was a busy road with plenty of people strolling between bars. I stripped off my leather jacket and tossed it away, then walked casually, trying to blend in. Cop car after cop car tore past me, still looking for a woman on a motorcycle. I walked on, fighting the urge to look back. And finally, the sirens faded behind me.

I walked until I reached a skate park, still and eerie in the darkness, and slumped down on one of the ramps. *What the fuck am I going to do?*

I had nothing. I didn't have my passport, money, or transport. I had no way to run and nowhere to run *to*.

I needed help.

I pulled out my phone: thank God *that* had been in my pocket, at least. *Calahan?* My thumb hovered over his name. The FBI weren't stupid; Calahan would be the first person they'd question. If he was caught harboring a fugitive, his career would be over, and I couldn't do that to him. And the same went for Caroline, and Kate...*all* my friends were in law enforcement, and they'd be screwed if they helped me. *Hailey?* She might be able to help, but she and Konstantin were in Europe for a month.

I hugged my knees and rested my head on my arms. Anyone else would have friends outside of work, people they could turn to. I had no one. *This is what happens when work is your entire life.* I hadn't felt so completely alone since my parents died. My mind plummeted down, down, *down*.

And then, right as it was about to hit bottom, it caught on something. One slim, silvery thread.

There was one place I could go where the FBI would never think to look for me. One person I could ask for help.

My mind recoiled. *No!*

Yes, I was attracted to him. Yes, I... felt things for him. But that made it worse, not better. He was still *Bratva,* still the enemy. I couldn't go to him for help. I was FBI, and the FBI's job was to hunt him.

But now they were hunting *me.*

I tried to think of another plan: something else, *anything* else. But I was out of options.

"Fuck," I said aloud, and climbed to my feet.

A few hours later, I was on the street outside Gennadiy's mansion. I'd been there so many times, sitting in an FBI car, watching the place. It felt wrong, walking up the driveway, like walking onto a stage when you've only ever been hidden in the wings.

There was a big iron doorknocker. I lifted my hand to it. Hesitated. Grabbed hold of it. Hesitated again.

I hated going to him. But what I hated even more was that my heart was racing just at the thought of seeing him again. I crushed the feeling down, lifted the knocker—

Gennadiy swung the door open wide. He must have been watching me on a security camera. He gazed down at me, his eyes tracking over my leather pants, my tank top and bare shoulders, finishing on my eyes. He seemed to get stuck there for a second. Then he gave me that superior, cold glare and raised one eyebrow expectantly.

I took a deep breath. "I need your help."

25

GENNADIY

THE SIGHT OF HER STANDING ON MY DOORSTEP, SO SMALL AND vulnerable, nearly broke me. It took everything I had just to keep my expression stony and unyielding. But when she asked for my help, I almost crumbled completely. It wasn't just the fear in her voice; it was that she'd come to me, which meant she had no one else. All the feelings that had been building for months welled up, and I had to brace my hands on the door frame to keep from grabbing her and pulling her to me.

It didn't matter how I felt about her. She was still a cop. Still part of the system that tore my family apart. We were on opposite sides in a war that would never end. But all of those reasons I kept clawing at as handholds...they were feeling less like iron and more like smoke.

I stepped back from the door and waved her in. She walked beside me through the hallway, looking absurdly small in the cavernous space. In the living room, she stopped in the center, just...*lost*. I forced myself to keep my distance. "What happened?" I asked gruffly.

She told me about being set up by someone at the FBI. "We were wrong before," she said, wrapping her arms around herself.

"Whoever's behind this is trying to get rid of *me,* not you. They didn't manage to kill me, so now they're getting me thrown in jail. Then they can pay someone to shiv me in the showers." She gave a bitter little laugh. "They might not even have to pay. An FBI agent in jail? Someone'll do me for free."

Before I could stop myself, I'd marched over to her and grabbed her shoulders. "No one's killing you," I snapped. I just meant to reassure her, but my words put a knife through the whole *idea* of someone hurting her. She lifted her chin and looked up at me and—

Blyat'. I'd never looked into anyone's eyes and seen *that* before. *Hope.* My hands tightened on her shoulders, and *God,* I just wanted to crush my lips down on hers and let all her good and all my bad obliterate one another.

I turned away and stalked over to a side table. I knew what I had to do. "You'll be out of the country tonight," I told her.

"What?!" she asked behind me. Then, "I don't have my passport."

I didn't dare turn around. "I know someone who can make you a new one." The idea of never seeing her again was tearing a hole in my heart. I hadn't been ready for how much it would hurt. But this was the only way to keep her safe.

"I don't have any *money!*" she protested.

"I'll give you some," I said. I just about managed to keep the pain out of my voice. "Enough to get started. A hundred thousand." I poured vodka, my knuckles white on the bottle.

"You'd do that?" she asked quietly. "Why?"

I turned around. "You saved my life."

She stared up at me and *chyort,* there was a different kind of hope in her eyes. "Weren't we mortal enemies just a few weeks ago?" she asked.

Don't break. Especially not now, when I'd be saying goodbye in a few hours. "A hundred grand," I said coldly, "is a small price to pay to have you out of my hair forever."

She locked eyes with me, challenging me, and my expression almost faltered. *Yebat'!* She was too good at reading me. I pushed a glass of vodka into her hand and turned away, drinking and not tasting it.

"Where would I go?" she asked.

"Wherever you want," I said coldly. "I don't care."

26

ALISON

I STARED AT HIS BACK, AT THE WAY HIS MUSCLED SHOULDERS ROSE AND fell as he took slow, deep breaths. *Trying to calm himself because he's mad? Or because...* Had I seen what I thought I saw in his eyes? Or was it crazy to think that someone like him could have feelings for anyone?

It doesn't matter now. I turned away and started pacing, firing up my cop brain and getting practical. Where *would* I go? I'd always wanted to see Europe. Paris? Rome? Or somewhere cheaper, where the money would last a long time? Brazil? What would I do? A fake passport would get me into the country, but it wouldn't stand up to detailed background checks, so I sure as hell wasn't working for law enforcement ever again. That part of my life was over. *What else do I know how to do?*

My stomach lurched. *Nothing.*

My steps grew smaller. I could tend bar, or mop floors: something where people wouldn't ask too many questions. A job, not a career. I'd never be able to risk coming back to the US. I'd never see Calahan, or Kate and Hailey, or Caroline again.

I stopped in front of an antique mirror bigger than I was. The worst part wasn't being on my own or never coming back. It was that I still had no idea who'd done this to me, or why. Which meant that whatever they were up to, they'd get away with it.

I stewed and stewed on it. Then I looked up, caught myself in the mirror, and glared. "No," I said aloud.

"No, what?" asked Gennadiy, sounding genuinely confused.

I turned to him. "No, I'm not leaving the country. I'm staying. I want to find out who's behind this and take them down."

27

GENNADIY

I blinked. "What?! No!" I marched over to her. "They'll kill you!"

"I need to clear my name. Get my job back."

The anger blossomed inside me, dark clouds filling me. "It's just a *job!*"

She was getting mad, too. "It's not just a job! It's—" Her voice fractured for a second. "It's all I have!"

The shame in her voice hit me deep in my chest, and an uncomfortable echo rolled through me. All she had was her work. How different was that to me?

I tightened my lips and leaned down to her. "You're not thinking clearly. Take the money and get out of the country!" I hated the idea of never seeing her again. But I wasn't letting her get killed.

"No!"

The clouds were black, now, and shot through with lightning. "Why not?!"

"Because... Because if I go, then they win!"

I hurled my vodka glass into the fireplace. "*Blyat'!*" I roared. "*Ty samaya upryamaya zhenshchina, kotoruyu ya kogda-libo vstrechal!*"

Anyone else would have shrunk away and looked at their feet. She lifted her chin and stared up at me. "What does that mean?"

"It means you're the stubbornest woman I've ever met!"

The black clouds in my chest had turned ice cold. I was angry because I was terrified of losing her. All of the longing I'd been mercilessly clamping down on welled up inside me.

I glared down at her, trying to intimidate her into being safe. But she glared back up at me with total defiance. A single lock of hair had escaped her tight little ponytail and crept across her cheek, and she blew it out of her face with a furious little huff. Her sapphire eyes were harder than steel...but heartbreakingly close to fracturing...

Every man has his limit.

I took her face in my hands and crushed my lips to hers. She gave a little *mmf* of shock, and her arms flailed out to the sides for a moment. Then I buried my hands in her hair, and she groaned, her lips parting and welcoming me in. My body pressed to hers, and she was an intoxicating blend of soft and hard, feminine but athletic, vulnerable but strong. My fingers plowed her hair, finding the band that kept her ponytail in place and pulling it free. I felt her hair spill out across my wrists and fingers, and I wanted to see, but I didn't dare open my eyes in case I was dreaming.

The tip of her tongue brushed mine, and I growled low in my throat and kissed her harder, putting my hands on her ass and tugging her tighter against me. Our tongues danced together, and we twisted around on the spot: it was impossible to keep still. I started running my hands down the graceful lines of her back, and she sighed and flexed like a cat, which rubbed her breasts against my chest. *Yebat'*, I'd imagined this for months: I'd already felt every part of her in my fantasies, but now it was real: the cherry and vanilla scent of her, the warmth of her body through her thin vest top... I still hadn't relinquished control of her mouth, addicted to the soft sweetness of her, and every second I kissed her, I forgot a little more about everything else.

We started moving around the living room, spinning and stumbling like drunk ballroom dancers, neither of us willing to open our eyes. I had to feel her breasts, but I couldn't bring myself to stop kissing her. I put my hands on her hips and flipped her around so her back was to my chest, her head tilted back so that my lips could stay on hers. I ran my hands up her body, moaning as I finally touched her breasts. But it wasn't enough, touching them through her clothes. I started pulling her vest top up over her bra, feeling my cock swell against her leather-clad ass. *I'm going to fuck you so many ways, Alison.* First, with her sitting on the side table, her legs around my waist. Then on the couch. No, wait, even better: bent over the *back* of the couch, with her ass in the air—

I had to see her. I wanted to watch as I bared her breasts. I broke the kiss for a second and drew my head back—

Her eyes fluttered open, and she looked up at me, her eyes wide and blue and...

Innocent.

I froze, panting.

What's the matter? I'd known she wasn't one of us, that she was a good person, an innocent in a world of killers. It was one of the things that first attracted me to her when she'd gotten so angry about me burning down the theater. I'd wanted to grab the angel's ankle and pull her down into my world. Fuck all the goodness out of her, make her beg for my darkness, ruin her—

But that was when it was just about lust, before the feelings started. Now...

My stomach knotted. She deserved better than the Bratva, better than *me.* She deserved a good man, maybe even a cop, like her, and a nice, safe life with two children and a little house in the suburbs. Not a tattooed gangster whose hands were soaked in too much blood to ever be clean.

I'd wanted her so I could ruin her. Now I had to let her go, to make sure I didn't.

A little voice told me that wasn't the only reason. That there was something deeper I was afraid of, something right down at the center of my soul. I silenced it.

I let go of her and stepped back. "This was a mistake," I told her.

She whirled around to face me, staring in disbelief. She searched my face for an explanation, but I stayed stony and silent. Inside, I was raging and screaming at myself. *Blyat', what have I done?* Why couldn't I have just held on a few more hours until she was out of the country? Now she knew I had feelings for her, if she hadn't known before. *Why did I have to go and kiss her?!*

She turned her back, but not before I saw the blood rush to her face. She tugged her vest top back down to cover her bra, then pulled her hair back into a ponytail...only to realize she didn't have the band to secure it. I spotted it on the floor behind her, picked it up, and gently put it in her hand. She snatched it silently and fixed her ponytail, pulling it savagely tight. Even from behind, I could see the hurt I'd caused, her whole body tense with humiliation as she took long, calming breaths. It made my chest ache. But it was better this way, better than a long, drawn-out explanation. *Like ripping off a Band-Aid.* That's what I told myself.

I sighed and rubbed the bridge of my nose. We still had to finish the argument we'd been having. I still had to convince her to leave the country. "Alison," I said gently. "You can't stay here and fight these people."

Alison finally turned around and...*Chyort,* were her eyes damp? The anger bloomed in my chest, filling me. I wanted to kill whoever made her cry...but it was me.

"Whoever they are," I continued, "they're organized crime, and that makes them too dangerous to take on. You have to trust me on this; this is my world."

She took a deep breath. "I know it is," she said, her voice shaky but determined. "That's why I need your help."

The anger disappeared, replaced with horror. "*What?!* I can't help you! Have you forgotten what I *am?*" Without thinking, I stalked over to her. That was a mistake because, as soon as I got close, the longing was almost too much to take. I scowled down at her. "If Radimir knew I was even *talking* to you... Bratva don't work with cops!"

"One of your rivals already *is* working with the cops," she reminded me. "They have someone in the FBI, and they tried to frame you and put you in jail. Are you going to let that lie?"

I glared at her, then looked away. Of course I wasn't going to let it lie, but I could deal with them when she was safe.

"I'm doing this with or without you," she said.

I glared at her, furious. She didn't know the first thing about how things worked on my side of the line. She'd be dead in a day without me. But she just tilted her chin up, determined.

Work with a cop, to bring down other criminals? That went against everything I believed in. Alison was an honest cop, but she was still part of the corrupt system that took everything from me.

But if I didn't help her, she was dead. And I wasn't letting that happen.

I sucked in my breath and slowly let it out. "Fine," I said. "I'll help you. Just as..."—what did they call it on the cop shows?—"*partners.* We'll bring these people down. Clear your name. And then you go back to your side, and I go back to mine."

At that last part, I saw her swallow and blink, her cheeks reddening again, and I felt that brutal ache in my chest for hurting her. *Blyat'! Why did you kiss her, Gennadiy? Why did you have to be so weak?*

I sighed and tried to think of practicalities. "You'll need to stay here until we're done," I thought out loud. "It's the only place that's safe. Follow me." As I marched upstairs, it slowly sank in that we were going to be working side by side and living together in this house for however long this took. Being so close to her but having to resist her...*this is going to be hell.*

We came to a landing, and I waved my hand at four identical doors. "Take any of the guest bedrooms."

She stared. "You have *four* guest bedrooms?"

"In this wing. Get some sleep. Tomorrow, we'll talk to my brothers and make a plan."

She chose the second room from the left. As she was about to close the door, she turned back to me. "Thank you."

Despite what I'd just put her through, she meant it. I looked away, not used to gratitude, and gave her a curt little nod. When I heard her door close, I slumped against the wall. *What the fuck am I going to do now?*

28

ALISON

I WOKE LOST AND CONFUSED, COMICALLY SMALL IN THE EMPEROR-SIZED bed. Someone was knocking on the door, too lightly to be Gennadiy. I'd stripped down to my panties to sleep, and I didn't have anything else to put on, so I scrambled back into my vest top, then cracked the door open, hiding behind it.

She was about twenty-five, blonde and absurdly pretty, in a white blouse and black skirt. "Mr. Aristov thought you might need these," she told me in a heavy Russian accent, and passed me a dark green leather bag the size of a large purse. "And these." She passed me a bundle of clothes and then, when I'd put them down, handed me a stack of boxes. "Breakfast will be served downstairs whenever you're ready." And then she curtsied, graceful as a swan. I managed to stutter out a thank you, then closed the door and leaned against it, dazed. *Servants. He has servants.*

I touched my fingers to my lips, remembering the kiss. Why had he suddenly pulled away? It hurt more than it should have, maybe because when I'd melted into the kiss, it had made me acknowledge all the feelings I'd been denying. I'd been craving his touch for three months, and for thirty heart-stopping seconds, it had actually happened...and then he'd ripped it all away again. My chest ached, remembering it. *A mistake,* he'd said, brutally crushing the excitement that had been rising inside me. Had I been wrong, all the times he'd seemed to want me? Had I just been imagining it? My insecurities about my body woke and uncoiled. *Of course he doesn't want you...*

I took a deep breath and rammed the feelings down inside, then looked at the clothes. God, he'd bought me an entire freakin' wardrobe. There were jeans, vest tops, blouses, sweaters, and underwear, and a cute, bottle-green denim jacket that I fell in love with immediately. It was all high-end designer wear from achingly cool brands, so high quality that my own clothes suddenly felt scratchy and cheap. Everything was fresh from the store...but there were no price tags. Gennadiy's maid had cut them off just to save me a few seconds, even though that meant they couldn't be returned. Money really did mean nothing to him.

Wait...it was only eight in the morning. *How did he get these here so early?* Either he had access to some personal shopper service for the ultra- rich that delivered within hours...or he'd called up the manager of some store downtown and scared them into opening early for him. Neither would have surprised me.

There were skirts and summer dresses, some of which were actually really pretty. But nothing I could ever wear. I looked down at my ruined leg. *Not his fault. He's only ever seen me in pants.* The boxes contained shoes in three different sizes. The heels were far taller than I'd ever wear, but there were a pair of leather ankle boots that were badass. I opened up the leather bag and found it was stuffed full of toiletries: everything from toothpaste to shampoo. He'd even thrown in some tampons and pads.

I took a long, hot shower and dressed, choosing some black jeans, a white blouse, and the ankle boots, then went to investigate breakfast. I found my way back to the staircase and then downstairs. The maid who'd brought me the clothes was polishing the banister, and I thanked her again and asked her name: Milena.

I followed the smell of food and found the dining room...and Gennadiy, sitting at the head of the table, sipping coffee. Both of us froze, unsure how to play things. "Thank you for the clothes," I said at last.

"I'm glad they...fit." His gaze traced over my hip, following the tight denim so closely it felt like a caress. *I'm definitely not imagining that.* But then he tore his eyes away guiltily. *What's going on?*

I sat and, immediately, a man in chef's whites appeared from the kitchen. "What can I bring you for breakfast?" He had the same heavy Russian accent as Milena.

"Umm..." *How do you order when there's no menu?* "Anything. Whatever's easiest." The chef looked blank. "Uh...what do you have?"

He blinked at me, almost offended. "Everything! Pancakes? An omelet? Bread, cold meats, cheeses? Porridge with honey, or chia seeds, or goji berries? An English muffin? Poached eggs? Scrambled eggs? Eggs Benedict? Pastries, fruit? You're American: waffles with maple syrup? Bacon and sausage? *Steak?*"

I gaped at him. "Um. Could I get half a grapefruit and some toast, please?"

"Right away."

I looked at Gennadiy. "All your servants are Russian? Because you don't trust outsiders?"

"Yes, they're all Russian. And I don't trust anybody."

Just a few moments later, my breakfast arrived, and it was amazing, the grapefruit juicy and deliciously sour, the toast sliced thick and with just the right blend of crunchy outer layer and fluffy middle. I was on my last mouthful when I heard voices in the hallway. Male voices, and one sounded bad-tempered.

My stomach dropped. I trusted Gennadiy—mostly. But his brothers were something else. I was about to be outnumbered, behind closed doors, on their turf, and I didn't have the protection of being an FBI agent anymore. "Do we have to involve them?" I asked quickly.

"Radimir is my *Pakhan,*" Gennadiy told me firmly. "I'll try to convince him to help you. But if I can't..." He shook his head, worried.

The door flew open, and suddenly I was staring up into the cold gray eyes of Radimir Aristov. He was even taller than Gennadiy, and the family resemblance was obvious: the same sharp cheekbones and hard jaw. But where Gennadiy was all fire and anger, Radimir was pure ice. A man who'd built his billion-dollar property empire through ruthless deals and broken fingers. In his tailored three-piece suit, he looked like a Wall Street banker, and he was meant to be the legitimate face of the family, letting the others do the dirty work. But I had no doubt that he was capable of snapping my neck himself if he chose to.

Radimir stopped in the doorway, blocking everyone behind him. "What's going on?"

Gennadiy took a deep breath. "This is Alison Brooks. She's an FBI agent. She's...*the* FBI agent."

"The agent who's been on you," said Radimir coldly.

"Yes," said Gennadiy.

Radimir's eyes bored into me. "The one who confiscated two hundred thousand dollars of our money?"

I prayed for my chair to sink through the floor. It didn't.

"Yes," said Gennadiy, head bowed.

"The one who impounded *four million dollars'* worth of supercars, and ended one of our most profitable businesses?"

"Yes," breathed Gennadiy.

"Then I only have one question," said Radimir. He tugged his waistcoat straight. "What the *fuck* is she doing at your breakfast table?"

"Please, brother..." Gennadiy's voice was gentle. He used his foot to push out one of the chairs. "Take a seat. Hear what she has to say."

"Sit down with one of *them?*" Radimir looked genuinely concerned. "Gennadiy, what's the matter with you?" His eyes went to me, then Gennadiy, then flicked upwards, towards the bedrooms upstairs. His eyes widened. "Are you—"

"No!" said Gennadiy and I simultaneously, both of us flushing.

A soft mane of copper hair appeared under Radimir's arm, and then a woman squeezed through underneath it. She was gorgeous, with big blue eyes and curves I'd kill for. *Bronwyn.* Radimir's wife, as of six months ago. "Darling?" she said gently, "Gennadiy wouldn't invite her here without a good reason." She poured coffee from the pot into a mug. "Maybe it's worth giving her a chance..." —she added milk—" ...to explain?" She pressed the mug into Radimir's hands.

Radimir looked suspiciously at me, then longingly at the coffee. Apparently, he wasn't a morning person. At last, he scowled and took the mug from his wife, stepping into the room at last.

Behind him was Gennadiy's other brother, Valentin. With his longer hair and hauntingly beautiful face, I'd always thought he looked like an actor, or maybe the lead singer of a band. But he was the deadliest of all of them, the family's hitman, with a body count at least in double figures. He skirted the table and took up residence in the corner, watching me closely.

There was the clinking of chains and the patter of many feet, and then Mikhail, the brothers' uncle, arrived, together with his four dogs. Mikhail was older, with a little silver in his hair, but he still had the Aristov good looks, and he seemed to be the only member of the family who smiled. His dogs were beautiful: enormous Malamutes with white faces, gray and white coats, and big, fluffy tails. One of them cocked its head and blinked at me. *Who this?*

Mikhail sat down at the table, and his dogs planted themselves two on each side of his chair, alert and watchful. Bronwyn sat across from me and gave me a warm, encouraging smile. Valentin sidled over to the table and slid into a chair, silent as a cat. Only Radimir was left standing, glowering at me over the top of his coffee mug.

His wife turned and gave him a pleading look, and, as soon as he locked eyes with her, he just...melted. It was like the cold mask he wore slipped, and he was suddenly vulnerable. Bronwyn held out a hand, and he laced fingers with her, then sighed and sat down next to her, throwing little, loving looks at her. I'd never seen a man so besotted, and even though it was beautiful to watch, it made my chest ache a little. I'd never had anyone feel that way about me.

"Thank you," Gennadiy told his brother solemnly. Then he turned to me. "Tell them."

I laid it all out. How I'd been leading an FBI team tasked with bringing down Gennadiy. How someone had tried to kill me and frame him. How, when that failed, they'd ruined my career and forced me to go on the run.

"I'm sorry that happened to you, Agent Brooks," Radimir told me. "But I don't see why we should help you. You've been trying to put my brother in jail. You hurt our business." He leaned forward. "You're *FBI.*"

"She *was* FBI," Gennadiy told him. "Now they're chasing her. The enemy of my enemy is my friend. She saved my life. *And* she stopped me going to jail."

Hearing him defend me made something inside me lift, and I had to work to not let it show on my face.

"I don't like it," said Radimir. "You forget what we are, brother." He tugged the collar of his shirt away from his neck, exposing his Bratva tattoos. "We swore we'd never help the cops."

"We're not helping the cops, we're helping *her!*" Gennadiy snapped. His brothers stared at him, and I thought I saw his ears redden.

Mikhail frowned, his easy smile fading. He began watching me the way you'd watch a scorpion.

"Look," Gennadiy continued, "whoever's behind this is one of our rivals. That's why they framed me; they want me out of the way. They have someone inside the FBI: that makes them dangerous. Forget trying to help her: we need to find who this is and take them out, for our own sakes!" He looked at me, then at his brothers. "We're all in this together."

Radimir drew in a long, slow breath, considering. Then he nodded. Relief sluiced through me.

"It must be someone who wants *you* out of the way as well as us," Mikhail told me, scratching the head of one of his dogs. His eyes hadn't left me for a second. "Who—other than us—were you investigating?"

I hesitated for a second. Spilling who the FBI was looking into broke all the rules. But they were trusting me: I had to trust them. "Two families," I told them. "The Cantellis and the O'Donnells."

Gennadiy slammed a fist down on the table hard enough to make everyone jump. "*Blyat*! The fucking Irish!"

Radimir planted his elbows on the table and cupped one fist in his hand. "It's not the Irish," he said firmly.

"Of course it's the Irish!" snapped Gennadiy. "We played nice with them, and now they think they can take over!"

"Finn O'Donnell has a lot of men," said Valentin quietly, "and he doesn't do half measures. If we accuse him of this, it'll mean a fight."

Gennadiy scowled. "Fine by me!"

"We have a deal with the Irish," Radimir said tightly. "It isn't them."

"We should never have made that deal!" Gennadiy yelled.

The room went silent. The two men glared at each other for three, four seconds before Gennadiy dropped his eyes and shook his head. "Sorry, brother."

I could feel the depth of the love between the two of them, but I could feel the hierarchy in the family, too, and I tried to learn from it. *Never forget who the boss is. Got it.*

"Given that we know accusing the Irish won't end well, maybe it makes sense to eliminate the other possibility first?" Bronwyn's voice was like a gentle summer breeze, and the tension at the table eased. Radimir and Valentin both nodded.

"That makes sense," said Mikhail. But he was still studying me.

Gennadiy shook his head sulkily. "Deal with Emanuela?" He sighed and rubbed at his stubble. "I—Alright. Yes. It's a good suggestion. We'll go see the Italians first."

The meeting broke up. Gennadiy hurried off to make arrangements for the Cantelli meet, already talking into his phone. Radimir and Bronwyn strolled out to the gardens, his arm around her waist. Valentin slipped away before I was aware of it. That left Mikhail watching me from across the table. His four dogs mimicked him, and it would have been funny if I didn't know how many people he'd killed over the years. I swallowed and sat up straight, refusing to be intimidated. "Something on your mind?"

"I am concerned for my nephew." Where the other Aristov's

voices were silver and ice, Mikhail's Russian accent reminded me of smooth, warming whiskey. "Gennadiy has a particular hatred of your kind. Police. The FBI. The *system.*"

A particular hatred? Why is that, I wondered.

"For him to overcome that hatred," said Mikhail, "I think something even more powerful must be at work."

"You're wrong," I said. "There's nothing between us." I looked away. "He's made that painfully clear."

Mikhail gave a long-suffering sigh and rose from the table. "That," he said, "is even more concerning."

He started walking away, his dogs falling in beside him.

I frowned. "You're worried because he doesn't like me?"

"No," Mikhail said without looking back. "Because he cares enough about you to lie to you."

29

ALISON

I was still sitting there, processing that, when Gennadiy walked back in, brooding and scowly. As he slipped his phone into his pocket, his shirt drew tight over the hard slab of one pec, and I flashed back to the warm press of him when we'd kissed.

"What?" he asked, frowning at my expression.

I looked down at my coffee, my heart suddenly racing. "Nothing. Any luck getting a meet with the Cantellis?"

"We're meeting Emanuela Cantelli in an hour."

I looked up in shock. Emanuela was the most powerful Italian boss in the city...but apparently, when the Aristovs spoke, even she listened. I accidentally met Gennadiy's eyes, and suddenly I was falling upwards into gray so breathtakingly cold, it made my spine prickle. But the longer he looked at me, the more the gray ice seemed to change, fracturing and heating until it was like silvery, molten metal.

He tore his eyes away. "We're meeting her at The Fitzroy," he said. *The Fitzroy?* Crap. I'd heard about it, but I'd never been. The restaurant was a Chicago institution, ivy-clad stone and snow-white tablecloths, with eye-watering prices and a six-month waiting list.

Gennadiy's gaze flicked back to me and this time raked over my blouse and jeans. "Wear something...appropriate," he told me.

"Appropriate?"

His eyes seemed to gleam for a second. "A dress."

I shook my head. "I don't do dresses."

His eyes heated even more. "You do today." Then he seemed to catch himself, and he marched off.

A dress. Because I needed to fit in with the billionaires at The Fitzroy or because he wanted to see more of me? I looked down at my denim-clad leg. *Boy, would you be disappointed,* I thought bitterly.

I glugged the rest of my coffee and stalked upstairs to change. I checked through all the clothes Gennadiy had given me: maybe there were some smart pants or even a pant suit I could make work. But no. Three pairs of jeans and a selection of beautiful designer dresses that would have looked amazing on anyone normal.

I paced back and forth for a few minutes, the shame and hurt heating to scarlet at my core and turning to anger when it reached the surface. *How dare he?* How dare he ask me to wear—

His voice, startlingly close. "Alison? We need to leave. Soon."

I stared at the door in panic. He was right outside. "Coming!" I caught my flustered face in the mirror. *Fuck.* Maybe I should just march out there in jeans and tell him this was what I was wearing. But Gennadiy would dig his heels in and demand an explanation. He was as stubborn as I was.

I could feel myself breathing faster and faster. I couldn't remember ever feeling so vulnerable and exposed, like I'd shattered on the floor and he was about to sift through all my glittering, private workings. I wanted my gun. I wanted this to be something I could fight my way out of.

Fuck it. I pulled off my blouse, then wriggled out of my jeans. Picking a dress at random, I pulled it over my head. *Fuck it, fuck it, fuck it. Get it over with.* It was blue and probably very stylishly cut, but I didn't pay any attention: all I knew was that it put my legs on show, up to just above the knee.

I slipped on some heels and grabbed the door handle. And it was only as the door swung wide to reveal Gennadiy that I realized, too late, why I was so upset.

It had been a long time since anyone had seen my leg, but I remembered in perfect, gut-wrenching detail the look of horror and disappointment on a man's face when he saw. And even though he'd already pushed me away, I couldn't bear to see that look of disgust on Gennadiy's face.

I started to swing the door shut again, but Gennadiy frowned and caught it with one huge, powerful hand, thinking I was playing some game. And then his eyes licked hungrily down my body: over the delicate shoulder straps and the tight bodice, down over the flowing skirt, down to—

My soul shrank down to a tiny fetal ball. I summoned up all my layers of armor, but it didn't matter, he was too close, he was going to see me break, he was going to see that his fearsome opponent was actually pathetically weak. Gennadiy blurred behind sudden, traitorous tears. *Goddamnit!* I blinked furiously and glared up at him—

He was staring right at the hellish, ruined landscape the Molotov cocktail had left. His eyes tracked all the way down to my ankle, then up towards my face—

My chest closed up. I couldn't breathe.

He looked me in the eye and...he didn't look disgusted, or disappointed. He looked angry. I watched his shoulders rise, and his hands curl into darkly tattooed fists.

"Who?" he whispered.

I blinked, thrown. But my chest had eased enough for me to speak. "The Torrisis. A long time ago. Mistaken identity."

He closed his eyes, his face twisted in pain. Then he nodded. "Come on."

I stared up at him in dismay. "I can't go out like this! I'm—" I looked down at my leg. *Hideous.*

He turned away for a second. I heard him huff his breath out angrily, as if he was fighting with himself. Then he turned back to me, took hold of my chin, and lifted it, making me look at him. The scowling mask was gone: for a second, he was open, exposed. "Alison...you're beautiful. Scars don't make you less, they make you *more* because something happened to you, something bad enough to hurt you...but you were strong enough to stay a good person. The ugly ones...they're the ones who get twisted and scarred *inside.* What happened to them made them monsters, and you wouldn't even know it to look at them."

It felt like something enormous was lifting from my chest. I gave a quick little nod, unable to speak. A single tear broke free and trickled down my cheek, and I saw his eyes follow it down. His hand tensed on my chin. His eyes flicked to my lips—

And then he turned and stalked away. "Come on," he said tightly. "We'll be late."

I stood frozen for a second. *Beautiful.* The word melted into my mind, and icy, Russian-accented rivulets of water ran deep, finding the little girl who hadn't felt beautiful in twenty years, and I had to bite my lip hard. And then they found adult me: obsessive, flat-chested, man-scaring me, and my breath went shaky.

Gennadiy was already halfway down the stairs. I ran to catch up. *He thinks I'm beautiful.* But for some reason, he kept pulling away.

We crossed the immense hallway, passing beneath a servant dusting the chandelier. I reran his words in my head. *He was talking about himself. He thinks he's a monster.* A deep swell of sympathy rolled through me. Then I caught myself. *What's the matter with me?* He *was* a monster. I'd known that from the start. So why did hearing him say it feel so wrong? Because something happened to make him like this? Because he didn't *want* to be like this?

Outside, we climbed into Gennadiy's BMW. He gave the steering wheel an affectionate stroke as he started the engine. Meanwhile, I glanced around, frowning. I'd spent months following this car, knew every inch of the exterior. Being inside felt weird, like walking onto the set of your favorite TV show.

Gennadiy turned to me. "What do you know about Emanuela Cantelli?"

"Only what's in the FBI files. Runs a lot of the west side of the city.

Daughter of Franco Cantelli, inherited his empire when he died. She's really young, for a boss...thirty?"

"Twenty-nine. Have you met her?"

"No."

His lips tightened. If it hadn't been Gennadiy, I almost would have said he looked nervous. "Emanuela is...she can be...*difficult.*"

"Difficult?"

Gennadiy sighed. "You'll see."

Storms were forecast for later in the day, but when we arrived at the restaurant, the sky was still a glorious deep blue. I climbed out of the car and, as the door closed, I caught my first glimpse of the dress in the side mirror. I hadn't really looked at it before but...*wow.* It hugged me just right, and the way the front was structured, it almost looked like I had boobs.

Then I stepped back, and my legs came into view. My stomach knotted.

I looked up and found Gennadiy watching me. He didn't say anything, just gave me a little nod. Some curt, Russian version of *you got this.* And somehow, it meant more, coming from my arch enemy. I took a deep breath and straightened my back, standing tall.

"Gennadiy, you smooth bastard!" The voice came from behind us: male, Russian-accented, and deeply affectionate. We turned just in time for Gennadiy to be pulled into a hug by Yakov Beletski, his friend who ran the docks. I'd seen him plenty of times, but only ever through a camera lens or a pair of binoculars, never up close. Yakov thumped Gennadiy on the back and then turned towards me. "And who is the new lady you're—"

His jaw dropped as he recognized me.

"We're working together," Gennadiy told him.

Yakov grabbed his arm and steered him away from me, then spoke urgently to him in Russian. I picked out the words for *FBI* and also, weirdly, *spell.* He glanced at me and seemed to ask a question. Gennadiy shook his head firmly but his cheeks reddened.

"And speak English," Gennadiy told Yakov firmly, and towed him back to me.

Yakov stared at Gennadiy as if he'd gone mad. Then he sighed, softened, and gave me a warm, honest smile. "Yakov Beletski," he told me. "At your service." And he took my hand and gently kissed it. I felt myself smile. I liked him immediately.

"You old charmer," Gennadiy told him.

"Thank you for the tip on the cesium," I told Yakov solemnly.

Yakov waved it away. "Anything for a friend." He looked sideways at Gennadiy, and a smile touched his lips. "And his favorite enemy."

"Come on," said Gennadiy tightly. "You can prop up the bar and be our backup, if Emanuela is..." He and Yakov exchanged knowing looks. *Is what?* Why were they so wary of this woman?

Gennadiy led the way inside. Two men in maroon waistcoats pulled open the big double doors, and suddenly we were in a world of hushed voices, softly clinking tableware, and gentle piano music from a pianist in the corner. Gennadiy had been right about the clothes: I'm not sure they even would have let me in, in jeans.

A woman jumped to her feet on the other side of the room. About my height, in a spotless white suit with black details. She had long, richly golden hair that fell in a broad fan down her back and a perfect hourglass figure. "Gennadiy!" she called, loud enough to make heads turn.

Yakov split off from us and went to keep watch from the bar. As Gennadiy and I approached Emanuela, he murmured in my ear. "We need to do this carefully."

I nodded. I was trying to focus, but the combination of icy Russian accent and hot breath in my ear rippled all the way down to my groin. "I get it. She's got the entire mob behind her. You don't want to start a war."

Gennadiy winced. "Yes. But also..." He huffed and scowled. "Look, just let me do the talking. She needs careful handling. She's...fragile."

Fragile? She was standing there confidently, beaming at us, ignoring everyone else in the restaurant, with her power suit and perfect, pouting lips. She didn't *look* very fragile. But he knew her best. "Fine."

We arrived in front of Emanuela. She'd stepped away from her table to greet us, and her three bodyguards had stepped back, too, which awkwardly crowded the family at the next table. But she didn't seem to notice. "Gennadiy!" She gave him a million-dollar smile. "It's been too long." Her accent was American with just a hint of sultry Italian. But there was something else about the way she spoke, something I couldn't put my finger on. "Did you know it's my birthday?"

Gennadiy looked—I did a double take—he looked *worried*. First nervous, now worried. *What the fuck is going on?* "I'm sorry, Emanuela. I thought it was next week. I would have brought a gift."

Emanuela rolled her eyes. "It *is* next week, but close enough. And *you're* my gift!" She sprang forward, wrapped one arm around his back, and pulled him into a kiss.

30

ALISON

TIME SEEMED TO STOP, PROBABLY HELPED BY THE FACT THAT THE ENTIRE restaurant fell silent. Everyone was watching the kiss, even the waiting staff. It wasn't just a quick brush of the lips: Emanuela had clamped herself on like a limpet and was working her lips, moving and pressing. Her free hand was stroking Gennadiy's jaw, and from the way her cheeks were moving, it was obvious her tongue was in his mouth. I felt myself take a furious step forward.

Then it got worse: she opened her eyes and stared right at me. She started grinding her body against Gennadiy's, smooshing her full breasts against my man's chest while she let out theatrical moans and gasps, her eyes never leaving mine. She was soaking up my outrage and horror, basking in it...

Gennadiy pried himself free and staggered back, wiping his mouth with the back of his hand. "Emanuela!" he hissed.

Emanuela burst out laughing: a beautiful, musical sound. "Look at her," she said, looking my way. "She looks so *angry!*"

I opened and closed my mouth, flushing to my roots. I *was* angry, and humiliated, because...well, because... *What's the matter with me? He's not 'my man'. I don't have any right to*— "I see you two know each other," I said tightly.

Emanuela darted forward, so fast I flinched back. "We did things," she stage-whispered loud enough for everyone to hear. I realized now what it was I'd heard in her voice: there was a giddy excitement, like a child who's had too much sugar. "When I was the mob boss's daughter, and he was the *rough, evil Bratva hoodlum.*" She curled around me like a snake, her lips brushing my ear. "Would you like to know some of the things he did to me?"

I shoved her back. Not violently, it was just instinct, like brushing a venomous spider off you. But it was enough to make all of her bodyguards draw their guns and aim right at me.

"It's okay!" said Gennadiy, jumping between us and raising his hands defensively. "It's okay!"

Emanuela stepped back, grinning, and licked her lips. Then she nodded to her bodyguards, and they lowered their guns.

"We came here to talk, Emanuela," said Gennadiy.

"Talking is so *boring,*" said Emanuela. She picked up a steak knife and balanced it on its point on her finger, then flipped it into the air and caught it. "I'd prefer to talk about *her.*" She grinned at me over her shoulder as she strolled over to the next table. The family sitting there paled when they saw the knife in her hand, but they didn't dare move. "Where did you find her?" Emanuela asked. She sat down on the father's knee, and the poor man's eyes bugged out in fear. "Why doesn't she have any—"—she drew two circles in the air with the knife—"tits?"

"Emanuela!" growled Gennadiy.

It happened so fast. Emanuela's hand flashed down, and there was a short, sharp scream of pain. It was only when she stood up that I saw the knife buried in the father's thigh.

"Don't talk to me like that," said Emanuela. All traces of playfulness were gone from her voice, leaving a flat, eerie calm. And I suddenly realized what Gennadiy had meant by 'delicate.' Not delicate like a vase. Delicate like a bomb. *Oh fuck.* The head of the most powerful mob family in the city was completely, terrifyingly, unstable.

The restaurant had gone completely silent again. Emanuela

pulled the knife from the father's leg, drawing a whimper of pain from him, and started towards Gennadiy. There was a white cream gateau on a serving cart, and, as she passed it, she dug her fingers viciously into it to extract the strawberry slice on top, then licked it into her mouth. The knife hung from her other hand, dripping a trail of blood across the pristine tiled floor. She didn't stop until she and Gennadiy were just a few inches apart.

"Emanuela," Gennadiy said, with a level of calm I'd never be able to achieve. "Please." He glanced around the restaurant. "Could we talk in private?"

I blinked in shock. He was trying to limit the damage if she turned violent, even though it meant we'd be away from Yakov, our only backup. He was putting the lives of the civilians before ours. He *did* have a heart, however hard he tried to hide it.

Emanuela stared up at him emotionlessly, toying with the knife with one hand while she licked cream from the fingers of the other. The tension drew tighter and tighter—

"Fine," said Emanuela boredly. She dropped the knife and walked out of the room, not looking back. Her bodyguards scrambled to follow her. Gennadiy and I exchanged worried glances...and hurried after them.

31

ALISON

Emanuela led us through a maze of hallways, finally stopping in a quiet room with a huge, waist-high glass water feature at its center. It was in the shape of a flower, a gurgling pool six feet across surrounded by thick glass petals. Three of Emanuela's guards took up positions around the room. Another two waited outside to stop anyone from coming in. My chest went tight. Yakov wouldn't be able to help us: we were on our own.

Emanuela jumped up onto the edge of the water feature and sat there kicking her legs. "Talk."

Gennadiy took a deep, calming breath. "Someone tried to kill this woman and frame me for it. I need to know if it was you."

Emanuela cocked her head to the side. "Who is she to you?"

"She's FBI," grated Gennadiy. "She's the FBI agent assigned to catch me. Was it you?"

"So there are no personal feelings?" asked Emanuela.

"She's *FBI*," Gennadiy told her. "Of course not."

That stung. It was so...dismissive. So the kiss had been just a mistake, like he said.

Emanuela braced her hands behind her and leaned back,

stretching like a cat as she considered. She extended one perfect leg and pointed her toe at me. "Hit her."

Gennadiy and I both blinked at her. "What?" he asked, after a second.

"Hit her," said Emanuela, staring right into my eyes. "A good, big slap across the face."

"No!" snapped Gennadiy. I could hear him fighting against his anger, trying to maintain control.

"She's FBI. What's the problem?" asked Emanuela, her eyes wide with mock innocence.

Gennadiy snapped. "Emanuela! I'm not here to play games!" He advanced on her, but Emanuela didn't so much as flinch. She just watched him, delighted, and her bodyguards drew their guns and pointed them at Gennadiy.

"Do it," I said quietly. "I can take it."

"I know you can," said Gennadiy stiffly. "That's not the point." He glared at Emanuela. "I'm not doing it."

Emanuela grinned. "You like her," she said, thrilled, "that's why you're helping her. But you don't like her enough to *be* with her." She pouted at me sadly and stage-whispered. "*Is it because of the leg?*"

My face burned, and I gave her a death stare. She ate it up, loving my hatred.

"Emanuela! Did you order a hit on this woman, *yes* or *no?*" growled Gennadiy.

Emanuela rolled her eyes. "I deal with so many people, Gennadiy, it's hard to remember." She sighed and jumped down from the table, then snapped her fingers in the air, calling me like a dog. "Come here. Let me look at you."

Gennadiy gave me a worried look, but I shook my head: *it's fine.* I'd play along if that's what it took to get some answers. I walked slowly around the table to her, painfully aware that this might well be the woman who wanted me dead.

She smiled at me as I drew close. "Do you want to know a secret?" She put her lips to my ear. "Gennadiy's fucked lots of women." She looked sideways, at Gennadiy. "But I've never known him to *help* one."

Like an idiot, I followed her gaze and looked at Gennadiy.

Emanuela grabbed the back of my head and rammed it down, bending me at the waist over the rim of the water feature and dunking my head in the water. I screamed, which wasted most of my air.

I heard Gennadiy yell. "Let her go!"

Bent over and off balance, I thrashed and fought, my hair swirling like dark tentacles across my vision. But Emanuela had the strength of madness. I could feel my ears and the back of my head were still out of the water: maybe she wanted me to hear because it was just my face she was holding under. But *just my face* would drown me just fine. Already, my chest was tight with the need to breathe.

Through the thick glass, I had a distorted view of Gennadiy's legs running forward. He stopped right in front of the water feature, close enough to touch, but I couldn't reach him through the glass. "Emanuela, stop it!" he snapped. "Let her up!"

"No," said Emanuela.

I struggled frantically, but she bent one of my arms up behind my back to hold me in place, and with my feet clear of the floor, I couldn't get any traction. My lungs began to burn, and I'd never felt so powerless. She was smaller than me, she didn't have my martial arts training, and she was still going to manage to kill me. The panic clawed at my chest. *Please let me breathe!*

The distorted gray mass that was Gennadiy sprinted around the table, and I heard the click of a gun. He'd grabbed Emanuela and, I guessed, had his gun to her head, standing behind her so her bodyguards didn't dare shoot. "Let. Her. Go!" he snarled.

But Emanuela's hand didn't move. "You can't kill me, Gennadiy," she said calmly. "If you shot me, my men would kill you before my body hit the floor. And then they'd kill Radimir, and Valentin, and Mikhail. So you're going to stand here and watch her die. You wouldn't risk everything just to save her. Look: she's nearly done."

My vision was going dark at the edges. I could feel my lips starting to twitch as my body's need to breathe overwhelmed my brain. Any second, I was going to inhale and suck down a lungful of water.

Then I heard Gennadiy speak, and there was something different in his voice, a rawness I'd never heard before, like he'd been sliced open right down to the soul. *"Emanuela? Look into my eyes."*

I felt Emanuela twist behind me as she turned to look. The world went dark, and I felt water fill my mouth.

Emanuela let go. I erupted upwards, spitting out water, and sucked in a huge lungful of sweet, sweet air. Light rushed back into the world, but my brain was still oxygen-starved. I staggered sideways and would have fallen if Gennadiy hadn't grabbed my waist. I heaved in breath after shuddering breath and tried to take in what was happening. Gennadiy had a terrified Emanuela pinned up against the table with his body, one arm pressing his gun to her temple while the other held me. His expression was beyond frightening, beyond anything I'd seen before. "Now answer the question!" he roared at Emanuela. "Did you put a hit out on her? *Was it you?*" I saw his finger tense on the trigger.

"No," said Emanuela desperately. "I didn't order her killed."

"Why should I believe you?" demanded Gennadiy.

"Because maybe I'd kill her," Emanuela said in a small voice. "But I wouldn't put you in jail. I'd want you here." Her voice cracked. "With me." In that moment, all the theatrics fell away, and underneath there was loneliness. And longing.

My stomach flipped. I hated her even more, now. But I believed her.

Gennadiy let her go and holstered his gun. Emanuela stumbled away and watched us with big, scared eyes, silent for once. Gennadiy grabbed my hand and led me out of the room, pushing past the bodyguards.

I looked back over my shoulder at Emanuela. "You and her really...?"

Gennadiy winced. "A long time ago. I was young and stupid. I didn't realize she still..." he shook his head ruefully.

I got one last look at Emanuela before we turned the corner. I hated her, but there was a pang of pity, too. *What the hell happened to her, to make her like that?*

As soon as it felt like we were a safe distance away, Gennadiy stopped, took my other hand, and turned me to face him. "You're okay?" he asked.

The emotion in his voice made my throat close up. Then he brushed my wet hair back from my face, and it *really* closed up. I knew I was a mess: make-up ruined, hair a dripping swamp. But he was looking at me like I was the most valuable thing in the world. I nodded, not trusting my voice. And replayed what had just happened.

Look into my eyes, he'd told Emanuela. What had she seen there? Something that had convinced her that Gennadiy *would* risk everything to save me.

Which meant...*when he told Emanuela he had no feelings for me, he was lying, to protect me from her. Or from himself.* The fragile, silvery excitement that had been crushed when he told me the kiss was a mistake began to tentatively unfurl. I swallowed and stared up at him.

Gennadiy looked away, scowling. "Come on."

We walked back through the restaurant. A worried Yakov ran over to us. "*Chyort,*" he cursed when he saw me. "What did that crazy *suka* do to you?" He ran a hand through his hair. "I'm sorry. I was stuck out here."

"I'm fine," I told him.

"Emanuela didn't order the hit," Gennadiy told Yakov. "Thank you for coming along." He and Yakov embraced, and then he took me back to his car. We drove to his mansion in silence, water dripping down the back of my neck as I tried to process everything. He *did* feel things for me. Which meant the kiss *hadn't* been a mistake. So why was he pushing me away?

At Gennadiy's mansion, I changed back into jeans, a blouse, and ankle boots and fixed my face. By the time I was done, Gennadiy had rounded up his family, and we gathered again in the dining room.

"It wasn't Emanuela," said Gennadiy. "So it was the Irish. Finn O'Donnell. He's the only other person Alison was investigating."

"That's not good," muttered Mikhail. Radimir cursed in Russian. His wife, Bronwyn, was sitting beside him, and he pulled her a little closer. Only Valentin was silent.

"So what do we do now?" I asked.

"We confront the Irish." Gennadiy said viciously. "Ask Finn what the fuck he's playing at. And we show up ready for war."

The anger in his voice made my stomach knot. He was spiraling downwards: more brutal, more violent, and that path only ended in one way.

The family geared up, grim-faced. Valentin slid vicious-looking knives into scabbards under his long, black coat. Mikhail opened the doors of his big, black SUV and pointed, and the dogs obediently jumped in. *He's taking his dogs? What if they get hurt?*

Radimir hugged his wife, and she clutched him to her tight. "Come back safe," she told him, her voice quavering, and he closed his eyes and nodded, his head pressed against hers. My stomach flipped: Radimir was doing this for Gennadiy, who was doing it for me. *If something happens to him...*

Gennadiy nudged my arm. I turned to see him holding out a black handgun, no doubt with the serial numbers filed off. A criminal's gun. I hesitated, then took it.

Radimir took his own car, Mikhail went in his SUV, and Valentin rode with us. We drove in silence, as cold gray clouds filled the sky above us. Valentin spent the journey staring out of the window, toying with something on a chain around his neck. Just as we arrived, I finally glimpsed what it was: a silver bird, small and delicate, like it was designed to hang on a thinner chain around a smaller neck.

We assembled down the street from Finn O'Donnell's bar. The sky was getting darker and darker: we were in for a massive thunderstorm, any minute. "We don't go in shooting," Radimir told us sternly. "We give Finn a chance to explain. But be ready for anything." We all nodded.

We moved off down the street, with Gennadiy and me at the back of the group. Valentin still hadn't spoken. "Is he okay?" I murmured to Gennadiy.

Gennadiy frowned, thinking. "What's the date?"

I had to think for a second: a lot had happened in the last few days. "The thirtieth."

Gennadiy grimaced. "Tomorrow is a difficult day for him." And he moved forward in the group and put his arm around Valentin's shoulders. I stared, trying to reconcile the two sides of him: the brutal killer and crime boss who sank his opponents in Lake Michigan and the man who deeply, fiercely, loved his family.

Finn O'Donnell's bar was a beautiful old red-brick building four stories high, surrounded by vacant lots on all sides. The story I'd heard was that property developers had bought up and demolished everything else in the street to build high-end apartment buildings, but Finn had stubbornly refused to sell. As we reached the doors, Gennadiy gave Valentin's shoulder a last squeeze and then moved in front of me, blocking my path with his broad back. "Stay behind me," he told me over his shoulder.

"I know how to use this," I reminded him, showing him the gun under my jacket. "I've been on plenty of raids."

"I know." He faced the front. "Stay behind me anyway."

I rolled my eyes, but the worry in his voice made me secretly melt. Then Gennadiy pushed through the doors, and we were inside.

I wasn't ready for the wall of noise that hit us. It was barely noon, but the place was already crowded with people drinking and talking. There was a rowdy, happy, blue-collar atmosphere, like everyone was either about to break into a song or start a bar brawl.

Part of what made it so noisy was the layout. The first two floors were one huge, double-height room with pool tables and three bars, and old, rickety-looking balconies loaded with people looking down from above. Everyone was in jeans and t-shirts, and the Aristovs stood out a mile in their suits. One of the bartenders pulled out his phone and muttered into it. Finn was going to know we were coming.

People cleared a path for us—even in Irish territory, everyone knew who the Aristovs were—and we worked our way up the wide, wooden staircase to the third floor. We approached a heavy oak door guarded by three unsmiling men. One of them opened it and waved us inside, then all three of them followed us in and closed the door behind us.

And there, behind an antique desk, lounged Finn O'Donnell.

He was in a suit, but he didn't wear it the way the Aristovs wore theirs. More like Finn and the suit had negotiated, had a drink, and come to an amicable arrangement. He wasn't wearing the jacket, there was no tie, and his white shirt was unbuttoned at the neck and rolled up over his muscled forearms. He was kicked back in an aging leather chair, his feet up on the desk, and a glass of whiskey in his hand.

I hadn't been ready for how good-looking he was. I'd seen him in photos, but they didn't capture how deeply blue his eyes were, or how they sparkled when he smiled.

"Well, well, well," said Finn. "The entire Aristov family. I'm honored." He had a faint Irish accent, like a playful thread of gold running through his words. He looked at Radimir and cocked a suspicious eyebrow. "You didn't want to bring your wife along?"

"She's working," Radimir told him smoothly. "Planning an important book signing at the bookstore."

Finn stood up and walked around the desk. "And who," he asked, "is *this* lovely lady?" He stood right in front of me, thumbs hooked lazily in his belt like a cowboy, and looked deep into my eyes. His grin was teasing and cocky and just a little filthy. "Has anyone ever told you," he asked softly, "that the way you walk is pure poetry?"

"That's enough, Finn!" snapped Gennadiy.

Finn and I both looked at him. I blushed. For a second, there, I'd been lost in those Irish blue eyes. He wasn't a match for Gennadiy, not in my book. But damn, the man was charming.

"Is she yours?" asked Finn innocently.

Gennadiy gave him the same death stare I'd given Emanuela. *Is he jealous?* "I'm not anyone's," I told them firmly.

Finn smirked and leaned against his desk. "What do you want?"

Gennadiy took a long, calming breath. "Someone tried to kill her," he said, nodding to me. "She's—"

"FBI," said Finn. "Did you really think I didn't remember? I saw her at the dog track. So you're working with the Feds, now?"

"She's not FBI anymore, Finn. And we need answers. Someone *is* working with the FBI, and they tried to frame me for killing her." He paused, watching Finn carefully. "Was it you?"

The whole room tensed. This was it.

"No," said Finn in a bored, tetchy voice. "It was not."

"*Blyat'*," breathed Gennadiy, and he drew his gun and pointed it right at Finn. Radimir and Valentin cursed and did the same, and I pulled out my gun, too. Finn grabbed his gun from his desk. Behind us, there were rustles of clothing and sharp, metallic clicks as the three guards behind us drew *their* guns. Mikhail's four dogs, who'd been sitting like statues ever since we entered the room, became streaks of gray fur, darting between us to face off with the guards. The room filled with the low, chainsaw rattle of their growling. *That* was why Mikhail brought them.

I looked around. Nine guns leveled at heads. One twitch of someone's finger and we were all dead. *Fuck.*

And then I noticed something.

Finn's men were pointing their guns at the Aristovs. The Aristovs were pointing their guns at Finn. But Finn himself? He was aiming at me.

"Put your gun down, Gennadiy," said Finn tightly. "Or your woman dies."

32

GENNADIY

Blyat'. Cold fear like I'd never known, wrapped around my heart and squeezed. "You've got it wrong," I grunted to Finn. "We're just working together."

"Bullshit," said Finn. "I saw your face when I flirted with her. Put your gun down, or I put a hole right through that pretty face."

Chyort! His flirting had been a ploy, and like an idiot, I'd fallen for it. I'd never normally make that kind of mistake. *This is why having feelings for someone is a bad idea.* "If you hurt her, I will *end* you," I promised.

"Yeah," drawled Finn. "But she'll still be dead. Now put your gun *down.* I'll count to three."

There was a rumble of thunder, right overhead, and rain started to lash the windows. I knew I couldn't put my gun down. If I did, Finn would kill all of us.

"One," said Finn.

I held my gun rock steady. Finn was behind this whole thing; he had to be. I couldn't trust him.

"Two," said Finn.

If I lowered my gun, he'd kill all of us. My finger tensed on the trigger, ready to shoot as soon as he did. *I'm sorry, Alison.*

"Thr—"

I couldn't do it. I knew it was useless. I knew Finn would kill us all. But if there was even a tiny chance to save her, I had to take it. My arm dropped to my side. I heard Radimir draw in his breath in shock...and then he, Valentin and Mikhail lowered their guns, too. Mikhail snapped out a command in Russian, and his dogs stopped growling and sat quietly.

And I stared down the barrel of Finn's gun and waited for whatever came next.

33

GENNADIY

"Jesus," said Finn. "You really *do* care about her."

I glowered at him. I could feel my whole family staring at me.

Finn looked at each of us in turn. "All of the Aristovs, lined up in front of me. Do you know how many people would pay me good money to rid the city of you?" He let out a theatrical sigh. "But here's something not many people know about me. When I go into business with someone...I'm loyal to them."

He tossed his gun on his desk. Behind us, I heard his men lower theirs. I stared at Alison and my family in shock.

Finn pinned me with a look. "Let me say it again: I don't know anything about a hit on your friend, or framing you."

First, I just gaped. Then I felt my face heat, and I looked at the floor. *Chyort!*

Radimir nudged me and gave me a meaningful look. I grimaced, then lifted my eyes to Finn. "I'm sorry, Finn," I muttered.

Finn waved it away. "Ah, you Russians, always so serious." He clapped an arm around my shoulders, pushed a whiskey glass into my hand, and filled it, then did the same with the others. I sighed, and the hatred eased, just a little.

I stole a look at Alison. Her long, athletic legs in those tight black jeans. That soft black waterfall of hair. And the way she prowled around the room, graceful and sinuous. Finn had been right: the way she walked *was* pure poetry.

Alison looked up and caught me looking, then raised an eyebrow. I could see frustration in her eyes, but also hurt...and hope. She wanted answers. And Radimir was scowling at me from across the room: *he* wanted to know what the fuck was going on, too. *Blyat'.*

We talked business with Finn for half an hour, with Finn kicked back in his desk chair and lovingly ruffling Mikhail's dogs when they came over to curiously sniff at him. Mercifully, when it came time to leave, the rain was still hammering down, and we had to run to our cars, so I dodged having to talk to Radimir...for now.

As soon as we were inside my BMW, though, Alison turned to me expectantly. The anger flared and started to spin: I was mad at myself, and at what I knew I'd have to do. I started the engine, refusing to look at her.

"Gennadiy," she said, with a softness that hurt my chest, "we need to talk."

I shook my head, still not looking at her. "Nothing to talk about." The anger was still building. Wanting her this badly and having to push her away...I wanted to scream and smash and destroy.

I could feel her staring at me. "What happened with Emanuela. With Finn, just now."

I made the mistake of glancing across at her and, instantly, I was locked into those sapphire-blue eyes. A lifetime of suffering had hardened them, but right now, they looked perilously close to fracturing, full of cautious hope. I could do it, I could make her happy *right now.*

But she deserved better than a monster, all twisted up inside. To save her, I had to push her away. I had to hurt the woman I wanted to protect.

I took a shaky breath and turned to face her. I let the unfairness of it whip the anger faster and faster, using it to power me. *"Listen!"* I snapped. "I saved you because it suited my needs. I need you alive so you can find out who's behind this."

"The kiss—"

"The kiss was a mistake!" I leaned closer, hulking over her. "I'm not the hero of your story, I'm the villain. I don't save people, I kill them. I don't build; I burn things down. And I *don't* fall in love, even with—" I bit it back. I'd nearly said *even with you.* "With anyone," I muttered.

She was staring at me as if I'd slapped her, and the pain and betrayal in her eyes nearly broke me. I just wanted to grab her face in my hands and kiss her...

Instead, I faced front and threw the car into gear. *I did what had to be done,* I told myself. And tried to ignore the voice that told me this was really about something else, about the dark void at my core. Out of the corner of my eye, I saw Alison sit back in her seat, blinking quickly. She wrapped her arms around herself and *blyat',* it nearly broke my heart.

I drove. The rain was torrential, now. Even with the wipers on full, the road disappeared between wipes, and the wheels sent up white fans of spray behind us. But I kept my foot hard down, desperate to be out of the car so I couldn't feel the pain I'd caused.

A car slammed into us from the side. The wheel flew under my hands, burning my palms, and I wrestled with it as the car fishtailed left and right on the wet road. *Blyat'!* My face flashed hot. I'd been driving too fast, given how wet it was. I must not have noticed someone pulling out—

"Gennadiy!" Alison yelled from beside me. She sounded panicked, for someone as cool-headed as her. *Why is she—*

There was a roar of automatic gunfire, and the side windows disintegrated as bullets tore through the car. I pushed Alison down and hunkered as low as I could. On instinct, my foot crushed the gas pedal to the floor, and the car surged forward. The gunfire took out the rear side windows and then the rear window as we pulled away from them.

I got my first glimpse of them through the driving rain: a big white SUV with a dark-haired man pointing a stubby submachine gun out of the passenger window. *Chyort!* They were accelerating, catching up to us. I looked around for Radimir's car or Mikhail's, but they were out of sight. *Chyort, chyort, chyort!*

The SUV came alongside us, and the gunman fired again, hosing the car. Unlike in the movies, cars aren't bulletproof. Bullets chewed through the doors, flew through the cabin, and ate their way out the other side. I could feel bits of plastic trim and leather hitting my face, arms, and ankles. Any second, a bullet would tear through us...

My blood turned to ice water. A bullet would tear through *her.*

I hooked the car left, and rammed them, but their car was bigger and heavier than ours, and it barely moved. Then Alison was taking off her seatbelt and climbing over me, her hair blowing in my face, her body warm against mine. She leaned out of my window, aimed low, and emptied her gun into one of their tires.

They swerved away, out of control. Alison retreated back into her own seat, panting in relief. But then I saw the SUV swerving back towards us, starting to spin. "Get your seatbelt on!" I yelled.

The SUV rushed towards us as she scrambled to get the buckle to lock in place. Then we were slammed sideways and spun around, the two cars tangled together as they pirouetted down the street. I saw a guy on a motorcycle swerve to avoid us and go tumbling off his bike. There was a series of bone-jarring thumps as we bounced off other cars, and then, finally, we stopped.

I twisted around to check on Alison. She was panting and white faced, but alive. "Are you hurt?" I demanded. "Are you hit?"

She shook her head, then pointed in front of us.

I looked. We'd come to rest just before a busy intersection. The SUV was nose-to-nose with us, and I was looking right at the driver and passenger. From their faces, they were Russian. From their builds and haircuts, former military. They were as shaken up as we were, and for a moment, we just sat there staring at each other.

Then the passenger lifted his gun. *Blyat'.* I looked around, but there was nowhere to hide. He'd cut us down, in or out of the car. I sat there numbly watching him reload. We were ten feet apart: he couldn't miss.

The engine's still running, I realized. God bless German engineering. I threw the car into gear and buried the gas pedal in the carpet, and the car leapt forward, ramming into the SUV and shoving it backwards. I kept the pedal hard down, pushing them down the street, into the intersection. I saw the gunman curse as his aim was thrown off. He took aim again, the barrel pointing right at Alison—

The SUV disappeared from view as a semi-truck crossing the intersection smashed into its side. I hit the brakes, and we screeched to a stop.

We sat there panting with adrenaline. Then I heard sirens wailing behind us. Alison turned to me. "Shit. The FBI's still looking for me. I can't let the cops take me in."

We scrambled out of the car, the rain soaking us instantly. My beloved BMW was a wreck, peppered with bullet holes, every window gone, and the nose concertinaed to half its normal length. But it had kept us alive. The sirens were getting louder, rising over the hissing rain that was plastering our clothes to our bodies. Alison ran over to the motorcycle that had gotten caught up in our crash. She hauled it upright and threw her leg over it. "Get on!"

I wasn't about to argue: it sounded like the cops were in the next street. I climbed on behind her and threw my arms around her waist. And then we were shooting forward and leaning hard into the corners as she powered down a side street and then threaded the bike through a series of alleys. We must have looked bizarre: a tiny woman leaning low atop the big sport bike and a hulking guy in a suit hanging onto her back.

The rain had made the asphalt perilously slick, but she was an expert, countering every skid. I hung on for dear life as the demon scream of the bike pounded my ears and the brick walls of the alley flashed by just inches away. *This is how she gets around?!* It was terrifying. But I had my body molded to hers, and the sweet smell of her hair was in my nose. If I was going to die, there was no better way to go.

The sirens faded behind us until, finally, we couldn't hear them at all. Alison slowed the bike and brought it to a stop in a narrow alley. With the buildings so close together and the storm clouds overhead, it was twilight-dark. The rain hammered down, soaking us and turning every fire escape and outcropping into a shining waterfall.

Alison turned the engine off, and the alley was suddenly silent aside from the crashing water. She twisted around on the bike, and we stared at each other, rain sluicing down our faces. The adrenaline was still racing through my veins, making every little detail clear and bright: her rain-soaked black jeans that clung to her legs, the white blouse that was now almost transparent, the wet locks of hair that fell across her face. Without thinking, I put my big, clumsy hand on her cheek to push them out of the way, and she was so cold... I cradled her face, warming it with my palm and—

All the feelings I'd been denying came welling up at once, overwhelming. I was off guard, I couldn't fight it—

I let out a growl of anger and brought my lips down on hers.

34

ALISON

FOR A SECOND, I WAS TOO SURPRISED TO DO ANYTHING. I THINK I MIGHT have let out a very un-me whimper of shock, and then his hard lips were forcing mine open, and his tongue was darting in to freakin' *own* me. The kiss wasn't delicate or sweet; it was months of pent-up desire all hitting at once, overwhelming and glorious, and I sat bolt upright in the saddle as the raw sexual heat of it lashed down to my groin like a bullwhip. The heat expanded outward, and I sagged, my eyes closed, now, melting into it. As the shock that *this is real, it's finally happening* died away, I finally began to respond, my lips moving on his, feeling my softness against his hardness, my tongue making little flicks against his.

He growled, trying to pull me closer. But I was still awkwardly twisted around on the saddle, I couldn't come any closer unless I—

It took both hands on his chest, pushing hard, to break the kiss. "Wait," I panted.

Gennadiy glared down at me, eyes glazed with lust and caveman-stubborn: *No wait. Want now.* I gulped because I could feel that if I didn't get back to the kiss *right now,* he was just going to grab me again, and the idea sent a wave of heat rushing right down to my toes and back up to my face. As fast as I could, I hooked one leg up and over the bike, twisted around on the saddle, and got the other leg up and over, so I was sitting facing him. "Okay," I said, breathless.

His hands captured my cheeks, and he kissed me again, hard and deep, and this time the kiss twisted and moved, both of us urgently seeking the other one. Waves of pink pleasure rippled down through my body, layering and building in my core into a tight ball of glowing heat. I was so small, next to his hulking body: he was kissing down into me, and the kiss was lifting me up, up, *up,* a fragile, silvery excitement unfurling inside me until it felt like my ass was going to lift right out of the saddle.

Then he growled and ran his hands down my neck and over my shoulders, his palms warm through my soaked blouse. His hands traced down my spine, hungry but slow, as if he was filing away how every part of me felt. They closed on my ass and squeezed hard, and I yelped against his lips. Then they tugged me roughly along the saddle towards him. I felt his knees opening my thighs wide and then.

"*MMF!*" I was squished up against him, and I could feel every movement of his powerful chest, his breathing shaky with lust. I could feel my nipples, pebble-hard from the excitement, scraping against his body through a couple of layers of wet cotton. And I could feel the hard length of him throbbing against my inner thigh. I knew, right then, that this wasn't going to be just a kiss, that we'd already passed some point of no return and were now plunging headfirst towards him inside me and me clawing at his back. The thought made the heat inside me go weighty and dense, my ass tightening in his hands and my pussy stroking needfully against his cock.

He growled again and pressed harder against me, but it wasn't enough, even with our clothes soaked by the rain: I could feel him scowl against my lips. He needed to feel me skin-on-skin.

Without breaking the kiss, he grabbed the collar of my blouse and wrenched it open right down to my jeans, buttons popping and flying. Then his fingers pushed the cups of my bra up, and suddenly his heated palms were gliding over my cool, rain-slick breasts. I trembled and squeezed the bike between my ankles. His hands made circles, lifting my breasts and stroking my nipples against his palms, and I panted against his mouth. Then he broke the kiss and lowered his head, and—

I threw my head back and gave a strangled groan as his hot mouth captured my breast, his tongue lashing over my hard nipple and coaxing it even harder. My eyes were closed, and the rain was hammering down on my upturned face. It should have felt cold, but all I felt was heat, like the rain sluicing down our bodies was the only thing stopping us from burning up.

His tongue traced my nipples, exploring the tips, the sides, and every little bump around the areolae. His fingers pressed against my breast, gentle but eager, relishing its softness. A glow spread through me and something deep in my chest, something that had been there ever since high school, eased. I didn't feel small or inadequate with him. I felt...perfect. We sat there for long minutes with me leaning back over the handlebars and him hulking over me, worshipping my breasts. My toes danced and splashed against the floor of the alley, and I thrashed and panted, scarlet pleasure lifting me higher and higher, until I couldn't take it anymore. "G—Gennadiy!" I croaked, tangling my fingers in his hair.

He understood. He felt the same need as me. All the months of fighting had been leading up to this, like we'd both been straining on the two ends of an elastic rope, building up more and more energy, and now we'd been catapulted together. It wasn't a want, it was a need.

He stood, swinging his leg over the bike. I started to stand up, too, but he didn't give me the chance: he grabbed me around the waist and lifted me up and off the bike. He pulled me against his chest, and I threw my arms around his neck and hung on, my legs wrapping around his waist. He cradled my ass and walked us to the wall of the alley, every step stroking my groin against his washboard abs.

My back pressed against the brick wall, and he kissed me again, long and deep. Then he started unbuttoning my jeans. *How the hell is he going to get them off?* I wondered: the jeans were *tight* and the fabric was sopping wet, and I was in an awkward position, and anyway I had boots on...

Answer: *with sheer brute force.* Gennadiy peeled my jeans over my hips and down my thighs, and my heart gave a little jump when I realized he'd hooked his fingers into my panties and those were going, too. As he slowly stripped me, I started running my hands over the hard swells of his shoulder muscles and then down over his chest. His shirt today was deep blue, and the rain had turned it translucent, a blue-tinted fog cloaking the dark swirls of his tattoos and the rich caramel of his skin. I started unbuttoning his shirt, exposing a tantalizing vertical slice of him and then, as I tugged the shirt free of his pants and spread it wide, the full, rugged majesty of him, a hard body painted with the story of his life. I'd seen him topless before, when I watched him at the docks with Yakov. I'd even guiltily doodled some of his tattoos on a notepad, telling myself it was to help me research his background. But now I could see every detail: crosses, numbers and stars that I knew charted his time in the borstal and the rise of the Aristovs, but other designs, too: serpents that coiled around his biceps and disappeared around his back; figures that looked like angels but with dark, bat-like wings. He'd painted hell across his body: to intimidate his enemies, or scare his underlings? I smoothed my hands across the dark ink, feeling each breath under my palms.

By now, he'd hauled my jeans and panties down to my shins. He pulled off my ankle boots, and they clattered to the ground, and then the whole mass of fabric was over my ankles and smacking wetly to the concrete. My legs kicked free, one smooth and one ruined, and I felt my stomach go tight, even though he'd already seen them once.

But then he set me gently down on my feet, knelt, and laid a kiss first on the scarred thigh and then on the normal one. He started alternating, crisscrossing his way down my legs, all the way to the toes and then all the way up again, pink ribbons of pleasure twisting together with silvery, heady joy. I blinked and blinked, but it was fine because so much rain was racing down my cheeks, you couldn't even tell I was crying.

He reached the crease at the top of my thighs and kissed along it, then ducked his head and flicked his tongue along my pussy lips. I gasped and threw my arms out either side of me, dragging my fingertips against smooth, wet brick and rough lines of cement as the tip of his tongue tasted me, traced my shape and then nudged me open. He was shockingly gentle, and I felt my legs weakening as the heat inside me turned to slickness. He was running his hands up and down my hips and ass, now, his tongue spearing up into me and his upper lip rubbing at my clit. I grabbed at his shoulders, digging my fingers into his muscles and rising up on my tiptoes as the pleasure rocketed higher. "I—" I broke off, not wanting to say it. Then his tongue circled my clit, and I groaned and *had* to say it. "I need you," I panted.

He drew back just enough that he could look up at me. Dark hair soaked with rain, pale gray eyes hooded with lust, the denizens of hell dancing across his chest. A man has never looked so unapologetically wicked. "Tell me," he said.

I stared down at him. I was standing virtually naked in a dark alley in the middle of the city. On some level, I knew I was supposed to feel unsafe, or at least nervous. But I didn't, not even a little bit. Being next to Gennadiy was like bathing in the protective light of a campfire. If anyone braved the rain and wandered along this alley, one growl from Gennadiy would send them fleeing. "I just told you," I said, my voice tight with need.

Gennadiy rose to his feet, but before he was fully standing, he scooped my ass into his hands and lifted me with him, pulling my legs around his waist again and pressing me back against the wall. "I want to hear you say it," he said, his Russian accent making each word a little kiss of ice that melted against my skin. He pressed the tip of his middle finger between my pussy lips and then pushed it up into me in one long, silken thrust. I moaned, watching the darkly-tattooed finger disappear into me, right up to his palm, just as he'd promised in the phone call all those months ago. My legs, wrapped around his waist, jerked in shock and then relaxed, my knees dropping either side of him and my ankles tugging at his ass. His finger was knobby and thick, and *God* I was so wet. As he hooked his finger just a little, my mouth opened into an 'O' of pleasure. I grabbed his hair, knitting my fingers through his wet locks, and turned his head so I could mutter in his ear. "I need you to fuck me," I said desperately.

His whole body tensed with the excitement of hearing me say it. But then I felt him steel himself. *"More,"* he demanded.

Our rivalry was still there, I realized. And he had to win, even at sex. But I wasn't about to give him the satisfaction. Blood rushing in my ears, I whispered, "I need you to fuck me, *you Russian bastard.*"

He gave a growl of lust and pulled his finger from me. He grabbed at his belt. shoving the leather viciously through the buckle and then ramming his pants down his thighs. His cock sprang up, the tan shaft a shade darker than his skin, the plum-sized head smooth and purple-pink. I had a brief second to stare at it, insides fluttering at the size of him, and then there was the rubbery sound of a condom going on, and the head of his cock was parting my sticky lips.

He looked deep into my eyes, wanting to see my reaction...and then he pushed up into me. I sucked in my breath at the silken stretch of him, at the wavefront of tight pleasure that moved with him as he filled me. Our eyes were locked, our breathing in time. He pulled his hips back a little, then pushed forward again, going deeper, and I groaned and bit my lip. His hands squeezed my ass cheeks, lifting me a little more, and he thrust again, and then his groin kissed up against mine, and he was in me to the root. He stared down at me, his expression victorious. He'd conquered me, like some warlord who finally beds a rival country's queen. *I won.*

I tightened around him and then, for good measure, squeezed with my thighs. I was the queen who seduced the warlord, leaving him powerless. I stared up at Gennadiy. *Are you sure?*

He looked down at where we joined, comically shocked. Then he looked into my eyes, his mouth open in awed lust. His eyes narrowed. *I'm keeping you.*

And then he started to fuck me. Slow, buttery-smooth strokes that made me moan, then tremble, then arch my back and thrust my hips forward to take even more of him. He moved faster, panting in my ear, ramming me against the wall but using his hands to shield my ass from its scratchy surface. The rain sluiced down our bodies, deliciously cool as our bodies lit up with savage, sexual need.

My hands roamed over his shoulders and back, glorying in the wide, hard bulk of him. I'm small, but I'd never *felt* small with men. The knowledge that I can usually kick the man's ass changes everything. Hanging there, though, sandwiched between Gennadiy and the wall, my legs open and up around his waist and his wet, rock-hard body slamming against me, I finally knew what it was like to feel small and fragile...and it was amazing.

His thrusts sped up again, his hips hammering between my thighs, and I dug my fingers into his shoulders. Each quick out-stroke drew more fluttery, silvery pleasure to my core. Each hard thrust compressed it, making the ball of heat inside me glow hotter and brighter. I let out a low groan: my orgasm had just appeared on the horizon, and we were riding a wave, thundering towards it...

My eyes had fluttered closed. I opened them and saw him scowling down at me, each slam of his hips shaking raindrops loose from his hair. He was scowling, determined...

Determined in a *very particular way.*

My eyes widened as he drove into me again. *He wants to—*

His pubis rocked against my clit, and my thoughts blew away like paper in a hurricane. It took me a moment to focus and think clearly again. *He wants me to come first.* He was still trying to win. He had his rival spread and vulnerable, pinned up against a wall, and now he was going to make her lose control before he did. He wanted to claim me, *own* me. And with that gorgeous, imperious face glaring down at me and those pale gray eyes melting me, demanding submission, the idea wasn't exactly unappealing. The tattooed demons on his chest glistened and flexed as his muscles moved, almost as if they were alive, and with that much angry, evil maleness pressed between my thighs, I *did* feel like some innocent, virgin queen being taken by a conquering warlord. All I had to do was give myself up to it.

But that stubborn streak inside me wouldn't let him win. As we closed in on my orgasm, I started grinding my hips, circling his cock. His brutal, perfect rhythm stumbled as his control began to slip. I pulled him closer, raking my nipples along his chest, and his eyes widened. His mouth became a tight line. "*Blyat*'!" He slammed into me faster, but I could tell *he* was rushing towards his climax, now, too.

I was desperately trying to hang on. I scratched my nails down his back, tightened my ankles behind his thighs. *He* was going to come first. *I* was going to win—

He gripped my ass hard, fingers digging in with just the right sort of roughness, and dipped his head to lick my nipple. The hot ball of pleasure at my core detonated, earthquaking through my body, and I felt myself begin to spasm around him. I grabbed his naked ass with both hands and pulled him deeper, whispering in his ear, "*Give it to me, Gennadiy, all of it.*" And he groaned as he shot and shot inside me, both of us coming together.

35

GENNADIY

WHEN WE FINISHED, WE STARED AT EACH OTHER, PANTING AND uncertain. *What now?* I don't think either of us had ever lost before. Or was it possible that we'd both won?

We dressed, stumbling and shaky-legged as we tried to drag soaking wet pants up our legs. I'd ruined Alison's blouse, so I gave her my suit jacket to wear, which was comically huge on her. Then we climbed back on the stolen bike and rode back to the mansion. With the wind whipping against our soaked bodies, it was freezing, and by the time we got home, both of us were shivering. I took Alison straight to my bedroom and pushed her into the big, walk-in shower fully dressed, and we stood under the hot spray until our teeth stopped chattering, then peeled our sodden clothes off and let the heat soak to our bones.

We wrapped towels around us and went to the bed. The idea was just to sit down for a moment, to rest before we dressed. But it had been a long couple of days with not much sleep in between, and even though it was only mid-afternoon, we were both exhausted. I flopped back on the bed, thinking I'd just rest my eyes for a minute, Alison pressed close to my chest, cuddling in like a sleepy cat, and both of us were asleep in seconds.

∽

I was woken by my phone buzzing: Radimir. I answered, still half asleep. "*Are you okay?*" he demanded. "There was a shoot-out, they found your car, wrecked—"

"I'm fine," I whispered. "Somebody attacked us. We got away. I'm sorry, brother, I should have called. I was—" I looked down at Alison, asleep on my chest. "Distracted."

Radimir went quiet. "You're with her right now, aren't you?"

I went to deny it, then closed my eyes, ashamed. I'd lied enough to him. "Yes."

Radimir sighed. "How long have you had..." I heard the snap of fabric as he tugged his waistcoat straight. "*Feelings* for this FBI agent?"

I swallowed, looking at her half-uncovered breasts, at the little tattoo of a bird on her lower back. "A while," I mumbled.

"Gennadiy..." I could hear the anger in his voice, but I could hear concern, too. He was worried about me. "I'm telling you, we can't trust her."

"And I'm telling you, we can," I said stubbornly, and ended the call.

I stroked Alison's hair. *Blyat'!* What had I done? I'd sworn to stay away from her, to protect her. But then I'd touched her cheek in the alley, and it had been so cold and...

I braced for the rush of guilt that would make me tell her *this was a mistake,* that would make me push her away all over again, but it didn't arrive. Looking down at her slumbering face, all I felt was...good.

A slow shock spread through me. Finally giving in to my feelings had let me see something: this was right. Me and her. Working together, fucking, her asleep on my chest. The whole thing. Maybe this was the only way it *could* work, for opposites like us. Either we destroyed each other or...we joined.

I had no idea how we were going to make it work, but I knew I wasn't giving her up again.

Now I just needed to figure out what to say to her. Luckily, I had some time while she was still—

At that second, she shifted and stirred. I felt my heart rate rocket. *No! No no no no!* I wasn't ready yet! I stroked her hair and made little *shh*-ing noises. But it was too late.

Alison opened her eyes and looked up at me.

36

ALISON

I ROSE UP THROUGH LAYERS AND LAYERS OF DEEP, WARM SLEEP, THE BEST I'd had in years. I opened my eyes, still warm and hazy, and then I saw the dark green canopy of Gennadiy's four-poster bed above me, and Gennadiy's upside-down face staring down at me, forehead creased with worry.

My cop brain kicked in and insisted that I start planning, solving, *doing*. I sat up and stared at him, breathing hard. *Why is he worried? What happens now? Is he going to push me away again? Does he actually feel anything for me, or was this just about fucking his enemy? Is a man like him even capable of—*

He leaned in and kissed my forehead. And my brain went *fzzt* and refused to work. I hadn't ever even remotely conceived that he could be that tender. From the look on his face, neither had he. "Why did you do that?" I thought out loud.

"You were thinking too much," he told me. Then he grabbed one of my ankles, and I yelped as he pulled me down the bed, and I went flopping onto my back again. He knelt astride me, hulking over me like a big, clumsy bear, caging me in with his arms just like that very first time at the casino. Except now, those pale gray eyes were full of concern.

"It is *possible*," he said, his Russian accent polishing the *s*'s, "that I owe you an apology."

I blinked up at him.

"The kiss was not a mistake. Neither was the one in the alley. And neither was the one on the bed."

"What one on the—MMF!"

His lips were on mine, hungry and demanding, and my eyes closed as I floated up into warm bliss. I could feel where the kiss was meant to end, the tiny lift of his lips...and then he growled and came back for more, his tongue dancing with mine as if addicted. Both of us had started to pant before he finally drew back.

"You, Special Agent Brooks," he growled, "are the first thing I think about in the morning and the last thing I think about at night. You're maybe the only person on the planet who understands me, and I understand you. I started off wanting to kill you; now I'm terrified something's going to happen to you. When you hurt, I hurt. When you're not around, I miss you." He shook his head. "And that's why I am *not* letting you go."

That fragile, silvery excitement that had risen, been stomped into the dirt, and tentatively risen again? It bloomed, sprouting a whole canopy of glittering branches and leaves. He kissed me again, this time hard and possessive, and I felt myself lifting up off the bed and rising up past the clouds. I felt something slotting into place, deep in my soul. All along, I'd thought he was my nemesis, but that wasn't it: he was the other half of me, the half I'd always been missing. That's why he *got* me. That's why we were always competing, because we were the same.

When we finally came up for air, I stared up at him, double-checking that he was serious, that he wasn't going to pull the rug from under me again. He gave me a solemn little nod.

I started to get up—I needed space, I needed to process—and he reluctantly lifted one of his arms to let me out. I slid out from under him and stood, clutching the towel around me to cover myself. Then I started to pace in the space passing between the four-poster bed and the polished copper bathtub. *Us?* Could that work? Yes, I'd been fantasizing about kissing him almost since day one, even when I hated him. Yes, my feelings for him had been growing steadily and accelerating this last month. But this was still a lot to take in. I started to pace, thinking. "Why did you push me away?"

He watched me from his position on the bed. "You're a good person, Alison. I thought you deserved...a good man."

I took a deep breath. He *was* evil. And from what I'd seen, he was spiraling, getting more and more ruthless and violent. But I'd seen the good he tried to hide. "I'm a big girl, Gennadiy," I said firmly. "And I choose *you.*"

I saw the relief in his eyes. Then he stood up, towering over me, and put his hands on my shoulders to stop me pacing. He smirked. "One thing you most definitely are *not* is big." And he patted me on the head.

I frowned up at him. "Pat me on the head again and I'll break your arm," I growled.

He gave a little nod, and we stood there looking into each other's eyes. When I thought of how we must look, the hulking, tattooed Russian gangster and the little FBI agent gazing up at him, I wondered if we were crazy. But, God, those pale gray eyes were the most beautiful thing I'd ever seen, and that full lower lip, still slightly smirking, made me go weak. *Goddammit. I have it bad for this guy.* "What do we do when I go back to the FBI?" I mumbled.

"I don't know," admitted Gennadiy. "Let's worry about keeping you alive first. Who's trying to kill you? It isn't the Italians. It isn't the Irish. Who else were you investigating?"

I shook my head tiredly. I'd been wondering the same thing, but, "I was only investigating you. And before this case and while I was off it, the Italians and the Irish. That's it."

"There must be someone else. An old murder investigation, a cold case?"

"No, no one."

"There must be!"

I shook my head again and opened my mouth to tell him there wasn't. But then I froze because...there *was* one other person. It didn't make any sense...unless I'd been horribly, terrifyingly wrong about them.

"Have you ever heard the name Viktor Grushin?" I asked slowly.

Gennadiy's face fell. Then he climbed off the bed and strode over to his closet. "Get dressed," he told me. "We need to talk to Mikhail."

37

ALISON

I HURRIED BACK TO MY ROOM—WRAPPED IN A TOWEL BECAUSE I couldn't face putting my soaking clothes back on again—and pulled on a bra and panties. I stood looking for a moment at all the beautiful dresses Gennadiy had bought for me, then looked down at my ruined leg. I was feeling better, but...no, I wasn't there yet. I grabbed a fresh pair of black jeans instead, a vest top, and a thin, deep blue sweater because the temperature had dropped, and ran for the door. When I opened it, Milena, the maid, was standing there. "Mr. Aristov said you had some wet clothes?"

She was already carrying Gennadiy's soaking wet suit and shirt. I thanked her and gratefully handed her my dripping jeans. "There's a blouse, too, but the buttons are, um...ripped off." I passed her it, flushing.

Milena didn't so much as raise a perfectly made-up eyebrow. "I'll get it replaced," she assured me, curtsied, and scurried off. I watched her go, blinking. This whole servants thing was going to take some getting used to.

Downstairs, Gennadiy told me that he'd called Mikhail and the rest of his family, and they were on their way. While we waited, his chef fed us steaming bowls of home-cooked tomato soup and toasted cheese sandwiches that were absolutely amazing, the bread crunchy and salty with butter, and the centers molten and dripping with strings of tangy cheese.

Bronwyn—Radimir's wife—arrived first because she'd come straight from her bookstore, and I grabbed the chance to get to know her a little. She was American, too, and she and Radimir had only been together a matter of months, so she wasn't used to the lifestyle, either. In fact, it was harder for her because she'd been a civilian with no contact with organized crime at all before Radimir had walked into her bookstore. "Aren't you...scared?" I asked her in the hallway.

"*Of* him?" she asked. "Never. *For* him? All the time. But...the Bratva's part of who he is. I figured I could fight it, maybe lose him to it...Or I could become part of it and be there for him when he needs me." She gave me a brave smile. "It's working...so far." Then her smile faltered. "What happens next...we're working on that."

What happens next. Children? Was she wondering whether to bring kids into Radimir's world? I tried to figure out how to ask, but, at that moment, we heard the other Aristovs arrive.

We hurried back into the dining room as Valentin walked in, silent and brooding, his eyes everywhere. Then Radimir, icily cold...until he spied Bronwyn and pulled her to him, taking both her hands in his and smiling at her with childlike joy. And finally, Mikhail arrived, surrounded by his dogs. For once, he wasn't smiling. "Gennadiy said something about Viktor Grushin," he told me. "Start talking."

We all sat, and I slowly laid out what I'd learned: that Viktor Grushin was a former spy turned anti-Bratva cop, that he'd successfully smashed the gangs in Moscow and then faked his own death. I pulled out my phone and showed them the photo I'd taken of his new, fake identity.

"He's *alive?!*" Mikhail shook his head, visibly shaken. His dogs butted their furry heads against him to comfort him, and he absently stroked them. "I never thought..." He muttered something in Russian, and Gennadiy stood and brought him a glass of vodka, which he drained in one gulp. He sighed, staring at the floor while the rest of us exchanged shocked looks.

When Mikhail finally raised his eyes again, his expression was hard, his voice cracked and bitter. "Viktor Grushin," he told me, "is not what you think."

We all leaned in to listen.

"You said he was a spy," said Mikhail, "and he was. But not some heroic James Bond. His specialty was overthrowing governments in the Middle East and Africa. Assassinating leaders, rigging elections, poisoning opponents. He stoked rebellions, started wars...people starved and died, just so our government could have another puppet leader. Grushin would do anything to complete his mission. When he finally came home, some idiot in the government thought it would be a good idea to put him to work dealing with *us,* with the *Bratva.* But they didn't understand the sort of man he is."

Mikhail looked right at me and spoke slowly and carefully, so I didn't miss a word. "Viktor Grushin," he said, "*did* take down the gangs, but not by becoming a cop. He did it by becoming worse than any of them. He became a predator who preyed on criminals." He waved his hand at me. "You FBI, you think that the Bratva is as bad as it gets. *Viktor Grushin* is as bad as it gets. He had no code, no honor. He didn't care about collateral damage. He gunned down entire restaurants, just to eliminate one person. He would snatch the children of gang leaders from their schools, and of course, the teachers would let him, because he was with the police. Then he would call the parent and *break the child's fingers* over the phone until the gang leader came out of hiding, at which point Grushin would kill him and move on to the next. I once—"

Mikhail broke off, his shoulders slumping. He gestured, and Gennadiy poured him another vodka, but Mikhail didn't drink this one. He just turned the glass around and around in his hands, staring at it. "I once had a friend named Prokopy Ivakin," he said quietly. "His wife, Katya...before she was with him, she and I—" He fell silent again, and Gennadiy and I looked at each other: he looked as shocked as me.

"One night," Mikhail continued, "Grushin and his men came for Prokopy. They interrogated him, trying to get all his contacts. He wouldn't talk so...Grushin took Katya and..."—Mikhail's voice became savage—"he raped her, in front of her husband. He didn't stop, even when Prokopy talked. And afterwards, he shot them both." As he knocked back the vodka, I thought I glimpsed tears in his eyes. My chest ached for him. *Oh, Mikhail...* And at the same time, I was cringing at how I'd hero-worshipped Grushin.

"I didn't know any of this," muttered Radimir, sounding sickened. "I heard talk of him but not...the details."

"The three of you had already left for America, thank God," Mikhail told him. "Grushin is one of the reasons I followed you." He sighed and continued. "What the government didn't realize was that a man like Grushin wasn't going to take down the gangs for a paltry government salary. He'd been close to Crown Princes and dictators for too long; he wanted to be rich...but even more, he wanted power. The whole time he was crushing the gangs, he was stealing their money, taking over their operations. He didn't create his own gang: that would have been noticed. He operated like a parasite, using blackmail to control people high up in the remaining gangs, and no one ever knew who the traitors were until it was too late." Mikhail pinned me with a look. "Viktor Grushin is the one man the Bratva fear, the one man we hate more than the cops."

Everyone sat in stunned silence for a moment. "What happened to him?" asked Gennadiy.

Mikhail sighed. "He amassed so much money and power, and *kompromat* on important people, that the government got scared. Rumor was, they were going to have him killed. When I heard he'd died of a heart attack, I thought that's what had happened."

"But he wasn't dead at all," I whispered, stunned. "He must have known the government was coming for him, so he faked his death. Got a new identity and came here."

Mikhail nodded. "And if he's in this city, and he has people in the FBI, then he's building a new network, right here in Chicago."

"He doesn't want anyone to know he's alive," said Bronwyn. "His mole at the FBI probably keeps watch on his file. When they saw you digging into him, they alerted Grushin, and he tried to take you out."

"And he tried to frame *me* to get me out of the way," said Gennadiy. "Because he doesn't want the Aristovs interfering in whatever he's doing in Chicago. He's out there, somewhere, getting stronger every day. Soon he'll be too strong to stop." He looked meaningfully at Radimir. "We'd never even have known Grushin was in the city, if not for her."

Radimir leaned forward. "We helped you," he told me. "Now it seems you can help us. Whatever Grushin's doing, it's a threat to us. We need to find out what he's up to and stop him. Then maybe we can clear your name, too."

I realized Valentin was looking at me, too. All of them were. I swallowed... and nodded slowly. It felt like I was stepping through a mirror, into a backwards world: I'd run to Gennadiy, a cop who needed a criminal for protection. Now the criminals had a mystery to solve...and they needed a cop to solve it.

I thought hard. Then, "If we can find the assassin Grushin sent to kill me, maybe we can get him to lead us to Grushin," I looked at Mikhail. "You told me Grushin doesn't have a gang of his own, so who did he send to kill me in my apartment?"

Next to me, Gennadiy tensed. I could feel the vengeful anger throbbing from him. "The men who shot up my car were Russians. Looked like mercenaries."

"Which means he probably hired a Russian hitman, too," said Mikhail.

I turned to Valentin. "That's your area. Think you could figure out who?"

Valentin was silent for a moment. I could tell he was still hurting: whatever anniversary was tomorrow, it cut deep. But then he seemed to steel himself, and he nodded slowly. "There's a bar where all those guys hang out. I can take you there. Would you recognize him if you saw him again?"

I thought about it. It had been dark, and he'd been wearing a ski mask. "Maybe," I said uncertainly. "He'd sure as hell remember *me*."

"We'll be right there with you," said Gennadiy, and slipped a protective arm around me. I flushed, but a warm bomb went off in my chest. Mikhail caught my eye and gave me an *I told you so* look. Radimir, though, frowned coldly at me. Working with me was one thing, but an FBI agent *in his brother's bed?* I wondered if he'd ever trust me.

Everyone stood and started moving towards the door. But Mikhail blocked Gennadiy's way for a second. "I've seen Grushin in action before," Mikhail said quietly. "You haven't. Don't underestimate him." I could see the fear in his eyes. Grushin had taken his friend from him...and a woman he'd loved. He didn't want to lose his family, too.

Gennadiy squeezed Mikhail's shoulder. "I won't," he said. "Now let's go get some answers."

38

ALISON

THE BAR WAS BEHIND AN UNMARKED METAL DOOR, HALF COVERED BY peeling posters. I shook my head in disbelief: I'd ridden down the street a thousand times and I'd no clue there was even a bar there, let alone that it was an underworld hangout.

Inside, the place was long but incredibly narrow, only about ten feet from wall to wall. The ceiling was low and covered in pipes and ducting, giving it the feel of a submarine. The lights were red, which made the place even more claustrophobic and unsettling. Nine men were gathered at small tables, drinking, and every one of them froze instantly when we walked in. It went so quiet that I could hear the panting of Mikhail's dogs and the click of my heels. Everyone around us was a trained killer, most of them probably former Russian military. And every one of them was *terrified* of the Aristovs. *Is this what it's like, being a gangster?*

Gennadiy scowled and put his hand on my back. "Is he here?" he asked tightly. I'd felt the anger building in him ever since we left the mansion. I hadn't realized, until tonight, just how mad he was about the attempt on my life. Back when it happened, he'd been hiding his feelings for me. But now...I could hear the vicious edge in his voice, and so could the men. A few of them cursed under their breath. The

Aristovs were terrifying enough, but *Gennadiy* Aristov, out for vengeance?

I forced myself to focus and think like an FBI agent. *Those three* were too tall. *Those two* not tall enough. *He* was too wide. That left three who were all solid possibilities. I pointed to them, and the Aristovs moved closer, surrounding them and herding them into a line-up.

I stepped right up to the men and looked at each one in turn. They glared back at me, silently fuming and jumpy with fear.

It wasn't the first time I'd been face-to-face with murderers, but there was something uniquely disturbing about knowing that one of these men tried to kill me. I don't think I would have been able to do it if Gennadiy hadn't been next to me, brooding and watchful, his face absolutely thunderous.

I looked at their eyes, the only part that had been visible through the ski mask, but they were all too similar. I sniffed, wondering if I'd remember their scent, but none of them was wearing a strong cologne. *It could be any of them.*

At that moment, one of the men took a swing at me, a vicious right hook that would have broken my cheekbone if it had connected. My martial arts training kicked in, and I swayed to the side, grabbed his arm and twisted, and he was bent over the bar with his arm up behind his back before he knew what was happening. Gennadiy stormed forward, furious, but it was already over.

Radimir muttered something under his breath that I couldn't hear, but he sounded impressed. Gennadiy gave me a rare smile, and I felt a warm glow of pride.

"So it's him?" asked Valentin, already reaching under his coat for a knife.

"Wait," I said. I was looking down. Being bent over the bar had made the guy's pant cuffs lift, and it gave me an idea. "I kicked the guy, hard, in the shin. There'll be a bruise." I used the tip of my shoe to lift his pant cuff a little more. "There isn't one. It's not this guy. But we can check the others—"

The third guy in the line-up bolted. He moved so fast, he was already halfway to the door before any of us could react.

Mikhail gave an order in Russian, and there was a thunder of scrabbling paws and a rush of gray fur as all four of his dogs took off after the man, streaking under tables like furry missiles. As the man reached the door, two dogs leapt and closed their teeth on his arms, dragging him to the floor. As he screamed, a third dog gripped his throat. The fourth stood on his chest for good measure.

Gennadiy, his face a mask of cold fury, marched over to the man, picked him up and slammed him face-down on a table, scattering bottles and glasses. I pulled up the man's pant cuff, just to be sure. *Yep.* There was a vicious purple bruise there. "This is him," I said.

Gennadiy looked at the bartender. "Do you have a back room? Somewhere we won't be disturbed?"

"Of course, Mr. Aristov," said the bartender, and pointed to a door. "The storeroom, right in there." He looked at the rest of us. "And drinks, for your family, while they wait!" He started pouring glasses of vodka, his hands visibly shaking.

I stared, stunned. If I'd been there with the FBI, the bartender would have been yelling about the damage and telling us he was going to sue. It was a whole different world on this side of the line.

Gennadiy grabbed the assassin and dragged him into the storeroom. He glanced back at me, and the look on his face was raw, protective rage. "Wait here," he told me.

And he closed the door.

39

GENNADIY

THE STOREROOM HAD WHITE LIGHTS, MERCILESSLY BRIGHT AFTER THE red-tinted bar. I could see the sweat on the assassin's forehead, the rapid movements of his chest. He knew he was in trouble.

He just didn't know how much.

I pushed him so that he was sitting on a stack of beer crates. I could feel the rage building inside me. *He tried to kill her. He came with a gun in the night and tried to kill her...* I forced myself to move slowly and carefully as I stripped off my suit jacket and shirt and laid them neatly over a box in the corner. No sense in ruining good clothes.

I turned to the assassin. I'm used to the anger that swirls in my chest. I've carried it for over two decades. But tonight, it felt different. *Focused.* I wasn't used to it feeling so personal. I wasn't used to having someone I cared this much about. "Where is Viktor Grushin?" I asked, struggling to keep my voice level.

The assassin didn't bother lying. He just shook his head.

Fine. I'd tortured lots of men over the years. I'd never found one I couldn't break.

I slammed my fist into his jaw, knocking him sideways, then knocked him back the other way. I worked on him for a full minute while the rage spun faster and faster in my chest, and when it was time to stop, it took me another few punches before I managed to hit the brakes and step back.

I've always been able to control the anger. Recently, it felt like it was controlling me.

I stood there panting and scowling, looking down at the blood that misted my chest. "Where is Viktor Grushin?" I asked again.

He panted and spat blood, but he wouldn't answer.

Okay.

I went at him again, letting the anger flood through my veins. I kept imagining her lying there asleep in bed as he crept through her apartment...

This time, when I managed to rein myself in, he was wheezing on the floor, his ribs broken. *"Where is Viktor Grushin?!"* I roared.

He stared up at me, terrified. But there was a deeper fear in his eyes, a fear of something worse. A slow realization rolled through me: he wasn't going to talk. *Ever.*

I growled and punched him a final time, knocking him out. Then I dug through his pockets, found his phone, and pressed his finger to the sensor to unlock it.

I turned to the door...then looked back at the man on the floor, unsettled. Mikhail's words came back to me. *Don't underestimate Grushin.*

Grushin had this guy so scared, he'd rather die than talk. A former spy, a *Bratva*-hunter.

What if we were out of our depth here?

40

ALISON

THE DOOR OPENED, AND GENNADIY WALKED OUT, STRIPPED TO THE waist. Valentin grabbed a bar towel and threw it to him, and Gennadiy nodded gratefully and wiped the blood from his hands. I peeked past Gennadiy, and my hand went to my mouth when I saw the assassin: he was a broken, bloodied mess. "Did he...talk?" I managed.

"No," said Gennadiy, pulling his shirt on. "But I got what I needed." And he pulled out his gun and pointed it at the assassin.

"*WAIT!*" I grabbed his arm. "Jesus, you don't have to kill him!"

Gennadiy shook me off. I could feel the anger throbbing through every tight muscle. "You don't understand how our world works," he told me. And he leveled his gun again.

I jumped between him and the assassin. "You can't—Look at him, he's defenseless!"

"Alison," said Gennadiy tightly, "Move."

"No!" My heart was hammering in my chest. This was *murder,* and I was still an FBI agent at heart.

Gennadiy scowled at me for several seconds while the others watched in tense silence. Then he sighed. "Fine," he said tightly, and holstered his gun. Then he nodded towards the exit. "Come on."

I let out a long sigh of relief and walked over to him. We started towards the exit—

Gennadiy turned around, pulled out his gun, and emptied it into the unconscious assassin. Then he grabbed my hand and pulled me out of the bar.

On the street outside, I pulled free of his hand and stood there gaping at him. "What—What— *Why?!*"

Gennadiy turned away from me, his hulking body taut with anger. I could see his shoulders rising and falling as he took big, shuddering breaths, trying to calm himself.

When he finally turned back to me, the raw emotion in his eyes made my heart forget to beat. A deep, protective need, so strong it overwhelmed him. "Because the way I feel about you," he snapped, "I'm not interested in subtlety or second chances. I want the whole city to know and be afraid. I'm sending a message: if someone tries to hurt you, I don't put them on the floor, I put them in the ground!"

The first shock was what he'd said. The second was that there was a tiny, secret part of me that went warm at the idea of him slaying anyone who touched me. I swallowed and nodded. Gennadiy cursed under his breath, then wrapped me up in his arms and pulled me tight against him.

The other Aristovs must have been giving us a minute, watching from the doorway, because as soon as we went quiet, they trooped out and joined us. We formed a tight huddle on the sidewalk. "The assassin was too scared to talk," Gennadiy told us. "But I got his phone." He showed us the call log. "He called someone before and after he tried to kill you. I'm guessing that's Grushin's number. If we can get a hacker on it, maybe we can find out who else Grushin's been calling, and find out what he's been doing."

"Did you check his banking app?" I asked. "We can see how he got paid."

I was just doing what we'd do in the FBI, but Gennadiy looked impressed, and fired up the app. "Twenty thousand paid in, a few hours before he showed up at your apartment," said Gennadiy. Both of us spoke at the same time: "*We should look into the account he was paid from.*" Then we both blinked at each other, surprised. We were on opposite sides, but we worked well together.

"Let's go home," said Gennadiy, and led the way to the cars. I fell in beside him, deep in thought. *He killed that guy because he hurt me.* Could I really be with someone who killed so easily? And he was only getting worse over time, ruthlessly expanding even though the Aristov empire was already huge, brutally killing anyone in his path. It only ended one way: with Gennadiy dead in some gun battle. I'd lose him.

I felt my fists bunch. *No. Fuck that.* I wasn't going to lose the only person who got me. The only one who made me feel safe, and beautiful, and complete.

Three months before, when I'd stood outside the burning theater, something inside me had hardened into unwavering resolve. Now, I felt it happening again.

Once, I'd sworn to take Gennadiy Aristov down.

Now, I was going to save him.

41

ALISON

Back at the mansion, Gennadiy was pulled straight into a phone call and then had to race off to the casino to solve some problem there. I'd always known he was busy, but now that I was on the inside, I was starting to see how massively overstretched he was, and there didn't seem to be anyone he could hand things off to. It slowly hit me that the Bratva wasn't like a business, or even like the FBI. You can hire more managers, train more agents, but you can't just magic up more brothers or uncles, and family were the only people Gennadiy trusted enough to delegate to.

I explored more of the enormous house and stumbled upon a whole crowd of Russian men in suits sitting, cleaning their guns: Gennadiy's security. They showed me their area, which took up most of one wing of the first floor. There was a barracks, a break room, and even a small shooting range.

I went back to the staircase and climbed all the way up to the top floor, trailing my hand along the thick, wooden banister. I found Melina changing the sheets in one of the bedrooms. "Need a hand?" I asked from the doorway.

She stopped and stared: apparently, she wasn't used to being asked that. Then she shook her head politely. "No, thank you. It's my job." And she carried on, tucking corners with ruthless precision.

Further down the hall, I stopped when I glimpsed a pair of legs through a window. A wooden door with an ornate brass handle led out onto a long stone balcony that stretched along the back of the house, looking out over the gardens. And from that balcony, a narrow stone staircase led up. The legs I'd seen were climbing up the stairs. *But what's up there? This is the top floor!*

I opened the door and went out onto the balcony, blinking in the sunlight. I was just in time to see the legs at the top of the staircase before they turned a corner and disappeared from view. There must be some sort of roof terrace up there. But at least I knew who it was: I'd caught a glimpse of a long coat. *Valentin.*

Back inside, I followed the staircase down to the first floor...and heard a dog yowling as if in pain. I froze...and heard another one howl, this time in absolute agony. I raced down the hallway...and pulled up short in the doorway.

The room was big, with black and white tiles that were very old, but scrupulously clean. An old-fashioned tin bath sat in the middle of the room, full of soapy water. It was surrounded by Mikhail's four huge Malamutes, barking and howling and in various states of being washed. And in the middle of it all, kneeling next to the tub and stripped to the waist, was Mikhail himself, issuing orders in Russian and being ignored. As I watched, one dog excitedly jumped into the tub, jumped out dripping wet, and yowled plaintively. The other three decided this was a good idea and joined in, throwing back their heads and group-yowling. Bathtime was either the worst torture imaginable or the most fun ever: they weren't sure. Mikhail shook his head and sighed, then laughed.

"Want a hand?" I asked. I'm not good at sitting idle.

Mikhail twisted around to look at me. "You'll get wet," he warned.

I pulled off my sweater and put it down on a chair, leaving me in a tank top. Then I knelt next to Mikhail. He was an intimidating sight, up close. He might have been a little older than the others, but his back and arms rippled with muscle, and he was still lean. One of the dogs bounded up to me and nuzzled my ear, and I shrieked and giggled.

With two of us, it was a little easier to corral the dogs one by one into the tub, shampoo their fur, and then rinse them. But only a little. There was a lot of dramatic howling, splashing, and dogs bounding after bits of foam that floated through the air.

We worked in companionable silence for a few minutes. Then, "I saw Valentin just now," I said. "Heading up to the roof."

Mikhail nodded. "That's his...what is it you call it? His *happy place.*" His Russian accent was warmly comforting. "He spends all his time up high: balconies, fire escapes, rooftops. Watching his targets. Like an... evil Batman." He laughed.

I nodded, and we shampooed and rinsed for another few minutes. Then, "I wasn't ready for Gennadiy to just...kill that guy," I blurted.

Mikhail nodded, suddenly somber. "You come from a world where even criminals have rights. Our world is brutal, and it can be cold." He scratched a wet dog behind both ears at once, and it panted in joy. "But if someone hurts someone we love, there are no courts, or rights, or plea bargains. That person is dead. Gennadiy *will* kill anyone who harms you. As would Radimir, for Bronwyn."

I nodded slowly, thinking. I wasn't sure I liked it, but, at the same time, there was something about it that felt warm, like Gennadiy was wrapping me up in his arms. I used a jug to pour clean water over a dog's back, rinsing away the suds. "Gennadiy's getting worse, isn't he? More ruthless, more violent? We noticed it even at the FBI."

Mikhail's jaw tightened. "He's angry. He's been angry for a long time." He seemed to be about to say something else, but closed his mouth and ruffled a dog's coat instead, making the shampoo foam.

My cop instincts kicked in. I thought back to what Gennadiy had said when he saw my leg for the first time. "Once, he sort of implied something happened to him. Something that made him all twisted up inside. Is that true?"

Mikhail turned and stared at me, looking shocked...and then impressed. "You really are an FBI agent. *Yes,* that is true. But it's a story *he'll* have to tell you." Mikhail waggled a dripping finger in the air. "And he won't want to."

I nodded silently. Gennadiy could be stubborn.

But so could I.

42

ALISON

THE NEXT MORNING, AS SOON AS THE BANKS OPENED, I MARCHED INTO the manager's office and flashed my badge. "I need to see the transactions on this account," I told him, showing him the number of the account that had paid the assassin. "Right now."

Normally, I would have filled out some forms, connected to a database, and dug into the accounts without ever leaving my desk. But using official channels would light up big red flashing alerts that I was suspended and my access had been revoked. I was hoping the old-fashioned approach would work: I'd even stopped at a store and bought a new pant suit so I looked more like an FBI agent again.

I was in luck: the manager's eyes went wide with fear when he saw my badge, and he couldn't cooperate fast enough. He even brought me a cup of coffee while I looked through Grushin's transactions. My badge might scare men away, but it has its uses.

My good mood evaporated when I started looking through the transactions. I had to check twice, thinking I'd miscounted the zeroes. The bank account was supposedly for a private medical clinic on the edge of town—obviously a front for whatever Grushin was actually doing. He was using it to launder money, dumping in funds and claiming they came from patients. But it was the *amount* of money that shocked me. There were two to three deposits every week, each between two and five million dollars. Grushin was bringing in about half a billion dollars a year. *What the hell is he doing?* I wished Caroline was there to bounce ideas off.

I arrived back at the mansion mid-morning and found Gennadiy just coming out of the shower. He'd been at the casino all night and had just come home to change his clothes. I sat on the four-poster bed, watching him dress, while I told him what I'd found out. "He's making hundreds of millions, and it looks like he's been here for at least a year. What's he selling? And how did we not notice it at the FBI? And why does he want so much money, anyway? Mikhail said it's power he really craves."

Gennadiy shook his head as he pulled on a forest-green shirt. "I don't know. It's..." He rubbed at his eyes. "Troubling."

I was trying to think, but it was hard not to be distracted. Shafts of warm sunlight from between the drapes lit up patches of his smooth, caramel skin and slid over the hills and valleys of his abs. I watched longingly, as his body slowly disappeared under the shirt, like watching a stripper in reverse. He fastened his cuffs, then moved on to the buttons. But he was operating on no sleep and had three buttons done before he realized the first one was in the wrong hole. "*Blyat'!*" he muttered.

I walked over and stood in front of him, dwarfed by his big body. I gently pushed his hands aside and started redoing the buttons for him. "You need to rest," I told him.

"I'll rest when all this is done."

Hmm. That sounded a lot like something *I'd* say. I'd never seen a workaholic from the outside. I finished the buttons and then laid my palms on his chest in a way I hoped was comforting. He scowled down at me suspiciously, and I swallowed: I felt like a mouse, trying to calm a grumpy bull. But I was determined to help him. "You...work a lot," I said gently. "Harder and harder. Building the business, destroying your enemies. I think...you've got this anger inside you, and it drives you." I looked down at my ruined leg, thinking of my parents, my missing childhood. "I know what that's like. But with you...it feels like the anger isn't fading, it's getting worse."

Gennadiy cocked a brow. *So?*

I took a deep breath. I didn't want to make him mad. I knew he wouldn't hurt me, but I wouldn't get anywhere if I got him riled up. "What is it?" I asked, so quietly it was almost a whisper. "Where does it come from? Maybe I can help."

He grimaced and started to say something: to snap at me, maybe. But he bit it back. Then again, and again, he bit it back. He took a deep breath and then took my cheeks in his hands and looked down at me. My heart lifted: he was trying so hard to make this work. "Thank you," he said. "I know...I know that you mean well. But it isn't something I can talk about."

He leaned down and kissed me, soft and tender, and I felt myself melt at the revelation that he could be so gentle. But I also recognized it for what it was: a way of changing the subject.

He broke the kiss and headed for the door. "I have to go. There's some problem with a gun shipment. But I'll try to look into Grushin's phone number, too. There's a hacker I know—"

I put my hand up: *stop*. "You have enough to do. Let me take this. I know a hacker, too." I sighed, thinking. "Plus, I really need to check in with her boyfriend."

43

GENNADIY

BEFORE I LEFT, I FOUND VALENTIN AND ASKED HIM TO START surveillance on Grushin's front business, the medical clinic. Then I headed across town, but almost immediately, I got stuck in traffic. Crawling along was even more frustrating than usual because, with my car totaled, I was having to drive Radimir's big Mercedes. None of the controls were where I expected them to be, and I felt clumsy and useless. I missed my BMW.

I glared at the bumper of the car in front. *I don't have time for this!* I felt like I was trying to keep about a hundred plates spinning. We had to find out what the hell Grushin was up to and stop him. But I still had the casino to run and countless other operations to manage, and they all seemed to be hitting problems at the same time.

And then there was Alison.

Just thinking of her made my whole chest *lift*. After months of watching her flit around in my rear-view mirror and the edges of my vision, she was finally *mine*. I was almost drunk on it: I wanted to spend all day, every day, with the warmth of her body against mine, breathing in the scent of her hair.

And yet...we'd been together *one day,* and already, I was fucking it up. As soon as she'd asked about the anger, I'd shut down. *This is what I get for falling for an FBI agent.* She'd figured out that there was something broken in my soul. And now she knew she was onto something, she'd never let it go. Those cop instincts ran bone-deep in her, and she was at least as stubborn as me.

She was right. The anger was driving me, and it demanded more violence, more territory, a bigger empire, every day. I was pushing too hard: muscling in on the cartel's supply lines last month was probably why they tried to kill me at the jazz club. I knew this path only ended one way, with me lying dead. But...

I couldn't stop. Stopping meant letting the anger slow and fade, and I couldn't do that, for the same reason I couldn't talk to Alison about it. I didn't want to face what was underneath the anger.

I shook my head and cursed. The traffic *still* wasn't moving. I was burned out and cranky from lack of sleep, my head was throbbing...*I need coffee.* And I was right beside the entrance to the Conroy Mall. I could go in and get a caffeine hit, walk around in the air-conditioned coolness for a few minutes, and maybe clear my head. It wasn't like I was getting anything done sitting here.

Five minutes later, I was wandering through the mall, coffee in hand. I'd asked for a triple shot, and the caffeine was roughly massaging my brain awake. Maybe that's why I had the revelation. I looked around at the people, and I finally knew why I'd always liked the place.

It was the normality. People with regular lives, with wives and husbands and kids. Guys buying lingerie for their girlfriends. Fathers buying toys for their kids.

I wanted a taste of that. Maybe, unconsciously, I always had. The Bratva, building the Aristov empire, everything I'd poured my soul into for years...it wasn't enough anymore. I wanted more. I wanted *her.*

But, God, how was that going to work?! She was a cop, at heart. A good person. Becoming part of our world would taint her, corrupt her...and even if she was willing to go through that change, I wasn't sure I wanted her to. Her goodness was one of the things I adored about her. *Blyat',* I just wanted to lock her in a room in my mansion, away from all harm...except she'd karate kick me in the balls, if I tried it. I closed my tired eyes for a second and rubbed at them. This relationship stuff was complicated.

Time to get going. I took a sip of my coffee, steeling myself, opened my eyes and—

On the other side of the food court was a face I recognized. It was impossible. But it was him.

"Hello, Gennadiy," said Viktor Grushin.

44

ALISON

I figured the FBI would be tapping my phone by now, so I used a burner phone to call Calahan. That meant that I must have come up as *Unknown Caller* on his screen, but he still answered with a frantic, *"Alison?!"*

My stomach lurched. Time had sort of gotten away from me since I went on the run. It had been almost two days. "Yep," I said guiltily. "I'm okay."

Calahan gave a groan of relief, and I heard him yell to Yolanda that *she's okay.* Then he tore into me, which, to be fair, I deserved. "Where have you been?!" he yelled. "You couldn't have *called?* I thought you were *dead!"*

"Sorr—" I started, but he wasn't done.

"There was a car chase through the middle of Chicago, a BMW got swiss-cheesed, the FBI are *still* picking through the scene, a woman with dark hair was seen riding off on a motorcycle, I was hoping it was you, but I didn't know—"

I tried to get a word in. "I—"

"The FBI has been all over me, but I told them you hadn't contacted me. Except in this case, it was *actually true* because you couldn't be bothered to *pick up the phone!"*

Calahan finally finished his rant and panted for breath. And I closed my eyes, chastened. He'd always been protective of me and I'd left him terrified because I'd been too busy solving the mystery, as always. *Solving the mystery...and fucking Gennadiy.* I winced. "I'm sorry, Sam. I should have called."

"You think?!" But I could hear that he was simmering down, and I knew the anger was just because he cared. He sighed. "What the hell is going on, Alison?"

I looked around. I was standing in the living room, right where Gennadiy and I had kissed for the first time. "A lot's happened," I admitted. I took a deep breath and moved outside, into the mansion's gardens. Wandering across the manicured lawns, I told him everything, from the night I'd confronted Gennadiy about burning down the theater all the way up to now.

There was a long, slow rasping. I imagined Calahan rubbing his stubble. "You fell for him?" he asked disbelievingly.

I opened and closed my mouth a few times. "Not all at once. It took months. It sort of...snuck up on me."

"Alison, the man's a killer. How many guys has he killed, now?"

One more, as of last night, I thought. *To protect me.* "A lot," I admitted.

"And from what I hear, he's getting worse," said Calahan. "He's out of control."

He sounded just like me when I'd been convincing my boss to let me go after Gennadiy. I closed my eyes. So much had changed in the last few months. "He's not just some monster," I muttered. "He's..." I sighed. "I think there are reasons he is how he is. Maybe I can..."

"Change him?" asked Calahan.

I closed my eyes and said nothing. I knew how it sounded.

"I don't want to fight," Calahan told me. "And I'm not here to lecture you. I just want you to be safe."

"I know. Thanks." I meant it.

"How can I help?" asked Calahan.

I looked at the piece of paper that held Grushin's phone number. "I have something I could use Yolanda's help with..."

"Hold on." I heard Calahan walk across the room. "You're up," he murmured, and there was the sound of a soft kiss. Then I was put on speaker.

"What do you need?" asked Yolanda.

I fiddled with the paper, nervous. "I need to know all the calls this phone number made."

"*Pfft,*" said Yolanda. "Easy. Read me the number."

"I'm a fugitive," I stressed. "If they find out you helped me, you could go to jail."

"What are friends for? Now read me the number."

I read it out. I heard Yolanda's fingers skittering across the keyboard, then a final, triumphant thump of the Enter key. "Easy," she told me. "Got a list of names and addresses. I'll send it over."

I slumped in relief. "Thanks, Yolanda."

Calahan came back on the line. "This Grushin guy sounds like bad fucking news. You want me to jump on a plane?"

I nearly had a heart attack. "*No!* Jesus, no, Sam, don't come to Chicago. You could lose your job just for talking to me!"

"Okay, okay," he grumbled. "But Alison? Be careful."

45

GENNADIY

AT FIRST, I THOUGHT I WAS DREAMING. I HAD DOZED OFF RIGHT IN THE middle of the shopping mall, and I was having a nightmare. Any second, I'd wake up.

But no. Grushin was right there, ten feet away, and coming closer. His gray business suit matched his silver beard, the deep red tie like a slash of blood on his chest. He was in his early sixties, but he'd kept all the muscle he'd picked up in the military, and he had a lean toughness, like he considered fat a weakness.

I blinked, trying to process. *He's here. He's right here.* It wasn't just that he'd tried to have Alison killed, or that he'd murdered Mikhail's old lover. He was the arch enemy of all Bratva: it was like seeing the devil himself walking the earth. I felt the comforting weight of my gun in its holster. *I can kill him. I can kill him right now, and he can never hurt anyone again...*

Except I couldn't. We were right in the center of a shopping mall, and I could count at least four security cameras. Not even Conrad the wonder-attorney could get me off if I executed someone on video. But Grushin couldn't kill me, either. He must have tailed me from the mansion and waited until I was in a public place.

He was here to talk.

I slowly sat down at one of the food court tables. Grushin sat down across from me. He gazed at me with undisguised contempt, like he was still the noble cop the media had portrayed him as, and I was the criminal trash that needed cleaning up. And I glared right back at him, the raw hate boiling up inside me.

It was funny, but when I'd first met Alison, I'd thought I'd hated her. Now I knew what real hate was. This man was everything I'd assumed she was: corrupt and uncaring, part of a broken system. And what he claimed to be, the honest, noble cop? Alison actually was that. Only she'd wound up framed and on the run, and he'd wound up a rich man.

"Gennadiy Aristov." He spoke in Russian, and he had the tone of a teacher disciplining a pupil. "It was always a regret that you and your brothers fled the country like rats before I could catch you."

"We didn't flee," I said testily. "We came to the land of opportunity."

Grushin leaned closer. "You were last on my list. Do you know why?" He smiled. "You've never been real Bratva. You have no heritage. Your parents, your grandparents, they weren't in the brotherhood. You're just three brats who decided you were going to be gangsters. And then you pulled your fool of an uncle in to join you."

I knew he was using spy tactics, trying to get in my head, but it still stung a little. Once, I'd thought Alison was my nemesis but now I saw that it was Grushin. He was the opposite of me in every way: coldly emotionless where I was angry, solitary where I relied on friends and family.

"Still, I'm willing to offer a deal," Grushin told me. "I'll leave the Aristovs alone. You can keep your businesses. I won't touch you and your brothers. You can keep what you have." He sat back in his seat. "All you have to do is hand over the woman."

I felt the anger surge inside me. *The woman.* He wouldn't even dignify her with a name. But I was confused, too. Early on, he'd tried to kill her because she was the only one who knew he was alive. But now I knew, and all my brothers. Killing her wouldn't keep his secret. So why did he want her?

It didn't matter because the answer was simple. "Go fuck yourself," I told him.

He put his fingers lightly on my arm, and it was like a spider was walking there. "If you don't, I will take your empire apart, piece by piece. I'll smash you like I smashed the gangs in Moscow. Every business, gone. Every deal, undone. And I'll come for your family, Gennadiy. Everyone you care about. Now *give me. The woman.*"

And this time, I heard it. He was so masterfully deceptive, that he almost kept it out of his voice...but not quite. There was a trace of stress when he talked about her.

He was scared. Not of our family, with its guns and power and billions. He was scared of her. So scared, he was willing to leave the Aristovs alone, just to get her off his back.

I suddenly understood. The only thing that scares a corrupt cop is an honest one.

I leaned in. "No," I told him, loudly and clearly.

He frowned and stared. I knew he was analyzing me, picking up on everything from my breathing to my body language, and I didn't care. "You're in love with her," he said with disgust.

Hearing the word was a shock. My mind had been skating around that word for weeks, calling it everything but that. But now it was right there in front of me and...

I scowled at him. I still had no idea how to be in a relationship or how I was going to be close to her without dragging her down with me and getting her killed. But there was one thing I was sure of.

"You're fucking right, I'm in love with her," I told Grushin. The rage rolled through my body in trembling waves, and I couldn't stay sitting anymore. I stood, sending my chair tumbling backwards, and leaned over the table. "You know, you were right about the Aristovs. We're not Bratva royalty. We don't come from a long line of criminals. But that means we don't play by the rules. I'm going to find out what you're doing in my city. I'm going to stop you. And if you touch my woman, I will take off your head with a fucking fire ax."

I turned and stormed away, not looking back. Grushin was terrifying and beyond powerful but now I had one slim hope. He was scared of Alison because she might expose him.

We'd wondered what the hell he was doing to make so much money. Now we knew it wasn't the usual drugs or gambling or protection rackets, because those things he could just bribe the authorities to ignore. It must be something so bad, he couldn't have it brought out into the daylight because the public would *demand* that the authorities stop it.

Our only chance was to become like Alison, to become cops. To expose whatever Grushin was doing before he killed us all.

46

ALISON

I GROANED AND TILTED MY NECK ONE WAY, THEN THE OTHER, THE muscles so knotted with tension they felt like concrete. I'd been hunched over a desk all day, painstakingly sifting through everyone Grushin had called.

There was nothing more I could do until Gennadiy got home, so I wandered through the mansion again. I found Mikhail in the living room, rolling around on the floor with his dogs as they played tug-of-war with a knotted rope. I moved on and found myself in the kitchen. *Wow.* It was enormous, with shining, stainless steel surfaces and appliances, and a massive stove for when the chef needed to cook six different dishes at once. I opened a door and found a walk-in freezer stocked with sides of beef and legs of lamb, and next to it a pantry. I gazed up at the shelves, which went right up to the ceiling. There were bags of potatoes, crates of vegetables and exotic fruits, canned goods, and all the flours, grains, and spices needed to cook and bake almost anything.

The pantry door had swung closed behind me, and I was just about to open it to leave when voices entered the kitchen, one deep and Russian and one soft and calming. Radimir and Bronwyn.

"...important to you," Bronwyn was saying.

"It's important to *Mikhail*," said Radimir. "He keeps saying it's the responsibility of the Pakhan to think about the next generation." I peeked through the crack in the door. They were standing six feet from me, right in front of the pantry. Radimir, in his three-piece suit as always, was hulking over his wife as she leaned against the kitchen island. I bit my lip. Should I open the door and let them know I was there?

"But it's important to you, too," said Bronwyn gently.

Radimir scowled and glanced around, checking there was no one listening. *Aw, shit.* Before I could do anything, he was speaking. "If you'd asked me a year ago, I wouldn't have even considered having children. But now..." He put a hand on Bronwyn's belly, and his voice became almost wistful. "...with you..." He looked deep into her eyes. "But the only thing that matters to me, *Krasavitsa*, is that you're happy."

Bronwyn bit her lip and then reached up and brushed her fingers across his stubbled cheek. "You know...if we do want a baby, there's something we're going to need to do a lot of."

"Didn't we come in here to make you a sandwich?" Radimir teased.

"The sandwich can wait," muttered Bronwyn, and tilted her head up, and his lips were on hers in a second. Then his hands slid under her sweater and— *Oh. Um...* I felt my face heat. I was going to be stuck here until they finished.

At that moment, the chef bustled in, carrying a carton of groceries. He pulled up short in the doorway. "Sorry, sir."

Radimir shook his head, scooped his hands under Bronwyn's ass, and picked her up, making her yelp in surprise. "Guest room?" he muttered under his breath.

"Guest room," Bronwyn panted.

They swept past the chef and out into the hallway. I slumped in relief. *Whew.*

Then the chef opened the pantry to put away his groceries and jumped back, startled, when he saw me lurking there.

"Don't mind me," I told him sheepishly. I ducked under his arm and hurried away.

As I left the kitchen, something occurred to me: *where's Valentin?* I'd been home all day, working in a study just off the hallway, so I knew when people came and went. Valentin had come back from surveilling the clinic an hour ago, and he hadn't gone out again, but he was nowhere to be found.

Then I remembered what Gennadiy had told me at the Irish bar. The anniversary that had been weighing on Valentin...it was today. And suddenly, I knew exactly where he'd be.

I went straight up to the top floor, then found the door that led out to the stone balcony. As I climbed slowly up the stairs, not wanting to spook him, something hit me: I'd thought of the mansion as home, just then.

The stairs led up to a small, flat section of roof with a low parapet, hidden from view from the front of the house. And that's where I found him, sitting on the parapet with his legs dangling into space. He glanced up when he heard me, and I saw the raw pain in his eyes. He didn't invite me closer, but he didn't tell me to get lost, either.

I swallowed and climbed the final few stairs, then looked down. *Ulp.* I'm not scared of heights, but this was three floors straight down onto flagstones, and that would make anyone nervous. I very nearly turned around and went back downstairs. It was getting cold, it looked like the rain was about to start up again, and I could ask the chef to brew some coffee, or maybe a hot chocolate...

But Valentin looked so alone. *Why isn't Mikhail comforting him? Or Radimir?*

I edged closer to him, then stood right behind him, but he still didn't speak. Maybe he didn't trust his voice not to shake.

Okay. Only one thing for it.

Very carefully, I stepped up onto the parapet and then slowly sat down–

One of my boots rocked sideways, and my leg shot out from under me. My ass came down hard on the edge of the parapet, and I slid, too scared to even scream–

Valentin twisted and grabbed me under the arms, an inch from disaster. "Careful!" he told me. Then, as I got myself safely seated, "Gennadiy would kill me if I let anything happen to you!"

I nodded my thanks, panting in fear. Then, as I processed what he'd said, a warm glow spread through my chest. When my breathing had settled, I asked, "Why do you spend so much time up high?"

He glanced across at me. "There are security cameras everywhere these days," he told me. "But they all point down."

That's why we've never caught him, I realized. "You don't have to worry about cameras here, though," I said gently. I looked around. We had a fantastic view of the gardens. Was that why he came up here? Did he find them calming?

Valentin sighed. "Things are easier, from up here."

I frowned, confused. And then I followed his gaze and realized where I'd gone wrong: I hadn't been looking far enough. Valentin wasn't looking at the gardens, or the streets around us, or anything nearby. He was looking at the city in the distance, with its swarms of ant-sized figures crossing crosswalks and colorful snakes of cars stopped at stop lights. It wasn't about being high up. It was about keeping everyone at a distance.

I looked at the silver bird he wore around his neck, too small and delicate to be made for a man. "What was her name?" I asked quietly.

He slowly turned and looked at me, and I sensed his armor opening, just a little. "Ruslana," he said. "Her name was Ruslana." He turned away, looking off into the distance again, and I thought that was it. But then I felt his hand tentatively move towards mine. I took it, squeezed it, and we stayed like that until the rain started.

I'd only just come down from the roof, the first few drops of rain still glistening in my hair, when Gennadiy burst in, eyes wild. I felt my heart lift. "What's going—*MMF!*"

In one movement, he'd grabbed me by the waist, pulled me to him, and was kissing me. I pinwheeled my arms for a second in shock and then melted into it. His tongue traced my lips, and then he was kissing me hard and deep, his hands running up and down my sides as if reassuring himself that I was real, that I was there. My back whumped into a wall, and he pinned me there, his big hands stroking down my legs and over my ass, and the kiss changed, becoming charged and hungry. Each touch of those strong fingers sent another ripple of urgent pleasure down through my body, becoming molten, liquid heat when it reached my groin. This man had the ability to take me from idle to redline in five seconds flat.

He finally broke the kiss and put me gently down, and I stood there shaky-legged and tender-lipped. "I just–" Gennadiy stared into my eyes and squeezed my shoulders so hard it was almost painful. Then he tugged me close again and this time just hugged me, burying my face between his pecs. A different sort of warmth spread through me, and I closed my eyes. This was what I'd been searching for when I used to take those epic, hot showers. Exactly this.

It was a long time before he released me. His forehead was creased with stress, and his cheeks were dark with stubble. He hadn't slept in two days, and I wondered when he last ate. He was pushing himself too hard, just like I always did. "What happened?" I asked.

He sighed and sat me down on a big leather couch, hunkering down in front of me. "I saw Viktor Grushin," he told me. "He's coming after our businesses, after *us*: all of us are targets. He'll destroy it all if we don't stop him."

I let my cop brain process that for a moment. Something didn't feel right. "Why would he risk exposing himself just to threaten you? That doesn't make sense." I frowned. "Unless there was an 'or'." I searched Gennadiy's face: he was a good liar, but I'd spent so long watching him, I knew every tell. "There *was* an 'or,'" I muttered. Gennadiy looked away guiltily and my jaw dropped open as I got it. "He wanted *me!*"

Gennadiy grabbed my hands, his voice like iron. "He's not having you."

Sick fear was rising in my chest. I'd come to him for help; I thought we could be allies. I never wanted *this!* "He's going to destroy everything because of me!"

Gennadiy pulled my hands together and closed his bigger hands around them. "No, he's not. Because we're going to stop him. Together."

He gathered the rest of his family and brought them up to speed. "We have to figure out what he's doing," Gennadiy told them. "Grushin made it clear we're all targets, now. You should all come and stay here, in the mansion, until this is over." Radimir nodded and squeezed Bronwyn's hand.

"I checked out Grushin's clinic," said Valentin. "Pretty fancy place: has a whole spa where you can get pampered while you recover from your nose job. Looks like a legit business. I climbed the fence and went dumpster diving, but all I could find was normal medical waste. Then I thought maybe it was some sort of pill mill and they were selling prescription meds, so I photographed all the packaging, but it was just anaesthetics, antibiotics...the only one I hadn't heard of was something called tacrolimus."

"That's not something you could sell on the street either," said Bronwyn. "I'm prescribed it for my arthritis; it's just an immunosuppressant."

Gennadiy clapped Valentin on the shoulder and nodded his thanks to Bronwyn. "So the clinic is like the casino: a legit front Grushin uses to launder money."

I turned it over in my head. "It's a pretty good way to hide big transactions. People pay hundreds of thousands of dollars for medical treatment. What if...Grushin's selling something, something really valuable? His customers pay through the clinic, it gets recorded as liposuction or a facelift, and no one's any the wiser."

"So what's he selling that's so valuable?" asked Radimir. "Technology? Information?"

We were all working together, bouncing ideas off each other, and, for a moment, it was almost like being back in the FBI. I felt a whisper of something, but I couldn't put a name to it.

"Some of the clients are probably real patients," said Bronwyn thoughtfully. "But some will be his customers. Could we get hold of a patient list?"

I shook my head. "Patient records are confidential. Even if I was back at the FBI, it'd be tricky to get that kind of information." I sighed. "Grushin's smart, I'll give him that."

"What about the numbers from Grushin's phone?" asked Gennadiy.

I showed him the list of numbers Yolanda had given me, the printout now a rainbow of highlighter ink. "These are all numbers in Moscow; probably contacts he made while he was working there. So, whatever he's selling, I'm guessing he's getting it from Russia." I pointed to the next few rows. "These are numbers here in Chicago. This is a company that does welding. I have no clue what that means. And this one is a small local transport company...I thought maybe distribution? But that makes no sense if his clients pick up their stuff from the clinic."

Gennadiy nodded. "Good work." A glow of pride spread through me. Even Radimir looked grudgingly impressed.

"What are the other numbers?" asked Valentin, pointing to the last few rows.

I sighed. "Those are numbers with no registered name or address. Burner phones, probably local criminals. I highlighted the ones Grushin calls a lot."

Gennadiy nodded thoughtfully. Then his finger stabbed at one of the highlighted numbers, and he went pale. "That's..." He trailed off, pulled out his phone, checked a number, and then double-checked it.

"What?" I asked, worried. "What is it?"

His voice was strangled. "One of the numbers is Yakov Beletski's."

47

GENNADIY

I sagged forward, and my palms thumped the smooth wood of the dining table. I could barely breathe. *Yakov!* My best friend.

"Could I have the room, please?" I grated. Everyone nodded and made themselves scarce until only Alison was left. She put her hands on mine and looked up at me with big, apologetic eyes.

I shook my head. "I needed to know," I told her.

She nodded sadly and started to leave, but I grabbed her wrist. "No," I said tightly. "Stay." She nodded and squeezed my hand, and I squeezed it back... *Blyat'*, I used to spend every day planning how to slip away from her. Now, I couldn't stand being separated from her. And she was becoming essential to the Aristov family, too. I could feel her being drawn into our world, getting used to breaking the law, just as I'd worried she would. But the truth was, we needed her. We didn't stand a chance against Grushin without her.

"What are you going to do?" she asked gently.

I shook my head. "I have no idea." Yakov had always been my rock. He was exactly the person I'd go to for advice in a situation like this. I took a deep breath...and felt the cold metal of my gun press against my chest. I squeezed my eyes shut. Traitors in the Bratva always met the same fate, but...*I can't. Not Yakov.*

Alison slipped her arm around my shoulders. As I inhaled, I caught the soft, vanilla scent of her skin and all my senses woke...but like when I'd comforted her in the graveyard, it wasn't sexual. This was about support. She's s0 *many things to me...*

Radimir burst into the room. "We need to get to the casino. Right now."

The fear in his voice made me not ask questions. Yakov would have to wait. We ran to the cars.

The casino was in uproar. My staff were arguing with men in suits. The state police were there, herding gamblers away from the gaming tables. The gamblers were clutching handfuls of chips, which they were being told they now couldn't cash in, and everyone was yelling at everyone else. Worst of all, a news crew was filming the whole thing. I snatched a piece of paper from one of the suits and read it.

We'd lost our gambling license.

"That's impossible," I told Radimir. "We *earned* that license. Legally. We ticked every fucking box."

"This is Grushin," said Alison. "He's doing exactly what he said he'd do. He must have bribed the head of the gaming board."

Mikhail shook his head. "Not possible. I know the man. *We* looked at bribing him, but he's a Boy Scout. Wouldn't take a bribe. Grushin must have some other hold on him."

The men in suits started hustling me out of the casino. As my family was pushed towards the glass doors, I could feel the anger building into a scalding hurricane. The casino's my proudest achievement, and Grushin had taken it from me in just a few hours. "You were right," I admitted to Mikhail. "I underestimated this guy."

We were shoved through the doors and onto the street. A whole swarm of news crews saw us and ran towards us. "Go," I whispered to Alison and pushed her away. The FBI was still looking for her: I didn't want her on the front page of every news website. She nodded quickly and split off from us, becoming just another anonymous gambler in the crowd.

Reporters surrounded us, yelling questions. I straightened my jacket and stepped forward, telling everyone how this was just a mistake, how our legitimate business had been unfairly targeted, and how we'd be appealing the decision. But between questions, I kept catching Radimir's worried glances. This was very, very bad. Not only was it a PR nightmare for our family, but losing the casino put a huge hole in our finances. It wasn't just a money maker; it was how we laundered a lot of our cash, and if it wasn't operating, we couldn't turn our illegal money into legal funds that Radimir could invest. I could feel sweat beading on my forehead. This side of the business was *my* thing, and it was me who'd turned down Grushin's ultimatum. It was up to me to fix this, and I had no idea how. My chest had gone tight: *Jesus, I can hardly breathe.*

The reporters turned to Mikhail for a moment, and he gave them one of his warm, engaging smiles, batting their questions away effortlessly. Radimir took the opportunity to pull me aside. I spoke before he could. "I know this is my fault," I told him. "If I'd handed over Alison..."

But to my surprise, Radimir shook his head and scowled, then nodded to where Alison was watching from across the street. "I don't like cops," he told me, "But I can see how you feel about each other. Handing her over wasn't an option, any more than I could hand over Bronwyn." He glanced between Alison and me, then tugged his waistcoat straight. "But I need you two to stop Grushin before he does any more damage."

I nodded, shocked. Then I locked eyes with Alison, and she gave me a little nod of support. I sucked in a breath, and this time, my lungs actually filled. For the first time, I realized I had someone I trusted to share the load.

But would it be enough?

48

GENNADIY

ALISON WENT TO WORK. FIRST, SHE CALLED HER HACKER FRIEND IN NEW York and asked her to look into the head of the gaming board, to try to figure out the hold Grushin had over him. Then she took over the dining room and started pinning names and photos to the wall, mapping out everything we knew about Grushin. My stomach knotted when I saw Yakov's name there. *How could he do this to me?*

I watched Alison as she tapped away on a laptop, utterly immersed. Only last week, she'd sat in the FBI office looking up at pictures of Valentin and Radimir and *me* on the wall, figuring out *our* network. Now she was working to save us.

She stood, crossed her arms, and stared at the map of names and faces. She began to do that thing where she rose up on her toes like a dancer and then sank back down as she thought, and I watched, hypnotized. Then she darted forward and added another detail. God, she was good at this. It was what she was born to do. But—my chest tightened—I couldn't see any way that could work. Even if we managed to stop Grushin and clear her name, she couldn't go back to the FBI if she was in my bed every night. And I couldn't give up the Bratva any more than I could give up breathing.

Valentin appeared from the shadows, silent as always. "It's eleven. You asked me to come get you."

I nodded. I'd been worried that if he didn't remind me, I'd let the time slip past and then put it off until tomorrow. That's how much I was dreading this.

Valentin put a hand on my shoulder. "I could go on my own," he offered.

I shook my head. "No." My voice was raw with pain. "I need to be there." I pressed my hand to his and turned to look at him. *My baby brother.* The guilt flared, and for a second, it cut through the anger, viciously sharp enough to steal my breath. I thought of Grushin, and the cops, and everything else that made me mad, whipping the anger faster and faster until that vulnerable center was hidden and I could breathe again.

I knew I couldn't go on like this. The guilt got worse every day, which meant the anger had to whirl faster and hotter to block it out. Soon, the rage would destroy me: I'd pick a fight I couldn't win and wind up bleeding out on the floor of some bar. I couldn't take Alison down with me. But I didn't know what else to do. I couldn't deal with the guilt, couldn't even talk about it. I couldn't take that much pain. *What am I going to do?*

I sucked in a deep breath and pushed the feelings down inside. Then I nodded to Alison, and the three of us headed to the car. My problems would have to wait. It was time to confront Yakov.

As we drove, Alison filled us in on what she'd been working on. "I've been trying to find patients who used the clinic. I thought if we could find enough, maybe we could figure out which ones are regular patients and which ones are Grushin's clients. But I could barely find anything." She rubbed her eyes. "The only name I turned up was a guy called Clayton Tuxworth, a tobacco billionaire from North Carolina. There was a story on a gossip site about him visiting the clinic a year ago. His lawyers made the site take it down, but I found it in an archive. He *could* be a client, or he could just be someone with gallstones. No way of knowing. He's, like, seventy, so it fits that he'd have health problems."

I nodded. "Well done." I tried to smile, but I couldn't. Not with what I was about to do.

We pulled up at the docks, but it took me three breaths to summon the strength to climb out of the car. Then I focused on the control center in the distance and just went for it, head down and walking fast, because if I stopped, I was worried I wouldn't start again. At this time of night, the docks were deserted and eerily quiet. We passed under the huge gantry cranes and then between the stacks of brightly-colored shipping containers. "Are you sure he'll still be here, this late?" asked Alison.

"Yakov hasn't left these docks before midnight in all the years I've known him," I told her sadly.

Valentin gave me a sympathetic look. I'd asked him to come along as backup, just in case.

As we reached the control center, I glanced up at the roof, remembering all the times we'd sat up there in lawn chairs. Valentin looked around. "I'll keep watch out here," he told me.

My chest aching, I led Alison into the darkened building, then up the stairs to Yakov's corner office. I slowed as we reached the hallway just outside and drew my gun. I nodded to Alison, who drew hers. For all I knew, Grushin could be in there with Yakov right now, or Yakov could know we were onto him and have a shotgun ready.

I took a deep breath...and opened the door.

Yakov was deep in paperwork, his gold-rimmed glasses perched on the end of his nose. When he saw me, he jerked upright, startled, then gave me a wide smile. "Gennadiy!" He turned to smile at Alison, happy but confused. "What's going on?"

I blinked, stunned. Yakov was many things, but a good liar wasn't one of them. Was it possible that...*he doesn't know?!* The weight on my chest shifted, wanting to lift but not daring to.

Yakov noticed our guns. "Gennadiy? What is this?"

We moved into the office. "Yakov, we found out who tried to kill Alison. It's Viktor Grushin."

I was braced for him to pull out the gun he kept taped under his desk. Instead, he just...crumbled. His head fell forward into his hands, and he suddenly looked every one of his fifty-three years. "B*lyat'*," he moaned. "Oh, God. Gennadiy, I had no idea he was behind all this." He looked at Alison, shaking his head. "I'm sorry."

I felt myself slump in relief. "But why would you work with that piece of shit? After everything he did to the Bratva back in Moscow?"

"I had no choice!" said Yakov. "He came to me six months ago. He blackmailed me."

"With what?"

Yakov shook his head. "He knows things, Gennadiy. Things he should have no way of knowing." He took a deep, shuddering breath. "He knew about my daughter."

I felt myself frown. "You don't have a daughter."

Yakov just looked at me sadly.

"You...*do?*" I said, amazed.

"Fifteen years ago, there was a woman...we weren't together long, but a year later she came back with a baby, *my* baby. She never asked me for a thing, but I gave her money, I wanted her to be happy and safe and well away from"—he waved his hands at our guns—"all of this. She lives in Seattle with her husband. She sends me a picture of our daughter, now and again. I have *no idea* how Grushin knew she existed."

"I do," Alison said quietly. We both turned to look at her. "The baby's in your FBI file. And Grushin has someone inside the FBI."

Yakov cursed. "Grushin told me that if I didn't cooperate, he'd send men to her house and..." He buried his face in his hands. "She's *fourteen!*"

I holstered my gun and put my hand on his shoulder, my voice soft. "It's okay. I would have done the same." I was relieved he hadn't been knowingly betraying us, but the fact that Grushin had been using my best friend, and we'd had no idea, was scary as hell. "What were you doing for him?"

"He wanted the Coast Guard patrol routes for specific dates and times. He must be smuggling something in across the lake." Yakov shook his head. "I'm sorry, I've no idea what."

"What was the next date Grushin asked about?" asked Alison.

"Tomorrow night, midni—"

Yakov jerked, and his chair rocked on its wheels. A red flower bloomed across his white shirt, and, at the same time, the sound of a rifle shot echoed through the docks.

Yakov looked at me, full of regret...and then he died.

49

ALISON

BOTH OF US DIVED TO THE FLOOR. ANOTHER SHOT CAME THROUGH THE window and smacked into the wall behind Yakov's desk, passing right over our heads.

We lay there panting for a moment. My stomach had shrunk down to a cold, hard knot, and my heart was slamming so hard it hurt. I was staring at the little black hole in the wall, my brain playing a loop of what would have happened if I'd dived a half-second slower. I looked at Gennadiy. He was staring at his best friend's body, his breath shaking with emotion.

A third shot came through the glass, this one lower: it bit a chunk from the edge of Yakov's desk. Why was the sniper still firing? We were out of sight, now, safe below the level of the window.

Then it hit me: the sniper was trapping us there, preventing us from getting up. Someone else was on their way to deal with us.

Gennadiy must have realized the same thing at the same time because he glanced at the door. And then he crawled in front of me, shielding my small body with his big one. My heart skittered. *No!*

Footsteps in the hallway. Gennadiy had his gun out and ready, but he was awkwardly crouched, unable to stand up because of the sniper. Whoever was coming would cut him down as soon as the door opened. I had my gun out, too, but I couldn't see past Gennadiy: he was deliberately blocking me. Protecting me, no matter what.

The door opened. Over Gennadiy's shoulder, I glimpsed two men in black ski masks, both with guns raised. My throat closed in fear. I grabbed at Gennadiy, trying to pull him out of the way, but it was too late—

There were two shots, and the men fell to the floor. Valentin walked in from behind them, calm and efficient. "The shooter's dead, too," he told us. "He was up on a crane. I'm sorry I didn't see him before he..." He looked at Yakov's body, his face forlorn.

Gennadiy stood up, then reached down and offered me his hand. I took it, and he effortlessly pulled me up to standing. "You did great, brother," he told Valentin sincerely. Then he turned to Yakov.

As soon as Gennadiy saw the body again, he muttered a curse under his breath. He walked around the desk and stood there looking down at his friend, his broad chest rising and falling in fractured rhythm as the loss hit him. I hurried over to him and stood beside him, then tentatively took his hand in mine. He squeezed it almost painfully hard, but I didn't let go.

I could feel my eyes prickling. I'd only met Yakov a few times, but I'd liked him: a rare, warm soul in this brutally cold world. For Gennadiy, though, the loss was gut-wrenching. I could feel the agony throbbing through his grip. In all those months watching him, I'd seen how he and Yakov felt about each other, the sort of friendship that doesn't allow for ceremony or bullshit, the sort where you're always honest with each other. And I knew what it was like to have someone you loved suddenly torn from you.

Sirens, in the distance. "We'd better go," said Valentin gently.

Gennadiy's jaw was firmly set, but his eyes were shining. "Rest, now," he whispered. He reached down and closed Yakov's eyes. Then he turned and stalked off towards the car.

50

ALISON

BACK AT THE MANSION, THE ARISTOVS AND I GATHERED IN THE DINING room again. I looked at Gennadiy, worried. He'd been silent, driving home. I'd asked a few times if he wanted to talk about Yakov, but he'd shaken his head.

"We don't have to do this right now," I whispered. "You just lost a friend."

Gennadiy frowned and glanced around the table. "We learn to...compartmentalize," he told me. The men all nodded. Bronwyn and I stared at each other, open-mouthed.

"Grushin must be watching us," said Gennadiy. "He must have tailed us from here, figured out we were going to the docks, and sent someone ahead of us."

"I didn't see anyone following us," I mumbled. I thought hard for a moment. "*Shit!*" Everyone looked at me. "It's the FBI," I groaned. "We put GPS trackers on your cars months ago." I looked at Gennadiy. "That's how I always knew where to find you. It's how I knew where the money drop was, even when you thought you'd shaken off your tail." I sighed. "And thanks to Grushin's mole in the FBI, if they know where we are, he does too."

Radimir slammed his fist on the table, making everyone jump. "*Chertovski* FBI!" He glared at me.

Next to me, Gennadiy started to rise in his seat. I grabbed his shoulder. The last thing I wanted was the two of them fighting. "I'm sorry," I told Radimir solemnly. "I should have thought of it sooner." *Then maybe Yakov would still be alive,* I added silently, my stomach twisting in guilt.

Radimir sighed and shook his head. "*I'm* sorry," he said. "It's been...a long day." But I could tell he still didn't fully trust me.

Gennadiy slowly sat back down. "I'll reach out to Yakov's woman in Seattle and...let her know. And I'll make sure she and her daughter are looked after." The others nodded in agreement. Gennadiy's face was a mask of pain: he'd lost his best friend, the casino had been shut down, and Grushin was gunning for him and his family. He hadn't slept in two days, and it was nearly one in the morning. The poor man was broken.

Now that I was still and safe, what happened in Yakov's office was starting to sink in. When Gennadiy pushed in front of me, he'd been ready to *die* for me, without thought, without question.

Something that had been out on the periphery, ever since the strip club, slid into place in my soul and engaged, filling me with a fierce, warm glow. My breath trembled. I felt protected. I hadn't realized it, but I'd been searching for that feeling ever since the foster home, ever since my parents died.

I felt myself frown, determined. *My man* was hurting. And I was going to do whatever it took to help him.

"Putting it all together," said Bronwyn, "what do we know?" She counted off points on her fingers. "Grushin faked his own death and came to the US. He set up some sort of business here in Chicago, something that's making millions every week. He's smuggling something in from Russia to Canada and then across Lake Michigan to Chicago, using the information he blackmailed out of Yakov to avoid the Coast Guard patrols."

"But we don't know what he's smuggling," said Radimir. "It can't be drugs, not unless he's bringing them in by the ton, and we would have noticed that, street prices would have plummeted."

"Guns?" asked Valentin.

"Still wouldn't make that sort of money," said Gennadiy. "Not unless it's top-secret military stuff. We know it's something *bad*. Something the public will demand is stopped if we expose it."

"We only know when one shipment is coming in," said Bronwyn. "Midnight, tomorrow night. That's our only chance to find out what's going on. And we've got no idea where the boat's delivering to. There are, what, twenty, thirty miles of shoreline? How do we find it?"

I could feel the worry from all of them. Grushin was threatening their entire empire, as well as their lives. And the more they worried, the more pressure it piled on Gennadiy. At the heart of all this was whatever illegal operation Grushin was running on the Aristov's territory, and that meant, however much the other Aristovs helped, Gennadiy felt this whole thing was his responsibility. It was too much pressure for one person, especially when he was grieving.

I looked around the room. The Aristovs were all silent, despondent. Out of their depth. Mysteries weren't their world.

They were mine.

I stood up. Five heads turned towards me. "I know how to find it," I told them. "We'll stop Grushin the same way I was going to stop you. Police work." Then I looked at Gennadiy. "I'll start first thing. But right now...it's time to sleep."

The words didn't sound right, coming out of my mouth. *Me?* Put something off until *tomorrow?*

But for the first time, there was something more important than solving the mystery. I had someone to take care of.

I took Gennadiy's hand and stepped back from the table. He stared at me, then looked at his family, then back to me. His eyes flared with frustration. "You sleep. I need to work."

He turned away from me, and my stomach lurched. *Am I doing the wrong thing?* I didn't want to embarrass him in front of his *Pakhan*. But then I saw Bronwyn giving me a big, approving nod, and I tugged his hand. "No. Gennadiy Aristov, you need to *sleep*."

He turned to me again, and this time his eyes went wide in shock, and just a bit of arrogant horror. *How dare she?* He glared, just like he had so many times when we were enemies...and I glared right back at him.

He softened...and melted. Just like I'd seen Radimir do with Bronwyn. He rose from the table and allowed me to tow him out of the room.

"What are you...where are we *going?*" he muttered in the hallway, cranky and confused and resigned, all at the same time.

"To the kitchen," I told him, and marched in there. I opened the pantry and rooted around for the bottle I'd seen in there, keeping hold of him with my other hand to make sure he didn't escape. "Okay! Now upstairs!"

He sighed, staring down at me. I was comically small, next to him, and I knew I couldn't drag him if he decided to stay put. But I lifted my chin, defiant...and he nodded and fell into step beside me.

I led him up to the top floor, to his bedroom. I turned on just a single light by the bed, so the room was mostly shadow. Without words, I pushed his suit jacket off his shoulders and began unbuttoning his shirt. His breathing became husky. When he was topless, I knelt in front of him and helped him slip off his shoes and socks, then unbuckled his belt. I heard him inhale tightly, and I saw his cock twitch through his pants. I shoved them down, along with his boxers, and now he growled.

I looked up at him. "Don't get excited," I said dryly. "That isn't what I've got in mind."

He frowned down at me, his cock half hard and rising. But I stood and pushed at him, guiding him into his bathroom and then into the walk-in shower. I turned on the spray and pushed him in. Then I stripped off my own clothes and followed him. When he realized I was naked, too, he tried to grab me, but I slipped out of his hands and started washing him, instead, slicking my hands over his shoulders, his back, his chest, working my way down his body. His cock rose more every time my body brushed against his, but eventually I got him to stand still and be tended to. When I turned off the water, he looked…maybe five percent more relaxed than he had been. *Well, it's a start.*

"Why are you doing this?" he asked me as I toweled him dry.

"Because you're under unbelievable pressure, you just lost a friend, and you haven't slept in two days. Because I know what it's like to think you can solve everything by working harder. Sometimes you need someone to tell you to stop."

"You know this because you had someone like that?"

"No," I said. "Because I didn't."

He looked down at me and scowled, and I felt his protective anger lift me like a wave. I nearly melted right there, but I had a job to do. I pointed. "Lie down on the bed, on your front."

He reluctantly lay down. I pulled on a bathrobe so I didn't keep distracting him with my nakedness, grabbed the bottle of almond oil I'd taken from the kitchen, and climbed onto the bed next to him. I was used to him towering over me when we were standing up, but he wasn't any smaller lying down. As I shuffled over and straddled him, I felt like a bird hopping around on the back of a rhino. My eyes roved over the contours of his back, with its twisting, dark tattoos, then down over the ass I'd admired so many times as I'd followed him around, hard and loaded with power. Lower down, on his right calf, I saw something I hadn't noticed before, a raised scar, maybe from a bullet. *So* that's *why he favors his other leg.*

I put my hands on his shoulders and then poured a little almond oil over the back of my hand: a little trick to help heat the oil before it touched his skin. I smoothed the oil over the globes of his shoulders until they shone, then started massaging him. He cocked his head curiously, then closed his eyes.

His muscles were like tire rubber, barely giving at all. I went to work, pressing my thumbs deep as I pulled with my fingers, kneading him like dough. As I dug deeper, I started to find the knots and work each one free. The room went quiet except for our breathing. He'd tense under me, then grunt as I bore down on the knot, then sigh as the hard fibers melted to taffy. "*Blyat'. Ty obuchen koldovstvu, zhenshchina.*" he muttered at last.

"What does that mean?"

"*You're schooled in witchcraft, woman.*"

I continued all the way down his back, helping work the tension out of him. "Now roll over on your back," I told him.

He rolled over, and I started on the fronts of his shoulders. Now we were staring into each other's eyes, and it was intimate...but not sexual, even if his eyes did keep dropping to the neck of my robe. This was about helping him, healing him. I moved down to his pecs, smoothing my hands over the wide slabs of his muscles and working the tension loose. I could feel his body changing, like a coiled spring slowly unwinding. His breathing slowed and eased, becoming deeper and more regular. He was relaxing, letting go. And then I started to hear a hitch in his breathing, a judder where there'd been smoothness. Things were coming to the surface.

I kept going, kneading the big knots and then the small knots and then the tiny ones, breaking down the walls all his tension had put up. And then...

"Yakov always remembered my birthday," he said. "Even though I never remembered his. He bought me these dumb fucking gifts. A hat that holds beer cans. A backscratcher."

I didn't say anything, just kept going. My job was just to help him get it out.

"Before I opened the casino, I had to do research." His voice was rough with pain. "Yakov and I took a car, and we drove all the way to Vegas. Three days in a car with him, and then back again! And a week of getting drunk every night and losing all our money. I fell in the pool and ruined my suit." He paused. "Best week of my life."

I was just smoothing my hands over him, now, calming him as the enormity of the loss hit him.

"He was always pleased to see me, you know?" Gennadiy whispered. "He was always—"

He closed his eyes, and I threw my arms around his neck and pressed myself close. I held him like that for a long time, his head on my shoulder.

"Thank you," he managed.

I nodded. I knew it wasn't over: he'd be grieving for a long time. But at least I'd helped him start.

Even now, though, I could feel that he hadn't let go all the way. Touching him like this, I felt so close to him, so entirely in tune with him, that I could feel the anger, rushing like a river, just under the surface.

I knew what it was like to feel that non-stop. To have it driving you, demanding that you keep working, keep pushing. The difference was, I'd found something to stop mine: *him.* I hadn't been aware of it until now, but my anger had dropped away when I'd felt the warmth of his protection. I'd been angry at the world for taking my parents and leaving me alone, but I wasn't alone anymore. Gennadiy's anger was still there, and still building every day. "Why do you carry all this...rage?" I whispered.

Any other time, I think he would have pushed the question away or changed the subject. But right then, with us staring at each other in that safe, silent room, it was impossible to lie. "Because it protects me from something worse," he said softly.

I stared down into his eyes, feeling my heart cracking. He *wanted* to tell me. He just couldn't.

I lay down, putting my head on his chest, and cuddled in beside him. I could already hear his breathing changing. He would sleep, now, and that was good.

But—my stomach knotted—unless he let me help him, I wasn't sure I could save him.

51

ALISON

EARLY THE NEXT MORNING, WHILE THE REST OF THE MANSION SLEPT, I left Gennadiy slumbering peacefully and went to work. I found a map of the lake and started narrowing down where Grushin could bring his merchandise ashore: somewhere out of the way enough that it wouldn't be seen, but not *so* out of the way that trucks and deliveries would stand out. It took me back to my early days in the FBI, in New York, when Calahan had first taught me this stuff. *I wish you were here now, Sam.*

The house's staff gradually appeared and seemed a little thrown that someone was up before them. They were followed by Mikhail, who was up early to walk the dogs. "I hope I didn't overstep last night," I said. "Taking Gennadiy away from his *Pakhan.*"

Mikhail shook his head, grinning. "Radimir respects strength. And he knows you were doing it because you care about his brother. You may be the only person who can order Gennadiy Aristov to bed...and that, I think, is why you may be perfect for him."

I flushed and looked down at my work, but I was smiling.

Mikhail's dogs circled him impatiently, doing their best to tangle their leashes. "All of this," Mikhail said, indicating the map. "Can you solve it?"

I sighed. "It would help a lot if I still had all the FBI's resources. What I really need is to get into City Hall's records to find out who owns what, but I can't exactly summon up a court order."

Mikhail nodded thoughtfully. "I have an idea. I will see you in an hour." And he led his dogs away, yapping and yowling excitedly.

I hadn't planned to stop for breakfast, but the chef looked so offended when he realized I'd been up for two hours and hadn't eaten that I agreed to freshly-made waffles with crispy bacon and maple syrup, together with a big mug of coffee. He kept returning to refill the mug, too, so by the time Gennadiy came downstairs, I was wired.

Gennadiy came up behind me and practically lifted me out of my chair, rotating me in his arms and pulling me into a long kiss that started gentle and grateful and ended urgent and hungry. I had to come up for air before he pulled my clothes off in front of the chef. "*Later,*" I whispered. Then, "How are you feeling?"

"Better," he said. There was a longing in his eyes. God, it was heartbreaking...he *wanted* to take that final step, to unburden himself and let the anger go, but he couldn't. *What could be worse than always being angry?*

He looked at the map I had spread out, and I explained how I'd identified six areas along the waterfront Grushin could be using. "That gave ninety-seven properties. I've eliminated seventy-one. That leaves twenty-six possibilities."

Gennadiy shook his head in admiration. "This is how you catch the bad guys."

I shrugged, embarrassed but proud. "Ninety-nine percent of police work is knocking on doors and shuffling papers...but it's what gets things done." I yawned and stretched, which I noticed made his eyes flick straight to my chest. "But it's not going to do us any good unless we can figure out which one of these properties Grushin owns."

At that moment, Mikhail walked in with Valentin...and gestured to him, like, *Ta da!*

I blinked. "Your idea is Valentin?" I looked at my mug. "I'm sorry, I must need more coffee. I don't get it."

Mikhail perched on the edge of the table and grinned that infectious grin. "Men like Valentin must have a special talent. The ability to sneak in and out of places unobserved."

"Mikhail said something about City Hall?" said Valentin helpfully.

Oh crap. That was the idea? Trespass and burglary? And when we found the place, presumably we'd be doing some breaking and entering of our own, to go along with the hacking of Grushin's phone records. Not to mention the assassin Gennadiy shot in cold blood, the three men Valentin killed last night, and my own illegal search of Grushin's bank account. What really worried me wasn't even the number of laws we were breaking: it was how normal it was starting to feel. But what else could I do? I didn't have the FBI to lean on anymore. I sighed. *"Please don't hurt anyone,"* I stressed, and told him which records I needed.

Just two hours later, he was back. To my relief, he hadn't had to use violence, just an open skylight, a phone call to draw a clerk away from her desk, and a fire alarm to cover his exit. I took the wad of files and started working through them, but Gennadiy shook his head. "I want to help," he said seriously. "Teach me."

So I did, showing him how to use the information in the files to trace the real owners, even when they hid behind a string of holding companies. He picked it up fast, but sometimes, when I demonstrated a technique, he'd frown. "What is it?" I asked at last.

He shook his head. "Just another thing I need to update," he said breezily.

I froze as it hit me: I was teaching him exactly how not to get caught. My stomach flipped. *Which side am I on, here? 'Ours?'* To his credit, when I got stuck, he helped me, too, explaining a few secret criminal techniques I'd never come across. We worked well together.

It took us the entire day, but just before ten in the evening, we finally found it. An old warehouse that was owned, through a series of shell companies, by Grushin's fake Polish identity.

"Grushin's boat will arrive there in two hours," said Gennadiy. "Let's go find out what he's smuggling."

52

GENNADIY

AFTER THE DOCKS, WE WEREN'T TAKING ANY CHANCES: WE TOOK FOUR of my men with us, along with Valentin. The cars we used were freshly stolen, so we knew the FBI wasn't GPS-tracking them. Grushin wouldn't know we were coming.

We arrived a little after eleven and parked down the street, then crept closer on foot. It was overcast, so there was no moonlight, and no wind, so Lake Michigan was millpond-smooth.

We found the warehouse easily enough, a shabby concrete block right on the water's edge with a rusting metal roof. The place was completely quiet, not even a guard. Maybe they never left anything of value there.

We settled down to wait. I'd brought binoculars and Alison and I passed them between us, searching for boats that might be heading for the warehouse. But there was almost nothing moving on the lake.

Then, at 11:45pm, Alison nudged me. "There!"

She passed me the binoculars, and I followed her pointing finger. A boat was heading straight down the lake, towards the warehouse. I tensed, ready...then, as it came closer, I sighed and shook my head. "It's a Coast Guard patrol," I told her. The Coast Guard boat veered off a few minutes later and followed the shoreline. It was nearly midnight, and there were no other boats even in sight. "We should stay, just in case," said Alison. "Maybe they'll show up late. Unless Grushin changed the date."

I looked at the warehouse. "We might as well take a look inside." With the lake so calm, it was easy to spot boats moving. Valentin could give us at least a half hour's warning if anything showed up.

Alison nodded. We crept over to the warehouse's side door, and Valentin picked the lock. We agreed he'd wait with my men and call us if a boat looked like it was heading our way.

Inside, the warehouse was pitch black. We didn't want to risk switching on any lights in case anyone did show up, so we had to use the flashlights on our phones. Picking our way through the place in the dark, side by side, with our flashlights sweeping around was nerve-wracking and also, weirdly...*fun.* Like we were some detective couple in a TV show, creeping around some derelict house trying to solve a murder. I glanced sideways at her. She'd put her hair up into the tight little bun that drove me crazy, and my flashlight's glare revealed little glimpses of her ass in those skintight black jeans, her perky little breasts pushing out her sweater...and that grimly determined frown. My FBI agent, who'd crack the case no matter what.

It wasn't a fun place to be. But there was no one in the world I'd rather be there with. Working with her, *being* with her, felt right, like I'd found the missing half of me. Yes, the Bratva was corrupting her, just as I'd feared, but, somehow, she was managing to keep her moral core. Maybe she could be my conscience, my balance. And yes, our world was dangerous...but with all her training, she could handle the danger better than any woman I'd ever known. She was the perfect partner for me.

And then reality kicked in. I couldn't be with her. I couldn't *stop,* and *live* like a regular person. I had to keep pushing and pushing until it killed me, because if I let the anger fade...the guilt would consume me.

We picked our way across a big concrete loading area, nearly tripping over coils of chain. Then we came to a railing, beyond which the floor was covered in what looked like black, shiny plastic. For a moment, I thought we were looking at a wall-to-wall store of plastic-wrapped drugs.

Then the floor moved, just a little. We both shone our flashlights directly on it and—

It was *the lake*. The whole back half of the warehouse was built over the lake, and we were looking straight down into the water. That meant a boat could be sailed right in here and unload out of the rain...and out of sight. There were some stairs that led right down to the water and two catwalks made of metal mesh for people to stand on while unloading.

At that moment, my phone rang. I grabbed it. Valentin. "What's up?" I asked. "A boat?" I looked out at the lake, but there was still nothing in sight.

"No, Grushin's men!" Valentin told me. "They just pulled up, two cars and a van!"

That made no sense. If they were here to meet the shipment, where was the boat? "Okay, we're on our way out," I told him.

"No! They're coming to the side door! They'll see you! Should we rush them?"

Fuck. I didn't want to get into a shootout if I could help it. Even if we won, and even if Alison came out unharmed, we *still* wouldn't know what Grushin was doing here. "No," I said quickly. "We'll hide. There's no boat coming; they must be here for something else. We'll wait until they go."

I looked around. There wasn't anything to hide behind in the concrete loading area; it was just a big, open space. But downstairs, next to the water: they wouldn't need to go down there. I grabbed Alison's hand and hurried down the steps. Then I pushed her under the staircase. There wasn't room for two of us to squeeze in, so I ran to the matching staircase on the other side of the warehouse and ducked under it.

I heard the side door open and, a second later, the lights flickered on. Now there really *was* nowhere to hide. But as long as they didn't come down here... We exchanged nervous glances from across the warehouse and tried not to make a sound.

And then something weird happened. The black water in front of us started to bulge upwards in the middle, like the lake had become solid. I stared...and then, as the water started to splash around the edges, my perception shifted. Something black and curved was rising up out of the lake.

We'd got it wrong. The boat had shown up right on time. We just hadn't been able to see it because it had been slipping silently under the water. Grushin was using a submarine.

Footsteps from above. The shipment had arrived...and Grushin's men were coming down here to unload it.

53

ALISON

THERE WAS NO TIME TO CALL VALENTIN. THERE WAS NO TIME TO DO *anything*. Any second, Grushin's men were going to start down the stairs and see us. There was only one place to hide.

I scrambled out from under the staircase and dived into the lake, fully clothed. Across the warehouse. I saw Gennadiy do the same. At least it was early September and the water wasn't too cold.

I swam under the catwalk, where the shadows would hide me as long as I kept still, and started treading water. The first of Grushin's men clattered down the metal staircase, then another and another. They gathered on the catwalk, right above my face. Apparently, my side of the warehouse was the unloading side. *Great.*

Now that the lights were on, I could see the shape of the submarine. It wasn't some huge thing, like the nuclear submarines navies use. It was only about the size of a small truck. And it didn't look like something a navy would build, either: there were dents where some of the metal panels had been hammered into place, and exposed pipes secured by cable ties. This was homemade and barely hanging together: it probably needed repairs after every trip.

One of the companies Grushin had been calling did welding. *That's* what that was for.

I'd heard of drug smugglers building their own submarines and using them to get their product into the US, but I'd never thought someone might use one to smuggle across Lake Michigan. The Coast Guard boat we'd seen made sense, now. Grushin hadn't wanted their patrol routes from Yakov so he could avoid the Coast Guard, it was so the submarine could sail right behind them, in their sonar blind spot.

The men above me were laughing and joking in Russian while they waited for the people on board to unseal the hatch. They weren't in any hurry...but I was already starting to get tired. There was only about an inch of air between the surface of the water and the underside of the catwalk, so I couldn't tread water normally. I had to arch my back and half-lie so that my lips stayed above water, and that made it very hard to kick downwards and stay afloat. If I could have grabbed the edge of the catwalk and clung on, I would have been okay, but I didn't dare: if one of the men glanced down and saw my fingers, we were dead. Worst of all, the submarine had churned the water up, and every few seconds, a wave would fill the gap beneath the catwalk and swamp me completely, cutting off my air. I was already getting tired.

That's when I had a horrible realization: no one was coming to rescue us. Gennadiy had told Valentin to stay put. They wouldn't have been able to see the submarine arrive. They had no idea we were in trouble.

To take my mind off the tiredness, I focused on what was going on. A hatch had opened in the top of the submarine, and a bearded man threw ropes to men on the catwalk to hold the thing in place. He gingerly climbed out, down a ladder, and across a makeshift gangplank to the catwalk. *The cargo will be next...*

But then a woman in her twenties appeared, looking around fearfully. As she climbed down the ladder, another woman emerged from the hatch. *Jesus, it's sex trafficking.* Grushin was selling Russian women to American men.

Then a boy emerged, no older than ten. *What?* And then a man in his thirties. *What the hell is going on?*

I was getting seriously tired, now, my thighs burning from

keeping me afloat. Every time a wave broke over my face, my body went into panic mode, and I had to force myself not to scramble out from under the catwalk to breathe. *Just a few more minutes. That must be almost all of them.*

But the people kept coming. Mostly men, but some women and a few children. Nine of them in all. Nine people, plus the pilot, plus a couple of men with guns who came out last. The submarine wasn't big: they must have been packed in like cattle. I tried to imagine being stuck in the windowless metal tube for the hours it must have taken to cross from Canada, knowing that a single leak or fault in the homemade engineering would send you straight to the bottom of the lake...and that no one would even know to look for you. I shuddered.

I was praying that once all the people were out, everyone would leave. But apparently, there was a whole procedure for shutting down the submarine and making it safe, and the men weren't in any hurry. I started to really panic: my muscles were cramping, and my legs felt like lead. I looked across the warehouse to see how Gennadiy was doing. He looked to be suffering, too, but at least on his side, without any men around, he could wrap his fingers around the edge of the catwalk to rest his legs occasionally. His eyes were locked on me, willing me to keep going.

And I did, while the pilot climbed back aboard and vented gas and closed valves and then scribbled notes on a notepad. But then my left leg really started to cramp and—*come on, come on*—now the pilot was fixing the rubber seal on the edge of the hatch—*come on, please!* —and then another wave hit me in the face, and I needed so badly to cough, but I didn't dare, and my lungs were burning—

My muscles cramped again, and this time, I sank. As the catwalk moved away from me, I panicked and clawed my way upward, swimming with one leg. I managed to get a gulp of air, but after a few seconds, the adrenaline rush faded, and my limbs felt as heavy as lead. The men were finally leaving. *Just another minute!* But then a wave came out of nowhere and went up my nose, and I was choking on lake water—

I sank again. This time, when I clawed, my muscles didn't have enough energy to get me to the surface. For a moment, I hung in place, thrashing but not moving, using up what air I had left. Then everything went black, and I was sinking down and down and down.

54

GENNADIY

I COULD SEE HER WEAKENING, SEE THE WAVES MERCILESSLY SMACKING her in the face, but I couldn't do anything to help. If I swam out from under my catwalk, the men would see me and kill us both. I had to hang there, watching the strength fade from her, and it was agony.

It took me straight back to another time, two decades ago, when I'd had to stand and watch helplessly, and the guilt burned even through the anger, searing my soul from the inside out.

She sank, and my heart almost stopped. Then she recovered, and I breathed again. My eyes were darting non-stop between Alison and the men: they were packing up, getting ready to go...

She started to sink again.

The last of the men turned away, and before he'd even reached the stairs, I'd let go of the catwalk and pushed off hard, swimming as fast as I could for the other side of the warehouse. With the submarine in the way, I couldn't go straight across: I had to curve around it. My legs were already aching from treading water, but I ignored the pain and kicked, wishing I didn't have my suit flapping around me.

I reached the back of the submarine and turned, heading straight for Alison's catwalk. *Where is she?* She must have slipped under the surface—

The lights went out.

I froze for a second. I hadn't thought of that: of course, when the men left, they'd turn the lights off. And with no moonlight, it wasn't just dark, it was *black. Blyat'!* I started swimming again. All I could do was keep going and hope I was still heading in the right direction. *Where is it? I should be there by now...*

My hand whacked into the metal catwalk, hard enough that any other time I'd have yelled. But I was too busy feeling along it, sweeping my arms underneath to find her, *frantic.* "Alison! *Alison!*"

My hands clawed at nothing. She wasn't there.

I took a lungful of air and dived, going straight down from the catwalk, arms sweeping around me, praying for a touch of her hair, a brush of fabric, anything.

Nothing. I dived deeper, hysterical. *I've lost her. Oh, Jesus, she's gone.*

And then my fingers dug into muddy grit. I'd reached the bottom. *No, no, no, please—*

Something bumped my leg, I twisted around, and grabbed at it. Fingers. A hand. I squeezed.

It didn't squeeze back.

I pulled the body to me, and it was her; I could feel the bun at the back of her head. I kicked for the surface with her hanging limp in my arms.

I surfaced next to the submarine, nowhere near where I needed to be, and had to grope my way back to the catwalk in the darkness, then claw my way up onto it one-handed while hanging onto Alison, then finally haul her out of the water. She still wasn't moving. I tilted her head back, pinched her nose and put my lips on hers, then blew into her mouth. It was so dark that I couldn't even see if her chest was rising. I had to feel for it. *Yes, it's moving.*

Five breaths and she still wasn't responding. I felt for her breastbone and started chest compressions, like Mikhail taught us when we were kids. *Twenty-eight, twenty-nine, thirty.* Still nothing. I could feel tears wetting my cheeks. *Come back to me. Please.*

I straddled her and went back to chest compressions. *One. Two. Three. Four.* She lay there, silent and still and terrifyingly cold under my hands.

It started to creep in, then: the reality that I'd lost her. And it wasn't like the loss of my parents, or even the loss of Yakov. It was like someone was tearing out a part of my soul. She'd become a part of me, and me a part of her. We needed to be together.

Fifteen. Sixteen. Seventeen. Eighteen. She didn't move.

I felt her slip away from me, and as the pain hit, I suddenly knew how wrong I'd been. I'd had her, I'd had a shot at a future with her, and I'd been ready to let her go, just so I could hang onto my anger, just so I didn't have to face the guilt and pain. *You stupid fucking bastard, Gennadiy.* No pain could be worse than this.

Twenty-two. Twenty-three. Twenty-four. Twenty-five. Give me another chance, please!

Twenty-seven. Twenty-eight. Twenty-nine. Thirty.

I put my lips on hers and breathed—

Her body spasmed, and she choked. I rolled her onto her side and heard her coughing up lake water.

"Are you okay?!" I blurted into the blackness.

She coughed and rasped, unable to speak. But she found my arm in the dark and patted it. *She's okay!*

The lights flickered on. I looked up, blinking in the sudden light, and pointed my dripping-wet gun at the loading dock—

Valentin's head appeared over the edge. His eyes widened when he saw the two of us, and he scrambled down the stairs to help.

I looked down, and now I could see Alison, soaking wet and bedraggled but *alive* and as the relief swept through me, I grabbed her and crushed her to my chest.

Valentin drove us to the ER, where the doctors checked Alison over and monitored her for four hours. They finally decided she was okay to go home, as long as she was watched closely.

That wasn't a problem because I was never taking my eyes off her again. I hadn't let go of her hand since we left the warehouse. And as soon as we got somewhere private, I was going to finally tell her the truth about the anger...and what lay beneath it.

55

ALISON

WHEN WE ARRIVED BACK AT THE MANSION, IT WAS ALMOST FIVE IN THE morning. I was wet-haired, wrapped in a blanket, and smelled of lake water, and all I wanted to do was collapse. But Mikhail ushered us towards the dining room. *Really? A war council, now? Can't it wait until morning?* And Gennadiy seemed to agree: he wouldn't let go of my hand and kept glancing towards the hallway and the stairs, as if he really needed to get me alone.

Mikhail circled the table, pouring a vodka for each of his nephews in turn and clapping them on the shoulder. It was obvious his family meant the world to him. *But why doesn't he have a wife or children of his own,* I wondered. His dogs went with him in a kind of furry entourage, surrounding each nephew with woofing affection, paws on shoulders, and furry heads butting up for head scratches.

Mikhail poured vodka for Gennadiy. For Valentin. Then for Radimir, who was sitting there holding hands with Bronwyn while he spoke to her in a low voice. She seemed to be flipping between flushing at whatever he was saying to her, and throwing worried looks at Gennadiy, Valentin, and me, maybe wondering *what if it had been Radimir* who nearly died tonight? Mikhail started to pour a shot for her, but she shook her head.

I thought Mikhail was done, but then he circled around the table, put a glass in front of me, and poured a shot into it. I looked around in shock. Radimir looked up at the wall, at the notes and phone records, and map, all the work I'd done to find Grushin. And then he looked at *me,* pale and half-drowned...and nodded somberly. The others were nodding, too.

They trusted me. Accepted me. I felt myself choking up.

They all raised their glasses, and I slowly raised mine, too.

"Welcome to the family," said Radimir.

I felt my eyes prickling and quickly knocked back the shot to cover myself. I expected it to burn, but it was smooth, like liquid ice with a flame frozen inside. Apparently, I'd never had the good stuff. Then Mikhail's dogs surrounded me, and any tears were hidden by a rush of furry heads butting my legs, wet noses in my hands, and tongues licking my cheeks.

When I'd given out an amount of head scratches and ruffles the dogs deemed sufficient, and they'd padded back to Mikhail, I explained what I'd seen at the warehouse. "Grushin isn't smuggling goods, he's smuggling *people.*" I hesitated. "I thought it was sex trafficking, but...there were men. And a child. I don't get it. It can't be for labor, the money doesn't come close to adding up."

Radimir nodded. "Life is cheap. A person is worth thousands, maybe tens of thousands. Not millions."

"Ransom?" asked Bronwyn. "Could they be hostages?"

I thought back to the people I'd seen. "Going by their clothes, they didn't look like they were from rich families. Even if they were, why would he be moving them from Russia to the US?" I sighed. "I asked my hacker friend to check the head of the gaming board's bank account. She didn't find any bribes. In fact, he could have done with a bribe; his wife's hospital bills had almost cleared him out."

"Maybe Grushin blackmailed him," said Radimir.

Mikhail snorted. "I told you, the man's a Boy Scout. He doesn't have any dirty secrets."

"Maybe Grushin threatened his family, then, like he did with Yakov," I said. But it didn't sound right. It was one thing to threaten a gangster, who couldn't go to the police. This guy was a respectable, high-up official. I looked at the web of information on the wall, feeling the case pulling me in. "There's something we're missing," I muttered.

"And it can wait until morning," said Gennadiy. "You need to sleep." And he stood up.

I started to argue and then caught myself. He was right. And he was—I melted inside—he was *looking after me,* just as I'd looked after him. I nodded goodbye to everyone and let him lead me up the stairs to his bedroom. He took my hands in his and turned me to face him. There was a look on his face I'd never seen before. *What's going on?*

He squeezed my hands, struggling to find the words. "I am...*violently* in love with you. Even when we were enemies, all I could think about was having you. Now I can't imagine a life without you in it."

The words, carved into weighty, silken ice by his accent, resonated through me. The fragile, silvery filigree that had been growing inside me for months vibrated and sang. I tried to answer, but I didn't have the words, and I wouldn't have been able to get them past the lump in my throat anyway. I just nodded hard.

"I'm..." He gave a long sigh, and when he spoke, I don't think I'd ever heard him sound more Russian. "I am not used to *this.*" He gestured between us. "And even less used to *talking.* But..." He took a deep breath. "I want to tell you why I'm angry. Why I can't stop. Because I've realized there's only one thing that scares me more than facing this, and that's losing you."

I nodded and guided him to the bed. He sat on the edge, and I knelt behind him, my arms around him as I listened.

He told me what happened when they were kids, when Radimir was fifteen, Gennadiy fourteen, and Valentin twelve. How their father, a good man, had tried to expose corruption in the Russian government, and one of his co-workers, a man called Olenev, had stabbed him to death to silence him. And then he'd framed the three brothers for their father's murder, and with the help of a corrupt prosecutor, had them sent to a brutal borstal in Vladivostok. All three of them were tortured, starved, and beaten by the staff for three years.

I got it, then. Why the Aristovs hated the justice system so much, why they'd chosen to live outside it. No wonder Gennadiy had hated me...just as I'd hated gangsters.

"When our mother tried to visit us," Gennadiy said, his voice shaking, "the warden raped her. When she was dying of cancer, we weren't even allowed to say goodbye."

I remembered the two of us holding each other beside Master Sun's grave, and I pressed myself to him, hugging him tight. "That's terrible," I told him.

He nodded stiffly. "But it wasn't the worst thing that happened to us."

He turned his head to look at me, our faces only a few inches apart. We were close enough that he could speak in a murmur, and I think that was the only reason he could get the words out. But we were so close, I could see every bit of pain in those pale gray eyes, and it was absolutely heartbreaking.

"It wasn't just the guards," he told me. "The other kids were all violent offenders. There was one, called Svetoslav, eighteen, a big tattooed piece of shit, who hated me as soon as he met me. He tried to break me from the very first day. He didn't just want to hurt me; he wanted me to crawl to him. But I wouldn't give in. Our father—" His voice cracked. "Our father always told us that if you lose your dignity, you have nothing. So I wouldn't give in, even when he beat me almost to death. So, after a few months, Svetoslav found another way."

He swallowed. "They came for me after lights out. Dragged me to someone's cell. I thought they were going to kill me." He closed his eyes for a second. "I wish...I wish they *had* killed me. But they locked me in there, alone. Then Svetoslav struts around the corner and I assume he's there to beat me. I stand tall. And then I see he's dragging Valentin."

I could hear Gennadiy's breathing speeding up as decades-old panic resurfaced. "I start trying to talk to Svetoslav. Telling him that it's okay, I'll bow down to him, to not take it out on Valentin. But he just ignores me. He drags Valentin into the cell next to mine. I can see them through the bars, but I can't reach them. Valentin's trying to fight; he's being brave, but he's only twelve. I start *pleading* with Svetoslav not to beat him, saying he's just a kid, but he ignores me again."

Gennadiy stopped. Closed his eyes again. The room went silent.

"And then," Gennadiy said, his voice like a wire drawn too tight, "Svetoslav starts pulling Valentin's clothes off."

I felt my stomach drop through the floor.

"I scream *no,*" said Gennadiy. "I keep screaming it and screaming it, until my throat is raw. But Svetoslav doesn't stop. I promise to do anything he wants. I tell him I'll bow down to him, I'll be his fucking slave. I say...I say do it to *me,* instead. But Svetoslav isn't interested anymore. He wants me to see what happens when I defy him. He wants me to be an example to all the other kids: don't be proud, or this will happen to someone you care about."

Gennadiy's face had gone pale, and his eyes were distant. He was *there.* I tightened my arms around him, rubbed him gently, trying to anchor him here, in the present.

"Valentin's screaming," said Gennadiy. "Screaming in pain and... screaming for me to help him. And I'm standing pressed against the bars, reaching into their cell, fucking clawing for Svetoslav, but I can't reach. I can't help him. I can't help my baby brother."

He wasn't crying. I think he was too focused on struggling through the story to cry. I was crying for both of us, silent tears coursing down my cheeks.

"I killed him," said Gennadiy. "A week later, I got Svetoslav alone in the showers, and I broke his fucking neck. But it didn't change anything." He met my eyes, and the pain in his face was beyond anything I'd ever seen. "I let it happen, Alison. I let it happen to my baby brother. I was six feet away, and I couldn't stop it."

He hiccoughed and sniffed, and now the tears did come, flooding his eyes and spilling over, and I clutched him tight. "It wasn't your fault," I told him gently. "It wasn't."

I kept holding him, and after a while, I felt his body ease a little.

But when he drew back so that he could look at me, the pain in his eyes was still there. "I've told myself that so many times. But it doesn't help."

I nodded slowly. "Maybe what you need is to talk about it with Valentin."

Gennadiy's eyes went wide with horror. Then he shook his head fiercely.

"It might help, even though it's been a long time. What did he say when it happened?" I asked.

Gennadiy looked away.

I frowned. "You didn't talk about it?" Then, with dawning horror, "You've *never* talked about it?!"

Gennadiy scowled. "We don't talk about things like that."

I wasn't sure if he meant *men* or *Russians,* or *Bratva.* Probably all three. "Gennadiy..." I took his face between my hands. "Listen to me. You have to." He tried to look away, but I wouldn't let him. "This has been eating you up since you were a teenager, and probably eating him up, too!"

He tore out of my hands and marched away across the room. I watched his muscled back rise and fall as he fumed. He shook his head, trying to deny it. Eventually, he turned back to me. "I never thought I'd trust a cop," he muttered. "But I trust you." He rubbed at his stubble. "This is really what I need to do?"

"Yes," I said firmly.

He blew out a long breath. And nodded. Then he came back to the bed and pulled me into his arms. We were both exhausted, and as soon as he lay back on the bed and his chest became my pillow, I felt sleep descending like a blanket made of lead. As we drifted off, he stroked my hair. I glanced up at him, and I could see him frowning, thinking.

I hadn't freed him of the guilt, not yet. But for the first time, he had a plan.

56

ALISON

I woke to daylight and a space in the bed where Gennadiy should have been. For a second, I panicked. Then I saw the note on the pillow.

Wait here. I will return with breakfast.
G.

I grabbed a quick shower and then climbed back into the bed naked. I felt comically small in the immense four-poster but it was divinely comfortable, with my back against a wall of thick pillows I figured were probably goose down and my bare feet unable to stop stroking the decadently smooth sheets.

The door swung wide and Gennadiy entered, in just a pair of boxers and carrying a tray. There were plates heaped high with waffles and three sorts of fresh berries, and individual jugs of maple syrup. There was a pot of coffee, cups and saucers, sugar and milk and cream, cutlery and napkins held by silver napkin rings. I had an image of Gennadiy asking the chef if he could do breakfast in bed, and the chef taking it as a challenge. "What is all this?" I asked, as Gennadiy set the tray down on the bed.

"You drowned," he said seriously. "You deserve a little luxury." He sat down on the bed and poured me a cup of coffee, then added two lumps of sugar.

I stared at him. "How did you know—"

"You forget, all the time you were watching *me,* I was watching *you.* Do you know how many times I've watched you sitting outside my house drinking takeout coffee?" He passed me the cup. "And... this is thank you. For last night."

I sipped and nodded. *You're welcome.*

"And..." He looked at me thoughtfully. "Our first time was up against the wall, in the rain. A woman like you deserves to be fucked in a proper bed on Egyptian cotton sheets."

I narrowly avoided spitting coffee all over those Egyptian cotton sheets, which made him grin. My heart fucking *took off,* seeing him so light and happy. I knew I hadn't fixed things, not yet. But I was getting a glimpse of how things could be if he did manage to let go of the anger, and it was glorious. I reached for one of the plates of waffles.

"No no," he told me. And poured maple syrup over it, then cut off a perfect, bite-sized chunk of waffle and berries and...

"Oh, no, you don't have to—*mmf."*

He wagged the fork at me knowledgeably. "A wise woman once told me: we all need someone to tell us to stop, once in a while."

I swallowed. "I don't recall anything in there about being hand-fed."

"She was wise, not perfect."

I snaked my hand down and tickled his side. He jerked, wide-eyed, like no one had ever tickled him before. "Martial arts," I teased. "I know all the sensitive spots."

He captured my wrist in his hand and pinned it to the bed. Then he captured my other wrist and used one big hand to hold them safely in my lap. "Be a good girl," he warned. "And eat your breakfast."

I stuck my tongue out at him, but let him feed me. I felt giddy and silly. *We could be good together.*

Until I go back to the FBI and we're on opposite sides again.

Nope. Not thinking about that. Not right now.

He ate, too, and we worked our way through both plates of waffles. As he lifted away the tray and put it down on the floor, the sheet slipped down around my waist. Instantly, his eyes locked on my breasts. I pulled the sheet back up to cover me, and he pulled it down again. I smirked: whenever he saw my breasts he was like a big, out-of-control bear, and as someone who'd always been self-conscious about my flat chest, it was oddly flattering. I went to lift the sheet again and this time he grabbed my hands and pressed them to the bed. "Stop it," he growled. "I'll tie you down, if I have to."

An unexpected surge of heat went straight to my groin. If he'd said *tie you up,* that would have been one thing, but *tie you down* sounded deliciously wicked. It made something rebellious rise inside me, an urge to fuck about just so I could find out. I felt my face heat. *What's happening? I've never been into that.*

He'd leaned closer, while I was thinking. "I love your breasts," he told me. He moved closer still, his mouth just a few inches from my breast, and each Russian-accented word was a warm little gust against it. "They're so perfectly shaped." I gasped and he moved a little closer, his lips almost brushing my nipple. "I *obsessed* over what they'd look like, if I ever got your clothes off. Dreaming about doing this." His lips suddenly closed around my nipple and I jerked and inhaled...then moaned as his tongue started to lash the soft bud. His hand started squeezing my other breast, his thumb stroking the nipple, and I began to grind my hips. I closed my eyes and let the pleasure take me, two harmonized drumbeats of perfect sensation that vibrated straight to my core.

He opened his mouth wider, taking in more of my breast, and his hand grew rougher. The drumbeats shifted, becoming darker and more insistent, and I began to pant, open-mouthed and needy. His mouth left my breast and an instant later, his lips found mine, his tongue searching out my tongue and dancing with it. Both of his hands worked my breasts and I was pinned against the wall of pillows, helpless. I knew that he could feel, from my ragged breathing, how turned on I was. Then he plunged one hand down under the sheets and between my thighs, and found my heated, sticky lips, and that was his confirmation.

He growled and inserted one knee, then the other between my thighs until he was kneeling there, his legs spreading mine wide. He was kissing down into me, deep, hot, conquering kisses that sent ripples of pleasure right through my body, crumbling my defenses. I went dreamily passive, my tongue lightly teasing his and my fingers dazedly tangling in his hair. His fingers pushed under me and traced the shape of my lips, slowly at first and then faster and faster, and I could feel myself slickening and opening. Then a thick, tattooed finger was pushing up into me, stretching me, and my breathing went trembly.

He began to finger-fuck me with slow, deliberate strokes, his other hand and his kisses still keeping me firmly pinned to the pillow wall, I went crazy, thrashing against him as the pleasure built, my heels drawing wide half-circles on the soft sheets and my ass grinding against the bed. I was so used to scaring men away, of always being the one who could win in a fight, but right now I was pinioned and powerless to do anything but enjoy it and it felt amazing.

But he wanted more. He broke the kiss and I slowly opened my eyes...to find him staring down at me, eyes hooded with lust and a smile on his face that was pure, calculating evil. My eyes widened...

He threw the sheets off the bed, leaving me completely naked. Then he hooked his forearms around my thighs and tugged. I yelped as I slithered down the bed, my back on the sheets and my hair fanning out above me. My lower half was lifted up into the air, my legs parted and—

I cried out as his mouth came down on my pussy, his tongue teasing while his upper lip ground against my clit. I had time for, *"What are you—"* and then his tongue thrust deep into me and my mouth opened in a silent gasp. He growled, long and low, and the vibrations made me arch my spine off the bed. Then he started licking me. Long, firm strokes that traced the shape of my lips and sent pink ribbons of pleasure rippling to my core. Then quick little circles around my clit that snapped those ribbons tight, cinching the pleasure so it was denser and hotter. I began to moan, kicking my legs in helpless pleasure either side of him as a climax started to build.

His hands were holding my ass rock-steady in the air as he leaned forward to devour me: with his hulking strength, it felt like he could hold me there all day, if he chose to. I couldn't even reach him: all my hands could do was grab handfuls of the sheets as the pleasure circled higher and higher inside me.

His thumbs began to stroke the sensitive skin of my inner thighs and my breathing hitched, the orgasm close, now. I thrashed and panted, arching my back and feeling the cool air of the room waft over my sensitive, spit-wet breasts. God, he knew exactly where to touch me and exactly where to flick and swirl his tongue to push me up and up and up.

He lifted his mouth from me for a second. "I always dreamed of having you like this," he murmured. "Flat on your back and helpless, begging me to let you come."

I panted and half-opened my eyes. The sight of him, kneeling over me like a tattooed colossus, was almost enough to send me over the edge. "I don't..."—I fought to untangle my thoughts—"recall... begging." A fresh wave of heat went through me, twisted and dark. It wrapped the orgasm like black silk ribbons and cinched it even tighter.

Gennadiy's eyes gleamed. He licked me again, teasing my clit and watching my reaction, giving me just not *quite* enough sensation to crest my peak. When he spoke, his lust made his accent stronger than ever. "Beg me, *Agent Brooks!*"

I felt all our teasing competitiveness come back, but with a deep, trusting love replacing the hate. It took hold of me, rocketing me upwards. "Never!" I told him, like some sort of haughty princess.

"Then you don't get to come," He gave me one last, mocking lick and then lifted his mouth from me.

I glared...and scissored my legs behind his head, pulling him to me and pressing myself hard against his lips. "Sure about that?" I asked.

His eyes widened in shock, then narrowed in mock-anger. *You'll pay for this.*

I tightened my grip. I didn't fear the consequences, I wanted them.

Staring right into my eyes, Gennadiy thrust his tongue deep, his upper lip grinding against my clit, and—

I arched off the bed and tossed my head against the sheets as the orgasm tightened and tightened...and then exploded, sending trembling waves all the way down my body and making me helplessly rock and grind against his face as he licked and licked. I rode him through it and then loosened my legs from around his head. He let my ass slide gently out of his hands and I collapsed on the bed, pleasure-drunk and glowing.

I heard him get off the bed. Then his heavy footsteps as he walked around to the head of the bed. His hands closed on my bare shoulders and I was roughly flipped onto my front.

His lips brushed my ear. "My turn, now."

I was still ten thousand feet up, basking on a fluffy pink post-orgasm cloud, so I just sort of grunted. Then I was tugged forward and upwards, onto my knees, and something was wrapping around my wrists.

I opened my eyes.

I was kneeling with my arms stretched out in front of me. Gennadiy had unfastened one of the golden, silky ropes that secured the four poster's curtains and slipped its loops over my wrists. As I watched, he cinched the rope tight, securing my wrists to the smooth wooden post.

Oh yeah. Consequences.

I tried to wriggle free of the ropes and found I couldn't. *Well of course he knows how to tie people up.* That shouldn't have been a surprise. What *was* a surprise was the needy thread of heat that shot straight down to my core and made me secretly crush my thighs together.

"Your safe word," Gennadiy told me, "can be *duck.*"

I craned my head around and glared at him...and then I gave him a curt little nod.

I expected him to fuck me but instead he slid around on the bed and inserted his legs under me so that I was on my knees, bent over his lap. I could feel his cock hardening through his boxers beneath me.

"Someone," he told me, "needs a lesson." He ran one big, tattooed hand over my upraised ass cheek. "Don't they?"

"No," I said, innocent and just a little taunting. *He's just kidding, right?*

"I've been wanting to do this since that night in my office," he told me. He squeezed my ass and I jerked. "Ready?"

He's definitely just teasing, there's no way he'd actually—

There was a rush of air and then the crack of skin on skin. An instant later, the pain arrived, a white-hot, spreading shock. My mouth dropped open...and then my lips went slack because a different feeling overtook the pain, a kind of heat I'd only ever had hints of before, trembly and all-consuming.

His hand cracked down again. Another flash of pain. Another rush of heat, spreading across my ass like a forest fire. What *was* that?!

Three and I instinctively tried to tug my hands free, so I could protect myself...and when I found I *genuinely couldn't,* the heat rose even higher, washing over my entire body.

Four and the pain wasn't even pain, anymore, it was a flash of lightning that preceded the thunder-roll of pleasure through my body.

Five, six, seven and my entire world narrowed down to his big, tattooed hand cracking against my ass in slow motion.

Eight and he suddenly thrust his other hand underneath me and began to rub my sopping folds. *Nine* and I was helplessly writhing and twitching in his lap and *oh God I'm going to come.* *Ten* and with the final spank my body tensed...and then shuddered and spasmed as the shock climax rolled through me. When I finally stopped moving, I craned around again and stared at him, awestruck. It wasn't just the near-instant orgasm. My own toxic anger, already calmed just from being near him, had dropped away to nothing, as if I'd just ridden my bike or had a sparring match. I felt almost drunk, and somehow cleansed.

"Are you going to be a good girl now, Agent Brooks?" he asked me.

"*Yes, Sir,*" I breathed.

He slid out from underneath me. I heard the whisper of cotton as he pulled off his boxers and then the sound of a condom being rolled on. Then he was in me from behind, driving up into me and finding me wetter than I'd ever been. We both groaned together as he filled me, *stretched* me. His hands gripped my shoulders and pulled me back onto him and I inhaled as I took him to the root.

He began to thrust, just gently rocking at first, and I bit my lip at the sensation of his heat and size, so deep inside me. I caught movement out of the corner of my eye and realized there was a mirror on the wall. I drew in my breath as I saw the woman on her knees, her wrists bound to the bedpost, and the hulking, tattooed gangster fucking her.

His hands slid forward along my body and squeezed my breasts, then stroked down my sides and grabbed my ass. He held me firmly in place and started to really fuck me, long hard thrusts that shook my whole body. Every *slam* of his cock into me released a new wave of pleasure, filling me up until I was moaning, gasping, pushing my hips back to meet him. An orgasm was racing towards me, unstoppable.

I looked at the mirror again, barely recognizing myself: eyes half-closed in pleasure, mouth open and panting. Behind me, Gennadiy was putting his entire body into each thrust: first his broad shoulders pulled back, biceps bulging as he drew me back onto him. Then there was a rippling of his abs as his core delivered the power. His hips lunged forward as he rammed into me and then that hard ass dimpled as he went hilt-deep in me. I could have watched him forever.

His thrusts got faster and the pleasure started to run away with me, an out-of-control cascade. I could feel strands of hair sticking to my sweat-damp forehead and my moans were filling the room. The blood was rushing in my ears, the orgasm close, and I could hear his breathing tightening: he was close, too.

He pounded me even harder, his hands sliding down into the creases of my hips...and then my eyes snapped wide as his fingertip circled my throbbing clit. "Come for me, Alison," he growled.

And I did, helpless in the face of *that* order in *that* accent. The climax shook me with wave after wave of pleasure and as I fluttered and clamped around him, I felt him push deep and explode deep inside me. We rode it together, our bodies pressed tight, until we both finally slumped, panting and sated. He untied the rope from my wrists and I looked at the faint pink marks in wonder. I'd learned something new about myself.

Gennadiy pulled me into his arms and we lay on our sides with my head against his chest. As our bodies cooled, it should have gotten cold but he stroked his hands up and down my back, all the way from shoulders to thighs, and I felt blissfully warm. It was only when I tried to shift position that I felt how firmly he was holding me. Gentle, but *firm*.

I tilted my head back so I could look up at him. He was gazing down at me, his gray eyes serious. "I hope you don't have plans," he told me.

"For this morning?"

"For the entire rest of your life." If it was possible, his grip got even firmer. "I didn't think I needed anyone. I didn't want to need anyone. But you...you are what I've been missing all along."

I gulped, my heart soaring into the stratosphere. And that's when I remembered that there was something he'd said that I hadn't, yet. "I—" I hesitated. I hadn't realized what a big step it was for me. How I could only say it now, when all those defenses I'd built up in the foster system had finally come down. "I love you too," I whispered.

He kissed me, slow and sweet. And we were still kissing when someone banged on the bedroom door. "What is it?" called Gennadiy.

"We need you downstairs," called Radimir from the hallway. "It's bad."

57

ALISON

WE DRESSED, AND I WALKED DOWNSTAIRS HAND-IN-HAND WITH Gennadiy on legs that were still a little shaky. Outside, the sky was concrete-gray, and a heavy rain was hissing down.

By now, I knew to head for the dining room. The entire Aristov family was there, looking grim. "All three banks we bank with have frozen our assets," Radimir told us, "Aristov Incorporated, our personal accounts, the cash in safety deposit boxes...everything. With the casino shut down, we have lost access to all our money. We can't buy product, we can't pay our men...*Blyat'*!" He looked at me helplessly. "The Italians, the Armenians, even the cartels, we can fight. But not this."

I nodded. The entire system was being turned against them, and it would crush everything he and his brothers had built.

"This is Grushin," said Gennadiy. "He must have ordered them to do it."

"Three different banks?" asked Radimir. "He'd have to bribe someone senior at all three of them."

Mikhail shook his head as he petted one of his dogs. "I've met some of those people. They make millions in bonuses every year; they aren't interested in bribes."

"Blackmail, then?" I asked.

"They can't *all* have deep, dark sex secrets!" said Bronwyn.

For the next three hours, we tried to figure it out. Mikhail helped with what he knew about Grushin's old techniques from back in Moscow, and the others shared their knowledge about the Bratva and other organized crime in Chicago. They were doing their best to help, but I was the cop, and they were looking to me to figure this thing out. And I couldn't. I paced up and down in front of the web of information I'd assembled, but none of it made sense.

The chef brought in a pot of coffee, and Bronwyn put a box of fancy-looking pastries on the table to keep us going. "Figured we needed a treat, with everything that's going on," she told me. "These are from this little bakery in New York, try one."

I picked one up, but I was too deep in the problem to eat. How had Grushin managed to order around the heads of three different banks? "It's not bribes. It's not blackmail." I brought the pastry closer. It had delicate, flaky pastry crusted with caramelized nuts. "Damn, these smell good."

Bronwyn was already munching on one. "Konstantin's girlfriend introduced me to them," she mumbled, mouth full. "I'm turning into that bakery's best customer."

I looked up and stared at her as a light went on in my head. "What if we've been looking at this all wrong?" I asked. "What if all these people he has influence over are his customers?" I leaned over the table. "What if they're buying something...*bad*. So bad, they can't ever risk it getting out. And they know that if Grushin goes down, *they* could go down."

"So what's he selling?" I thought back to the people on the submarine. "Maybe it *is* sex trafficking."

The Aristov men all scowled in disgust, which made me like them even more. "But Grushin is making millions per transaction," said Gennadiy sadly. "People just aren't worth that much."

"And, the sort of people we're talking about are *old*," said Mikhail. "The head of the gaming board is nearly eighty. If he bought himself a beautiful young Russian woman, his heart would pop."

Bronwyn coughed, and we all looked at her, thinking she was politely trying to get our attention. But then she put her hands to her throat, and then to her chest.

Radimir was at her side in a heartbeat. "*Krasavitsa?* Are you choking?"

Bronwyn was rapidly turning pale. Sweat was breaking out on her forehead. "Does she have allergies?" I asked.

Radimir caught his wife as she slumped sideways in her chair. "Bronwyn?!" He listened. "She's barely breathing!" He turned to Valentin. "*Get the car!*"

Gennadiy knocked the pastry out of my hands. And it slowly dawned on me that Bronwyn had been poisoned.

58

GENNADIY

WE ALL PILED INTO RADIMIR'S MERCEDES, AND VALENTIN SPED US TO the nearest ER, running every light, the tires fighting for grip on the soaking streets. Radimir sat in the back seat with Bronwyn in his arms, begging her in Russian to hold on.

At the hospital, the staff got Bronwyn onto a gurney and barreled her through the waiting area. Radimir ran alongside her, muttering to her in Russian even though she couldn't hear him and squeezing her hand, while the rest of us chased along behind.

"Is she pregnant?" a nurse asked him. He was so distraught, he didn't even hear her. "Sir! Is there any possibility your wife could be pregnant?"

"No," Radimir told her. "We were just about to start trying for a baby, but she needed to talk to her doctor first. She's on medication for rheumatoid arthritis."

We reached the curtained-off treatment area, and doctors started trying to thread a tube down Bronwyn's throat to help her breathe. "I need you all to wait in the waiting area!" the lead doctor told us. "Let us work!"

Radimir stepped back out of the way but stayed in the corner, a brooding statue. The rest of us reluctantly withdrew. We found

Mikhail in the waiting area: he'd had to follow in his SUV because the Mercedes had been full. He'd had to leave his dogs at home, for once, and it felt strange and wrong, seeing him without them.

I took a seat in a plastic chair, slipped my arm around Alison's waist and pulled her close. She rested her head on my shoulder, and I rested my chin on the top of her head, cold waves of worry breaking through me one after another. *Bronwyn!* I'd been worried when she first appeared in our lives. *Chyort*, I'd argued for killing her, because what she knew could have put my brother in jail. But everything changed when I saw cold, calculating Radimir falling in love. I'd never thought I'd see him love someone: I hadn't been sure he was even capable of it, after what we'd been through in Vladivostok. But she'd completely melted that frozen heart and transformed him, in a way I didn't understand at the time.

I looked down at Alison. I did now.

A nurse I recognized from the huddle around Bronwyn burst out of the curtained area and yelled down the hallway in medical jargon. A moment later, another nurse ran to her, pushing a cart of equipment. *What does that mean?!* My chest tightened. Bronwyn was so different to our family, with her gentleness and her books and her enormous sandwiches. And maybe that was why she was exactly what our family had needed. She'd become someone I really liked, someone I'd die to protect. If she died...

I felt so fucking useless: Bronwyn had been in my mansion, where she was supposed to be safe, and that bastard Grushin had nearly killed her anyway. He must have intercepted the bakery delivery...God, all of us could have eaten those pastries. *Alison* nearly ate one! I tightened my arm around her.

It was a race against time, now: could we stop him before he wiped us out? And I was way, way out of my comfort zone. Billionaire bankers, who could wipe out our empire with the stroke of a pen? City officials being somehow controlled by a former spy? This wasn't my world. My hands tightened into fists. *Just give me someone to shoot!*

Radimir suddenly emerged from the curtained area and marched towards us, chest shuddering as he fought to control his anger. We all jumped up. "What's—" I began.

"Her heart stopped," Radimir said, his voice strangled. "They're trying to restart it. They made me leave. I was in the way."

He began to pace, eyes down and shoulders hunched. I understand anger, and I should have known to leave him alone, but I wanted to help. I put a gentle hand on his shoulder.

He whirled to face me. "It's your fault!" he snapped, shoving me in the chest. "This is your mess! Your side of the business! Your fucking FBI agent!"

I staggered backwards...and took it. A few months before, I would have yelled back at him. Now I understood what he was going through: I remembered kneeling over Alison in the warehouse, begging her not to leave me. Alison reached out and squeezed my hand.

Radimir went to stand by one of the big glass windows, staring out at the rain. There was silence for a moment. Then he rubbed his face with his hands and turned to me. "I'm sorry," he croaked. "I'm sorry, Gennadiy. I just don't know—"

I nodded.

Radimir's voice was shaking. "I don't know what I'm going to do if she dies..."

A doctor ran out of the curtained area. "Mr. Aristov!" He stopped in front of Radimir. "We've managed to get her heart going again...for now." He led Radimir back towards the treatment area.

The rest of us reluctantly shuffled back to the waiting area, pale and drawn with worry. As we sat down, Alison rubbed her hand across my back. I turned to her...and pulled her into my arms, crushing her against me.

And then all we could do was wait.

59

ALISON

I KEPT LOOKING AROUND AT THE OTHER FAMILIES IN THE WAITING AREA, there because their kid broke an arm playing baseball, or their uncle had a stroke. We were there because some guy *poisoned* one of us. And we couldn't even go to the cops: the FBI were still hunting me, and even if they weren't, the cops would be happy to let one gangster kill another, just like my boss had said. I'd never realized how lonely this life was, outside of the safe, secure system we all take for granted. We were completely on our own: that's why family was so important to the Aristovs. *And for me.* I was one of them, now.

A half-hour after we arrived, a lady in her seventies raced in, nimble despite her walking stick, and asked where her granddaughter was. Gennadiy went over and embraced her, and introduced me: she was Baba, Bronwyn's grandmother, who'd raised her after her parents died. Then three of Bronwyn's friends showed up, scared and desperate for news. Radimir emerged briefly to tell us that it was still touch-and-go and took Baba in to see Bronwyn. I caught one tiny glimpse of her through a crack in the curtains. She looked waxy and gray, and there was a tube going up her nose. *Ah, Jesus...*

For five hours, we all paced and waited. And then Radimir came staggering out through the curtains, looking like he was about to collapse. "She's going to be alright," he croaked. "She's responding to the treatment."

There was a chorus of relieved sighs, and we all hugged Radimir. I saw him give Gennadiy an especially hard squeeze, and Gennadiy patted his back: *It's okay.*

An hour later, we were allowed to go in and see Bronwyn. Gennadiy, Radimir, and I were in with her when she opened her eyes. Radimir threw his arms around her and held her tight. "*Krasavitsa!*" he breathed. "I thought I'd lost you!"

Bronwyn shook her head. But when he drew back, her eyes were full of tears. "The baby," she whispered.

Radimir took her hands. "You weren't pregnant."

"But I *would* have been. If this had happened a month from now..." Her face crumpled. "This would have killed the baby, Radimir, how can we—"

She started sobbing, and Gennadiy and I quietly withdrew to give them some privacy. A little later, Radimir came out. "She's sleeping," he told us. "The rest of you should go home. I'll stay with her and call you if anything changes."

Gennadiy nodded. "We'll come back tomorrow."

"When you do," said Radimir, "can you bring Bronwyn's medication? She'll need another dose tomorrow. It's in her purse."

I nodded, glad to have something practical to do.

We said goodbye to Bronwyn's friends, gave Baba a ride back to her apartment, and then headed back to the mansion. By now, it was late afternoon. We were met at the door by all of Mikhail's dogs, who'd picked up on all the panic when we left. They butted up against us, sniffing and demanding answers. *Where red-haired one? Why she no with you?!* We ruffled their coats, scratched their ears, and tried to reassure them.

Upstairs, I found the guest room Radimir and Bronwyn were using and grabbed the medication from Bronwyn's purse, putting it into mine before I forgot. Gennadiy followed me in and put his arms around me from behind. Alone together for the first time in hours, I finally said what I'd been thinking all afternoon. "I don't know if we can beat this guy."

Gennadiy pulled me back against him. "We will," he said firmly. "You're going to find him. And then I'm going to break his neck for what he did to Bronwyn."

I slowly nodded and felt another bit of FBI Agent-me slip away.

"Come on," said Gennadiy. "Take a moment. Eat something. My chef makes this onion soup—"

A shout in Russian from downstairs, from one of Gennadiy's men. We ran to the stairs and looked down. The whole mansion was lit up red and blue from flashing lights outside. Then a voice, amplified through a loudhailer. "This is the Chicago Police Department! We have the place surrounded. Come out slowly and with your hands in the air!"

60

ALISON

WE RACED DOWNSTAIRS AND FOUND MIKHAIL AND VALENTIN LOOKING as shocked as we felt. "What the *fuck* is going on?" asked Gennadiy. He parted a window blind with his fingers and peeked through. "*Chyort*, that's not good," he muttered. "Cliburn is out there." He looked at Mikhail. "Don't we have an *understanding* with the District Attorney?"

Mikhail nodded somberly. "Cliburn happily takes his money every month." He sighed. "It would seem that Grushin has made him a better offer. Or he's another of Grushin's clients."

I cursed under my breath. I wasn't sure if I was an FBI agent, mad at how the justice system I'd always believed in had been corrupted, or an honorary Aristov, mad at how one of those corrupt players had double-crossed us. Maybe both?

At that moment, my phone rang. "What the hell is going on?" yelled Calahan in my ear. "I just heard Chicago PD are raiding Gennadiy's mansion!"

"I'm aware," I said tightly.

"Please tell me you're not in there," begged Calahan.

A long, guilty silence.

Calahan blew his breath out. "What do you need?"

I loved him for wanting to help, but... "There's nothing you can do," I told him. "FBI New York doesn't have any jurisdiction here. You could lose your badge, Sam. Stay out of this." And I ended the call.

"You have three minutes!" yelled the cop on the loudhailer. I felt my stomach drop. *Jesus, this is really happening. We're going to be arrested.*

Gennadiy looked around at the mansion and cursed under his breath. "We'd better go."

He walked off down the hallway. Mikhail and Valentin followed him, but I just stood there. "Go? Go *where?* Out the back way? We're surrounded!"

Gennadiy looked over his shoulder at me. "You think we don't plan for the day the police come to our door?"

Frowning, I followed him. He led us into the kitchen, where his chef already had the door to the pantry open. Gennadiy thumbed a button on the underside of a shelf, and a section of the tiled floor dropped away, revealing a set of stone stairs. I stared, open-mouthed. I'd hidden in that pantry and had no idea what was right under my feet.

Avgust, Gennadiy's head of security, ran up to us. "We'll stall them for as long as possible."

Gennadiy squeezed his shoulders. "No shooting. Go quietly. Say nothing. Conrad will get you out." They embraced. Then Gennadiy was hustling me down the stairs. Mikhail gave a short, quick order in Russian, and his dogs shot into the room and followed his pointing finger down the stairs in one long train of gray fur. Mikhail followed them, then Valentin, and Gennadiy brought up the rear, closing the trapdoor behind him.

The stairs led down to a tunnel: not some dirt-walled, prison-escape thing but a concrete-lined passage big enough to stand up in; there were even *lights*. There was also a rack at the bottom of the stairs with five black holdalls, each one with a paper luggage tag. Gennadiy grabbed *V, M* and *G*. I stared at him, amazed.

"I'm sorry I didn't make a bag for you yet. Take Bronwyn's." And he threw me the *B* bag.

The tunnel ran for about a hundred yards and ended in a metal spiral staircase. Valentin went up first and gingerly lifted the manhole cover at the top, gun drawn...then climbed out and waved us up. When I emerged, I saw we were on a footpath in a small park, down the street from the mansion and hidden from it by thick foliage. When everyone was up, Gennadiy led us down the footpath to the street, where a blue minivan was parked. He felt under the rear bumper and pulled out a key, and we all piled in. As we pulled away, I heard the distant bang of the police breaking down the mansion's door. "Pretty slick," I admitted.

"I had to allow for the possibility that one day, you might actually catch me," Gennadiy told me. He looked at the dog on my lap. "Sorry, it's a little cramped."

I cuddled the dog close and ruffled its fur. It turned and licked my neck. "I consider it a definite plus," I said seriously.

Valentin drove us across town and finally stopped in a strip-mall parking lot. *We did it,* I thought, still a little dazed by the whole thing. *The cops have no idea where we are. We beat them.*

I caught myself. *When did the cops become 'them'?*

We climbed out. The rain had eased to a light drizzle that dampened our faces and made the dazzling, blue-and-white lights of the strip mall feel shockingly cold and stark. Gennadiy took me to one side. "We should talk about what to do next."

"What is there to talk about?" I asked blankly. "We track down Grushin."

"That might not be possible anymore." He was trying to keep his voice calm, but I could hear the fear underneath. Fear for *me*. "The mansion and everything in it is gone, seized by the cops. All our bank accounts are frozen. My men have all been arrested, and by now the cops will have gone to the hospital and taken Radimir, too." He waved his hand at the four of us, at the minivan. "This is *it!* This is all we are, now!" I looked around at our sad little circle: it was terrifying, how far and how fast the Aristov empire had fallen.

Gennadiy took the *B* holdall from me and tugged open the zipper, showing me what was inside. "There's twenty thousand in cash in here. Bronwyn's fake passport won't work for you but I can get one made that will. By tomorrow, you can be out of the country."

I shook my head. "I want to stop this guy."

His self-control snapped and he grabbed my face between his hands. "And I want you alive! *Blyat'*, Alison, for once in your life, don't be stubborn!"

I stared into his eyes, an awful, cold certainty setting in. "If I say *yes,* you'll come with me?" He didn't answer. "*Both* of us get out!" My voice started to shake. "Right?"

He dropped his eyes. "You know I can't leave Radimir."

I nodded sadly. I understood. But that meant... "I'm staying," I told him.

He sighed, exasperated, and scowled down at me...and then he pulled me into a tight, tight hug. At last, he drew back, brushed my hair from my face, and kissed me reverently. "I must have been a saint in a previous life," he said, "to deserve you."

I hugged him again, and then the four of us sat down on the hood of the minivan to figure out what the hell we were going to do. The sun was going down, and the temperature was starting to drop. I pulled my thin denim jacket tighter around me and, as soon as he saw I was cold, Gennadiy wrapped me up in his arms. But inside, a deeper chill was rolling in. We had nothing, no more leads. And the clock was ticking: by now, an APB would have gone out on all of us. It was only a matter of time before we were arrested.

I dug in my purse to see if I had a charger because my phone was running low. But the first thing I found was the carton of Bronwyn's medication. *Crap.* She was probably under police guard at the hospital now. I turned it over in my hands...

And suddenly sat bolt upright. "I know what Grushin's doing," I said.

Everyone looked at me.

"You remember that tobacco billionaire," I asked, "the one who went to Grushin's clinic? We need to find him. Right now."

61

ALISON

Fortunately, Clayton Tuxworth wasn't exactly publicity-shy. Since stepping down as CEO of his tobacco company, he spent his days playing golf, giving speeches, and brokering multi-million-dollar deals, and all of it was documented on social media. It took all of five minutes to find out that he was attending a black-tie reception at a hotel across town.

We screeched to a stop outside, the minivan ridiculous in the sea of stretch limos. The press were there and they stared as we marched up the red carpet: Gennadiy, scowly and intimidating in his charcoal-gray suit and dark red shirt; me, marching alongside him in my ankle boots, jeans and denim jacket; Valentin just behind us with his long coat flapping in the wind; Mikhail looking like some dignified statesman come to sign a treaty; and following behind him, four enormous Malamutes. Security stepped forward to stop us and then faltered when they recognized Gennadiy: no one wanted to offend an Aristov.

We burst into the hotel's ballroom. The guests were at circular tables, getting tipsy on champagne and whiskey and serving themselves from a buffet table that ran the entire length of one wall, loaded with whole roast chickens and hams, cheeses, fruit, and desserts. At the far end of the room, the guests of honor sat at a long table, with Tuxworth right in the middle. He was in his seventies, lean, with a deep brown golfer's tan and sleek, chin-length white hair. I counted four private security guys spaced out around the room, and they looked a lot more formidable than the hotel guys outside. We weren't getting close to him unless.... "We need a diversion," I said as we marched towards him.

Mikhail nodded. Without breaking his stride, he turned to his dogs. "*Uzhin*," he said, and pointed to the buffet table.

The dogs became four streaks of gray fur. Screams and laughter rose as they barged under tables and past legs, tails wagging furiously. Two of them decided it would be faster to go *over* the tables and sprang up onto them, paws scrabbling at snow-white tablecloths and sending glasses of wine tumbling. They jumped from one table to the next, leaving a trail of destruction, and then jumped onto the buffet table just as the other two arrived from below.

Chaos erupted. All the hotel staff and two of the four private security guys raced over to the buffet as the dogs trotted up and down the table, stepping on gateaux and scattering cheese plates, tipping over salad bowls, and spilling sauces in their eagerness to reach the meat. One stood on the edge of a serving platter of cold cuts and flipped it, catapulting sliced meat onto tables, the floor, and people's laps, and the dog bolted around the room, determined to locate and wolf down every piece. Two dogs decided the roast chicken was theirs and began attacking it from both sides, tearing off drumsticks with their teeth. And one dog sunk its teeth into a huge cold roast ham and started backing away, dragging it along the table and growling at anyone who came close.

The four of us marched towards Tuxworth's table. One security guy ran to block us, and Gennadiy felled him with a single punch. The other came from my side, and I twisted and flipped him over my shoulder. Then we were standing in front of Tuxworth, who was half scared, half outraged. "What the *hell* do you think you're doing," he demanded, "coming in here and—"

I grabbed his shirt and ripped it open all the way down the front.

All of us stared at the long, vertical incision scar that ran down his chest.

"What do old, rich guys want more than anything else?" I asked bitterly. "Another ten years of life. Those people on the submarine: Grushin *is* trafficking them. But not for sex. For their organs."

62

GENNADIY

MIKHAIL RECALLED HIS DOGS AND, AS WE WALKED OUT OF THE HOTEL, Alison laid it all out for us.

"We were wrong, right from the start," she said. "We assumed Grushin's clinic was just a front, a way of laundering money from his business. But it *is* his business. There aren't enough organs legally donated to even cover all the people who really need one. No one's giving you a heart if you're already in your seventies...unless you buy one. If you're a billionaire, paying five, ten million dollars for more life is nothing." She pulled out Bronwyn's medication. "Immunosuppressants. They had them at the clinic to stop people rejecting their new organs."

I shook my head slowly. It had been right in front of us, but it had taken Alison's FBI brain to figure it out. I grabbed her hand and squeezed it, insanely proud of her, and she gave me an embarrassed smile.

"And if you're powerful," said Mikhail, "Grushin steps in and saves your life for free. Cliburn, the District Attorney, is an alcoholic. What's the betting Grushin got him a new liver?"

"Or if the person's got a relative that needs a transplant," I said, remembering something. "The head of the gaming board: his wife was ill."

"And once the operation's done, you're an accessory to murder," said Alison. "Grushin *owns* you. That's how he's amassed so much power, so quickly. Jesus, he must have done this for hundreds of people across the state. Most people rich enough to afford it are going to have some sort of power he can use. He's not doing it for the money, he's doing it for the influence."

I fell silent as we reached the minivan and climbed in. Innocent people who'd done nothing wrong being smuggled into the US, killed, and their organs stripped out. Just so some elderly rich guy could live a few more years. The rich, eating the poor. "*Blyat'.*" I felt the rage slowly building, taking hold of me. I am not a good man. But some things are wrong, even to me. "We have to stop him." I looked at Alison, took a deep breath, and said something I thought I'd never say. "We need to go to the police."

But Alison shook her head. "Grushin controls the DA. Plus, those people who came off the submarine, the next batch of donors: Grushin will kill them to cover things up if the authorities get close. We have to get them out first. And then we have to take Grushin alive so he can testify."

I rubbed my stubble. "Someone at the clinic might know where they're being held. Let's go."

63

ALISON

THE CLINIC WAS ON A PRETTY, LEAFY STREET JUST OUTSIDE THE CITY. BY the time we got there, the sky was turning from orange to deep blue. We parked down the street and, as we got ready, everyone was tense.

Everyone except Mikhail. "Feels like old times," he said in that richly smooth, Russian growl. "When we started out, we had no money, no fancy cars. Just the Aristovs against the world." He turned to me. "And now you, as well." He grinned at me, and I smiled back, a warm glow spreading through me. Mikhail opened up his holdall, pulled out a shotgun, and racked the slide. "Now let's go to work."

The clinic had to look like a legitimate business, so it only had light security: a rent-a-cop with a handgun. I pulled out my gun and pointed it at his head, and he immediately put his hands up. We left him with one of Mikhail's dogs growling at his balls, daring him to move.

Most of the staff had gone home for the night, but a nurse pointed us to the head surgeon. Gennadiy grabbed him by his lapels and walked him backwards down the hallway, through a set of doors, and into an empty operating theater. He threw the man on the operating table, knocking over a cart and sending kidney bowls and scalpels clattering. "*Start talking!*" he roared.

The surgeon panted, white-faced. "I didn't know. I swear." He hung his head. "Not at first. I used to be on a hospital transplant team. Then Grushin found me. He had blackmail information on me; he knew about an affair I'd had. He offered me a job here, for a lot of money." He shook his head. "I thought I'd just be patching up gangsters who'd been shot."

"When they do a normal, *legal* transplant," I said, "it's a race against time to get the organ where it needs to go." I had to fight to keep my voice level. "That's the big factor in it being a success, right, how fresh the organ is? So ideally..." My voice shook with anger. "Ideally, you'd transplant from a person who's still alive."

The surgeon couldn't meet my eyes. He nodded. "The donors are brought in unconscious, on ventilators. The rest of the staff think they're brain dead."

"But they're not brain dead." Gennadiy got right in the surgeon's face, angrier than I'd ever seen him. "*Are they?!*"

The surgeon flinched. "They're just s—sedated. Alive, until...we take the organs."

"Jesus," I whispered. I was thinking of the kid I'd seen get off the submarine. "They must hold the donors somewhere, alive, until they can schedule the client for surgery. Where?"

"I don't know," said the surgeon. Gennadiy wrapped his hands around his throat. "I don't! But I know it's close! They're here within a half hour."

"How do they show up?" I asked.

"In an ambulance. From a private patient transport company: the ambulances look kind of beat up."

A memory scratched at the back of my brain. "ACS Transport?" The surgeon nodded. I turned to Gennadiy. "That's the other company Grushin called. I presumed it was freight shipping; I never thought of *patient* transport." I looked at the surgeon. "Anything else you can tell us?"

He shook his head. "I've only been working here a few months. Grushin moved me from the New York clinic."

We all stared at him. "*What?!*"

His eyes flicked between us nervously. "There are three. New York, LA...and Chicago is the newest."

My jaw dropped. It was so much worse than we'd thought. *Three* clinics. Who knows how many people Grushin had already killed?

As we walked back to the car, Gennadiy said, "So now we raid this transport company? Find out where they're picking up the donors?"

I shook my head. I was doing internet searches on my phone, checking a theory. "The surgeon said the ambulances looked beat-up. I think that maybe...yes, look." I showed him my phone screen. "ACS Transport filed for bankruptcy years ago. Then someone bought it. Now it has no website, no news stories, it doesn't exist...but it's still dropping off patients. I think Grushin bought it, and *that's* where he's storing the donors. It has everything he needs: space, basic medical facilities, and ambulances to drop them off at the clinic without anyone getting suspicious."

"Then let's go," said Valentin.

But to my surprise, Gennadiy shook his head. "If that's Grushin's hideout, it won't be like the clinic. He'll have armed men there to guard the donors." He looked around. "There are only four of us. We need backup."

"Konstantin?" asked Mikhail. "He helped us before."

"His men are in New York; it'd take too long," said Gennadiy. "We need someone local."

"And someone we know for sure *isn't* working for Grushin," I said sadly. Then I drew in my breath as the solution hit me.

Gennadiy saw my expression and narrowed his eyes. "Who?" he asked suspiciously. And then he realized, and his face fell. He looked at me pleadingly. "Oh no. Please..."

64

GENNADIY

A half hour later, I was glaring at a familiar set of double doors.

"We don't have a choice," said Alison, running a calming hand over my back.

"I know," I said tightly. "That doesn't mean I have to like it." I took a deep breath...and opened the doors.

This time, it was night, and Finn's bar was packed full and deafeningly loud. Finn himself had decided to take a turn tending bar and was filling a beer glass while flirting shamelessly with the pretty blonde he was serving. When he saw us, his face split into a wide, teasing grin. "Gennadiy! Saw the cops breaking down your front door on TV. Did they let you go already?"

I glowered at him and jerked my head: *we need to talk.* He leaned in and whispered something to the blonde, which made her giggle. Then he vaulted over the bar, grabbed her waist, and pulled her into a kiss. When he moved away, he tangled his fingers with hers, looking back at her and keeping the connection until the very last second. The blonde looked like she might swoon. Even Alison looked a little swoony. I glowered even harder.

Finn slapped me on the back and led the way to a private lounge, grabbing a bottle of whiskey from the bar as he passed. The lounge was full, but one look from Finn and it emptied instantly. He fell into a leather couch, swigging from the bottle as he did, and looked at us expectantly.

Alison filled him in on what Grushin had been doing and why we needed the Irish. Finn grinned. He couldn't *stop* grinning. "So what you're saying is...you need my help."

"Yes," said Alison.

He gave her a filthy smile. "Much as I love to hear the word *yes* from your sweet lips, I want to hear it from him." And he looked at me.

I felt the anger rise and swell in my chest, a hurricane that just needed to be given a target. But then I thought of the people from the submarine. The women. The child. I took a deep breath...and crushed the anger down, crystallizing it into a weapon to use against Grushin. "Yes," I told Finn. "I need your help."

Finn grinned...but it wasn't quite as smug as I'd expected. He must have known what it took for me to say that. He stood and called for his brothers. "Alright, then. Let's go get the bastard."

65

ALISON

ACS Transport was a low, ugly building on a run-down industrial park south of the city. There was grass growing in the parking lot, and the neighboring buildings were all boarded up: it was the perfect place for a hideout.

We circled around the back and found a loading dock and two ambulances, both with fading paint and sagging suspension. Valentin picked the lock, and we stacked up outside the door, guns at the ready. Finn had brought six men with him: I wasn't sure which were brothers or cousins and which were just on his payroll because they were all dark-haired and broodingly good-looking. I just knew I was glad of the backup.

Valentin opened the door, and we rushed inside. There was a garage area where an ambulance was half-disassembled, probably being stripped for parts to keep the other two running. The van from the warehouse was there, too. The place smelled of engine oil, damp, and disinfectant.

A shot rang out, and we ducked for cover. Gennadiy shot back, downing a guy half-hidden behind the van. But more men ran in from deeper in the building and opened fire as well. Gennadiy pulled me protectively behind him. "You and Mikhail go and find the donors," he told me, pointing to a hallway. "We'll take care of the guards."

Part of me automatically wanted to argue, resenting being kept away from the action. But he had a point; we had to make sure the donors were safe. I nodded and hurried off with Mikhail and the dogs, but I threw one last, worried look back over my shoulder as I ran. *Please, Gennadiy, be careful!*

We found an office and then a couple of basic treatment rooms with gurneys in them. But there was no sign of the donors. We kept going, past more offices and then a break room. And surprisingly quickly, we reached the end of the hallway. *Where are they?* The only place left was the garage where the firefight was going on, and they weren't there.

My chest tightened. What if we were too late? What if Grushin had already killed them and taken their organs?

I looked at Mikhail, but he looked as worried and confused as me. We backtracked, and then he put a hand on my arm to stop me. He went into the break room to grab something he'd seen: a t-shirt, too small to be an adult. *The boy!* But where was he now?

Mikhail bent and held the t-shirt out to one of his dogs, muttering a command. The dog sniffed twice, then charged to the end of the hallway and sniffed at the wall, thumping its tail excitedly.

I took a closer look at the wall. Its paint wasn't exactly the same color as the others, as if it had faded less. A big photocopier was pushed up against it. "Help me move this," I said, and together we heaved it out of the way.

Behind the photocopier, a fake wall had been built. A section near the floor had been hinged, like a human-sized cat flap. I pushed it gently open...and looked right into the face of the boy I'd seen at the warehouse. I felt myself sag in relief. Then I looked behind him, and my stomach knotted. All of them were there, men and women packed together in a bare, windowless space only about ten feet square. There was bottled water and a bucket in the corner for a toilet. *Jesus.* "Come on!" I waved them over. "We're getting you out of here!"

One by one, they crawled out through the hole. The little boy started to cry, mumbling in Russian, and Mikhail, normally so happy, looked completely overcome. He scooped the boy into his arms and held him, shh-ing him and talking to him in Russian. "He wants his mother," he said to me. "There, there, little one. It's going to be okay."

One of the women heard the gunfire from the garage area and nervously plucked at my sleeve. "You...from other gang?" she asked.

I looked down at myself. I guess I didn't look much like an FBI agent anymore. In fact, maybe *another gang* was closer to the truth, now. "You're safe now," I told her.

But the gunfire from the garage area didn't seem to be dying down, and that was the only way out. Something must have gone wrong, and that thought made me go cold inside. *Gennadiy!*

66

GENNADIY

FUCK.

It had all started well. We'd rushed in and taken care of two of Grushin's men straightaway. But we'd pushed deeper into the garage too quickly, and when another four men popped up out of nowhere, I'd been cut off from the others. The gunfight had turned into a stalemate, and I was pinned down behind a rack of spare tires.

Footsteps. I froze, listening. One of them was creeping around the rack from the left. I whirled that way. Then I heard more footsteps, this time from the right. They were coming at me from two directions, knowing I couldn't face both ways at once.

All I could do was keep stubbornly facing to the left, the patch between my shoulder blades itching, knowing I'd be shot in the back any second. I stood there motionless, gun raised, waiting...

Grushin's man leaned around the rack, and I shot him in the chest. Then I dived for the floor and rolled over to look behind me, knowing I'd be too late. And I was. Another man was already standing there, aiming down at me, and I couldn't get my gun on him in time. I winced—

There was a gunshot, and the man crumpled to the floor.

Finn swaggered into view, smirked, and offered his hand. I sighed...and took it. "Thank you," I told him.

From there, the fight started to go our way. A few minutes later, Valentin took down the final one of Grushin's men...and he managed to take him alive.

I left them for a moment and ran to the hallway where I'd last seen Alison. She was crouched next to a photocopier, gun up, guarding the donors, and when I saw her safe, a huge swell of relief closed up my throat. I grabbed her and pulled her into my arms, then crushed her against my chest so hard she *oof*ed. Then I took her cheeks between my hands and kissed her.

I went back to check on Grushin's man. The others had formed a circle around him, and Valentin was attempting to question him. "Where is Viktor Grushin?" he hissed, a knife to the man's throat.

The man shook his head.

Finn picked up a tire iron and stepped forward. "Tell us where your boss is, or I'll start knocking out teeth."

But the guy still wouldn't break. It was just like the assassin I'd interrogated at the bar: Grushin had him so scared, he'd rather die than talk. Anger and violence weren't going to get us anywhere.

I sucked in a long breath of calming, cool air, dug deep...and squatted down next to him, waving Valentin and Finn aside.

"I know that you're scared," I began. "Grushin's probably threatened people you care about." *Blyat',* I'd sat in police interrogation rooms a thousand times, but I'd never realized how hard it was on this side of the table. I kept thinking about what this man had done, all the innocent lives he'd helped to snuff out, and it was like a sparking live cable dangling over a pool of gasoline. I had to work *so hard* to keep a grip on my anger.

I forced my voice to be calm...and continued. "But even if Grushin gets away, we've still destroyed his operation here in Chicago. He's going to be pissed at the people who let it happen, and you're the only one still alive. Do you think he's going to care that you didn't talk?"

The guy looked at me sullenly, saying nothing. Every instinct wanted me to grab his throat and crush the life out of him. But then we'd have nothing. I looked at Alison, and she nodded.

"We're your best chance," I told him. "If you tell us where he is, we'll stop him. He won't be able to hurt you or your family."

Then I crouched there silently, waiting. I looked at Alison and she was staring at me, stunned. I was shocked, too. Just a few months ago, I wouldn't have been able to do that.

Grushin's man took a long breath. "He's at his townhouse," he said. "403 West Brenton."

I let out a long sigh of relief, nodded and rose.

"Kill me," said the man.

I froze, staring at him.

"If I'm the only one alive, he'll know it was me who talked," said the man bitterly. "This is the only way he doesn't go after my family. Kill me."

I exchanged a horrified look with Alison.

"Come on, just do it!" snapped the man, his eyes tightly closed. "Just fucking do it!"

I put my gun to his head and fired.

Everyone stood there silently for a moment, shaken. Then Alison spoke up. "If we want to get Grushin, we have to do it now. This guy's a master at disappearing, and as soon as he hears we hit this place, he'll run, and we'll never find him. We have one shot at taking him. And we need him alive. The only way we expose this whole thing is with him in front of a Grand Jury."

"What do we do with them?" asked Mikhail, nodding to the donors.

"Liam, take 'em to the bar," said Finn. "Get them some food and show the little one my pinball machine. The cops can pick them up when this is all over."

I nodded in thanks, warming to him a little more. "Alright," I said. "Let's finish this."

67

ALISON

As we raced through the darkened streets with Valentin at the wheel, I dialed Caroline. "Don't hang up!" I said as soon as the call connected. "I need your help!"

"Where *are* you? What's going on? Jesus, Ali, there's an APB out for you! I could lose my job just for talking to you!"

"Look, there's a lot to explain, and I don't have a lot of time. But I need you to get Halifax and Hadderwell and Fitch and a tactical team and come to 403 West Brenton, right now. You can take me and Gennadiy into custody as well as the guy who's *actually* behind all this." I didn't know how things were going to go when we got to Grushin's house. This way, if it went well, the FBI could show up, and we'd all be heroes. And if it went badly...at least they'd still catch Grushin. "But please, Caroline, I need you to trust me and do this for me. Right now."

For a few seconds, there was just panicked breathing as Caroline debated. I sat there digging my fingernails into my palm. Then, "Okay. Okay, I got you."

I slumped in relief and thanked her, then ended the call. About five minutes later, we pulled up outside 403 West Brenton, a beautiful old red-brick townhouse.

We crept around the back, and Valentin picked the lock. Mikhail stationed his dogs outside to catch anyone who ran. Then Gennadiy slipped through the door, with me tight behind him, a hand on his shoulder. Ahead was a hallway, scrupulously clean and lavishly finished, with aquamarine walls and polished wooden doors. It was surprisingly quiet, except for classical music coming from upstairs. *Where are the guards?* We passed a dining room with a table big enough for ten, and a study lined with books. Every wall was flawlessly painted, every doorknob polished to a shine. Grushin must have spent millions on the place, and I guessed he had similar homes in New York and LA.

The Irish spread out, searching the first floor and then descending silently down the stairs to check the basement. They were back in under a minute. "Servants' quarters and a guard room," Finn told us quietly. "Empty." *Where is everyone?* As one, we all looked up the wooden staircase, towards the music.

Gennadiy crept up the stairs, gun raised. My heart was hammering: I'd been on plenty of FBI raids, but I'd never had so little idea what we were walking into. It was only the feel of Gennadiy's shoulder, solid and warm under my hand, that let me keep my feet moving.

We'd reached the second floor and were fanning out when it happened. There was a noise like someone slamming a sledgehammer into a solid block of iron, over and over again, right next to your ear. The wooden banister next to us disintegrated, and I smelled burning wood as splinters and chips sailed past my face. Two of the Irish fell to the floor. I thought a bomb had gone off, some sort of booby trap.

Gennadiy shoved me sideways into a bedroom, and we fell full-length on the floor with him on top. The destruction followed us. It was as if God was reaching down with an invisible finger and sweeping it across the room, obliterating everything it touched. Its path cut across the carpet, digging holes right down through the floorboards, then diagonally through the bed, pulverizing the mattress and exploding the pillows into clouds of feathers.

I finally realized we were being shot at, with a heavy machine gun, from the next floor up. The gunner was swinging his aim around, trying to hit us through the open door. I watched, wide-eyed, as the bullets crept towards us.

Gennadiy grabbed me and crawled, hauling me with him over to the far wall. But the bullets came mercilessly closer and closer. He flattened me against the wall and pressed me there, covering me with his body, determined to protect me as long as he could—

The bullets stopped an inch from his leg. The top of the door was blocking the gunner's fire. The gunfire swung back the other way, chewing a line of plaster from the wall as it crept back out into the hallway. Then it finally fell silent.

I was still smooshed between Gennadiy's big body and the wall, and I just stayed there for a moment, my ears ringing. I was panting in fear and coughing, too: the air was full of plaster dust, feathers, and smoke. Out in the hall, I could see one of the bullets lying on the blood-soaked floor: Jesus, it was the size of a *pen!* No wonder anything hit by that thing got shredded!

"Valentin?" yelled Gennadiy. "Mikhail?"

A second went by. Then they yelled back in Russian from another room. My heart started beating again.

"Nobody move!" ordered Gennadiy. He looked at me and shook his head. We'd walked right into a trap. Grushin must have seen us coming, maybe on a hidden security camera, and had pulled his men upstairs to lie in wait. Now no one could leave the rooms they were in: the machine gunner upstairs would tear them apart as soon as they stepped out into the hallway.

I heard a car outside and crawled over to the window. The bedroom looked out over the side of the house, and I saw Caroline's blue minivan coming down the street. "The FBI's here!" I told Gennadiy in relief. They could back us up and come in and get Grushin. But first we had to make sure they didn't walk straight into the same trap we had.

We both looked at the door. I'd be dead as soon as I set foot in the hallway. But the windows were old-fashioned sliding ones. They had security locks to stop them opening too far, but maybe... I heaved the window open. The gap wasn't wide enough for Gennadiy, but I could just squeeze through. It was dark enough outside that the ground below was just a black void, but it couldn't be more than an eight-foot drop.

Gennadiy shook his head and boxed me in with his arms. "You're not going out there alone! Grushin could have men out there!"

"It's the only way!" I told him and pointed towards the front of the house. "The street is *right there!* In two minutes, I can be back with the FBI tactical team!"

Gennadiy scowled and glowered at me, then sighed. "*Be careful!*"

I looked up at him and nodded, a sudden lump in my throat. If you'd told me a few months earlier that my mortal enemy would be making me feel so loved, so protected, I'd have said you were crazy. "Always," I told him.

I had to wriggle out of the window feet-first. Gennadiy held my hands as I dangled, supporting me until the very last moment. When I was ready to drop, he squeezed my hands as if he didn't want to let go.

"I got this," I promised.

He frowned stubbornly...and then reluctantly let me go.

I dropped. Six feet, eight feet, *oh shit,* I'd underestimated how big the house was: the drop was more like ten feet—

I hit the concrete and heard something snap. OW. *OW!*

I fell sideways, picking up some bruises, and came within an inch of cracking my skull on an ornamental stone handrail. I lay there for a second, panting and shaken. *That didn't go great.* But I was alive.

I gingerly stood up...and grating pain flashed up my left leg and made my stomach churn. *Fuck.* Okay, I'd deal with that later. I waved to Gennadiy that I was okay and then hobbled down the passageway at the side of the house, out of sight of the window.

I emerged at the front of the house, and there was Caroline, climbing out of her minivan. I stumbled the last few feet and almost fell into her, wrapping her up in a hug. "Thank you, thank you, thank you," I breathed. The others were probably right behind her. The tactical team might be another few minutes, I'd just have to hope Gennadiy could hang on for—

I caught movement out of the corner of my eye. I twisted around...and saw Viktor Grushin stepping out of the shadows just down the street, no more than twenty feet from me.

Shit! How did he get outside? He must have an escape tunnel, like Gennadiy. I stumbled in front of Caroline and raised my gun, the guilt clawing at my chest. *She isn't even a field agent: what have I gotten her into?* "Stay behind me!" I told her frantically. Then to Grushin. "Stop right there! Let me see your hands!"

Grushin stopped and lifted his hands, grinning. My eyes searched the street behind him. He wouldn't come out alone, he'd have a bodyguard or a—

A brutal, burning pain erupted in my lower back. I staggered forward, and the pain in my ankle made my legs fold, sending me to my knees. My head went light, and it was more than just the pain. I felt for the source of the pain, and my hand came away dripping blood. *I've been shot!* A sniper? But I hadn't heard anything...

The gun dropped from my fingers and clattered to the sidewalk. My muscles didn't have any strength anymore. *Caroline? Is Caroline okay?* She'd been standing right behind me...

I rolled over onto my back and found her looking down at me, tears in her eyes. "I'm sorry," she sobbed.

And then I saw the knife in her hand and understood.

68

GENNADIY

ALISON DROPPED FROM THE WINDOW, AND MY STOMACH LURCHED WHEN I saw her ankle give way. But then she was up and hobbling off towards the front of the house. *Chyort!* My woman was so brave. I lost sight of her as I hurried down the side of the house. But at least she was safe now, with her FBI friend.

Footsteps, climbing the stairs from the first floor. Were the FBI coming in already? I skirted the edge of the room, trying to make sure I stayed far enough back from the door that the machine gunner upstairs didn't see me. But the instant my shadow fell across the floor, bullets tore into the carpet and splintered the floorboards. I flattened myself to the wall. *Blyat',* that thing was lethal. There was no way I could leave the room or even get close to the door, but by hunkering down and leaning, I managed to peek out...and what I saw made my stomach drop. Men in black ski masks were coming up the stairs. Grushin's men. They must have been hiding down the street, waiting until we were trapped inside. *How did they know we were coming?*

They had us split up and boxed in, rats in a trap. They could take each room in turn and wipe us out. Worst of all, they were down there on the first floor...with Alison.

Forget Grushin. I had to get down there and check she was okay.

At that moment, the first of Grushin's men reached the landing and started firing into my room. I dived full-length behind the bed as bullets tore into the wall above me. *Blyat'!*

Unless I could think of a way out of this, I wasn't going anywhere.

69

ALISON

Caroline is the mole.

Maybe it was the blood loss—already, it was a spreading red lake beneath me—but I couldn't make my brain focus on anything aside from the betrayal. I'd thought she was a friend. My *only* friend. But she'd been Grushin's inside woman from the start. She'd taken the bullets from Evidence to frame Gennadiy, and the cocaine to frame me. She must have told Grushin my address so he could send the assassin to my apartment. That's why she'd hugged me so hard when she showed up afterwards: she'd been wracked with guilt. And she warned Grushin we were coming for him tonight, that's how he'd laid the trap and waited down the street. It was all so fucking obvious, now. The only thing I didn't understand was...

"Why?" I rasped.

Tears were flooding down Caroline's cheeks. I just didn't understand it. *Money?* Did he bribe her? She'd always been such a warm, kind person. Either I'd utterly misjudged her, all this time, or—

Oh. Oh *fuck*.

Jack. Her kid with a heart condition. The one who'd suddenly gotten better, a year ago. "Grushin gave him a new heart," I whispered.

Her face crumpled, and she dissolved into sobbing. "*He was going to die!*"

Oh God. Grushin had shown up on her doorstep and offered to save her kid. What would *I* have done? What would any mother have done? And once she'd accepted his offer, he owned her.

The toe of a leather shoe hooked under my cheek, and I was flipped onto my front. There was a nuclear flash of pain from my ankle, and I screamed, and then the wound in my back opened up, and I gave a guttural grunt, tears springing to my eyes. I lay there terrified to move, because the slightest movement hurt so much.

Viktor Grushin stared down at me, shaking his head. "I don't understand why he'd want someone who's so much trouble," he told me. He glanced towards Caroline. "Come inside. Once they're all dead, you'll help me burn the place down. We can make it look like the Aristovs had a fight with the Irish." He started strolling towards the house. Then, as he passed me, he—

NO GOD NO PLEASE—

—grabbed my broken ankle.

I screamed long and loud as he dragged me along the ground behind him. Before we even reached the house, the pain and the blood loss had made my vision shrink to a dark tunnel.

My last thought before I passed out was a horrible realization. Caroline hadn't told the FBI we were here. Which meant no one was coming to save us.

70

GENNADIY

GUNFIRE FROM THE DOORWAY FORCED ME BACK BEHIND THE BED AGAIN. I shot back, and Grushin's man ducked behind the wall. He wasn't getting in, but I wasn't getting out, either. I lay there on the floor panting. I didn't care that I was about to die, as soon as the guy brought some friends. I was thinking of Alison, downstairs. I had to get to her.

More gunfire, but this was further away, and I realized I was hearing it through the wall. "Valentin?" I yelled.

"It's Finn!" And he banged on the wall, only a few feet from my head. He must be in the bedroom next to me.

Then I heard Mikhail's bass roar. "Valentin's with me! We're at the end of the hall!"

I looked at the wall next to me, building a mental map. Finn was next door, Mikhail and Valentin next door to him. So close! If only we could go out into the hallway and meet up! I looked despairingly in their direction...and then the ugly, flowery wallpaper caught my eye, and I focused on the wall itself.

What if...what if we didn't go out into the hallway?

"Finn," I called through the wall. "Keep them busy!"

I heard him curse under his breath, but then he must have

dodged towards the door because the machine gun opened up again, pounding our ears. And the guy at the door to my room drew back, out of the way.

I pulled out my phone and dialed Mikhail. When he answered, I put my lips right to the phone so he could hear me over the gunfire. *"Break the wall!"*

I looked around and saw the bed I'd been hiding behind. The frame was made of painted iron, and I heaved it up and unscrewed one leg. That gave me a foot-long chunk of iron with a screw thread pointing out of one end. It wasn't exactly an ax, but it would have to do. I slammed it into the drywall, and it made a satisfying dent. I started frantically swinging it, shattering the plaster and caving in the thin drywall. It started to work, chunks tumbling to the floor and a hole beginning to form between two of the studs. The deafening sound of the machine gun covered what I was doing. But as soon as it stopped and Grushin's man in the hallway came back, I was dead. Standing there hacking at the wall, I was completely exposed.

I kept frantically swinging, panting with effort, drywall dust filling my lungs and sticking to my dripping face. I finally broke through the second layer of drywall, and I could see Finn's room. He was still acting as our decoy, jumping forward to catch the attention of the machine gunner upstairs, then pulling back as the bullets chewed up the floor by his feet. "What's the matter, you fucker?" he was yelling as he danced back. "Can't shoot straight?"

I felt a little more of the hate slip away. He was brave as hell.

I swung the bed leg again and again, shoulders burning. I had a person-sized hole in my side of the drywall, now, and I was just getting started on the second layer, when suddenly everything went quiet. The gunner must have gotten suspicious because I heard him shout in Russian. *Check what they're doing.* Fuck. The hole wasn't done.

I backed off from the hole just as the guy in the hallway peeked in. He saw my half-finished escape route, and his eyes widened. Then he raised his gun.

Blyat'! I'd had to put my gun away to work on the hole. *I was so close!* I felt the anger rise, blossoming outward in a slow-motion explosion...and for once, I let it. I poured gasoline on it, thinking about Alison, alone downstairs, about Valentin and Mikhail...

Sometimes, you have to be calm and smart. Sometimes, you have to get angry.

I hurled the bed leg at the guy in the doorway, put my head down, and ran at the half-finished hole. A shot rang out, but missed. I was running full speed, now, too angry to worry about how much it would hurt. I hurled myself at the wall, a human wrecking ball...

I crashed through the drywall and went tumbling across the floor in Finn's room, trailing a cloud of drywall dust. I lay on my back for a second, coughing, my head and shoulders throbbing from the impact. Then Finn reached down and offered me his hand, and I grabbed it and let him pull me to my feet. On the opposite side of the room, Mikhail and Valentin were climbing through their own hole. I nodded to them, relieved. *Together again.*

With four of us, we actually had a chance. When the machine gunner upstairs stopped to reload, we rushed out into the ruined hallway. Finn, Mikhail, and I dealt with Grushin's other men while Valentin raced up to the next floor. There was a single shot and I heard a body fall. A moment later, Valentin came back downstairs. "It's safe," he told us. "But Grushin's not up there."

My chest tightened. That meant he was downstairs...with Alison. "Come on!"

I led the way back down to the first floor, only to find it swarming with Grushin's men. And there, coming through the front door, was Grushin himself, Alison held in front of him as a shield. She was grimacing in pain and—*Blyat'!*—She'd been wounded. Blood was dripping from a wound on her back, a lot of it.

The fear clawed at me, and I rushed forward, but Grushin and his men opened fire, and Valentin had to pull me into the shelter of the kitchen. The bullets meant for me shattered a stack of plates by the sink, scattering porcelain shards.

We tried to force our way out of the kitchen door, but a barrage of gunfire drove us back. Even when Finn's remaining men joined us from upstairs, it wasn't enough. We were outnumbered and pinned down. My chest went tight. *Alison!* She was bleeding out; she'd die if I didn't get to her!

Grushin's voice came from the entrance hall, coldly mocking. "I told you this is how it would end, Gennadiy. Your whole empire destroyed and everyone you loved dead."

I looked desperately at Finn, Valentin, and Mikhail, and they looked grimly back at me. There was no way to reach her, and we were probably dead ourselves in another few minutes. I took a deep breath and stuck my head out of the kitchen for a split second. Bullets shredded the doorframe, and I had to pull back, but for a brief instant, I locked eyes with Alison through the carnage. The fear I saw on her face made my heart go cold. She could feel it. She knew she was running out of time.

71

ALISON

It's funny how undramatic dying can be. I'd always thought I'd go quick: one misjudgment on my bike and a truck slamming into me, or some criminal emptying his gun into my chest. But this was like a heavy, warm blanket settling over me, coaxing me to sleep as the life drained out of me drop by drop. My ankle and the stab wound in my back still hurt, but it felt like the pain belonged to someone else, at the other end of a long tunnel.

My head lolled: if Grushin hadn't been holding me upright, I'd have ragdolled to the floor. But through half-shut eyes, I saw Gennadiy being forced back into the kitchen, bullets plucking at his suit jacket. Grushin's men pushed forward to finish him. This was the end. *No. Please no...*

There was a bang behind us, and everyone turned.

The front door was open and sagging on its hinges. And in the doorway was a familiar, disheveled figure, his tie askew under his FBI body armor. *Calahan?!*

"FBI!" he yelled. And started shooting. And right behind him, shooting over his shoulder, was a woman in her sixties, her silver hair pinned up tight and a savage expression on her face. *Carrie?!*

Three of Grushin's men fell immediately, and, now that they were being attacked from two sides, the rest of them panicked as they tried to return fire. Gennadiy and the others began to push forward again, towards me. "What are you doing here?" I yelled to Calahan. "I told you not to come!"

"When did I ever do as I was told?" yelled Calahan.

As more and more of his men fell, I could feel Grushin's mood shifting from confidence to panic. He put his gun to my head and backed away, pulling me in front of him. Gennadiy ran forward and stood shoulder-to-shoulder with Calahan. "It's over, Viktor! Let her go!"

But neither of them had a clear shot, not with me hanging limply in Grushin's arms. I tried to struggle, but the wound in my back burned and spasmed, and I cried out in pain.

Grushin opened the side door and dragged me out into the garden, then started moving towards the front of the house.

I was going to live just long enough to be his hostage and help him get away with this whole thing.

72

GENNADIY

I HAD HIM RIGHT IN MY SIGHTS, BUT I DIDN'T DARE SHOOT, NOT WITH Alison's head lolling and swaying in front of his. *Blyat'*, she looked so *pale!* I glanced helplessly at the two FBI agents who'd shown up, but there was nothing they could do, either.

We advanced down the side of the house, following Grushin as he backed towards a car. With every step, I could feel the tension ratcheting higher in my chest. Sirens were wailing in the distance. Grushin was going to get away, and the cops would turn up just in time to arrest us and stop us from going after him. Grushin would go into hiding, his friend the DA would cover things up, and the clinic would be running again within a month. I growled and pushed forward, closing the distance to Grushin, but he pushed his gun warningly against Alison's temple, and my steps faltered.

I just need one little break, I prayed. *One chance. Just one.*

And then, as Grushin reached for the handle of his car door, I got it.

Alison's blonde-haired friend came lurching out of the bushes in front of the house, tears flooding down her cheeks, and plunged a knife into Grushin's side. He tottered sideways, letting go of Alison...and that's all I needed.

I launched myself at him and tackled him to the ground, then started punching him. The fury I'd honed for so many years roared to life. *For Alison! And Yakov! And Bronwyn!* My fists smashed into his face, left then right then left, the rage whirling faster and faster. *The casino! Our money! All the Bratva he'd killed and terrorized back home! All the people he'd killed, to take their organs!*

This ended *now*. I was going to destroy him completely, so he could never hurt anyone again.

I glanced up and saw Mikhail running towards me. *Mikhail!* Grushin killed his friend and the woman he loved. My fists swung again and again, blood flying.

"Stop!" yelled the male FBI agent. But I didn't.

Valentin reached me and put a hand on my shoulder, trying to pull me away, but I shook him off. Then Mikhail was on my other shoulder, but I twisted away from him, too. *He deserves it. He deserves to die.* I pounded Grushin's face, on and on—

And then I glanced up and saw Alison. She was lying on her back on the front lawn, with the older, female FBI agent crouching next to her. She needed me. And she needed Grushin alive to clear her name.

A week ago, I wouldn't have been able to pull myself back. But now...

My fists rose, trembling, dripping blood...and paused. I knelt there sucking down the cold night air, clawing at the anger inside me, willing it to slow and slow...and stop.

Immediately, the guilt rushed in, eating away at my vulnerable, unprotected core. It hurt so much I hunched over, fists clenching tight. I knew I couldn't take it forever.

But for her...I could take it for a while. Until—I looked across at Valentin—until I could do what needed to be done.

I stood and ran over to Alison, then knelt down beside her and wiped my hands on the grass. *Blyat',* she looked so fragile! I just wanted to pull her into my arms, but I didn't dare risk moving her. "Will she be okay?" I asked, brushing my fingers across her cheek.

"She's lost a lot of blood," said the older, female FBI agent, her voice tight with worry. "The paramedics are on their way."

Alison murmured something I couldn't hear. I leaned closer, my heart pounding. "What did you say?"

She was mumbling, spacey from the blood loss. "*Did I catch the bad guy?*"

I glanced around at Grushin, bloody and battered, but alive. And then I looked down at myself. I grabbed her hand and squeezed it. "Yes," I managed around the lump in my throat. "You did."

EPILOGUE

Alison

After that, things went hazy for a while.

I remember being loaded into an ambulance as the street filled up with police cars. Gennadiy was trying to climb in beside me, a cop was trying to handcuff him, and Calahan was arguing with both of them. Then everything went black.

When I came to, it was daylight, and I was in a hospital bed in a quiet room. One leg was in plaster, I was hooked up to an IV, and I could feel a dressing on my back. I tried to move, winced and groaned, then tried again.

"For once in your life, would you just *stop?*" pleaded a familiar voice.

I twisted around to look. Calahan, looking even more disheveled than usual, was sprawled in a chair next to my bed. "Gennadiy?" I asked immediately.

His mouth tightened. I think maybe he was still hoping that he could talk some sense into me. But then he looked into my eyes, and whatever he saw there made him sigh in resignation and then soften. "Gennadiy's fine. I mean, he's at the center of a major police investigation into all the bodies that you two left at that ambulance company, and at Viktor Grushin's house, but–"

The door opened, and Gennadiy marched in.

"...he does have a *very* good defense attorney," grumbled Calahan.

Gennadiy swept his hands under my shoulders and lifted me to him, pressing me to his chest and resting my head against his shoulder. He only loosened his grip when the machines beside my bed started to beep accusingly. Then he gently laid me back down and gave me a look of such fierce, possessive love that I melted.

"Are you going to jail?" I asked, worried.

"Conrad got me out on bail," Gennadiy told me. "As for jail..." He looked at Calahan and rubbed his stubble. "The situation is...fluid."

Calahan sighed. "About a billion people want to take statements from you. You might want to start thinking about what you're going to say."

I nodded gratefully.

Calahan ran a hand through his hair. "The DA wanted to throw the book at the Aristovs. But now the DA himself is under investigation by the Justice Department. As is everyone who Grushin gave a new organ to at all three clinics. It's going to take months to shake out, and meanwhile, the case against the Aristovs is falling apart. Especially because Caroline has testified that it was Grushin who tried to assassinate you, and that she switched the bullets to try to implicate Gennadiy, and stole the coke they used to set you up."

"Is *she* going to jail?" I asked.

"For a while," said Calahan. "But she's cooperating in the case against Grushin. If she gets a good lawyer..."

I made puppy-dog eyes at Gennadiy.

"The woman conspired to assassinate you," he reminded me. "She set you up. She *stabbed* you!"

"And saved me," I argued. "She did the right thing...eventually. And she has kids!"

Gennadiy cursed under his breath. "I'll get Conrad to recommend someone good."

"What about you and Carrie?" I asked Calahan.

Calahan shrugged. "Well, we broke a lot of rules...but Carrie managed to spin it that we were helping an agent in danger, whose own office had been compromised. The FBI is embarrassed enough that it'd rather the whole thing just went away. We'll be okay." He stood. "I'll give you two some time alone. Try and rest, okay?" He walked over to Gennadiy, stopping when they were almost chest-to-chest. "And as for you..." His voice became like steel. "Treat her right. Or jail will be the least of your worries."

Gennadiy gave him a solemn nod. When the door closed behind Calahan, he leaned over the bed and put his big, warm palm on my cheek. His thumb brushed my lower lip. "You scared me." He smiled, but there was a tremor in his voice. "Maybe...try not to drown, or get shot at, or stabbed, just for a week or so?"

"I'll consider it," I muttered. And kissed him.

Four days later, Gennadiy was pushing me around the hospital gardens in a wheelchair. It was my first time outdoors since I was stabbed. September had brought an end to the thunderstorms, and the crisp, cool morning air felt amazing against my face. Then a familiar figure wandered towards us, and my heart forgot to beat for a second. *This is it.*

"Hey," said Assistant Director Halifax. He nodded politely to Gennadiy. "Mr. Aristov. May I have a word with Alison?"

Gennadiy scowled at him. He'd make an exception for me, and maybe for Calahan and Carrie, but, to him, the FBI was still the FBI. "You want me to stay?" he asked me.

I shook my head. "No. Thank you."

Gennadiy wheeled the wheelchair over to a bench so that Halifax could sit down. "I'll be just over there," he told me, nodding to a nearby tree. But he was glaring at Halifax when he said it, and I didn't miss the threat in his voice.

Halifax sat down on the bench and passed me one of the two coffees he was carrying. "I've got news."

"The charges, or my job?"

"Both. Which do you want first?"

My mouth was suddenly dry. Ever since I woke up, I'd been imagining this moment, playing out all the different ways it could go. I sipped my coffee. He'd remembered how I liked it. "The charges," I said, my voice tight.

"All charges against you have been dropped."

I took a breath. It felt like an iron band around my chest had just disappeared. I took a gulp of coffee to cover myself. "And my job?"

"Given the extenuating circumstances, Grushin's arrest and all the arrests it's led to, the Director feels it would be a mistake to lose such a good agent. There'll be a reprimand in your record, and you'll need to complete a probationary period, but..." He smiled. "You can come back, Alison."

And that's when I realized that, unconsciously, I'd been hoping I'd be fired. Because now I had to choose. Halifax's eyes followed mine to Gennadiy.

"You don't need me to tell you that there are rules," he said gently.

I nodded silently. My eyes were going hot.

"You don't need to decide now," Halifax told me. "Think it over while you heal. Take a week."

I tried to imagine life without the FBI. It felt like a crack was forming, starting on the surface and winding deeper and deeper, until it terminated right in my soul and a whole, cliff-sized wedge of me broke off and tumbled away into the ocean, leaving huge areas of me vulnerable and exposed. For my entire working life, I'd been catching bad guys and solving cases, going for beers with cops or FBI agents, and then falling asleep thinking about a case. I didn't know how to do anything else. I didn't have anything else.

Then I looked at Gennadiy. Somehow, I'd found the one person in the universe who was the same as me, who got me. Who knew what it was like to stay up until three in the morning because you had to solve this problem, who wouldn't hate me for working flat-out. But who'd look after me, who'd drag me off to bed when I really was overdoing it. And who'd let me do the same for him. Who'd always protect me, no matter what. Who'd risk everything to save me.

A new life, without the FBI, was terrifying.

But a life without Gennadiy was unimaginable.

I sniffed, blinked back tears, and shook my head. "I don't need a week," I told Halifax. "I resign."

One Month Later

Gennadiy

"So this is your favorite place?" asked Alison. She was blinking, her eyes still adjusting to the gloom after the bright sun outside.

"My favorite place," I confirmed. Not long ago, I wouldn't have even considered telling someone that, or even admitting to having a favorite place. A lot had changed. I squeezed her hand and led her forward, through shafts of sunlight that lanced down into the dark space like lasers, revealing dust motes that danced and swirled as we breathed.

I took Alison's hand and guided it. She suddenly yelped as her palm brushed a warm, velvety nose.

"Heaven's Tears," I told her. "But we call him Cloud."

As our eyes adjusted to the dark, we could make out a beautiful gray stallion with cream patches. Alison gasped as the horse snorted against her palm and then lowered his head for scratches.

"He likes you," I told her.

"He's amazing," whispered Alison.

"He's the second most beautiful thing here," I murmured, running my eyes over her. The jodhpurs showed off every graceful curve of her long legs, and the tight white blouse made those high little breasts absolutely mouthwatering. With her black hair swishing in its ponytail and her ass bouncing up and down in the saddle, I knew I wasn't going to be able to take my eyes off her all day.

"Even standing still, he looks fast," said Alison.

"He was a racehorse," I said. "Until a guy called Spartak burned our old stables down. Cloud survived, but..."–I showed Alison the burn scars– "He'll never race again."

Alison nodded sadly, running her hand over the horse's back. I could feel them bonding.

"He still loves to run, though," I said. "Don't worry, we'll start you off on someone slower. Let me show you how to put a saddle on."

∼

By the end of the day, we were sore and laughing and pleasantly exhausted. As the sun set, we walked back towards the car, where Valentin was waiting to drive us back to the city. I was still waiting for my new car to arrive, so I'd asked him to give us a ride. I could have just hired a car, but—my chest went tight—I'd wanted him here for a reason.

Alison saw my expression and gently slipped her hand out of mine. "Why don't you go on ahead?" she said. "I'm going to go back to the stables and see the horses. Take as long as you need."

I nodded silently. She understood. She always did. I sucked in a breath and looked around. Valentin and I were all alone, with fields all around and no one to hear us. It would never get any easier than this.

I blew out my breath and started walking towards the car. The guilt and self-hate that had been festering for decades bubbled up inside me, dark and toxic. Twice, I nearly veered off and headed for the stables instead. But I had to do this. Because if I felt this way, how did *he* feel?

Valentin looked up as I approached and frowned at my expression. "Brother?"

I swallowed and put a hand on his shoulder. "We need to talk," I rasped.

∼

There was some woodland near the stables, and we wandered deep into it. The sunset made the trees throw out long, black shadows, and the darkness made it easier, somehow.

I started in halting, awkward little rushes of words, scowling at the ground as I talked. I could feel the familiar weight of everything I was—Aristov, Russian, a man—trying to silence me. *We don't do this. We don't talk about these things.*

But I could see Valentin throwing quick little glances at me that looked almost hopeful. That pushed me on...and the more I spoke, the more I felt like I was wriggling free from under all that tradition. It hadn't been protecting me; it had been trapping me.

"I never meant for it to happen," I told Valentin. "If I could go back and bow and scrape to that bastard Svetoslav, so he didn't rape you, I would. In a heartbeat."

"I know that." Valentin grabbed my arm. "Gennadiy, I don't blame you. I never did. But–" He looked at me, his eyes full of pain, and his voice hitched. "Afterwards..."

"We never talked about it," I said guiltily.

"I—" Valentin looked away. "I thought–"

My stomach dropped as realization hit. "No!"

"—I thought you were...disgusted with me."

I threw my arms around him and hugged him tight. "No! Brother, no! I just felt so guilty that it happened! I never felt that about you, *ever!* You're my brother, I could never..." I squeezed him even harder. *All these years!*

We stood like that for a long time, until the sun had sunk below the horizon and the sky had turned from copper and scarlet to deep blue. Then we trudged back to the stables, our arms around each other's shoulders. Something had lifted from both of us, but more than that...we'd opened a door that should never have been slammed shut. We knew we could do this again if we needed to.

I could feel a space in my center, where the guilt had been, and it felt new and jarring and tender, after living with the guilt for so long. It slowly dawned on me that I could fill it with something else, now. Something good.

As we neared the stables, I saw Alison emerge from them. She was walking with that graceful prowl, her jodhpur-clad legs pale in the light of the rising moon. Valentin patted my back affectionately and gave me a tiny push, and I was off and running, covering the field in big, eager strides. I grabbed Alison's waist, and she whooped as I picked her up and whirled her around.

I knew what I wanted my future to be.

One Week Later
Alison

I groaned in ecstasy. I had a waterproof pillow positioned *just-so* to cushion my head on the edge of the tub, the water was hot enough to soak all the tension out of my muscles, and the bath bomb Bronwyn had given me made it smell like I was drifting through a tropical paradise full of fruit and flowers.

I'd never had a big bathtub before, and I'd never had the time to indulge in a proper bubble bath. But one thing I had plenty of right now was time: five weeks on from leaving the FBI, I still had no idea what I was going to do with my life. And seeing Bronwyn's minor obsession with baths had made me curious. Now I understood.

"This is your fifteen-minute call," murmured Gennadiy as he walked past. He looked down at my bare, gleaming shoulders and the tops of my breasts, just visible above the bubbles, and his eyes gleamed.

"I don't have to get out yet," I mumbled dreamily. "I can be ready in ten minutes." I let myself sink a little lower in the tub until my lips were brushing the surface. "Maybe five *bububub*."

Gennadiy smiled indulgently—he was smiling more, these days —and perched on the edge of the tub. "Five minutes might be pushing it. Not even you could get ready in five."

That sounded like a challenge. "Wanna bet?"

He cocked his head. *Are you kidding?*

"Five minutes," I insisted.

"And if you lose the bet?" he asked. He was trying to sound casual, but I could hear the lust in his voice.

"You get to tie me up," I said immediately. And flushed.

"And if I lose the bet?"

I hadn't thought that far ahead. "I get to tie *you* up. And ride your face like a horse."

Gennadiy threw back his head and laughed, then nodded. We grinned at each other. The rivalry was still there, and it bound us together even tighter.

Ten minutes later, I erupted out of the tub, sending Gennadiy ducking for cover. I whipped a towel over my body, pulled on a bra, and then rolled on my back on the bed, pulling hold-ups up my legs. I jumped up, grabbed a dress, and pulled it over my head while my feet felt their way into my heels. I leaned forward over the mirror, grabbed some lipstick, and carefully applied it, then brushed a touch of blusher on my cheeks. "Done," I said breathlessly.

"Four minutes and fifty-eight seconds," Gennadiy said doubtfully. "But it doesn't count."

"Why not?"

"You're not wearing panties."

"A choice," I said breezily. "Not an oversight."

His eyes locked on my groin, and he cursed under his breath. "You do this deliberately," he growled. "You know I want you so much, I'll let you get away with anything."

I smirked and offered him my arm. He sighed good-naturedly, and we walked arm in arm to the door.

Every time I stepped out into the hallway and saw the line of polished wood doors and the long, scarlet carpet stretching the length of the east wing, I still had a wobbly second where I felt like I was in a movie. I wasn't sure I'd ever get used to living like this. I still got flummoxed every time Melina, the maid, curtsied to me, and I still kept asking, unsuccessfully, if she wanted help making the beds. But...honestly? Throwing my clothes in a laundry basket and then finding them back in my closet, washed and pressed, and hanging on hangers? Kind of magical.

As we walked downstairs, Gennadiy was rubbing my ass through the thin fabric of my dress, delighting in my lack of underwear. *I hope it's a short meeting.* Wearing dresses still felt new and strange. I still mostly wore jeans in public, but I was gradually building up my confidence and showing my legs more.

Downstairs, the Aristovs were gathering. We ran into Mikhail and his dogs first, and we spent a happy few minutes giving ear scratches and being batted by fluffy, excited tails. Then Valentin appeared. Like Gennadiy, he seemed a little lighter since the two of them had talked. I looked at the necklace he wore, the silver bird catching the light. Who was Ruslana? And was he ever going to be able to let go of her and heal that broken heart?

Bronwyn and Radimir arrived just as we were moving through to the dining room. I was still coming to terms with how Caroline had betrayed me, but just as I'd lost one friend, I'd made a new one. Bronwyn and I were getting to be close: both of us were new to all this, and she was helping me to navigate both the Bratva and the lifestyle that went with it. She'd made me an appointment with her personal stylist to help me dress the part but, just as importantly, we'd had some deep conversations over coffee at her bookstore. As Radimir and Gennadiy marched ahead, I pulled her aside. "How'd it go? Did you have the talk?"

Bronwyn nodded. "I told him I wasn't ready, after the poisoning. I told him I'm just not sure it's safe to bring a child into our world."

"How'd he take it?" I asked.

She smiled. "He said, *Krasavitsa, take all the time you need. I'll wait forever.*" Her smile became sad. "I just hope I can get past this. I want to make him happy."

"You already do," I told her firmly, and gave her a hug.

We took our seats in the dining room. Radimir was with Bronwyn at the head of the table, the king and queen. Gennadiy and I were at the far end, Mikhail on one side with his dogs, and Valentin on the other. I felt a big, warm swell of emotion. After years of searching, I'd finally found the family I'd always wanted.

Then, as one, they all turned and looked at me. *Wait, what? What's going on?*

Radimir leaned forward. "We called this meeting to discuss something with you."

I gaped, utterly thrown. I'd thought it was just a standard family meeting. I glanced at Gennadiy, and he gave me a reassuring nod. "O...kay," I managed.

Radimir took a deep breath. "When we first met, I didn't hide what I thought about an FBI agent so close to our family. But I have come to trust you. Without you, I doubt we'd all be sitting here today."

I nodded hesitantly. I had no idea where this was going.

Radimir put his elbows on the table and clasped his fist in his other hand. "Grushin was operating right under our noses. He was blackmailing Yakov; he had control of the head of the gaming board, the DA, senior people at the banks...and we had no idea. It took you to uncover all that."

"What we're saying," said Gennadiy, "is that maybe..." he looked around at his family, "maybe the bad guys need cops too."

"There are always people, within our organization and outside it, trying to steal from us," said Mikhail. "Or run their own schemes without our knowledge. Or even plan a coup. We would like you...to stop them."

I looked around at them, dumbfounded.

"You are already part of our family," said Radimir. "This is different. We are offering you a job."

"I've needed someone to share the load with for years," said Gennadiy. "I've never found anyone I can fully trust...until now."

I turned it over in my mind. A year ago, everything had seemed so simple. There were good guys, like Calahan and me, and bad guys, like the Aristovs. But now I'd seen a guy who was meant to be a cop corrupt the whole system, right up to the DA. And I'd seen that there were far worse people in the world than the Aristovs. If Chicago had to have crime, better that they were running things than people like

Grushin. I'd get to do what I loved: detective work, figuring things out, catching bad guys. Just in a different way.

It was a big step. *Am I really going to do this?*

I looked at Gennadiy. A chance for the two of us to work side by side. To solve mysteries, catch bad guys...okay, *worse* guys. To maybe even do some good.

I took a deep breath...and nodded.

When the meeting broke up, Gennadiy whispered, "Come with me. I have a surprise for you," and nodded to the hallway. As soon as we were out of sight of the others, he pushed me up against the wall. His hand was under my dress and roving up my thigh even as his lips came down on mine. I moaned as his hand brushed over the bare spot on my hip where the waistband of my panties would have been. Then his fingers were gliding sideways, over my naked skin, between my thighs... His tongue slipped into my mouth at the same instant his fingertip pushed inside me, and I groaned, my knees buckling.

"Your surprise can wait," he muttered.

I opened my eyes. "Wait, this isn't the surprise? There's an actual surprise?"

He looked down at me, eyes glazed with need. "Mmm. But now I'm distracted."

He kissed me again, and I moaned and pressed myself against him. Then I broke the kiss again. "What's the surprise?"

He mock-scowled at me...then sighed and smiled. "Fine." He wagged his finger at me. "But the second we're done with the surprise..."

I saluted.

He spanked my ass. "Come on."

He led me into the entrance hall and then outside. And there, gleaming in the moonlight...

"You found my bike?!" I shrieked, delighted. I hadn't seen it since the night I ran from the FBI.

Gennadiy rubbed at his stubble. "Local thieves had taken it, and sold it, but Finn knows a guy and he and I went and retrieved it last night." He actually smiled when he said Finn's name, now.

I ran over to my bike. Then I saw the white one sitting next to it. "Who's is that?"

In answer, Gennadiy swung his leg over it.

"You can ride?" I asked.

"Only a dirt bike, and that was when I was a teenager, stealing purses in Moscow," said Gennadiy. "I was hoping you could teach me."

I stared at him, imagining. The two of us, racing around the streets of Chicago, the wind rushing over our bodies as we pushed the limits...and then coming home and fucking, drunk on adrenaline. "Yes," I said seriously. "Very much yes."

He nodded to my bike. "Let's start now. There's something else I want to show you."

I held up my finger. "Give me one minute. I need to change." I turned towards the mansion.

"What's wrong with what you're wearing?"

"You want me to ride a motorcycle in a dress and no panties? In your mind, how does that end?"

He smiled, and his Russian accent thickened with lust. "I can think of nothing but good ways."

"Just wait." I ran back into the mansion and returned in my leathers.

As I climbed onto my bike, he stared at my ass. "Did you stop to put panties on?" he asked.

I gave him my best mysterious smile and started my engine.

Gennadiy directed me downtown and, at first, I thought we were going to the casino. But then he slowed and stopped, a half block away. I pulled off my helmet and looked around in confusion. Then I saw, and my jaw dropped.

The community theater, which had been a burned-out shell for months, was now a construction site. A banner proudly proclaimed a grand reopening early next year, funded by Aristov Incorporated. I climbed off my bike and took off my helmet, staring. "You're not turning it into a poker room?" I mumbled.

He wrapped his arms around me from behind and rested his chin on the top of my head. "I have enough poker rooms."

I twisted around and hugged him hard. Then I stepped back and just looked at him. I'd gotten used to heels, and I'd forgotten what it felt like to be my natural height, gazing up at him. I ran my hands up his arms and over his biceps, feeling my pulse accelerate. My eyes flicked to the left, to the mouth of a dark alley, remembering the last time we'd been on a motorcycle. "No," I told him.

He scrunched up his brow. "No, what?"

"No," I said, a little breathlessly. "I didn't put panties on."

His eyes narrowed in lust. He seized my wrist. And then we were running into the alley together.

The End

Thank you for reading! If you enjoyed *Heart of Rage,* please consider leaving a review.

Alison first appeared in *Hold Me in the Dark,* which is Calahan and Yolanda's story.

Radimir and Bronwyn's story is told in *Frozen Heart.*

Valentin's book will be next. If you sign up to my newsletter, I'll let you know when it comes out plus you'll receive a free ebook novel and novella I wrote especially for my subscribers. Sign up at:

https://list.helenanewbury.com

Made in United States
North Haven, CT
21 January 2026

87090394R00215